STONES IN
MY BRA

Judith Watkins

Copyright

This is a work of fiction. Names, characters, places, and incidents are either the product of the author's imagination or are used fictitiously. Any real-life characters or locations have been fictionalized in varying degrees for various purposes.

Cover design by Joe Robson

A huge thank you to everyone who has contributed a crumb of their characters and a sprinkling of their stories to form the ingredients of this novel. Lovely friends encouraged me in my baking and tasted earlier recipes, whilst long-suffering family helped with the washing-up. The kitchen, as always, was kept shipshape by the man of the house. A thousand flapjacks to you all!

Contents

1

Mindless Meditation

'*From Nought to Nirvana?* Sorry love - that session's fully booked. You're twenty third on the waiting list.'

I groan inwardly, but retain an outward appearance of Buddha-like calm. How will I ever achieve self-realisation if I can't get on the bloody course? And I need to get there quickly, tick it off my to-do list and move on to decluttering the attic and sorting out Small Child's verruca.

I've been coming to Spirit Mind Studio - Sheffield's latest New Age venue for three weeks now. But my spiritual progress has been negligible. I'm always running late, missing the best classes, and spend more time finding the family's dirty laundry than *the soul within.*

Refusing to give up, I scan the timetable for suitable alternatives.

'How about *Three Quick steps to Calm and Peace?*'

'No can do, duck - the teacher's off sick with stress.'

'*Accessing your Inner Astrologist?*'

'That one's cancelled due to *inauspicious circumstances* - a problem with Saturn, apparently. But I could squeeze you in to *Dancing away Depression* if you like?'

'Oh, sounds promising. Upbeat tunes? Beyoncé?'

'No. Whale music and sounds of the sea.'

'I don't think that's me somehow. What else do you have?'

'Well there are always spaces on *Mindfulness for Mums.* And it doesn't start while two o'clock, so you've got time to have an organic juice or one of them invigorating 'erbal infusions first.'

I scratch my head and sigh. *Mindfulness for Mums* is the only class I ever attend. But there's no option, so I settle down with a brew of Korean ginseng and ginger, distilled in a clear quartz singing bowl, and wait for the mindful mothers to arrive.

Soon, an entire range of northern motherhood is queuing outside the smoky-glassed studio. At the front, designer-clad, yummy-yogi-mummies pose Instagram-ready on one limb, followed by earnest-looking lycra-ladies with PhDs in meditation. Further along some give-it-a-go track suits line up open-mindedly. But I take my place at the back with the free-trial-membership-rabble in our jeggings and miscellaneous, baggy T-shirts.

Our instructor, white-robed and compassionate-eyed, bows us into the darkened, womb-like space, where we silently contemplate our mats, waiting for today's words of wisdom.

'Namaste beloved mothers. Let us begin the journey of letting go.'

I know the drill by now, so creak into lotus position, folding my flab, origami style, into my lap, before *omming* in lacklustre fashion as I settle down to *clear my mind* and *rest in the moment*.

'Today, dear ones, we're going to rid ourselves of unresolved psychological issues through a powerful visualisation.'

A bar of chocolate and a broken wedding ring flash unbidden into my mind.

The instructor chases away the image - 'Now I want you to breathe deeply and follow the flow of your breath as it goes in and out. In and out...'

After several minutes of heavy snorting I feel pleasantly light-headed.

'Let those inner voices fade away.'

Bloody voices! Until I started mindfulness they were just a background noise but now they're forever thumping around in my head. There's the Critic, my constant companion, with her mantra of *'fat, forty, frumpy'*, the Nag with her endless lists of *'shopping, ironing, duty sex...*' and the Temptress with her seductive advice of *'wine's good for you, reality TV's educational, running away - that's the answer!'*

'They're only thoughts and all thoughts drift by like clouds in the endless sky of your mind. Breathe out and let them pass.'

I exhale and the voices fade away.

'Now think of a stumbling block in your life.'

Well this is an easy task for me. I have so many stumbling blocks I don't know where to start.

'And surround it with a halo of light.'

A half-burnt candle flickers pathetically in the draughty room of my mind.

'Good. Really intensify that light.'

Deep breath. I can do this.

The candle becomes a small fire, then gradually a bonfire, then, before I know it, it's a raging conflagration, burning up decades of failure. It's surprisingly cathartic when, with a flash of golden light, those stumbling blocks turn to ash.

'Excellent. You're doing so well. Finally, send love to it and let it dissolve.'

I concentrate hard on dredging up some love. My head itches with the effort but my body relaxes and my mind quietens. All I can hear is the inhale and exhale of the room. All I can see is a comforting, velvety darkness. All I can feel is my body expanding into a loving unity.

For one beautiful moment, I feel a sense of peace, a second of stillness.

But then... *Will Delightful Daughter, ever leave home? When, oh when, will Devil Teen stop being confrontational? Will Small Child finally settle down at school? Will my dad's health get any better? Will I survive another twenty five years of marriage? Will I ever find the peace and meaning that I'm searching for? Who am I, behind all these labels I've given myself over the years? Am I just Midlife-crisis Mystic or is there something more profound?*

'And now bring yourself, refreshed and calm, back into your body, back to the present and, when you're ready, come back to the room.'

As I reluctantly open my eyes, I see the smiling face of my friend, Zen Mother, hovering over me.

'I thought you'd fallen asleep! I didn't want you to miss pick-up time.'

'No, I was just savouring the calm before the storm.'

Zen Mother puts out a hand and pulls me up. She's surprisingly strong for someone so petite. Her blonde hair is tied back in a sporty ponytail and her grey eyes, with their hidden sadness, look at me intently.

'Were you avoiding me earlier?'

'No, I just didn't want to queue jump.'

'Ok, so are you enjoying the classes? Have you had your Tarot cards read yet? Do you think you'll join once your trial's over?'

'Errr - kind of - no - not sure. I only seem to get to this class and membership's a bit pricey. How about you?'

'Yeah, I'm loving it. I go to all their yoga and qi gong classes. You should try those sometime.'

'Mm, maybe. It's just trying to fit everything in round work and family. It's hard enough escaping to our philosophy class on Wednesdays. Anyway, look at the time. We'd better hurry!'

As I dash into the yard, just seconds before the bell goes, I catch sight of Bubbly Brazilian, swaying gently to silent samba rhythms beneath headphones clamped tightly over her waist-length hair. She's in head to toe yellow and orange - a brilliant splash of sunshine on this watery-grey, spring day.

I circle round so as not to startle her and, on seeing me, she gives a shriek of delight, an exuberant 'Olá' and folds me into her ample bosom.

'I've missed you, my dahleeng! I've been waiting too long to hear your expert analysis of the royals' latest escapades. When I saw that front page photo of the Duke and Duchess I did a double-take. I could've sworn it was an older version of your daughter. She's the spitting image of Kate!'

But before I can launch into a detailed critique of my favourite royals, we're rudely interrupted by English Rose, the missing member of our Mothers' Musketeers.

'God, tell me they haven't come out yet. I couldn't get the bloody caramel in the millionaire's shortbread to set.'

English Rose collapses against the wall to catch her breath, her creamy skin flushed prettily pink underneath her chestnut bob. Looking at her I experience a stab of un-friend-like envy as I note her slender figure and line-free complexion. She looks barely more than a girl herself, despite having four robust and boisterous children who run her ragged.

'The bell went a few minutes ago but our lot aren't out yet,' I tell her.

I'm about to enquire after the fate of the shortbread but my attention's caught by Zen Mother at the far side of the playground. She's comforting a lone, distraught father. His tie-dye T-shirt, clogs and goatee beard mark him out as Luke's dad.

I ask Bubbly Brazilian, the fount of all playground knowledge -

'What the hell's going on there?'

'Oh poor dahleeng! The jungle drums say his wife's left him… for a woman! Apparently it's rocked his world and his manhood. But Ethan's mum's such a sweetie, she's taken him under her wing. Nothing fazes her.'

Knowing that Zen Mother has no partner on the scene, I ask -

'Is she making a move on him then?'

'No, no, my dahleeng. She's far too self-contained to want a man. She's just encouraging him to breathe and making him batches of lentil casserole.'

At that moment we're bowled over by the arrival of Sage, Clementine and Brie, three of English Rose's mob, all clamouring to be fed immediately from her Tupperware box of goodies. They break the news that our lot will be out late because Mrs Stickler is issuing *a note*.

I scratch my head. Surely not another cause-for-concern-letter? I try to remember when I last forced my water-phobic son under the shower. But then I relax - it must be a whole class issue. Maybe it's a ban on the latest card-trading fad?

As the torrent of children, released from their day's imprisonment, floods out from the dilapidated Victorian building into the potholed, inner city yard, I scan the faces anxiously for Small Child. He's my youngest - a school refusenik - a solitary individual with specific interests that none of his classmates share.

And finally there he is, at the very back of the line, scratching his head forlornly and limping on his verrucaed foot. His face lights up when he sees me.

'Mummy! Did you bring my Lego tractor down with you?'

'I did sweetheart, and I brought you a piece of my flapjack as well. Go off and play for ten minutes if you like.'

So off he hobbles to the rusty equipment already swarming with kids releasing their pent-up energy. Even with one leg out of action and a hand full of Lego, he scales the climbing wall in seconds. Meanwhile, I sink gratefully onto a nearby bench and tuck into my own piece of flapjack.

Before long I'm joined by English Rose. With a withering look, she hands me a dark green stone with flecks of pink in it.

'One of yours, I think. I picked it up after you'd been for a coffee the other day.'

Blushing slightly, I thank her and put it quickly into my pocket. Then she spies what I'm eating.

'Oh your famous flapjack. It's to die for! You must let me into the secret one of these days.'

'I promise I will. One of these days. Only not just yet. You have to give me a break - after all, you're the Kitchen Goddess whilst I'm Mrs Distinctly Average. This is the special recipe that allows me to shine. I'd like to keep it that way for now.'

Unperturbed by my mean-spirited answer, English Rose offers me her Tupperware treasures and I make a start on her melt-in-the-mouth shortbread. I know I shouldn't give in to temptation. Over the last few years a roll of flesh has been creeping over my waist band. But I'm ten years older than all my friends and, unlike them, I'm no single lady out to impress. Long-term marriage breeds indifference to a husband.

I stick another piece in my mouth and scratch my head contentedly.

'Mmm, this shortbread's heavenly. Who needs a man when chocolate does the trick? Still, now there's a spare man in the school yard, might *you* be interested?'

English Rose snorts.

'Luke's dad? He's a bit too vegetarian for me. I like a man who appreciates real food - a rare steak and a full-cream, pepper sauce. Plus, I'm always suspicious of beards. What are they hiding? I can't be doing with a weak chin - reminds me of my ex.'

'Well it's been two years since you kicked him out. Isn't it time you were moving on?'

'Yes, I know. But I'm having more fun cooking up desserts in the kitchen than I ever would cooking up a storm with a man.'

And it's true, English Rose seems so much happier since she got divorced. And Zen Mother's priority is her son - no man has yet scaled the walls she's built to protect them both. As for Bubbly Brazilian, she's perfectly content with her bachelorette life style. It makes me nostalgic for my own single days - the era of carefree travelling - a different time zone from my current endless wheel of duty and domesticity.

My reverie is interrupted by Bubbly Brazilian, who's finally succeeded in hauling Cristiano away from his favourite game of football. She's marching towards us, with a look of disgust on her face, waving Mrs Stickler's note in front of her like a red rag.

'Have you read this, my dahleengs? It's a nightmare and absolutely no joking matter when your hair's as long as mine!'

My heart sinks…

The silver lining is that a diversion to the chemist allows me finally to pick up a verruca treatment for Small Child. But my arrival home with a metal comb and a bumper-sized bottle of nit lotion doesn't go down well with my older two.

Devil Teen, with his mousy mop of curly hair, is unimpressed.

'Oh God, mother. Little poo-face strikes again. We've only just got over the trauma of thread worms.'

Delightful Daughter is horrified.

'Noooooo! This cannot be happening. I've got a bar shift in two hours. How can I de-louse myself in time? Give me that bottle. I hate my life!'

But before I can hand it over, Devil Teen starts another argument.

'It's not fair, mother. Why should she go first? Just because she's the eldest, she thinks she gets precedence. You should handle this in a democratic manner and draw lots for the order.'

'Ignore him. I haven't time to mess about. He's just being difficult and *apparently* he's got no homework, judging how he's been on the PlayStation non-stop since he got home.'

'Snitch.'

'Loser.'

As Delightful Daughter snatches the bottle from my hand and storms to the bathroom, Devil Teen makes an obscene gesture at her back and kicks his little brother for causing the problem in the first place. I slip off to the kitchen to sneak a biscuit from my secret, Will and Kate commemorative tin, cleverly hidden from the scathing eyes of my anti-royalist partner. For a blissful minute I daydream about life before children, of freedom and exciting adventures. Then, fuelled by a sugar high, I gather myself together and prepare to do battle with the head lice.

An hour later, with children fed, I make my usual call round on my father. A handsome man in his day, with an impressive Roman nose, he's been dogged by ill-health as long as I can remember. After my mother's funeral the widows of the neighbourhood descended upon him with food parcels and comfort. But his lack of communication skills turned even the die-hards away.

He shuffles to the door in obvious pain.

'Hi dad. You ok? Is your leg ulcer playing up?'

He runs his hand through his now thinning, white hair.

'A bit love. Never mind. You?'

'Could be better, dad - long story. What have you been up to today?'

'Shopping.'

'Great - did you buy anything special?'

'Some pikelets - had one with jam just now.

That's nice. Did you do anything else?

'De-frosted the rhubarb. You can make us a crumble for Sunday.'

'Oh, sure. Maybe *you* could learn how to do it?'

'No, love, match will be on.'

'Oh, okay then.'

'And Blades are playing now, love! So, settle down, if you're stopping. Half-time's nearly over.'

As we sit in silence on the settee, I wonder how on my earth my mother kept her sanity all those years - no conversation from the man apart from food and football. Marriage! It's a strange old institution, binding together the most unlikely of couples. And I should know with my own mixed marriage of Yorkshire and Welsh heritage. As newly-weds we used to celebrate our differences, but now rugby and the royal family are a source of constant irritation.

As I wonder what changed, those inner voices in my head chip in with their two-penny-worth.

'Well, look at you. No surprise he'd rather watch rugby.'

'If only you'd tidy the house, you'd make him happy.'

'He's not the only fish in the sea, you know...'

Then suddenly there's another voice and I realise with surprise that it's my father.

'Sorry dad. What did you say?'

'I said your mother says you mustn't be too hard on him.'

'What? Who?'

'Welsh husband. Mum's worried. Said - take care of each other.'

'Dad, what are you on about? You know mum died nearly ten years ago! Are you talking about a dream you had?'

'A dream, love? Yes, your mum was always my dream girl. Pass me those tablets now... GOAL!'

As I hand my father his tablets, I wonder whether perhaps his leg's infected. Blood poisoning can affect the brain. I'll ring the district nurse in the morning to check up on him.

But on leaving the house, a knot of panic lodges in the pit of my stomach.

The nits and the kids have retired for the night, and my beloved finally returns home after yet another business dinner. Head lice don't trouble him but apparently the expense of the latest royal visit does. He's sitting in bed having a late night snack of cheese on toast with a dash of Sheffield's own, Henderson's relish, and moaning about the cost of the monarchy.

'That Harry - swanning up here to open a factory - think of the costs! Surely you see they're a complete waste of public money. We could've propped up our national health system for the same amount, isn't it?'

For once I refuse to rise to the bait. I've got better things to worry about. And mid-rant, he suddenly realises he no longer has an audience.

'Is something up, my lovely? It's not those nits, is it? I know that lotion dries your hair out. But you'll be going to the hairdresser's soon, isn't it? I meant to mention your roots need doing - the grey's showing through again.'

'Oh for God's sake. I'm not bothered about my bloody hair, even though I obviously look like a hideous hag to you. Thank you very much! It's my dad I'm worried about!'

'Your dad? What's he been up to now?'

I find myself pouring out my worst fears - dementia, Alzheimer's, a slow decline into senility.

My husband listens, albeit one eye on the rugby scores, and nods in appropriate places - at least he's learnt that trick over the years. When I finally come to a halt, he gives me a half-hearted hug.

'Listen, my lovely. Your dad's fine. You've been thinking he'll drop dead for years now and he's still going strong. As you say, he's probably got an infection and a few antibiotics will sort him out in no time, isn't it? Now stop your worrying. It'll all be ok.'

'Maybe you're right. I'm just a bit overwrought. Letting things get on top of me.'

'Talking of which…'

He waves his toast in my direction and moves closer with an opportunistic wink.

'Do you fancy a bit?'

I ignore his unromantic gesture and sink back on my pillow, feigning sleep.

I know he's doing his best. I know I'm supposed to be on a journey of self-improvement, looking for my *higher soul* and seeking enlightenment. But it doesn't seem to be helping. I let the memory of a chiselled, Gallic jaw and seductive eyes fill my head. What if I'd made different choices - accepted a French rather than a Welsh proposal? Whatever happened to the handsome hotel owner of my tour guiding days?

I frantically retreat from the thought. How can I be so dismissive of these long years of marriage? How can I be so shallow? It all used to be so simple when I was younger. Everything was clear cut. I knew where I stood. I knew what I wanted. I knew right from wrong. And reviewing my past, I remember how, at the age of seven, I first met God in the greengrocer's…

2

God, the Greengrocer and THOSE Shoes!

I've returned to my childhood. I'm seven years old and my role so far has been that of Sacrificial Lamb.

Our Bev, my bossy, big sister - raven-haired and raven-hearted - has already bagged the part of wayward child, deciding it's *she* who's in charge. Once Our Bev's decided on a course of action, she's not to be swayed and luckily for her, she has a willing and obedient sidekick in her younger sister.

I've been whipped by a stick and made to hurdle make-shift jumps as I act as her personal pony. In her restaurant behind the garden shed, I've been force-fed wilted dandelion leaves and daisy heads washed down with puddle water and gravel. And the latest escapade - the opening of a clandestine salon underneath the dining room table - has resulted in my father being ordered to *slipper* us both. My mother was livid when she discovered the pile of beautiful, curly ringlets hidden beneath the table cloth and saw my near bald scalp. Now an emergency hairdresser's appointment with Aunty Babs down the road has left me with a crew-cut and the appearance of a boy.

As punishment, we're forced to accompany my mother on her never-ending round of the local shops. We've already stopped at Betty's Bakery for the weekly update on the postman and his *special* deliveries. Then at the butcher's Mother's made sure that Bill in his stripy apron hasn't short-changed her on the sausages.

Only now it's time to head to Mr Evans'. My mother turns to us with a stern face.

'Remember girls, don't speak unless you're spoken to. Stand up straight and for goodness sake, don't touch anything!'

She opens the door and we step into the smell of wood shavings and damp fields. My seven-year-old heart beats rapidly as I cling to the belt of her coat before I perform the ritual, vigorous feet-wiping on the mat inside.

Mr Evans, with his omnipotent, grey beard and judgmental eyes, exudes a sense of authority and power. Always dressed in his brown tradesman's jacket, leather hat on his head, he wields a mighty sweeping brush in his weather-worn hands. His voice is commanding and Yorkshirely brusque and the local housewives queue for his attention in terrified silence. There's no running gossip or friendly banter tolerated in Mr Evans' personal Garden of Eden.

His colourful displays of fruit and veg line up in precise rows. Those sour, green Granny Smiths that my mother buys lie polished and shiny next to the rosy-hued Braeburns. Beside them, the exotic Golden Delicious, temptingly sweet, but out of our price range, glisten seductively under our gaze.

'Get away from them apples!'

Mr Evans' voice booms, as Our Bev's hand lingers over the Golden Delicious.

'Beverly! What did I tell you?'

My mother has *that look* in her eye.

Mr Evans towers before my sister, brush raised in readiness. She drops her hand and he lowers his brush, scything through the customers' legs to sweep away the sawdust on the floor.

Then, turning his attention to the queue, he decides what purchases he will permit today. First to be turned down is a timid newly-wed.

'No thae can't 'ave them Maris Pipers. It's King Edwards thae needs for chips.'

Another trembling customer has her recipe instructions rejected outright.

'Making lemon curd? Then thae'll be needing four large lemons not two.'

No one contradicts him because his word is law.

We girls find ourselves backed up against the display of apples. Our Bev nudges me and I watch in horrified awe as her hand whips out from beneath her poncho, grabs an apple and disappears. She grins, then nods at me. But I can't! Our Bev glares at me. I shake my head. She nods again more urgently. I bite my lip. She kicks my shin. I glance round nervously. Then my hand darts out, encircles the treasure, and disappears back beneath the knitted folds. The deed is done. Our Bev nods approvingly.

And finally it's my mother's turn.

'The usual Granny's please.'

'Them's cookers thae knows, not eaters. 'ow about some Golden Delicious?'

My mother purses her lips.

'Thank you, but no.'

There's a collective intake of breath.

Mr Evans scowls.

'No?'

'That's correct. The usual please.'

My mother exits the shops with a triumphant smile on her face and the Granny Smiths in her bag.

But soon it's Monday morning and the only apples on my mind are the ones for the teacher. Every morning begins with a traditional assembly which includes a Bible story, a prayer and a hymn. I learn that apples are dangerous to eat (particularly if offered to you by a naked lady), that when it rains heavily an ark is preferable to an umbrella, and that spoilt younger children always get the best coats. I'm heartened by the fact that, even if you've been swallowed by a whale, you can live to tell the tale, that with a home-made catapult you can defeat a giant, and that a Good Samaritan will always cross the road to help you.

From these tales, I recognise that God is all seeing, all-knowing and, at times, worryingly vengeful. To get in His good books I learn to recite the Lord's Prayer by heart. I'm not sure what a trespass is, but I know all about temptation and forgiveness, and it weighs heavily on my young heart. And it's as I'm singing the words to our newest hymn that I finally realise the truth!

'God in *a workman's jacket* as before,
Sweeping the shavings from His workshop floor.'

Of course, it's so obvious to me now! He sees everything. He knows everything. He wears a workman's jacket and he's always sweeping the floor. Mr Evans is God!

He is, therefore, the only one who can deliver me from evil. But I've sinned against Him! I'm not good enough to go to Heaven. Surely he'll strike me down and I'll burn in Hell for all eternity?

After nights of sleepless torment, tossing and turning about my lack of perfection, I have black circles under my eyes and my mother is concerned.

'What on earth's wrong with you? You'd better not be sickening for something.'

When I finally confess, she tuts -

'Mr Evans isn't God! God would never drop his aitches! Nonetheless, I'm very disappointed in you. Did your big sister put you up to this?'

I glance up. Our Bev is in the doorway, making threatening gestures. I shake my head.

'Well, I expected better from you, my girl. There's nothing for it - you'll just have to own up and face the consequences.'

I'm not convinced by her argument, as God does a lot of *smiting* in the Bible, which doesn't sound very forgiving. However, the next day my mother marches me shame-facedly into the greengrocer's and I eventually find the courage to look God straight in the eye. My eyes start to tear and my lower lip wobbles. My heart's pounding and my mouth's dry. Am I to be mown down by his broom of retribution?

But God's in a merciful mood today. He tilts his hat backwards on his head, and his face breaks into an unexpected smile.

'Na then, laddie.'

He stops for a minute in confusion, looking at my shorn head atop my granny-knitted poncho. My mother shakes her head at him, irritated, and he continues.

'Na then, lassie. Stop thae blubbing! What thae did were wrong, and thae knows it but thae's only a littl'un and no one's perfect.'

Then, with an uncharacteristically cheery wink, He leans over the counter and hands me another forbidden apple. He turns to my mother with some unwanted advice.

'Na then, Missus, I'll add that to thae weekly bill too. And if thae can't afford Golden Delicious, them Braeburns are cheap but sweet. Seems little lassie 'ere knows 'er eaters from 'er cookers!'

For some reason, my mother leaves the shop muttering under her breath.

Her mood hasn't improved by Sunday morning and she's still concerned about my spiritual well-being. She's deemed my soul definitely needs saving this week - so it's off to church.

When Our Bev groans, Mother replies firmly -

'Yes, you too Madam! You may look like Snow White but don't think for one minute you've hoodwinked me.'

So Father's forced into his ancient wedding suit, whilst Our Bev and I are suitably dressed up in buttons and bows, hair brushed into meek submission. But underneath our calm compliance, our inner anarchists strain to escape. I'm clutching a handful of marbles in my fists and the ears of Our Bev's toy horse can be seen poking out of her coat pocket.

'Oh lamb of God that taketh away the sins of the world. Have mercy on us,' intones Crinkly Clergyman, as I battle to keep my eyes open.

He's a kindly soul but fast approaching death. His dog collar swings round his skinny neck and his stringy, white hair has emigrated from his head to his nostrils. He's certainly not a poster boy for Christianity.

We know that once we've bobbed up and down a few dozen times and Our Bev's charmed all around her with her voice of an angel, then Crinkly Clergyman will shuffle forwards to the lectern to deliver his sermon.

As the congregation is droned into a slumber, Champion the Wonder horse canters along the pew shelf, jumping over the hymn books and bibles, narrowly avoiding the cannon balls being fired at him. Father's head is nodding gently, oblivious to our antics, but Mother shoots us a warning look. Champion gallops back to his stable and all weapons are returned to the armoury.

Once the coast's clear, Our Bev fishes into her pocket, and with a finger to her lips, passes me half of a piece of flapjack she's filched from the pantry. It's Mother's secret recipe and its chewy, golden-syrup oatiness keeps our little mouths busy, as its brown-sugar butteriness melts on our tongues.

I slide closer to Our Bev in the hope of finding a soft cushion for my head but she elbows me in the ribs as Crinkly Clergyman clears his throat and gets ready to read out the weekly announcements.

'And finally, I'd like to introduce your new minister to you. He's come straight from Theological College and I'm sure you'll make him very welcome.'

I sit up in surprised anticipation as a gasp goes up from the congregation and Trendy Vicar walks out onto the stage and into my life. He's tall, dark and handsome, with a shoulder-length lion's mane of glossy, Vidal Sassoon hair and a pop star's moustache. He's shunned vicar's vestments for a white, flared suit with an impossibly big collar, purple kipper tie and - the piece de resistance - white platform shoes. I can hear Mrs Blue Rinse in the pew behind me tutting. Father's woken up, dazed and confused. And Mother's mouth is pinched in disapproval.

Looking as if he might be about to disco-dance down the aisle, Trendy Vicar shimmies to the lectern, raises his well-toned arms and gorgeous face to the heavens and in a deep baritone belts out -

'Praise the Lord! Hallelujah!'

He's certainly woken up the congregation, and whilst the stick-in-the-muds gaze on in horror, I feel an excitement rising in me, a bubbling lightness fizzing to the surface.

It's the fifteenth Sunday in a row. Trendy Vicar never fails to impress me. He's dramatic and passionate. He mixes the scriptures with music and theatre. He leaves the pulpit and paces up and down the aisle, thundering about precariously on his six-inch heels. He leads us in prayer, where my eyes never quite close, fixating instead on the angry, crescent-shaped scar branded on his left hand. I wonder idly if this is a result of some life-changing incident that brought him to the Lord. But before I can daydream further, he thumps the lectern, raising his voice to regain my attention, and his Casanova eyes pierce my soul.

With his seductive guidance, the messages behind the parables become clear:

- help is always available even when the situation feels desperate
- facing up to your fears is key
- showing compassion and love to others is the way forward

He makes me feel important, special, safe and loved, and gives me a sense that miracles can happen. As a result I've turned into Committed Convert and come away every Sunday with my heart singing, determined to be a model Christian and make the world a better place. The *Who am I?* and *Why am I here?* questions that my mother dismisses as childish ramblings are taken seriously for once. How safe it feels to be guided by a set of rules, a check list for living my life - and all conveniently set out in a handy, bedside book.

In my quest to be a good person I offer to feed the cat and wash the family car for free. I write prayers in my spare time and donate all my pocket money to sad-eyed orphans in Africa. I even sit, uncomplaining, through Our Bev's singing lessons and let her borrow my coveted *Tales of the Lost City of Atlantis.*

My parents are bemused by my newly-discovered religious zeal but unimpressed by Trendy Vicar's commando assaults on the pews. I overhear them talking -

'I'm their mother and want them brought up properly. All that tambourine-waving and happy-clappy nonsense - it's subversive. And that young vicar's far too handsome for his own good. He needs a large helping of humility. Thank goodness Beverly at least seems immune. But I think we should move to a more civilised church soon before any damage is done, don't you?'

'Up to you, love.'

So my mother, in her starched dresses and homage-to-the-queen hats, returns us to the boring predictability of traditional religion. For the moment the light within me keeps on shining but, without Trendy Vicar and his Charismatic Christianity to stoke its fire, the brightness fades. And it will be no match for the heartache which lies ahead.

3

Friendly Philosophers

'What would a wise man or woman do?'

Bob, our endlessly patient philosophy tutor, poses this question in the vain hope that we'll discover a fount of hidden knowledge within.

I glance round the room at the circle of would-be philosophers of all ages, gender and ethnicity. We're sitting in the lounge of a converted semi in the eclectic suburb of Nether Edge, where east meets west: suited professionals mix with boho artists and the local crown-green-bowling club opens its arms to belly dancers and Morris men alike. It's no surprise then to find nose-studded twenty-year-olds sitting next to hearing-aid-wearing pensioners with a few fellow mid-life-maniacs thrown in for good measure.

The problem that Bob fails to understand is that I have no inner wise woman. She's taken a long vacation - if she was ever there in the first place. All this time I've been attending with Zen Mother and I'm none the wiser.

The pink-haired girl with an eyebrow ring shoots up her hand. How come she's been allowed to have a piercing? She can't be more than fourteen. And how come she's only been to a few of these classes yet has already nailed the wise woman?

Those inner voices know why.

'You're slow and stupid.'

'You should do your homework.'

'Homework or Celebrity Sandcastles? It's a no-brainer!'

But I've been to enough philosophy classes to know these voices are part of my Ego-self and don't actually exist, although they've yet to take the hint.

The problem is there's such a lot to take on board. Confucius confuses me and Plato perplexes me but at least *Philosophy in Practice* finds the common ground between philosophers from all cultures, using their discoveries to help us in everyday life. Shakespeare and Rumi bring poetry for our souls, the books of the great religions give us deeper insights, and Galileo and Einstein show us the scientific view.

I realise that the question of *Who am I?* that's dogged me all my life has been addressed by many sages in the past. And, although I'm still no closer to the answer, at least I know I'm not alone in my search.

I've tried to recruit others too but Bubbly Brazilian goes nowhere if music is not involved and English Rose claims to be on a Sugar Craft course at college. Not for them learning about levels of awareness. I, on the other hand, have discovered that I exist in a waking sleep, on auto-pilot, engaged in daily activities without being fully present.

Zen Mother elbows me in the ribs.

'Pay attention. It's time for the lesson.'

Bob clears his throat.

'This week we're considering the Adveita tradition - an ancient Hindu philosophy and one of the classic, Indian paths to spiritual realisation. Adveita believes there's a spirit self - the Atman - within each living entity and this is linked to all other beings, so there's an experience of oneness, rather than duality.'

Interesting concept. I certainly don't feel oneness with any beings at the moment.

'It's like waves on the ocean. Each wave can be distinguished as a separate entity but is, in fact, part of a whole body of water.'

Waves, eh? I feel like I'm drowning in them.

'Or it could be seen that each person is a different item of jewellery but we're all fashioned from the same golden source.'

Only I'm the Bargain Basement earrings.

'Most humans are in a state of unawareness and don't recognise this unity, this *Eternal-I* but see their ego-led *Everyday-I* as the true self. This encourages them to act in a selfish, self-interested manner, rather than with the greater good in mind. So it's important to realise that we are not the voices in our head but the higher awareness itself.'

But the voices in my head are having none of this.

'He doesn't know what he's on about! And you're too thick to keep up.'

'You should be at home sorting out the family.'

'Enough! Swap philosophy for zumba.'

Bob strokes his white wizard's beard - a sign something interesting's about to happen.

'Ahem, now we're going to put this into practice. I'd like you all to find a balanced, comfortable posture, close your eyes and focus on the five senses.'

I shift uncomfortably in my seat. I've forgotten to tell the kids their granddad's TV's on the blink and I said he could come round to watch the football.

'Now, concentrate on the feeling of your body on the chair and the touch of the clothes and the air on your skin.'

Oh Lord - clothes - did I switch on the washing machine before I left?

'And become aware of taste and smell.'

Pizza! I hope Devil Teen's remembered to cook his brother tea.

'Next, connect to the hearing, starting first with noises close by, then allow the hearing to embrace the furthest sounds...'

As I close my eyes, the lack of visual stimulus gradually heightens my perception of sound. I focus first on my own breathing, then pan out into the wider world - the creak of a chair, the rustle of the breeze through the curtains, the bang of a car door, the distant hum of traffic.

Slowly all sounds cease and my head for once is clear and empty. A golden expanse fills my consciousness and its light stretches in all directions. I am but a speck of dust caught in its rays. I feel a connectedness to all people, a beautiful sense of oneness. Is this the essence of Adveita?

For a brief minute or two, I rest in *the now* until the very thought of why I don't get to this point more often, pushes me out of the *now* and back into my head once more. Bloody hell! I've forgotten what this week's task was - I wasn't listening.

Bob stretches and pulls down the sleeves on his leather-patched jumper.

'Now then, the task. I hope you all did it. Who's practised giving everyone their *full* attention when listening?'

There's an uncomfortable hush as the group members contemplate their shoes. I jump straight in, knowing it's better to confess my sin freely than have it dragged out of me later.

'Sorry, Bob. I forgot to do that because I was still thinking about the task from the week before. You know - *find the beauty in everything*. And I have to say that British weather used to depress me, but now I appreciate all those shades of grey in the sky. And when the number three bus is late as usual, instead of getting ratty, I look at a raindrop running down the shelter window and think how beautiful it is.'

Bob nods approvingly, glad that at least some ancient philosopher's wisdom is trickling through. I'm off the hook. I can relax now and watch the others squirm.

Zen Mother, goody two shoes - probably the only one of us who always does the tasks - offers her view.

'Mm, well I found it interesting. I like to think I'm a good listener.'

I curb my uncharitable thoughts, because actually she *is* a good listener. Maybe when she's stopped talking I can jump in with an example of how body language shows you *are* really listening. That'll impress Bob.

'But I found that instead of *really* listening,' Zen Mother says, 'I was already formulating responses of my own whilst the speaker was still talking.'

Mm, I didn't see that one coming. Maybe she has a point. I vow to try and really listen for the rest of the session.

Bob pauses silently for a moment before replying. He does this a lot. It's about letting answers and decisions be made from a position of stillness, rather than from a busy, preoccupied mind. I understand the logic behind this but all the same, it's intensely annoying. Just spit it out man, dammit! The well-thought out answer arrives after several minutes.

'Good.'

Eyebrow Ring has recently had her tongue pierced.

'What I found shhtriking is that I washh aware of my own voishh when shhpeaking. It washh like I washh the obshherver, notishhing shhomeone elshh shhpeak.'

'Excellent.'

Zen Mother chimes in again.

'When I really focussed on listening, I felt a much stronger connection with the speaker. Weirdly, it felt at times like I was the one speaking, as well as listening.'

'That's a very good point that we're going to touch on in a minute.'

Typical. Bob's got his favourites - he's always applauding them. *I* only ever get a brief nod for *my* contributions.

'Now this week we're going to listen to our minds and their unhelpful negative thoughts. We're going to make an effort not to criticise anyone.'

Thank goodness my lips are tightly sealed. No one will ever know my real opinion of them.

'By that, I mean, even *silently* in our heads,' Bob adds.

I concede defeat and lean back in my chair, just in time to catch a small orange stone that's rolled down the sleeve of my jumper. I quickly stuff it in my jeans pocket before anyone notices.

Back home I fail immediately at the task because, as I open the door, the smell of burning is all pervasive.

'For God's sake, can't you even cook a pizza?'

Devil Teen scowls, wrinkling his freckled nose.

'It's not my fault. Granddad couldn't work out the remote control. He said *Gran* thinks I ought to be less argumentative and more helpful. As if I don't do enough already what with school work and babysitting little poo-face! Anyway I went to help him and didn't hear the timer.'

Boy Scout stomps into the kitchen.

'I've just got in, isn't it? Tripped over a pile of shoes and found the house on fire and your dad tuning in to football when I need to watch rugby! Where have you been?'

'You know where I've been. It's my weekly class. It'd be nice if you paid attention for once.'

'It'd be even nicer, my lovely, if you tidied the house for once. It's a complete tip. Bloody philosophy and searching for the truth. I'll show you the truth, isn't it? You've been sitting on your bum all day, navel-gazing, whilst I've been working my socks off and come home to Armageddon! It's no wonder I jump at the chance of a night away.'

'Well bloody go then. I'm not your slave and at least I care about my dad. You never ring yours. You've no appreciation of your parents and no idea what it's like to lose one. You never put family first. You're so selfish.'

'Now you're just being hysterical, isn't it? Bloody menopausal woman. I'm going out to the pub to watch the match and get some grub. I hope you've cleaned up and calmed down by the time I get back.'

'Ok, go ahead and do that. It's not as if we'll miss you. You're never bloody here. One day I'll show you. You'll come home and find all the clutter gone and maybe I'll be gone too!'

After I sort out the chaos, stick another pizza in the oven and run my father back to leafy Totley, I try in vain to recreate the peace I found in today's practical exercise. But my head's full of angry thoughts. What we once loved about each other - my unfettered spirit and quirky fondness for royalty, his sense of order and passion for rugby - is now a source of constant conflict. My mind's spinning and those bloody voices just won't shut up.

'Bet he never really loved you.'

'Let's face it, he's right. You should really make an effort with the housework.'

'Ignore them. Make a clean break of it.'

My inner wise woman finally surfaces to advise caution and focussing on happier memories. So I drag myself to the bookshelf to look through those old honeymoon pictures and remind myself what love used to be like.

The albums are all jammed together higgledy-piggledy. I reach up and one comes crashing down onto the floor. It's from my pre-marriage days. It falls open at a photo of a hotel in Lyon, France. And once again I find myself staring into those familiar, come-to-bed eyes.

I shiver imperceptibly. Is this just a coincidence?

4

Sporting Behaviour?

After a sleepless night, I'm waylaid on the stairs by a plaintive 'Muuuuuum! I need a lift to the tournament tonight. Can you take me?'

This is the first that Small Child has told me about any competition, but I'm not a super sleuth mother for nothing. Years of parenting have honed my spying skills and my nightly sweep of his room has already ferreted out a crumpled information sheet, hidden under the half-eaten apple in his lunch box. This has given me a whole twelve hours' advanced warning of my expected taxi-driver and cheer-leader duties.

Although I'm still smarting from yesterday's marital stand-off, I feel I owe it to my son to encourage some paternal participation. I raise the subject over breakfast, making an effort to curb all negative thoughts.

'Did you know our little man's been chosen for the handball team? It'd be great if you could come along to watch.'

There's a grunt and a slight lift of an eyebrow.

'Well, if they want parents to watch, then they should hold the competitions *after* work hours, isn't it?'

'Can't you finish early for a change? You never come to any of his after-school activities. *Luke's dad* seems to manage it.'

'Listen, my lovely. I have *real* work to do, not like that arty-farty clog maker.'

'Free-lance book illustrator actually.'

'Whatever. He needs to get a proper job, isn't it? No wonder his wife left him.'

'Oh for goodness sake. It's probably just as well you can't come. *I'll* re-organise *my* day to watch *our* son, shall I then?'

'Great idea, my lovely. And while you're at it - get the scissors to that hair of his or he'll never see the ball coming, isn't it?'

I bite my tongue. At least Small Child has *one* supportive parent. My son's typically on the side-lines observing, so if participating in this tournament helps him make some new friends, then I'm all for it.

Small Child attends Bohemia City Primary - a school with children from 'interesting backgrounds' and an Ofsted record of barely 'satisfactory'. Being in the inner city, it has limited space and no green area, so the children's *sports enrichment* takes place either in the ramshackle hall or in the cracked, tarmacked yard. For this reason, I'm impressed their team's even entered for a non-mainstream sporting event.

I track Small Child down to the living room, where he's perched on top of the bookcase, and quiz him about this unfamiliar sport. How long's he been playing it? How did he get chosen? And what sports clothes does he need? Small Child is uncommunicative and replies unhelpfully -

'Dunno. We played it in lessons. I was only the sixth fastest but Mrs Stickler said she needed children with *reliable* parents. Oh, and she said they provide a kit.'

'Hmm, thank you - very illuminating. Who else is going? I presume Cristiano, Ethan and Luke? They're all good at sports. And Saffron's mum texted me to say she's taking Saffron and Akila. So is there anyone else who wants a lift? Because I can take three more if needs be.'

'No, don't think so. Mummy can you move? You're in the way of the TV.'

And on that note, I'm dismissed.

It's now three minutes past the end of the school day. I'm usually here before the bell goes but am delayed because I stopped to pick up some light refreshments, just in case … Small Child exclaims dramatically -

'Mum where have you been? Everyone's gone already! You're going to make us late!'

It is the *us* part of the sentence I focus on, taking in the extra faces looking up at me expectantly.

'Marek? Saeed? Aren't your parents taking you?'

Apparently not.

However, I'm not the only parent there. Luke's dad's also at the school gates looking as if he's had a complete personality transplant. Gone are his signature clogs, ethically-sourced T-shirt and fair-trade jeans, to be replaced by Italian loafers, Moschino shirt, sharp-fitting suit and designer stubble. Gone too is his old, battered VW, upgraded to a brand-new Audi. He's surrounded by a gaggle of excited boys - Luke, Tyler, Cristiano and Ethan - bedazzled by the all-singing-and-dancing Satnav and sound system.

In contrast, Marek and Saeed's faces fall when they see their ride. I quickly fling empty bottles, sweet wrappers and Nerf gun bullets into a plastic bag. Then I discreetly pocket a small quartz stone that's rolled under the front seat. Finally we're ready for off, although with three nine-year-olds trying to out-do each other in a funny-face-pulling contest, it's hard to focus.

As we stop at the first set of traffic lights on Eccy Road, Luke's dad pulls up besides us, with Ray-Bans on, windows down, cool music blaring out, and his posse getting down to the beat. The funny faces quickly turn to sad envy - Small Child's mum and her Radio Two grooves are just not doing it for my crew.

Trying to reclaim some street cred, I floor the accelerator and screech off in a cloud of smoke, catching the Audi unawares as I arrive in first place at the next set of lights. When Luke's dad takes off his sunglasses and gives me *the look*, I feign sudden interest in my rear view mirror. And, on green, I set off sedately, allowing the Audi to disappear into the distance and macho honour to be restored.

After twenty minutes we cross the border into the north of the city, where life-expectancy is ten years lower than those of us who live in the more affluent south. To try to make amends, the government's poured money into the area and when we pull into the car park, the boys all gasp at the sight of the futuristic, new-build school.

Bubbly Brazilian - in an eye-catching red jumpsuit - English Rose and Zen Mother have just arrived with Saffron and her best friend, Akila. Nearby, a group of smartly-suited youngsters are waiting. Meanwhile, I open the door for my mob to exit, and they pile out screaming and bulldoze their way through to Mrs Stickler and Mr PE.

As we go down the steps into the tournament area, I ask Bubbly Brazilian what's going on.

'Well my dahleengs, there are four teams competing tonight. Bohemia City, obviously, and that posh private school. Then there's the notorious Northern Academy and of course our rivals - Southfields Juniors.'

The parents groan at the name. Southfields' catchment area isn't far from ours but their social mix is much narrower and more affluent, so they rather look down on our lack of uniform, which Bohemian Citizens view as their right to exercise self-expression, creativity and freedom. In contrast, the privileged suburbanites regard our imaginative dress sense as undisciplined laziness on the road to anarchy. Despite weekly assemblies on equality, fairness and respect, both schools remain arch-enemies. So we must beat them and preserve our honour.

At this news, Luke's dad gathers our team together in a huddle and gives them a rousing pep talk about winning at all costs. I worry he's going to put undue pressure on Small Child, who's already nervous about letting the side down.

'What's going on with him?' I ask of the fellow mums - 'He's like a different man.'

'Well that's the point isn't it? He's trying to be a man,' says English Rose.

'Apparently, he's landed a top job with that fancy ad agency in town,' says Bubbly Brazilian - 'They're paying him a fortune. I think it's turned his head.'

But Zen Mother smiles patiently.

'It's just a phase. He'll come round.'

The competition's about to start and Mr Handball, the organiser, gathers the schools together. Team Bohemia has a grand total of seven supporters. In contrast, our rivals have brought an army of fans. Even The Northern Academy, now in special measures, has assembled an impressive range of followers. With their in-your-face buzz cuts and stick-on skull and crossbones tattoos, they might be bottom of the Schools' League Table, but at sport they have a chance to show the Education Secretary there's more to life than maths and literacy.

Mr Handball explains that in this schools' version, to encourage equal participation, there must be two girls playing in each team at any one time. I look around and count five girls for each school, apart from Bohemia City, which has just Saffron and Akila. I hope they're up to the challenge as they're going to have to play at least three matches and Saffron, who's never struck me as very sporty, is already out of breath from walking down the stairs.

I hiss at Small Child.

'How come *she* was picked?'

But he replies with evident awe -

'Don't worry Mum, she's got a wicked throw on her.'

Our first match is against the posh privates, kitted out in well-ironed tabards with school crest and Latin motto. Meanwhile, Mr PE has his hand in a large sack and, like a bad magician, keeps pulling out a series of well-worn, crumpled, polyester vests of varying sizes. Cristiano's is down by his knees, Tyler's can barely make it over his chest and Saeed's got his on back to front.

Small Child comes to complain.

'Mum my foot still hurts - that verruca's not gone yet and this vest's well whiffy. Do I have to wear it?'

I stand up-wind from him because if he, with his cavalier disregard for hygiene, can smell it, then it must be bad.

'You'll be fine, sweetheart. Anyway, it's too late to change now as the whistle's gone.'

The carnage begins and, despite Luke best efforts in goal, we're being massacred. His dad takes him aside and I can hear the words 'useless' and 'you'd better man-up!' I'm not sure I like this new, competitive dad very much.

'How much practice have you actually done in school?' I ask Small Child, as our team walk off despondently.

'We've played twice in PE.'

'Well that explains everything! Never mind - it's not the winning but the taking part that counts.'

Small Child rolls his eyes and replies.

'Tell that to Luke's dad.'

Luckily, we have a chance to watch some matches before competing again. It's a revelation to the team, as they start to pick up some tips. But it's little help for our next game against The Northern Academy, who psyche us out with an impressive rugby Hakka. A muttering goes round the spectators as their No 6 player comes on. He's all of 5 foot 10 and must weigh in around eleven stone. Luke's dad isn't happy.

'No way that kid's nine years old. He looks at least thirteen! I'm going to have a word with the ref.'

Zen Mother tries to placate him.

'It could just be his hormones you know. You should always try and give the benefit of the doubt. After all, Tyler's quite a strapping lad too.'

'Yeah, but that giant's twice the size of Tyler. I've been played for a fool long enough and I've had it with acting the nice guy.'

But before Luke's dad can demand to see a birth certificate, play's started and blood's flowing. Akila's been thumped *accidentally* in the nose but is sent back on because of the two-girl rule. Marek's been tripped more than once and Ethan comes off court, several bruises the worse for wear. Once again we've lost, but this time we've scored a few goals and, thankfully, it's break-time.

While the posh private school sets out trestle tables for a banquet, and the Southfields' crowd feast on their *simply the best*, we fumble vainly through our empty pockets. English Rose looks crest-fallen.

'I packed my bag full of goodies but when we swapped cars I forgot to bring it with me.'

I open my bag with a touch of smugness.

'Just as well that I remembered my royal biscuit tin. And I've also got enough flapjacks and fizzy drinks to go round.'

And for once Small Child smiles as if he's genuinely glad to have me as a mother, instead of obsessively checking my head for grey hairs and freaking out when he discovers I've developed yet another wrinkle.

Shortly afterwards, Posh Private Mum offers us the leftovers from their Fortnum and Mason's hamper and I discover her team has played several competitions in order to get through to the finals. How strange then that Bohemia City have gone straight in without playing any qualifying matches…

The break comes to an end but Luke's dad's still fuming about the Neanderthal nine-year-old.

'Seriously. Someone needs to say something. I'm sure I've spotted a couple of lager cans in that Northern Academy's black bin bag. I'm going to have a word with their coach.'

Once again Zen Mother comes to the rescue.

'I'm not sure it's such a good idea to mention it to him, what with his bent nose and thuggish expression. Wouldn't it be better to give our team some pointers instead? Our coach doesn't seem very interested in helping them improve. He's just making them pose for team shots all the time. You'd think he'd be more concerned with winning than photography. And as for Mrs Stickler, she's spent the entire tournament marking worksheets.'

But Bubbly Brazilian's had a better idea. I turn round to see she's got her playlist on speaker-phone, booming out Queen, whilst shaking her booty and getting the Bohemians to clap along.

'You got blood on your face, poshos. You big disgrace, Northern Academy. Waving Bohemian's banner all over the place. Southfields - we will, we will - rock you. Sing it Bohemians! We will, we will - rock you.'

Cristiano's mortified. But the rest of the team, pumped up by the music, are raring to go. Even Saeed, who's normally reserved, has got his hands in the air.

'I'm not sure we're supposed to encourage that sort of behaviour,' whispers Zen Mother.

I shrug my shoulders.

'No, well if anyone complains, we'll just say she's foreign and knows no better. Anyway, it's got those Southfielders rattled, which can only be a good thing.'

And indeed, our final game's the deal breaker - up against Southfields with their go-faster trainers and pre-planned tactics. They may have taken their dextrose tablets but we have the element of surprise and are fuelled up on Coke and Red Bull.

Luke scores first, much to the delight of his dad, who gives me a superior look. Then the Southfielders equalise, taking out two of our players in the process. Ethan and Small Child are sent onto court. I smile at my boy with a false brightness I don't feel. The pressure's on. And even though I know it's the taking part that counts, the voices are telling me otherwise.

'See your son's as hopeless as you are. He's going to let the side down too.'

'You should spend more time helping him improve.'

'To hell with all after-school activities!'

41

The clock's ticking down and Saffron, who's spent her entire time on court avoiding any action, has found herself, finally, with the ball. She's about as far away from the goal as she could be, but with a ritual cry that any Sumo wrestler would be proud of, she lobs it with incredible power right into Small Child's hands. For one agonising second it looks like he might drop it. Fear etches his face. I will him with all my mother's might to do what he needs to. He turns to face the goal. Hands trembling, he bowls a weak under-arm which bounces once, twice, then rolls meekly to the back of the net - the Bohemians win the game!

Mrs Stickler looks up briefly from her marking and gives a nod of approval while Mr PE runs round taking victory snaps, despite the fact we've only finished third overall. When I ask him if he's disappointed we didn't win, he replies with candid honesty.

'Oh no. We only entered at the last minute because one of the qualifying teams dropped out. We didn't stand a chance. Still, it was a great opportunity to get some publicity shots for the school website. It makes it look as if we offer lots of different sports. Ofsted like that kind of thing you know.'

We may not have won the tournament but Small Child has a huge grin on his face as he rushes through the front door, blonde hair swinging, to regale the rest of the family with news of his winning goal.

'That's great, big, little brother!'

Delightful Daughter, bends over to hug him, then remembering the recent nit incident, draws back and decides on a high five instead. Devil Teen's obviously impressed, despite himself.

'Well done poo-face! You might even get as good as me one day. Though you'll actually have to start playing rugby first, won't he dad?'

His father looks up distractedly from the match on TV.

'Oh … good on you, son. I'm sure your mam caught it on camera. See, you *can* win if you put your mind to it. Talking of which

I've just been reading that climbing's going to become an Olympic event, so we might make a champion of you yet!'

My father, here for his mid-week meal, pats Small Child on the head.

'Brilliant. I'll let Gran know.'

My heart sinks. I was kind of hoping this would all go away but the voices are here to remind me.

'What kind of daughter are you?'

'You should've rung the district nurse.'

'Let someone else take care of it for once!'

Later, as I put Small Child to bed, he gives out a long sigh.

'What's wrong sweetheart? I thought you had a good day?'

'I did mummy. It's just sometimes I think daddies get disappointed in us.'

'What do you mean by that?'

'Well, my daddy doesn't want me to climb for fun, he wants me to win an Olympic medal and Luke's dad tells him he should be more competitive. Luke says his father didn't use to care about winning. They used to have a good time together, drawing and making up stories. Aren't we allowed to do things just for fun, then?

'Of course you should do things for fun! Fun's really important. It makes life worth living. Now enough of your questions. Go to sleep. It's the weekend tomorrow. No school - so plenty of time for fun.'

I tiptoe out of his room but his words stay with me and that night, as I restlessly attempt to sleep, I wonder, like him, what *is* the point of us being here? I remember back to my childhood, that happy-go-lucky self who ran carefree over the moors and wrote stories for fun. Where did she go to?

And now I'm more than half-way through my life, with two, nearly independent kids and a small child who won't remain small much longer. I've been married almost twenty five years but somewhere along the line the fun's disappeared.

I think back to my tragic, teenaged heartbreak and then again to the French love I never fully committed to. And I contemplate, not for the first time, how things might have turned out differently.

5

Magic Mushrooms in the Cemetery

'Off to the library to do some revision, mum.'

Our Bev shoots me a knowing look. Lucky her - she's escaped education for a job at the riding school, leaving academia and the burden of my mother's expectations to me.

'That's good to hear, young lady.' She gives me a rare smile of approval. 'University's in your sights, as long as you don't get distracted…'

She turns to my father for reinforcement and, disconcertingly, he stares me in the eye.

'Your mother's right, love.'

My stomach churns - my conditional place means getting three top grades but my mock results have fallen short of that. I should be studying but as I leave the house, I take the path that leads away from the library.

You see, I'm seventeen years old and in with the *cool gang* at Bohemia City Comp. Their parents, unlike mine, are relaxed ex-hippies and the cigarettes on offer at their parties are not of the tobacco variety.

I'd like to say my mother's principled upbringing stops me inhaling, but bowing to peer pressure, I take a drag, then choke in a stream of tears. In the end what prevents a drugs habit isn't moral fibre but the physical inability to get to grips with smoking.

Instead I watch from the side lines as the hip crowd dissolve into incomprehensible giggles and go on scavenging trips when the *munchies* hit them. Whilst it's slightly perturbing being the only member of the group who's not constantly high, I don't care because I'm in love.

My John the Baptist look-alike, with his complicated background, uneasy family relationships and addictive personality needs saving from himself and I'm the one to do that. I am Protector of Lost Causes and it's my mission to keep him from harm.

He has long, dark, flowing locks - which my mother disapproves of - troubled brown eyes and a sensitive heart that only I understand. When sober enough he plays the guitar. Not the rousing calls to God of my charismatic Christian days, but melancholic, discordant chords that make my soul shiver in sadness.

Today we're meeting in the park. My heart lurches at the sight of him - he's so handsome - I can't believe he's hanging out with me! But he looks restless and more agitated than usual.

'Hey there. What's up? Has something happened?'

He's about to tell me, then changes his mind.

'No. I'm cool. Just waiting for Apple, then I'm all yours for the day.'

'Apple?'

'Yeah. You know. The dealer.'

'You said you were going to cut down during revision time! And it's a bit public here, isn't it? If my mother finds out you're taking stuff, she'll ban me from seeing you. It's bad enough you're not from upmarket Dore or Whirlow! Our Dad's not too keen on you either.'

A disarming smile lights up his face as he folds me into his arms.

'Just as well that *you're* keen on me, then!'

I breathe in his familiar, musky smell. Our bodies fit together so well. And if my mother knew *that* then she'd definitely ban me from seeing him! I sigh with longing.

'I hope this bloke's coming soon. Then we can go back to yours and *be keen* in private. Anyway, why's he called Apple?'

The Baptist smiles - 'You'll see. He's here now.'

A lanky figure, face hidden by curtains of greasy, dark hair beckons us over from the back of the courts. He's dressed in black and looks shifty.

'Nae then. Is that thae bird? 'Ow's about an introduction? Ey up Princess.'

He nods his head upwards in acknowledgement and I understand his nickname. He has the largest Adam's apple I've ever seen. I try not to stare and pretend I'm here for the tennis rather than illegal transactions.

Later, back at the Baptist's, I snuggle up against his bare chest. I don't care if he's from the wrong side of the city or that he smokes, I just care that he's here with me now.

'Do you want a drag?'

I shake my head - being with him is enough to make me high. It's not puppy love or teenage lust, but a sense of coming home. Whilst I get on well with my family, it sometimes feels so much is expected of me - good grades, a university education and a sensible job at the end of it.

The Baptist, on the other hand, accepts me as I am. He never tries to improve me - he thinks I'm perfect already! And unlike Our Bev, the homebody, he understands my wanderlust.

'Hey babe. I've been thinking.'

He caresses my arm.

'Why don't we take off after exams? You know, hitch round Europe.'

He pulls me to him and for a moment our souls entwine and dance in the darkness of his eyes.

'Really? Just the two of us?'

'Yeah, to the south of France to pick grapes or sell ice-creams on the beach.'

'Sounds great but the harvest isn't til the end of August and uni starts in September.'

'Well, forget uni and other people's expectations. You and me, kindred spirits, exploring the world together.'

I catch my breath. What could be more romantic than running away with the love of my life? But I hesitate a second too long.

'It's your mother, isn't it?'

'I just … She'd never forgive me. She's set her heart on me getting a degree. But we could still travel in the holidays.'

For a moment he looks sad, then, seeing my concern, kisses it away.

'Little Miss Sensible. You're right of course. But for now, the house is empty and there's plenty to explore here…'

The final term passes quickly and meeting up with the Baptist out of school becomes difficult as my parents waylay me in the hallway every time I try to sneak out. My mother insists on accompanying me to the library and once a week forces my father to take me to the pub as a break from homework.

It's a bastion of maleness but, as my father is a regular, my presence is tolerated as long as I stay quiet, blend into the flocked wallpaper background and sip any beverages from an appropriate *lady's glass*. It's the non PC past and underage drinking is the norm. I sit there silently knocking back the Babychams, trying to recall French vocabulary, as my father dissects the latest scores with his beer-bellied football mates.

When they've finished, we have our usual conversation.

'How's school?'

'Fine.'

'Geography?'

'Gave it up two years ago.'

'Really? Home to your mother then?'

'Sure.'

The Baptist's family, however, aren't so vigilant, and without me by his side, his meetings with Apple become more regular.

One lunchtime, I reluctantly pull myself away from his embrace.

'Come on. Let's do a bit of revision.'

'Let's not. This is much more fun.'

'I know but there's only a few weeks left, then all summer and a whole new life in Bristol together.'

He bows his head.

'Yeah, well. I'm not sure I'll get the grades, babe.'

'Course you will. I'm not going anywhere without you!'

And, over the long summer, I never stray from his side, much to my mother's annoyance. He's full of wild suggestions but, like a guard dog, I'm alert to danger.

'It's a beautiful evening. Let's climb on the roof and watch the sunset.'

'Er, it's a bit high and you're very high - maybe not such a good idea?'

'Come on! Take off your shoes and socks. We can dance together on the water.'

'Honestly, I don't think we should. It's the canal! It's deep and scummy. Why don't we lie on the grass and watch the stars instead?'

Distracted from this current idea, the Baptist lies back and gives a deep sigh.

'Look at those stars. How many billions of years have they been burning? And look at us pathetic humans. Our lives extinguished in mere decades. Don't you ever wonder what the point is? Why are we here? Where are we going? Who are we?'

His heartfelt questions take me back in time to my seven-year-old self, opening a door I've long since shut. Before I can answer, he continues.

'I thought I knew who I was. But it turns out my whole life's been a complete lie. I found out a while ago that I'm adopted. How do you like that?'

'What? When? Why didn't you tell me? I thought we shared everything!'

'I'm sorry babe. I've been wanting to tell you for ages … I just didn't know where to begin. I guess I was trying to sort it out in my own head first…'

Looking at his dejected expression, my heart goes out to him.

'Bloody hell. That must've been a shock.'

'Too right. Explains why my kid brother looks nothing like me. He's theirs of course. I'm the cuckoo.'

'No, you're not. Don't think like that. You're amazing! Your parents adopting you probably let them relax enough to have a child naturally. Without you, there'd be no little brother. You're the gift that gave them a family.'

'Whatever. I don't feel like a gift. I don't feel like anything. I just feel numb. It's like my identity's been taken away. Like I've been sucked into a black hole. Like I'm stuck in some bottomless void.'

'Is that why you've been smoking so much?'

'Guess so. It takes the edge off. Stops me thinking. You wouldn't understand… Anyway, boring. Let's climb that pylon.'

But he's wrong. I *do* understand. At least partially. I know what it's like to question your identity. To think you're not good enough -

that love's conditional on behaving a certain way. I've had many nights recently, lying awake, regretting not studying harder, and knowing I might let everyone down. I've stared into that pit of darkness too, but the thought of our future together has kept me going.

I can help him. I know I can. I'll make him feel safe and loved. Maybe together we can pass through this darkness? Maybe there's a way through to the light?

But how can we get there?

We go early in the morning, into the woods on a foraging expedition. The trees lean over us protectively with their sunshine-dappled canopy quivering with birdsong. The ferns underfoot rustle as small animals skitter out of our way.

I make The Baptist run along the deserted paths with their smell of earthy dankness until we finally collapse, exhausted and giddy, in a clearing. Looking up at the watery-blue sky with its patchwork of streaky-white clouds, I feel a sense of calm and acceptance.

'Who needs drugs when this can make you feel so alive yet so peaceful?'

I turn to the Baptist for confirmation but he's gone to some inner shadow world where I can't reach him.

'Yeah maybe, but it never lasts. The darkness is in me. Waiting. These babies, on the other hand, put a bit of colour back in life…'

He points at the tiny, brown mushrooms, clustered in a fairy circle under one of the trees.

'Just wait til you give them a try!'

'Are you sure they're not the poisonous ones?'

'Pretty sure.'

'Bloody hell. I'm not taking them unless you're 100% sure.'

'Boring. Adds spice to life if there's a hint of danger.'

'No, seriously, I'll be the first in the family to get into university. If I die before I get there, they'll not be happy!'

'Alright Miss University Star. I guarantee they're edible - ok?'

'Yeah, alright then.'

We meander back, hand in hand, a pair of nature-lovers, carrying the fruits of the forest with us in a rustic basket.

Once home, with the coast clear, he rustles us up a fungus delight. But these mushrooms aren't the type my mother usually puts in her omelettes...

Like a condemned man sitting down to his last supper, I eat, savouring every bitter, meaty mouthful and sit back to watch the effects. However, I find myself momentarily distracted by my finger nail.

I've never realised how amazing it is, with its shiny, keratin grooves and delicate hues of pink and white. And my hand is fascinating with its individual lines and idiosyncratic creases. Then my gaze catches the carpet - another object of intense beauty that I've not appreciated before. Each fibre dances and shimmies, and my hand sinks into the softness of its tender caress.

'Let's go to the cemetery,' announces the Baptist, and I'm pulled to standing and ushered out of the door.

Everything's in slow motion. Time has altered and stopped still.

I glide along with a sensation of weightlessness, and stop transfixed by the streetlights. Sounds, colours and smells intermingle enticingly in a hallucinogenic haze. The glow of the lamp calls to me, full-toned and welcoming in its orangeness, and my mouth fills with its taste of burnt toffee.

We enter the cemetery and the tombstones open their arms, whispering,

'Don't be afraid. We're the keepers of your loved ones.'

The church, silhouetted in the moonlight sighs -

'I'm just a symbol. The path lies beyond.'

The trees, haloed with shimmering light, extend their branches outwards in a protective embrace. The damp earth hums imperceptibly with tones of rich, charcoal coffee.

The impenetrable blackness of the sky stirs a memory deep inside me, a forgotten fear, perhaps. But the infinite darkness is dotted with shining starlight which ripples down, cloaking me in its loving radiance, and I feel a sense of profound peace and joy, a oneness with the universe.

I fold the Baptist in a tight embrace and know that we're safe and loved and held. If this is God speaking to me through a vision, then all is well.

Eventually, after a few hours, the euphoria wears off but the experience has been so profound that, unlike the Baptist, I'm in no hurry to repeat it. In fact, for weeks afterwards, I find myself moved, sometimes to tears, by the perfection of a raindrop and the magnificence of a sunset.

The halcyon days of summer roll on. The A-level results come in and, unlike my mixed-up boy, I get the grades I need. Somehow I've managed to fool them all.

The Baptist views my leaving as a treachery.

'You'll forget about me and find some clever, posh guy to talk foreign literature with!'

'Don't be silly. It's you I care about. I'll be back every few weeks and you can come and visit me. And next year, after re-takes, you can join me there.'

'I can't bear to be apart from you! I'll go to pieces. Let's just take off and travel the world. You know you want to. You're only going to university to keep your precious parents quiet.'

It's true, the people-pleaser in me wants to keep my parents happy, but it also wants to keep him happy too. And somewhere deep down, the *Who am I?* has the answer. But what that answer is I've yet to find out.

I sigh, trying to find a compromise.

'Look, give me time to talk to mum. Maybe I can transfer to Sheffield University? I'm not naturally clever. I've had to work hard to get those grades. How am I going to keep up with those students from private schools, anyway? And what's the point if you're not there to share my experiences? Besides mum would be delighted if I stayed here.'

'Yeah, but not if *Her Royal Highness* thought *I* was the reason. She's done her best to break us up as it is!'

'Look, she'll get used to you eventually. Come round with me now and talk to her.'

'You're kidding, aren't you? I'm going mushroom picking. Come with me instead, babe. I need something to calm me down.'

'What you need is to stay *sober* for a change.'

'It's never bothered you before.'

'I know. But if you're off-your-face, my mum's never going to agree.'

'I need to be high to deal with your mother.'

'Now, you're being unfair. She's not that bad.'

He moves towards me and for a moment I think everything will be alright.

'I'm sorry babe. It's just I love you so much. The thought of losing you is tearing me apart.'

'I love you too. But the answer isn't getting stoned all the time. Please help me talk to mum. Maybe I can persuade her that a year travelling will improve my languages.'

'Yeah, until she discovers *I'll* be going too!'

'Well it's worth a try, isn't it?'

But he pulls away from me and his face hardens.

'Look, parents are a lost cause, in my view. *You* talk to her. I'll see you later.'

'Please. *Don't go!*'

But he's already half-way out of the door.

'Great. Go and bloody drug yourself to death then. See if I care.'

'I bloody well will then. I'll take Apple with me. You go and find a posh nob to hang out with. That'll make your mum happy.'

We storm off in opposite directions and I spend a fretful day pretending everything's ok. My mother notices me mooching around. I suspect she knows more than she lets on. As always, her answer to any problem in life is to keep yourself busy.

'Now then young lady. It's about time you learnt some basic cooking techniques if you're going to be fending for yourself soon. How about I show you how to make my special flapjack?'

Despite myself, I can't help being curious.

'What? Your secret recipe? You're really going to show me how to make it? Our Bev doesn't even know, and she's the one who's half-decent at cooking!'

'Exactly. Beverly has different talents to you. You're never going to be a culinary wizard, which is why you're going to university - even if it is to study some ridiculous, communist language. At least you'll find a decent job at the end of it. So, anyway, I know you modern girls are all feminists, burning your bras, wearing trousers - no need for men anymore. But in case you ever want to impress, then you can never go wrong with the family flapjack. Nearly bagged me an earl, if I'd not let my heart rule my head… Well, enough of this nonsense. Roll up your sleeves and put your pinny on.'

Several hours and many attempts later, my mother's finally satisfied.

'There, my girl - even you can manage it! Just don't forget that special ingredient, eh? That's what makes it unbeatable.'

I can't believe the time's flown by so fast and that I've spent such a pleasant afternoon with my mother. For all our differences, I know she has my best interests at heart. I just need to pick the right time to tell her about my plans. And in the meantime, I can kiss and make up over a flapjack The Baptist won't be able to resist.

'I'm going out mum. I won't be too long.'

'Mmm. Well, don't go spoiling things, Madam. You've got a bright future ahead of you. Don't forget it.'

I smile at her.

'I won't mum. And thanks for today. It was fun.'

As I turn the corner to the Baptist's house, I have my first inkling that all's not well. A blue light's flashing in the distance. The house is empty but there's a crowd of neighbours outside.

A sickening feeling washes over me. I rush up to them.

'What's happened?'

'That long-haired lad's been taken to hospital.'

I back away in confusion. I should've gone with him! I should never have said what I did!

Out of the corner of my eye, I see Apple skulking behind a hedge. I accost him.

'What the hell's going on? Where is he? Is he ok?'

Apple swallows - his throat like a giant balloon.

'I told 'im not to pick 'em. They looked raight dodgy. Then he started chucking up and thrashing about.'

'But he's going to be alright isn't he? Isn't he ...'

There and then I make a pact with my absent God.

'Just let him be ok and I promise I'll start going to church again. I need him and he needs me. We're soulmates. We belong together. Those can't be my last words to him. I'll never forgive myself! Please God - do something!'

I stand vigil outside his hospital room all night, my nails bitten to a quick and my nerves shredded into a million pieces. I'm not allowed in - 'Relatives only. Too harrowing.' My mother comes to fetch me, physically prising me from the door. She holds me silently in her arms, as an agonised, animal howling and a tsunami of grief rock my body.

My future is shattered.

My roots ripped out.

My wings broken.

Tormented sorrow congeals like sticky tar in my lungs, suffocating every breath, forming a boulder of pain in my chest.

For my first love, my John the Baptist, with his soulful, troubled eyes, has taken one risk too many. The toxic hit from the wrong kind of mushroom causes his heart to give up. And my heart gives up too.

The light goes out and God is lost to me forever.

6

Showers, Shells and Shopping

'Mummy, can we go abroad like Cristiano? It's boring at home.'

Small Child has a point. There's not much to do in the holidays and it's all weather-dependent. If we stay, I'll just end up spending money to keep him amused. But the reality is we can't afford to go abroad. Gone is the freedom of my pre-kids travelling days. Luckily, there's a cheaper solution - free accommodation at my sister's.

'How about we stay with Aunty Bev in Scarborough? You can go in the sea, climb the cliffs and maybe go riding.'

'What about the souvenir shops, crazy golf and the Rib Ride?'

'Well, let's see - they're expensive but if you're good, you could go to the arcades.'

'Wow, brilliant! When are we going?'

The arcades are a deal clincher and, with no further convincing necessary, Small Child trades in the Med for the North Sea. Maybe the rest of the family will join me? Time for some much needed bonding? I bring up the idea that evening.

Disinterested husband is the first to decline.

'Oh, another school holiday, my lovely? No can do, I'm afraid. I've got important meetings on, isn't it? You go though and have a great time.'

Another black mark against him. *He* may have forgotten all about our argument the other day but *I* certainly haven't!

Then Delightful Daughter makes her excuses.

'Sorry Mum. You know I'd love to go riding with Aunty Bev, but my shifts clash and I need the money more than a break.'

Here I forget to bite my lip. I know I should let her find her own way in life, but I'm frustrated that she's over twenty now yet has no direction. Before I can stop myself, I blurt out my frustrations.

'Well maybe if you got a more suitable job, you wouldn't be so hard up! You got good A-levels after all. You could've gone to uni or done some travelling. I just don't understand why you're still at home.'

'Mum, you promised you'd stop going on about it. Do you want me to move out?'

'I know, I know. I'm sorry. And no, of course I don't want you to move out. This is your home. It's just you could do so much more. But, it's your life after all and besides, not all your friends went to uni, did they? I bumped into that girl with the green fringe the other day. You know, the one from Hillsborough, with the strong Yorkshire accent. What was her name? '

Devil Teen's ears prick up and he interrupts.

'She's called Jess. And her hair's purple now not green.'

Delightful Daughter gives him a quizzical look.

'And how would you know little, big brother? Since when did *you* start hanging out with *my* friends?'

Devil Teen flushes.

'Since I bumped into her at the hairdresser's where she works. She's been doing an NVQ course at college and wants to open her own salon. So at least she has ambition, unlike you, Big Sis.'

The conversation's starting to deteriorate so I jump in quickly.

'Look, all I want for you both is to be happy and find something you're passionate about doing.'

Delightful Daughter raises an eyebrow.

'Well mum, you don't seem exactly passionate yourself about working at the college. You're always moaning about it.'

'I know. I'm sorry. I'm a terrible role model! Don't follow my example. I used to love teaching. It's just that lately, it's low in the college's priorities. And, what with all the management changes, re-organisation, cuts and ridiculous paper work, the job's lost its appeal. But that's *my* problem. What *you* need is to find something that interests you.'

'Well, actually I was going to tell you, mum, I've been doing some voluntary youth work at church recently and really enjoying it. There's a course running in Sheffield next year so I might look into that.'

'Oh, that sounds lovely, darling. Go for it.'

Devil Teen undermines his sister's decision.

'Yeah, great if you want to spend the rest of your life living at home! Do you know how little youth workers get paid? It's just as well one of your children has got a sound career plan, mother. Me, I'm heading for the big bucks and a job in the city. So as soon as I finish school, I'm off.'

'Well, that's wonderful, sweetheart. But remember money isn't everything, you know. And, changing the subject back to the seaside - what do you think?'

'A difficult decision, mother, but sadly, I feel unable to go to Scarborough with you or little-poo here. As much as I love Aunty Bev, a house full of cats and route marches on the beach in the rain don't appeal to me. I'll stay home and do some revision.'

And although I know he'll likely spend more time on the PlayStation than his schoolwork, it's an argument he knows he's won. I smile ruefully at Small Child.

'It looks like it's just me and you then, sunshine. Or do you want to invite one of your friends along? How about asking Ethan or Luke?'

'No, thanks mum. They're not really *my* friends, are they? Just the kids of *your* friends. And, anyway, I don't think they're ready to have Aunty Bev sing them awake in the morning just yet!'

And for once I agree. Our Bev runs her own stables in Scarborough and finds animals more endearing than children. Happily single, she does her own thing - singing and keeping cats as company. But she's always pleased to welcome my kids to the house, as long as they behave. So, with my battered, old car duly packed up with a suitcase of clothes and another of Lego, we set off for the coast.

Our Bev, still annoyingly slim and rocking a dramatic streak of grey in her fringe, opens the door. She greets us in her best Lionel Ritchie voice - 'Hello, is it me you're looking for?'

Small Child grins broadly. He's fond of his unconventional aunt.

'Hi, Aunty Bev. How many cats have you got now? Can I go and stroke them?'

'Hello, littlest Squirt. At the last count there were five and three of them are in the back garden. So off you go, whilst I catch up with your mum.'

I navigate past the two remaining tabbies sprawled out in the hallway whilst Our Bev, humming *Tea for two*, makes an industrial-strength cuppa before we settle down for a chat.

'How's Our Dad, Squirt? I thought you might've brought him up for some sea air.'

I take a deep breath - she'd know how he was doing if she called him more often!

'Actually, I'm worried he's losing it. He says *mum* visits him every night. I mean, I know he's lonely without her. But it's been ten years now!'

Our Bev nods dismissively - 'Well, he's bound to get a bit confused at his age and at least it's another topic of conversation to add to food and football. Anyway, what about that husband of yours? I haven't seen him in Scarbs for ages.'

I pull a face. Trust her to change the subject! But she's right, he could've made the effort to come. My head replays the last few days. He never pays any attention to me! Like Our Bev, he dismisses my worries about dad and takes his own parents for granted. We spend most of our time apart and when we *are* together, we never have anything to say. My head hurts with all the voices chattering in my brain.

'Why would he want to come away with such a fat frump anyway?'

'You should make more of an effort.'

'I bet that French charmer would never have run out of conversation…'

I'm pulled out of my reveries by Our Bev uncharacteristically putting an arm round my shoulder.

'Come on Squirt, what's up? You look out of sorts.'

'Oh, I don't know. Just it's so rare to feel taken care of.'

'Isn't my favourite brother-in-law pulling his weight then?'

'It's not his fault. He's really busy. And he finds the kids hard work.'

'Yes, well, I'm with him on that one. Give me a house full of cats any day. And I suppose he expected to have all the little horrors out of the way by now but then you had your *accident* so it must've felt like double jeopardy.'

'Great, thanks for making me feel better! Unplanned maybe but I've never regretted it. It's just everything always lands on me. It makes me miss mum. She'd have had words with him.'

'I know. I miss her too. Not her tellings-off though. And she would've had a few things to say about you having littlest Squirt at such a grand old age!'

'Well, maybe so, but she'd have come round to the idea. She was a good Gran - much more chilled than as a mum.'

'That's true, she could be severe. Do you remember when she'd been rushed into hospital and I came straight from the stables in my jodhpurs? Anyone would've thought I'd turned up naked the way she went on about it! Here, look at these old albums. I've got some photos of us on the ward before she went in for her op. She's even wearing a hat and gloves - *just in case* - remember the Duchess of Kent was opening that new wing. And look, here are some of you in your atheist, leftie stage. Remember that ridiculous trilby and those hideous purple shoes?'

'They weren't hideous. They were cool.'

'Oh! And isn't that the hippy you went out with? The one that had the tragic accident?'

My heart skips a beat as I look into the soulful eyes of my first love. If only…

'Our dad definitely disapproved of him.'

'Why do you say that?'

'Well for a man of monosyllables, dad had a few choice words about *druggy* lads. In fact it's one of only two occasions when he got worked up. And you know full well what the other occasion was, don't you?'

I nod uncomfortably and quickly flick through the pages, trying not to dwell on the past.

'Who's that little boy outside the local shops?'

'You, courtesy of Bev's Beauty Boutique! That didn't end well. Set you off on a life of crime.'

Despite myself, I smile at memories of forbidden apples and childhood sins as we continue to reminisce about times gone by.

The next day looms early but not bright and I wake to seagulls instead of *Big John at Breakfast*. Yes, I'm definitely in Scarborough! Our Mum really liked it here, once she'd got over Our Bev's shock defection.

Thinking of my mother brings that familiar heart ache. Her death was so unexpected. Ironic too, as my father, with his long-established infirmity, was the one who was meant to go first. Sometimes I feel I've never properly grieved for her in my attempt to carry on the pretence of normal life.

And okay, my husband did his best to support me, dutifully hugging me every day, even though I felt his wrist discreetly turning to look at his watch. It wasn't his fault he never fully understood. He'd never experienced loss. Was that the start of us growing apart? The point when the stone in my chest became a permanent fixture? Maybe that accounts for my soul searching - an attempt to make sense of the senseless. But if that's the case, then I've not done a very good job so far!

But before I get dragged back into the *what ifs* of my past, Our Bev interrupts my thoughts. She's taken one look at the weather and decided that *auntly* duties are not on the cards this morning.

'Hmm, I think I'll let you two Squirts go down to the sands on your own. But make sure you don't bring back buckets full of stones! Every time you visit, I always find a collection of weird and wonderful rocks in the bedroom. It's most bizarre. Anyway, I've got to de-flea the cats and then practise for my church solo. I'll see you this afternoon at the stables.'

So much for family togetherness.

Wrapping up warmly in jumpers and cagoules, we head for the shore. It's 12 C and raining. But we're British, and immune to the weather. No blue skies, sparkling sea and golden beach to be found here. We enjoy our sky fifty shades of grey, our seas muddied, and our sand an honest, dirty brown. Small Child, unperturbed by the light drizzle, clambers up the cliffs and dashes in and out of the waves, collecting shells for his sandcastle. Meanwhile, I hunker down under the sea wall, scarf wrapped tightly round my neck, and wish I'd brought my gloves with me.

When hypothermia sets in, we head towards the Abyss of Hell - the Arcades. Ten minutes and £10 lighter I finally manage to convince Small Child that the claw of the *Stack 'n' Grab* machine is rigged. Undeterred, he rushes off to the video games to wreak on-screen carnage.

Then onto my nemesis - the traditional 2p coin pusher machines.

'Mummy, you've just spent £25! What will Dad say?'

The mention of his father brings me crashing back to reality. I wipe the sweat off my brow and steady my shaking hands.

'I don't think Dad needs to know about this, do you?'

Small Child smells the fear and senses an opportunity.

'I don't suppose so, mum. Shall we go to the souvenir shop next, before the crazy golf and Rib Ride, then?'

I concede defeat and in between rain showers, we dive into shops full of tat before hitting the golf course and ending our morning with a Rib Ride. After all, who needs Mediterranean heat and pistachio ice-cream? We're British, and bracing sea air and candyfloss are what our summer is about!

Home again, wind-swept and ruddy-cheeked, Small Child spontaneously hugs me.

'Thanks, mummy. Holidays with you in Scarbs are the best.'

It's a moment to treasure, for who knows how much longer he'll want to hang out with his old mum - Devil Teen's certainly past that stage. And maybe there's a lesson to be learnt here? Maybe I've been spending too much time in mindless meditation when I should just be grateful for what I have in the here and now?

After lunch we head for the stables, where our Bev plonks her nephew on a small horse. He looks at the stallion by its side.

'Why don't you have a go, mummy? Are you too old? Too scared?'

Our Bev raises an eyebrow.

'Do you want to prove your cheeky son wrong, Squirt? After all, you used to go riding as a kid.'

I'm about to shake my head as those voices remind me of my flaws.

'You'd only fall off and make a fool of yourself!'

'You should show a bit of decorum at your age.'

But then I have second thoughts.

'Go on, let them scoff. You ride away into the sunset!'

Nervously, I mount the horse and we set off walking before transitioning into an ungainly trot.

'Good work, Squirt. You've remembered a lot. I thought you'd have forgotten it all. You're doing okay, actually.'

Despite feeling vulnerable on top of this massive, snorting creature, I'm surprisingly pleased to be complimented by my big sister.

'But you still look uncomfortable. What you need to do now is to *think like a horse*, learn to *feel* it both emotionally and physically as it moves beneath you.'

'Really, Our Bev? That all sounds a bit weirdo psycho-babble coming from you.'

'Hmmph. I knew you'd say that, Squirt. But a *feeling* rider is a *more effective* rider, so just give it a try.'

I decide to rise to the challenge, and *go with the flow*. Smiling to myself I repeat the phrase 'I'm a horse. I'm a horse.' The horse beneath me seems unimpressed and tips me forward in the saddle. So much for my *horseiness*.

'Shut your eyes and concentrate on the feeling of movement. The horse won't crash into anything. It'll keep going round the paddock. Trust in the communication between you both.'

I'm not convinced, but I don't give up easily, so I cross my fingers tightly, close my eyes and hope for the best.

With my sense of sight removed, my other senses become sharper. I focus in on the sound of the horse's breathing, the faint rancid smell of the sweat on its flanks and the sensation of being not quite balanced in the saddle. I adjust my position slightly and loosen my grip on the reins and now I can anticipate when the horse's legs are about to move. I synchronise my rise and fall so that we're suddenly in harmony.

And then for one weird and magical instant it feels as if the horse and I have become one! Its legs are my legs and it responds smoothly to my slightest touch, changing pace and direction almost unbidden. We've become a mythical centaur - half-human, half-horse!

We are both one.

No judgement.

No duty.

No desire to escape.

Here in the moment.

In the light.

All is well.

I give a joyous laugh-out-loud, which breaks the spell. I fall forward again, shuddering into the horse's mane.

I open my eyes. Our Bev's looking at me with concern.

'Are you okay, Squirt?'

I wipe my face. It's wet with tears.

But I've no idea why I'm crying.

7

University, Death and the Russian Soul

University is a whole new world, where no one knows my past. It's a chance to reinvent myself.

Back home in Sheffield, my mother's trained me to speak *posh* but I soon realise my accent jangles amongst the plummy vowels of those around me. For I've moved on to a new, elite group of Public school southerners, with double-barrelled surnames. They all know each other but can't quite place me, despite Arabella Whittington-Smythe's conviction she's met me before.

'Didn't I see you at the Sandringham estate last summer? You're one of those Spencer gals, aren't you?'

I'm studying French and Russian but this is my first foray outside of Yorkshire, let alone the UK. For me, Bristol, with its elegant Georgian streets, arty cafes and alternative galleries is already a different planet. My new friends, with their weekend trips to New York and second homes on the Côte d'Azur find this endearing and have adopted me as their *pet northerner*. My accent's thickened accordingly, so if you want to know *summat abawt* whippet-racing or clog-dancing, then, *eeh bah gum,* I'm your expert.

I've invented a new persona - Intellectual Northern Atheist - and a penchant for wearing *interesting* hats and shoes. I'm vehemently anti-God since he's let me down so badly and am looking forward to spending some time in the Soviet Union, with its ideology of eliminating all religion.

Home, with its painful memories is somewhere I avoid, spending most of my holidays with Arabella at her country pile or Piers at his London pad. But it's Christmas again, I'm leaving for Moscow in the New Year, and the excuses have run out.

'Your idea of fun sucks, Our Bev. A *Higher Power* doesn't exist. I don't know how you can believe such mumbo-jumbo. And I can't think of anything worse than singing with the God-Squadders to old folk. For Christ's sake, you're only twenty-three! Get a life!'

'Well, Squirt, your life consists of going out late, then coming home hammered - as if that's fun.'

'Girls! Enough now!' says my mother - 'Whatever will the neighbours think? You'll wake your father. You know he needs to rest since his heart got worse. It's the season of good will. Please, make an effort to get on.'

Clearly, she's not going to let me wangle my way out of carol singing but if I ask nicely she might give us a lift.

'Moother, I'm not going if I 'ave to take t'boos. Can't thae gi'us a ride?'

My mother's not impressed.

'Listen, my girl, I'm not giving you a lift anywhere if you can't speak properly. What on earth's happened to you? University's meant to make you sound educated, not broad Yorkshire!'

Our Bev comes to the rescue, with an operatic version of the Beatles.

'Mum, we need a ticket to ride.

Please, give us a ticket to ride.

Otherwise Squirt won't sing,

Cos she don't care.'

My mother smiles despite herself and twenty minutes later we're deposited at the Home, where fellow members of the choir, kitted out in red, full-length garments, are waiting. They look askance at my drainpipe jeans, pink shoes and porkpie hat. But too bad. There's no way I'm wearing a cassock. I'll just stand at the back and mime.

I find myself next to Fred, a paunchy, red-faced plumber and his wife, a beautiful blonde woman, with dramatic bone structure and striking green eyes. It's only when she bumps into me and apologises in her mother tongue, that I realise she's Russian and might have contacts in Moscow to help me.

And fortunately, Mrs Tatyana Higginbottom is more than happy to pass Tsar Nicholas look-alike, husband-number-one on to me. I'm intrigued about her decision to leave her first marriage, so in the break, when the oldies are searching for their false teeth to chomp on Custard Creams, I quiz her about this unknown Russian she's sending me to meet.

'How come you left if he's so good-looking, creative and exciting? Fred and his U-bends don't seem half as much fun!'

'It's true' - Tanya says - 'Vanyushka was my soulmate. But he was a philanderer, a butterfly, flitting from flower to flower and never settling. What I craved for, what Fred can provide, is stability and a solid basis for a family life.'

'Really? Sounds boring.'

'Well, you're young. You'll change your mind when you're my age and want children. A woman has to be pragmatic. My Fred's not a man of many words but he's steady and reliable, with hidden depths - for he dared to travel behind the *evil Iron Curtain.*'

'Well let's hope it isn't so evil anymore and that Vanya shows me its better side.'

So, after the festivities have finished, I pack a suitcase with jeans to trade, a bilingual dictionary and a bathplug - ready for my adventure to the Soviet Union. I've become Reluctant Russophile, keen to discover the country and the people whose language intrigues me, but nervous to live in such an alien political system.

The big day arrives and my family accompany me to the airport as if it were my last trip to the gallows. They take it in turns to say a touching goodbye.

'Good luck. Spartak play well. Write to your Mum.'

'Goodbye-ee. Don't cry-ee! The cat's got your room now. Don't sigh-ee!'

'Remember, you're representing Britain, young lady. Don't let Queen or country down. And for goodness sake don't come back a communist! I can't believe you're going so far away! At least Beverly appreciates home! Still, once this is out of your system, you can get a nice teaching job. In the meantime, I'll send you a food parcel as soon as I can and updates on *the Family*. I'll put in some flapjack, shall I?'

Our delegation of twenty British students from various UK universities arrives on a chilly January day at Sheremetyevo airport. It's the era of strained relations. The Cold War hasn't yet warmed up and the stony-faced border guard is an example of how not to thaw international relations.

My initial impression of Moscow is of gloomy bleakness. Grim-looking citizens in drab clothing wait stoically in the browning slush for mud-spattered buses to take them home to their grey tower blocks.

No western privilege for us. We're all equal now. So, we too are housed in one of these blocks, which huddle together in ugly mobs on the outskirts. It's an international student hostel but we decadent westerners are taught in separate groups. We're not encouraged to mix with the correct-minded socialists from the satellite countries, for fear of contaminating them with our capitalist ideas. To ensure no fraternising of incompatible ideologies, we're strictly monitored.

At the end of each corridor sits a stern-faced, tight-lipped *dezhurnaya* behind an official looking desk. The dezhurnaya's the *watch dog* of the floor, with eagle eyes on our every move, diligently noting down who we associate with. It feels like I've walked in from the cold onto the set of a post-war thriller and that any moment I might discover a hidden bug in my night light.

I soon learn that dezhurnayas are identical in their middle-aged, stout grouchiness, with all female warmth and empathy bred out of them. They wear a standard shift dress of brown-flowered acrylic which crackles with static electricity as they lean forward over their desks, to spy on us.

But as time goes on and we get used to each other, the terrifying dezhurnaya on my floor starts to thaw. My Russian small talk's minimal and she doesn't understand my daily references to the weather but I stick a cheery grin on my face each time I pass and eventually my perseverance pays off.

She allows me to address her by name, Maria Ivanovna. And in return I'm given the title of *anglichanka s ulybky* - smiling English girl. Small gifts of tights and chewing gum pave the way for better East-West relations. She makes me hot, black tea from a samovar when I'm feeling ill and, in return, I share coveted pieces of flapjack from my mother's emergency packages.

Despite our segregation, we've infiltrated the softer Eastern bloc and now have Polish and Czech friends, who, for a small cut, change our money illegally and sell on our jeans. We're an international family of European, South-American and African comrades, united in our battle with guerrilla noun declensions and freedom-fighting verb conjugations. And who could ever forget Enrique, our Argentinian pin up? He of the chocolatey brown eyes and cow-lashes to die for. All the girls are in love with his luscious locks and sexy tango moves, so I'm amazed when one day he slides into the seat next to me in the library.

'Devushka, has anyone mentioned you look like Princess Diana?'

I'm surprised he knows who she is but I silently thank my mother for my genes and for her weekly commitment to writing.

'Mm yes. Is it because I'm tall, English and with a similar hair style? So, you like our royal family, do you?'

'Si, si, I love Lady Dee and all her beautiful outfits.'

'Oh well, maybe you'd like to see the latest clippings of her? My mum sends me an update in each letter. Look here's one of her in a tiara...'

And so a friendship's forged over a mutual fascination with Diana's wardrobe and the jewellery collection of Her Majesty. But despite my heart pounding, Enrique remains, sadly, *just a good friend*.

Another good friend is my dictionary, used to translate the instructions shouted at me by the Russian *babushkas* - grannies - on the street. They're even more formidable than the dezhurnayas and pass comment on any *inappropriate* behaviour.

Clothed in universal, unflattering shift dresses, their Baba Yaga faces peer out disapprovingly beneath black, Russian shawls decorated with red roses. They stand, hawk-eyed and judgmental, observing my strange, western behaviour. Then they regally spit out commands at me.

'*Devushka* - young woman. Don't sit on that wall! You'll get women's problems.'

'Devushka! You can't cross the road there!'

'Devushka! Wrap your scarf properly round your head!'

The last directive's actually quite helpful. For days now I've been suffering from terrible pain in my nose, and it's only once I cover up my face, I realise the problem is my nostril hairs icing up into frozen needles and viciously stabbing me with each inward breath.

The babushkas, unfortunately, can't explain the lack of bath plugs in the Soviet Union, and for some reason, not a single bathroom in the hostel possesses one. To be honest though, a bath's never on the cards. The cracked tiles in the bathroom, ingrained with dirt from pre-revolution days, don't entice me to linger over my ablutions. The water's a dubious rust colour, the drains have smelled better days, and the plumbing's, at best, unreliable. Still, a bathroom between five of us is a luxury.

We're starting to understand how privileged and decadent we are to Soviet eyes. They despise but envy us for our access to *Beryozka* shops, those Aladdin's caves of colourful, western consumer goods, forbidden to non-foreigners and which accept hard currency only. They're a far cry from the normal, Soviet shop with its plain, white packages labelled *Flour, Sugar, Tea*.

Quite often the shelves are empty, as food shortages abound, depending on what current political sanctions are popular. Queues are epic, but have their own special etiquette and you can even stand in several queues at the same time!

Indeed, shopping in the Soviet Union is a revelation. I leave my list of things to buy at home and never go out without a handy bag and a sense of adventure. For who knows what might vanish overnight from the shelves and what unexpected delight might be found around a street corner?

Cheese disappears for three months, then reappears when the EU needs to offload a surplus. Fruit's a luxury. Sometimes I fight off the hordes of babushkas to place my solitary, gnarled apple, with pride, on the counter.

The strange thing is, that whenever invited round to Russian friends' homes, their tables groan under the weight of delicacies never seen in any store. This is a result of foraging in the surrounding countryside, growing and pickling their own produce at their *dachas* - small summer houses - and *blat* - that shadow economy of bribery and barter, where everything can be bought from a useful contact for the right price.

It's hard for us to make Russian friends. The black marketeers actively court us, but their overtures are self-interested, in the hope of getting their hands on our jeans or pounds sterling. And most ordinary citizens view westerners with suspicion, or are worried the authorities will keep them under surveillance for associating with non-communists.

Some of us, like myself, have *inherited* Russians and they tend to be intellectuals, although it's hard to know what to call them, as they seem to have so many names. For example, *Ivan Denisovitch* is the person I meet formally first of all, but when I get to know him better, I call him *Ivan*. Once we get friendly, he becomes *Vanya* to me, and after a few vodkas, *Vanyushka* and I are already best mates. It's no wonder I find it so hard to follow the plot of a novel in Russian. It turns out there are only five main characters instead of the twenty I'd imagined!

So, Vanya, Tatyana's ex, the showman with a flirtatious manner, has taken me under his wing and made it his job to introduce me to Russian culture and traditions. He initiates me into the artistic underworld, where wild parties spring up in abandoned warehouses decorated in designer chic. I realise that all's not as it seems.

Underneath the veneer of puritanical communism, a thriving libertinism exists.

And once Russians get to know you, they go out of their way to help you. They offer to get tickets to sold-out shows, give up their free time to accompany you to the polyclinic, and pretend politely that you speak their language like a native. Weirdly though, as you move closer into their inner circle, they revert back to directness.

Vanya barks out orders at the table.

'Give me the bread! Pass the sugar! Open the window!'

He happily discusses me with his friends.

'I think her Russian's got worse recently. And it's time she got her hair cut.'

I interrupt in a feeble *what's to be done about it all* manner.

'Hello … I'm here in the room with you! Can't you just do the decent British thing and talk about me behind my back?'

But Vanya shrugs dismissively -

'I'm your friend. I don't need to say, *please* or *thank you* and I'll always be honest.'

And the proverb *a Russian will give his only shirt to a friend* rings true for me. The friends I've made here have, materially, so little but are prepared to sacrifice it all in the name of friendship.

Many of them live in *communalki* - communal flats. These are essentially one room within a larger flat, with a shared bathroom, kitchen and dimly lit corridor connecting them all. Sometimes an entire family, parents and two children, live and sleep in a room the size of my bedroom. The stress of living within such confined quarters, often sharing the communal areas with people you'd never choose to, cannot be underestimated.

Vanya uses the space between the panes of his triple glazed window to store his milk and perishable food, rather than use the kitchen fridge. His neighbours are quarrelsome alcoholics with a tendency to *borrow* possessions.

I admire the way he organises his room. Everything's kept to a minimum. Only necessary items and objects that bring him joy are allowed in his hallowed space. He has a small, wooden table, which we pile around to eat, drink and philosophise. And the bed's separated from his living area by huge bookcases which groan under the weight of his prized literary collection.

Vanya takes my education seriously, making me visit a museum or art gallery each day, and a film, theatre or ballet production every weekend. It's thanks to him that I start to see Moscow with different eyes. Its grey grimness turns out to be just the brown paper wrapping that protects the treasures of the picture book within.

I marvel at the Kremlin, that imposing red fortress with its signature, tall, star-topped towers and impressive white palaces. I fall in love with St Basil's Cathedral, whose gaudy cupolas flame like a colourful bonfire into the sky. I brave certain death and swim in the open air pool by the river. My sight's obscured by the rising steam over the surface as warm water meets air temperatures of -15 C and my hair's only protected from freezing and snapping off by a flimsy swimming cap.

I'm awe-struck by the magnificence which is the metro and dazzled by the beauty of the Bolshoi. I live my dream of riding in a troika through the snow-crusted forests of silver birches, but it's the golden onion domes which truly capture my heart.

Today those domes rise proudly above the beautiful, Orthodox Russian church in the village of Peredelkino, where the writer, Boris Pasternak, is buried. In the west, he's known for the film *Doctor Zhivago* but to Russians he's a talented poet.

As a small group of disparate Pasternak appreciators assemble by his grave, one after another, they recite stanzas from his banned poem *Hamlet,* finishing together on the melancholic but truthful line - *A mortal life is no walk in the park.*

A shiver runs down my spine as memories resurface of another, moonlit cemetery, and a oneness with nature and mankind. I recall that night with my first love and, hearing the poem, my heart aches again for my lost boy who, sadly, also found life to be *no walk in the park*.

Here in this small cemetery, it's hard to believe you're in a land of atheists. There's something incredibly moving and almost spiritual in the fact that complete strangers have come together at this snowy tomb, under clear, blue skies, uniting in one voice to show their love for a poet whose words inspire them.

The rhythm of the stanzas echo in my head like a hymn. It's both magical and mystical, a real example of the *russkaya dusha* - Russian soul - used to describe Russian identity and spirituality.

In this country, where religion's supposedly dead, it's moments like this that surprise me most. It's a connectedness that somehow embraces all people. Despite their often hard lives, Russians find a beauty in poetry, nature and in simple pleasures. *God* is never spoken out loud but here today at the great poet's tomb, there's a sense of the eternal and a stillness that speaks to the soul.

We wander into the village church with its typical onion domes. Its rounded cupolas are a deep blue and embellished with golden stars - such beauty in such a simple setting.

I'm expecting some kind of exhibition or potted history of the village. For whilst Russian Orthodoxy isn't officially banned, it's at best discouraged, and most of the churches I've visited so far are well-preserved museums. This place, however, has a sense of deep tranquillity, which is why I'm so horrified when I come face-to-face with my first dead body!

It's a little babushka with white hair and a well-lived in face. She's lying in an open coffin with flowers around her head. Her eyes are closed and she looks at peace. My startled glance acknowledges that this is, indeed, death. The house is there, but the householder has departed. This body's just an empty shell, an envelope with no letter inside. I wonder fleetingly where it's gone, before I stumble outside, in shock, away from this sudden, undesired encounter with mortality.

This isn't the sanitised, closed casket, out of sight, quiet departure from life that we expect in the U.K. It's an in-your-face, meet-your-maker, this-is-it-mate, which I find deeply unsettling.

I never had the courage to say a final goodbye to my soulmate. Is this how he ended his days, alone in some casket before being consumed by fire? Sadness and guilt overwhelm me as I try to compose myself.

In England, we'd all be terribly apologetic at such a dreadful mistake happening. How unfortunate there were no signs to prevent us chancing upon such a situation. We'd have a strong cup of tea to steady our nerves, then change the subject to talk about the weather.

But here in Russia, death is no taboo. Dinner table conversations don't ban the sensitive. No subject's left untouched. God may be officially dead but the yearning for something higher and more noble lives on.

Later that evening Vanya breaks out the vodka, and each one of the friends assembled makes a long and moving toast to life, the hereafter and the babushka. In my inebriated state I wonder aloud where the essence of the babushka's gone to. What's happened to the energy that animated her and made her alive?

And my Russian friends don't offer trite answers or change the subject to a safer topic. Instead there's a sincerity in their considered responses and a soulfulness in their speeches - a longing for a greater truth to be revealed.

Vanya raises his glass and makes a sombre toast.

'To life and death and love and awareness!'

I wonder if he's thinking of his ex and, oiled into bluntness by the alcohol, I ask -

'Do you miss Tatyana?'

He hesitates before answering.

'I let my green-eyed beauty slip away, devushka, and it's the biggest regret of my life! But this is the path I'm destined to walk and who knows where it might lead?'

Yes, the vodka comes out and, with it, the Russian soul walks free. Those questions that haunt me: the *why am I here?* the *what is the meaning of life?* aren't brushed under the carpet, like at home, but discussed seriously and thoughtfully.

It's a refreshing breath of air and somewhere, hidden out of sight, a small flame flares up in me once more.

8

A Mums' Night Out

'True love? What's that? Thirteen years and four kids I gave that man! And he was nothing but a cheat. I should've kicked him out a long time ago.'

English Rose takes another slurp of her Whiskey Sour and continues her tirade.

'The final straw came when I realised he'd taken my signature roulade from the freezer and passed it off as his own handy-work in order to impress his latest floozy. He didn't even appreciate it was crafted from 70% dark chocolate from Ecuador for God's sake!'

We nod, agreeing it's better to be on your own than stuck with a love rat.

Tonight, it's our termly mums' meet-up and we've invaded *La Mama,* a popular tapas bar, conveniently within walking distance and famous for its cocktails and Latin American beats.

Bubbly Brazilian's in her element. She's wearing a tight-fitting, cobalt blue, halter neck salsa outfit. It's covered in sequins and shows off her assets to electrifying effect. She's long since left her chair and is rhythmically stepping, front-back-side-back around our table, a tumbler of Caipirinha in her hand.

'You're better off without him, my dahleeng. It's just a shame you're on such acrimonious terms.'

I jump in to defend English Rose. In her strappy, flowered sun dress she looks so young and vulnerable.

'Well he did shack up in the end with Sage's best friend's mother, so you can hardly blame her! And anyway, you should give her some pointers, seeing as you and your ex are still such good mates.'

Zen Mother, who's wisely kept her own counsel, takes a sip of Tequila Sunrise - 'it's alcoholic but at least the orange juice will keep me hydrated' - and asks,

'Go on then. What's the secret of a good divorce?'

Bubbly Brazilian does a twirl, pauses for a moment then suddenly squats down, picks something off the floor and shimmies towards us.

'Has one of you dahleengs lost a little pink stone from an earring?'

I colour slightly and make a play of touching my ears.

'Oh, yes, it's mine. Thanks. How annoying! I'll take the other one out, so I don't lose that too.'

English Rose looks at me pointedly but I studiously ignore her, so she turns to Bubbly Brazilian, waiting for words of Latino advice.

'Well my dahleengs, Cristiano's father's a good man, as you know. I met him working in London. And somehow, despite your awful climate, he persuaded me to make my life up here. But it was all a pretence! I thought he shared my passion for dance and music and he thought I shared his love of football but in fact the only thing we shared is our love of Cristiano. So we carried on, going our separate ways.

Then seven years ago, my mother died and I realised life was too short for wasting. I did a lot of therapy - very non-British, I know - but it really helped. In the end, we sat down and talked. He agreed it wasn't working for him either but we both vowed to put Cristiano at the heart of everything. That's the secret, bury the hatchet and think of the kids. And so far, it's working. I love the freedom of being single. My ex takes Cristiano to football and that's when I go dancing. I'm really enjoying it too, since the new instructor arrived. He's amazing!'

We straighten up on high alert at the possibility of a new love interest for our friend. Being the matriarch of the group, I lead the interrogation.

'Sounds intriguing. Tell us more.'

'My dahleengs. He's simply the best. A master at mambo. He's won awards for his rumba and his paso doble's unsurpassed.'

'Yeah, yeah - enough of the dance - tell us more about the man!'

'Well, he's about your age and from Argentina. You'd like him actually as he's a royal family fanatic too. His favourite dance is the tango, obviously. And he has the most incredible chocolatey eyes, with lashes that supermodels would kill for!'

He's starting to sound familiar but surely this'd be too much of a coincidence?

'He's not called Enrique, is he?'

'Enrique? No. His name's Kiki. Why do you ask?'

'Just he sounds like a guy I knew in Moscow. But maybe all Argentinian men are gorgeous hunks with a love of tango and the crown jewels?'

'Yes, he's certainly gorgeous and for once I've found someone who shares my passion.'

'Oh, so when are we going to meet him then?'

'Well he's very busy over the next few months. He's involved with that new restaurant.'

English Rose leans closer at this news of culinary interest.

'A new restaurant? What kind of food? Can you get us tickets to the opening?'

'Calm down, my dahleeng. I'll do my best but it might be impossible. It's a brand new concept for Sheffield - a dance spectacular as you dine. Kiki's doing all the choreography. Then after the food, there'll be boogying until the early hours. It sounds divine.'

English Rose groans and makes inroads into her third Whiskey Sour.

'Forget the dancing. What about the food? Tell us about *that!*'

'Oh, I'm not sure, my dahleeng. I was so excited about the dancing, I didn't ask about the food.'

Zen Mother, takes another delicate sip of her cocktail, smoothes down her Senegalese kaftan, and smiles reassuringly.

'Well, I can tell you. See, Ethan likes to tune in to Radio Hallam and they've been talking about the restaurant on Big John at Breakfast's show. Apparently, it's a type of fusion food. It takes the best flavours of South America, adds in a dash of Asian spiciness and blends it with traditional, European cuisine. They're running a competition to name it. Apparently, the owner's got some previous connection to the city and is keen to get the locals on his side. You know, make it a restaurant for the people.'

I swig back another Moscow Mule and snort derisively.

'Well if it's got fancy food and dance, it'll have fancy prices too, so out of my budget for sure. And I can't see my darling hubby forking out good money unless it's for rugby international tickets! One of you lot will just have to hook up with a millionaire who can treat us all to dinner there.'

English Rose sighs.

'Chance'd be a fine thing! At the moment, on the one day a week my ex has my brood, the last thing I want to do is go on a date with some of the weirdoes you find on line! I've had a few disasters on those matchmaking sites. No, being single suits me - no one to please but myself. Bliss! I can just sprawl out on the settee with a good box-set, a cask-aged tawny port and some home-made macarons for company. It's my one stress-free day of the week.'

She turns to look at Zen Mother.

'How about you? How do you manage to stay so sane? Nothing seems to ruffle you. I know you've only got Ethan, who's so placid, unlike the hysterical screamers who live with me! But, all the same, you must get lonely sometimes. Don't you wish you had someone to share your life with?'

Zen Mother closes her eyes for a minute.

'Yes, you're right. I *have* been lonely, especially in the early days after my husband died. Ethan was just a baby then and everything seemed overwhelming. But you have to soldier on, don't you? Then about two years after the accident, the grief really hit me and I sank into a depression. Someone suggested I go to yoga and for some reason that really seemed to help.'

My heart goes out to her. She's been through a lot, yet always puts a positive spin on things. I should try to be more like her, make more of an effort with my mindfulness. If only I didn't keep getting distracted by those voices! I shake my head and return to what she's saying.

'I know it's not for everyone but it really grounded me and now it's a daily practice. In fact, I've started training to become an instructor. So, what with studying for that, going to philosophy classes, looking after Ethan and managing my impossible workload as a social worker, I haven't got time for much else! But, you know, there's been a shift recently. I never thought I'd look at another man again and I certainly don't want the shackles of marriage, but maybe now it *is* time to let someone into my life.'

I sigh in envy. How great it'd be to let someone into *my* life, someone who didn't *shackle* me and would appreciate me for a change! This thought resonates strongly and wakes the sleeping voices.

'Who'd be interested in **you***?'*

'You should be focussing on improving your marriage, not escaping it!'

'Have another drink and download a dating app!'

I take a slug of my cocktail but the Moscow Mules have re-awakened my Russian directness of old. Before I can engage my brain, my mouth opens.

'Yes, great, only don't let it be Luke's dad, will you?'

Zen mother blushes and responds in an un-Zen like manner.

'What have you got against him? He's lovely. We often chat in the playground and I've always found him delightful.'

I realise from her tone I should backtrack.

'Well, maybe I'm wrong. I hardly know him after all. It's just I didn't much like his behaviour at the handball tournament. He was a bit aggressive, I thought. And if you're going to get together with someone then it should be someone special who's going to treat you like a princess. You deserve the best.'

Zen Mother *rehydrates* with her Tequila Sunset and recovers her calm.

'Aaah, that's sweet of you. You're only looking out for me. But you're wrong about Luke's dad. He's just going through a hard time, so needs all the support he can get. But as for romance, I think that's the last thing on his mind! And besides, I've got it into my head that any new bloke should share my love of yoga. And that's definitely not him, so don't worry!'

At that moment, more sizzling tapas arrive at the table, courtesy of English Rose, who likes to sample everything off the menu. The smells wafting our way are so delicious that Bubbly Brazilian stops mid-cha-cha-cha and comes back to her seat.

'My dahleengs, the food here's so good. That new restaurant will have its work cut out to do better, I think.'

English Rose, surprisingly, disagrees.

'The savoury stuff here's great but it'd be lovely to have tapas of different puddings, although, it has to be said, that nothing could ever beat *someone's* flapjack. A secret recipe that *someone* refuses to share, even with their best friends!'

Someone keeps quiet, downs the rest of her cocktail and goes off in search of a refill. On the way to the bar, my phone pings. It's Delightful Daughter.

- Just dropped Granddad back. Is he okay? Apparently, GRAN'S pleased I'm applying for a course …

The voices answer for me.

'You know he's not okay, useless woman! You're just sticking your head in the sand.'

'You should've asked the district nurse to refer him for tests.'

'Make that a double Moscow Mule!'

When I totter back, the girls have obviously been talking about me.

'Come on, spit it out! What's wrong? Has my mascara run?'

'No, my dahleeng. We were just saying how that pink suits you. Very striking!'

'Ah thanks. My personal-dresser nine-year-old chose it, actually. I bought it for that factory opening with Prince Harry, so he notices me in the crowd, which is more than can be said for the man I'm married to!'

'Well at least you *have* a man in your life, my dahleeng. It's your silver wedding, isn't it, next year? That's amazing – twenty-five years of matrimonial bliss.'

'Well, twenty-five years, I'll agree with. But as for the matrimonial bliss, I don't know any more! We're stuck in a bit of a rut at the moment. Maybe we've been stuck there for much longer, actually. Maybe it all started falling apart when my mum died. You know, I was so busy holding it together, I had no energy for anything else.'

Bubbly Brazilian and Zen Mother nod sympathetically. They understand only too well what I'm talking about.

'It just seemed so unfair. *Dad* was the one with the health problems, not *mum*. It was all so senseless. Then, finding out I was pregnant for the third time, I was overjoyed - like the baby was sent to bring me happiness again. Only my husband didn't see it the same way. Being a dad again wasn't quite what he had in mind…'

'Oh, my dahleeng I'm sure it was hard for you both at first. But things must be getting easier now, surely?'

'Hmm, for *him* maybe! He doesn't have to run the house, feed the family, hold down a job he hates and deal with a demented father! I mean he *lives* at the Holiday Inn. And I don't think he even notices I exist unless I get in the way of the screen when he's watching rugby. I just keep thinking back to the past loves I had before I married him. Thinking how different life could've been. Is that really wrong of me?'

'No, no, my dahleeng. It's perfectly natural. But, congratulate yourself - you're still together, despite everything. However, I don't think you've ever mentioned your ex-boyfriends before and this is too juicy to let you get away with. Spill the beans! We're all ears, aren't we my dahleengs?'

So, before I know it, I'm revealing how the Baptist broke my heart and a certain French hotelier nearly captured it again. It seems slightly disloyal to be so open about these ghosts from my past but the cocktails have loosened my tongue and it feels good to share my secrets with friends I trust. After all, straying in your dreams isn't the same as straying in real life. All long-term married couples do it, don't they?

As I stagger into the bedroom and collapse still half-clothed into bed, my husband turns over in his sleep, rises slightly and puts a familiar arm around me. 'Susan, Susan, you're all I ever wanted,' he mumbles before pulling the duvet off me and slumping back onto his pillow. Unfortunately, my name is not and has never been, Susan!

I roll away from him, disgruntled, debating whether he too finds nightly solace reliving past romances. If it's true, then what's the point in us still sticking together? I glance over at this older, thicker-set version of the man I married and wonder, not for the first time, what I could ever have seen in him all those years ago...

9

Nuns, Cows and Elephants

'*India?* You've just got back from Russia! Has that Gandhi film turned your head?'

My mother is unimpressed by my post-university plans - 'You youngsters think it's all about *finding yourself*. What you *should* be finding is a *job*!

'Mum, I *will* - when I get back. Only I don't know what I want to do in life! Not a 9-5 job that's for sure. I want to see the *world,* not just Brid or Benidorm.'

'Look, my girl, be realistic. An *earl* used to write *me* love letters. Much good that did! Now when you've got *this*, whatever *this* is, out of your system, please, settle down! Your father's health's not good and Beverly's defected to Scarborough, so it'd be nice if *one* of my daughters stayed in Sheffield to save me from a life of football and food. And who's this young man you're going with? I'd be much happier if there was a group of you.'

'Mum, Arabella can't turn down the job in the city and Piers has to step into the family business, so it's just the two of us.'

'Oh dear! You're not .... You know … *together*, are you? Because these things can go terribly wrong when you're such a long way from home. Are you sure you're not better off working a summer season on the east coast?'

'Mum, I can go to Skeggy any time. It's *India* I want to visit. And me and him, we're just good mates, that's all. Don't worry, I survived the Iron Curtain, didn't I? I'll be fine.'

I say that with fingers crossed because, although the Enigma's sat next to me in lectures for three years, we've never really swapped personal details or spent time alone together. He's intelligent, certainly knows his stuff and can cut you down in any argument. He's tall, fair and spindly, never seeming quite at ease in his body. With his watery-blue eyes and weak, aristocratic chin he's your quintessential, stiff-upper-lipped Englishman. Still, my mother's forbidden me to travel by myself to far-flung, foreign shores, so The Enigma's my only option.

Doubts assuaged, she sends me - Intrepid Explorer - off to The Enigma's home, a large country mansion a short drive to the airport. As I walk with my backpack up the tree-lined alley to this near stately home, I wonder if I should go round to the servant's entrance instead.

I skirt past the manicured lawns with their amazing displays of topiary, and tentatively ring the bell. It echoes ominously around the building and then I hear the clattering of officious footsteps drawing closer.

To my surprise, the door creaks open to reveal a nun. Stern-faced and unsmiling, she ushers me in silently and suspiciously to the entrance hall.

'Wait there. I'll inform the Master,' she commands.

I feel I've entered some kind of Gothic tragedy and look round nervously for signs of skeletons escaping from cupboards. However, everything's clean and orderly. All the same, something's missing that I can't quite put my finger on.

A short while later, the pinched-faced Sister walks stiffly back, accompanied by a slow-moving, hunched figure of a man I presume to be the Master. He's an older version of the Enigma but grey-haired and with a heavy weariness about him as if some great tragedy's blighted his life, causing his shoulders to stoop and his feet to shuffle. He's followed nervously by my soon-to-be travelling companion.

The Master appraises me, a smile not quite reaching his eyes, and extends a formal handshake.

'Welcome to our humble home. Perhaps my son would like to show you round the grounds before supper?'

And with that, I'm dismissed.

The Enigma takes me on a tour of the house. It's huge and rambling, with large crucifixes on every landing. The walls are white and spartan but the overall effect's strangely dark and heavy.

'What's with the nun?' I ask with a newly acquired, Russian directness.

The Enigma coughs distractedly.

'Oh you know. When Mother …well when Mother …wasn't there any more, Father…'

He coughs again.

'Well it was difficult for him with five children, and erm, well, the Holy Sisters came to save us and, aah… they never really left us, I suppose.'

'Oh right,' I nod understandingly, not understanding anything.

Did his mother die? Or maybe she left? There's not a single family photo on display in any of the rooms, so maybe that's it? I'm curious to know, but aware that this isn't the time to ask.

'How about showing me the gardens?' I suggest.

It's supper time and Scary Nun slops unappetising, watery soup into my bowl. She growls at me like a dog asserting its alpha status.

'It's not much but the Lord should make you thankful.'

I'm about to start eating when The Enigma kicks me under the table. Scary Nun's looking at me askance. Her nose wrinkles imperceptibly as if detecting an unwanted smell.

'Are you not a believer, child? In that case, I'll have to pray for your sinner's heart to be saved from the fiery pits of hell!'

I realise then that everyone's hands are clasped to say grace, so quickly put my palms together and look contrite. After a few minutes of eating in uncomfortable silence I decide on a safe conversation opener. I ask the Master cheerily.

'So what are your other children doing now?'

He ignores my question as if I'd affronted him. The silence deepens until The Enigma rescues me with a, 'Oh they don't come home much anymore,' and that ends the social chit chat for the evening.

As we leave the soulless mansion for the airport the next day, I realise what's missing - there's a complete lack of a feminine presence, an absence of light and love. Maybe that's why the Enigma's keen to leave home. Maybe he's hoping, like me, to *find himself* in India?

And after a ride to Gatwick in the family Rolls, two plane flights, and twenty eight long hours later, India well and truly finds us!

Spices and petrol fumes lay waste to my nostrils. Street hawkers and taxi horns bulldoze my eardrums. A rainbow of saris, vibrant flowers and spectacular sun-sets seer into my eyeballs, forcing me to be fully aware of everything going on around me.

This is so different from my experience in the Soviet Union, where I had to dig deep to find the treasures of the country. Here, in India, the jewels are displayed openly on each corner. It's a kaleidoscopic feast of saffron and saddhus. Holy cows wander god-like through the streets, as the motorised rickshaws weave chaotically around them.

Delhi with its iconic imperial Red Fort, sprawling Jama Masjid Mosque and endless tombs and temples takes us time-travelling back to the past. A group of small, brown-skinned boys running barefoot through the dust-filled streets triggers a memory in my head, as if this isn't the first time I've witnessed this scene.

In Amritsar we marvel at the Golden Temple, a mesmerising base of elegant marble, blending into a shimmering layer of golden panels, all topped by a gilded dome. It floats at the end of a long causeway in a sarovar - a man-made lake - where its reflection dances gently on the surface. It's a reminder that here, in its cool waters, the material world meets the spiritual.

Our next stop is Shimla, summer capital of the British Empire built on the forested lower slopes of the Himalayas, and a strange meeting point of two very different cultures. The British came here in the 1820s to escape the intense heat and stamped their mark on it with examples of classic English architecture. A medieval style Town Hall vies with a baronial castle and a country church to grab my attention. The sense of dislocation intensifies as an orange-robed holy-man with ash-daubed forehead waits patiently outside the mock Tudor post office. On its roof, thieving monkeys clamber unchallenged - the undisputed rulers of their kingdom.

I lean against the wall and squint into the sunlight. Everything's turning slightly hazy and the world around me is disappearing - smells dampening, sounds dimming. In the distance I can make out some movement. Is that a horse-drawn carriage? A man in a long tail coat and top hat? A group of women gossiping in full skirts that rustle as they move? There's an overwhelming feeling of familiarity. I blink and look quickly at the Enigma, to confirm what I'm seeing but he seems to have noticed nothing unusual.

'Did you see that? I could've sworn there was someone in Victorian dress! I've got the weirdest feeling - a memory of walking these very streets. Maybe there *is* something in this reincarnation idea?'

The Enigma looks at me with concern.

'You're losing it! It's a trick of the light, obviously. All these buildings are just like the ones back home. So, of course you feel you've been here before. As for reincarnation, what's the point if you can't learn from your past lives? Look, when you die, you go to heaven or hell and that's the reality.'

'Well, that may be *your* reality but that's exactly the point! If you'd been born *here,* you'd be *Hindu*, not *Catholic*. You're just a product of your upbringing. Your religion's an accident of your birth not a consciously chosen path. At least I've given up on God for good reason! Still, there's something in the air here... I can't explain it, but it kind of makes me wish there *was* a higher power.'

'Too much sun! You should go and lie down. We've got a long journey tomorrow.'

'Yeah, you're right. I can't have been here before. It was just a coincidence.'

But the saddhu, eavesdropping nearby, waves his ancient, bony fingers excitedly in my face, proclaiming -'Mehmsaab. Remember this. Nothing in life is ever a coincidence!'

His words unsettle me. This entire country unsettles me, with its unfamiliar view of life and death.

Next stop is Varanasi, sacred city of both Hindus and Jains. It's an intense place, frenetic yet captivating. It's home to trinket sellers, snack vendors, holy cows, beggars and religious devotees. Its tight tangle of claustrophobic, narrow lanes recall a life unchanged since medieval times. Crowds of pilgrims sweep through them, spilling out onto the riverbank lined with its ceremonial ghats - the steps down to the sacred Ganges. Here at dawn they enter its holy waters to cleanse themselves of sin in one of the most polluted rivers in the world. And here, in plain view, corpses are burnt in the open air and Death catches up with me once more.

The funeral pyres burn ceaselessly all day as the dead pass on to their next life. Grieving families watch their loved ones being consumed by fire, comforted by the fact that this is believed to be the most spiritually appropriate way to release a soul from the body.

But I find no comfort in it! For me, those flames aren't cleansing and renewing but menacing and all-consuming. Is this what became of my free-spirited boy? Is ash all that remains? If the physical container can combust so easily, then why is it so hard to dissolve that ever present lump in my chest?

The smell of burning flesh makes me gag. I turn in anguish to The Enigma and see that he too is struggling with his emotions. It's time to leave.

'Let's get out of here. I can't cope with this!'

Mutely he agrees and we take the very next bus out.

At least the journey is a welcome distraction. Often we're the only white faces to be seen and we cause a commotion. The months in the sun have bleached my hair and I'm a target of interest wherever we go.

Unwittingly, we've morphed into the royal family. The Enigma, with his gentrified air, is the Prince Charles of our couple and the crowd parts before him. But I'm their beloved Princess Diana, and by far eclipse his popularity.

Unlike me, the Enigma takes things in his understated stride. He's comfortable with facts and figures but seemingly unmoved by the wonders we encounter that send me into paroxysms of delight.

He declares the soulful classical music we hear at festivals to be 'different', the Taj Mahal to be 'okay', and a heart-stopping sunset over the Ganges to be 'quite nice'. Breaking point for me comes in Leh, in the Himalayas, at the roof of the world. I feel a familiar stirring, a half-frightened, half-excited intake of breath, as I start to lose myself in the velvety blackness of the night sky and the brilliance of the stars that seem close enough to touch.

I sigh in blissful rapture.

'This is so immense and profound.'

'Mmm. It's not bad.'

'*Not bad*? You certainly know how to kill the moment! What's wrong with you? You're such an energy vampire. Why can't you ever lose yourself in the here and now? Are you emotionally incontinent, or what? The only time I've seen you really moved was watching those funeral pyres.'

I stop short because I seem to have hit a nerve. After an awkward silence where I recall his loveless home, I have a moment of clarity.

'Is it something to do with your Mum? What really happened to her?'

The Enigma's face crumples in distress. After an interminable silence, the truth finally comes out, and it's as if a dam's broken inside him.

'We never talk about it. She went out one day and never came back. But at school I heard them whispering about how she was found … hanging from the tree at the bottom of our rose garden.'

'Oh my God! That's awful!'

'Yes, I know. It's bad enough that we lost her. But suicide's a mortal sin in the Catholic Church. No doubt she's burning in hell right now. She didn't love us enough to stay...'

His shoulders heave and I see before me a small, wounded child whose heart has been shattered. I try to comfort him as best I can, aware that no words are adequate to heal his pain.

Sure, I've had my experience of death. But to lose your mother, how devastating would that be? No compass in life, no lighthouse guiding you safely past the rocks, no lifeboat to rescue you - just a cold, stormy sea and an anchorless boat. But he needs to know he was loved! We all do!

'That's ridiculous! How can you possibly believe that? Your mum obviously loved you. But with five kids under six, she must've been on her knees! No one realises how exhausting it is having children. Plus, her hormones were going haywire. She obviously wasn't thinking straight. Nowadays they pick up on post-natal depression much faster, but in those days, you were just supposed to get on with it. There wasn't any counselling, so it probably seemed the only way out.'

'Do you really think so?'

'Yes, I really and truly do.'

'But don't you think *I'm* to blame somehow? I was the eldest - if only I'd helped more, she'd be alive today.'

'That's ridiculous! You were only six years old! No, of course you're not to blame. You were a *child* and it was your mother's decision. But she only made it because she was *desperate*. You have to remember, she was ill. It wasn't her fault. It wasn't anybody's fault. It was just a tragedy. And I refuse to believe for one minute that she's burning in hell! You know I don't believe in God, but if I did, then I'd want Him to be a God of love and I think He'd be looking after your mum in heaven and giving her a great big hug. Now you just come here.'

He looks at me, eyes filled with hopeful tears, and shuffles towards me. I put my arms around him - probably the first time someone's hugged him in years - until he finally releases the grief of those past memories and sobs into the early hours of the morning.

From that day on, The Enigma changes subtly. His walk's lighter and his enthusiasm more noticeable. He buys a wooden flute to while away the long hours waiting for buses. He's talented and loses himself in his music. Before long, it's Prince Charles who starts drawing in the crowds, whilst Diana takes a back seat.

Our stay in Mumbai coincides with the Festival of Ganesh, the Elephant god, one of the myriads of Hindu deities that fascinate me. We sit companionably on the beach, watching the festivities. All around us joyous chanting fills the air, drums beat and showers of sweets and red poster paint fly everywhere.

We talk about continuing our travels, expanding our horizons, seeing the globe with fresh eyes. Then the Enigma puts his arm round me and I realise this embrace is on the verge of becoming something else.

I ask uncomfortably.

'Mm, what are you doing?

'I just thought, you know ... Erm, well ... I just hoped us travelling together might lead to ... you know ...'

I do know. But even though I feel for him, I can't go there, I let him down as gently as I can.

He laughs it off.

'Not your karma, eh?'

No it's not my karma. I've no idea what my karma is! I came to India to *find myself* but somehow, I seem to have got more lost! My head's exploding with a multitude of impressions, new ways of looking at the world and different spiritual perspectives. But what is the right path? Who is the right person to walk it with me? Maybe I should listen to my mother... Perhaps it *is* time to get a job?

10

Nine Perspectives on Life

I'm running my hands through a mane of glossy, dark hair. Gorgeous, brown eyes smile playfully at me, whilst lips, full of passion, whisper seductively into my ear.

'Bloody great! We've overslept, isn't it?'

I wake from my dream into the nightmare of my reality where different voices vie for attention.

'You must've turned the alarm off last night, isn't it?'

*'Yes, that's **you** he's talking to, stupid!'*

'You shouldn't drink so much, you can't take it anymore!'

'Just phone in sick!'

'Mummy, do I *have* to go to school?'

I skip breakfast and with a heavy heart set off for work. I've been at the college for years now, in a respectable teaching job my mother approved of. Mostly I've loved what I do but recently I've become jaded with both students and colleagues. We might now be in a state-of-the-art building, complete with all-singing-and-dancing glass atrium, but the song in my heart has died and the dance is now a shuffle.

Maybe it's a phase, a middle-aged malaise, a feeling of *is this all I've done with my life?* It's bad enough at home, with a husband who's always pointing out your short-comings, but when work's also underwhelming, then the whole of life appears unsatisfactory.

I open the staffroom door and notice my colleague's new haircut.

'Looking fab, Jenny.'

'Blatant lie. It's a disaster and the last time I model for the Hair and Beauty Department!'

'Oh dear! Well, any more thoughts on that course proposal?'

'Yes, loads. Lots of issues. More time needed. We can't possibly implement it as it is.'

'Oh, alright. Thanks. I wish I'd never agreed to it now.'

But as usual my mouth said 'yes' before my brain engaged and now I'm landed with extra stress and no help. Typical! I look hopefully at Mehmet. He can often be relied on for support. He nods sympathetically.

'I've proofread it for you and corrected all your typos, spelling mistakes and bad grammar.'

'Oh, thanks, Mehmet. I did it in a bit of a rush.'

'Yes, you can tell.'

Great! Mehmet's meticulous but not always tactful. Thank goodness for Nancy and her optimism.

'Brilliant. Well done!'

'Aaah, great. Can you give me a hand working on it then?'

'Ermm, I'd love to but I'm rather busy.'

'Really? I thought you were under hours this term?'

'Sorry, what are you implying?'

Oh dear! I'd forgotten Nancy encourages people rather than actually helps them. Thank goodness that Scott, the newbie in the staffroom, diffuses the situation.

'Calm down, Nancy. She's not implying anything. Now, who'd like a nice cup of tea?'

'*Tea*, Scott? A *whisky*'s what I need! My life's in *meltdown*!'

The door slams and Amanda, attention-seeker extraordinaire, flounces in. We exchange looks and pretend to be lesson planning, as she weeps about her health issues, and how her students hate her. Scott makes comforting sounds and drip-feeds her tea and posh biscuits filched from Nancy's secret stash.

Then Claire enters, power-dressing her way across the room, as befits her status of Head of International. She's followed by the ominous steps of Manuela, and nervous Nadim from the IT section.

This isn't a good sign.

Although Claire's a whirlwind of good-humoured activity, rushing from meeting to meeting and charming all, Manuela's a different matter entirely. When things go her way, she's a delight, but step out of line, then beware!

Today it's obvious that none of us are in her good books. She cuts to the point, upsetting some and annoying others.

'Are you idiots? None of you've inputted the registers correctly, despite last week's training course.'

'Oh God! It's all me! I know it. I can't do anything right. I'm hopeless!'

'Yes, but it's not only you, Amanda.'

Mehmet looks up indignantly.

'I think you'll find my registers are perfect.'

'Yes, that's correct, Mehmet. You're the only one who's bothered to check them.'

Jenny's annoyed too.

'Well, that's exactly why I didn't input mine! I had questions. The course wasn't clear. I said as much on my feedback form.'

'Ok, point noted, Jenny. At least you did it, unlike Scott. But the rest of you obviously need a remedial lesson. So, I've brought Nadim to supervise you. There'd better be no mistakes next week.'

With that she breezes out, leaving Claire to give us a rousing speech about mastering the register by the end of the day.

Pep-talk over, we return to our desks. But Claire hasn't finished with me yet. She comes over and sits down for a chat about the new course proposal. Suddenly, she shrieks and jumps up.

'Ow! I've just sat on something sharp. It's a pointy, purple stone. Where on earth's that come from?'

I flush and quickly rescue it from her.

'Oh sorry, it's mine. It must've fallen off my brooch the other day. Are you ok?'

'Sure, it was the shock of sitting on it. Not a great way of encouraging teamwork though. Just as well I've booked you onto that course this afternoon. It's about better staff bonding. Perhaps it'll revolutionise relationships in the workplace.'

I nod, unconvinced. Then I sit through an hour of Nadim avoiding eye contact and giving incomprehensible explanations. Afterwards I rush to teach my lower-level class and grab lunch before signing into the course.

As I enter the training room, I see about twenty staff members, picked from different college departments. They have an air of resignation. Yes, they may well have an afternoon off teaching but will a weak cup of tea and two chocolate bourbons compensate for three hours of boredom and the inevitable *cascading* back to colleagues?

As I queue for my free beverage, I notice the sign above the tea urn.

The Enneagram: Understanding yourself and the others in your life.

I've no idea what the Enneagram is and, apparently, neither do my fellow tea-drinkers.

Betty from Catering confesses -

'They're on to me! I know we went metric years ago but all my recipes are in pounds and ounces. Can't get my head round kilograms.

And I'm not about to either. I do my own thing. If they want to sack me, let them try!'

Ron from Engineering reassures her -

'No, it's not kilograms, love. It's some bloody initiative from Sharon in HR. Trying to show off to her boss. She read an article about it online, apparently. Thinks it's the next trend in improving staff motivation and performance at work.'

'Oh, I don't like the sound of that.'

'Never mind, love. Ennea-course that gets me out of teaching my NVQ1 horrors is good news to me.'

But we're soon to discover what exactly the Enneagram is, as our trainer, a petite, curly haired woman with a gentle smile, walks to the front. Ron peers at her with a hint of recognition.

'Bloody hell! Isn't that Sandra from Childcare? I thought she'd gone in the last round of cuts.'

Betty puts on her glasses for a closer look.

'Ooh, you're right. They took a big hit, like us. Their Nursery Provision and our Sugar Craft were taken off the programme. Mind you, it hasn't done her any harm. She looks ten years younger. And, by the way, isn't she good pals with Sharon?'

'Well that bloody explains it then. Jobs for the boys. Everything on the cheap at this place.'

And it is indeed Childcare Sandra, with a new care-free, college-free career. She skips to the lectern.

'How lovely to see so many familiar faces and have the opportunity to introduce you to the Enneagram. Now, you may be wondering what it's all about and I can tell you it's a system used for mapping human nature. It has mystical origins, connected to the Sufis. You know, those folk that whirl around for a living. So, it can be viewed in a deeper spiritual context. You see it's believed we all have a pure essence inside us but we mask it with one of the nine types of ego personality.

Ron groans theatrically.

'What bollocks! This is going to be a complete waste of time.'

'Oh, hi Ron, how are you doing? And no, I'm not going to waste your time. I'm not focussing on that aspect today. I suspect the college has little interest in the development of your *enlightenment* and more in the development of your *productivity*. No, today, I'm running through a series of exercises that'll help you find out your personality types and those of your colleagues and give you some ideas about how to communicate more effectively.'

'Still sounds like bull to me.'

'Well, maybe you could hold your judgement for now and enjoy the break from those NVQ1s? I heard them kicking off as I was passing the workshop. You're probably better off here with a cup of coffee and a Hob Nob.'

And to be fair, Childcare Sandra's left the college but remembers its students only too well, so Ron shuts up and settles down.

We start by learning there are nine distinct personality types on the Enneagram and, as Childcare Sandra's keen to point out, in the spirit of the college's Equality and Diversity policy, none's better or more desirable than another. However, within each type, you can be unhealthy, average or, healthy.

Knowing more about your personality type allows you to better understand your behaviour, and that of others. This hopefully leads you to be the best version of yourself and to be more considerate and compassionate towards others.

Sandra concludes her introduction by telling us -

'The types are given numbers to avoid attributing value judgements, but of course, over time, they've also been given some names. I've got them here on my Power Point, with a few key descriptors. So, have a look and see if any resonate with you. But don't worry if they don't as we'll be doing some activities later to find out more.'

I look carefully at the label on the screen, wondering which one I am and which those close to me might be.

1 The Perfectionist - responsible, independent, hard-working with high standards but can appear judgmental.
Mm, well I try to do everything to a high standard, not that my beloved would agree. But I'm certainly not obsessed with punctuation like Mehmet.

2 The Giver - outgoing, friendly and helpful but can be resentful and manipulative.
The positive aspects could definitely be me or any teacher, wife and mother for that matter. But I don't recognise the negative traits at all.

3 The Performer - self-confident, ambitious, successful but can be too busy 'doing' to enjoy just 'being'.
Teaching's a type of performing, I guess but I'm never full-on like my Brazilian buddy. And unlike Claire, I'm content to stay at the chalk face.

4 The Tragic Romantic - intense, dramatic and creative but can be self-obsessed and demanding.
I feel I could be creative but whilst my life's often a drama, it's never as extreme as Amanda's, although I've certainly fallen for some dramatic types in the past!

5 The Observer - quiet, intelligent, reflective but can appear emotionally distant.
I'm definitely not one of these! I'm a people person and need to get involved rather than stand back and watch from the side-lines, unlike Small Child and geeky Nadim. Maybe my dad's a Number Five? That would explain a lot!

6 The Questioner - productive, imaginative and a great trouble-shooter, but can be suspicious and inflexible.
My tendency to rush in without thinking things through means I'm probably not a questioner. It's Jenny who's the 'Yes, but…' member of our team. Could English Rose belong here too?

7 The Epicure-Enthusiast - cheerful, energetic and charming but easily bored and self-centred.
Well, I'd like to think I'm a happy-go lucky person but unfortunately

that's not always true. As for having gourmet tastes, I appreciate a five-star restaurant but am equally as happy with a takeaway curry. And whereas Nancy's a designer shopper who enjoys the fine things in life, I'm more of a bargain basement girl myself.

8   *The Boss - an intense, protective, hard worker, but can be confrontational and unaware of others' feelings.*
I admit to having a bossy tendency every now and then but I'm no match for alpha-female, Manuela, and I generally follow the party line, unlike Betty from Catering. Maybe Devil Teen is an Eight? It would explain the constant arguments.

9   *The Peacemaker - warm, accommodating, but hates conflict and can procrastinate.*
 Well, in my eyes, a little bit of conflict makes life more interesting, but Scott would disagree with me and I reckon Zen Mother and Delightful Daughter could be in this category too.

After a few exercises exploring the different personality types, I've a good idea what position my colleagues occupy but the jury's still out for me until I get the handout giving more detailed negative and positive qualities of each type

When the less evolved traits of Number Two, the Giver, are discussed, it's like someone's punched me in the stomach! I recognise myself so well.

- *thinking people take me for granted and don't care about me*
- *using flattery to get round people*
- *agreeing to help, then resenting it*

What a revelation! But now the key factor's how to be the best, rather than the worst of my type? And how to use this awareness for better relationships with those around me? I return to the staffroom in a lighter mood, vowing to understand and appreciate others more.

As I open the door, no one even bothers to ask me about the course. Typical! Never mind. I decide to make Amanda feel better after her hard start to the day, so improvise a small, white lie.

'I've just seen your students and they told me they'd had a great lesson with you!'

'Oh thanks, yes. They said I'm a fantastic teacher. Honestly, why do I get so worked up? By the way, could you give me a hand with these registers? I don't have a clue what I'm doing.'

'Sure, yeah. No problem.'

I seethe silently to myself as I fill in and backdate all Amanda's registers. Then I type up the key points of today's course. I'll make them into a slide show later and offer to present it at the next staff meeting. That'll get me in Claire's good books, so I can leave early next week for my *date* with Prince Harry.

It's late when I arrive home to discover Devil Teen in front of the PlayStation and Small Child cowering behind the settee. As I walk in, with my coat still on, my youngest runs tearfully towards me.

'Mummy, it's horrible. He's shooting everyone and there's blood everywhere!'

'What on earth's going on?'

Devil Teen glances up from the screen.

'Nothing. Little-poo's being a pain. I told him to play upstairs with his Lego, so it's hardly my fault he's traumatised.'

'Err, is that *Call of Duty*? You know you're not supposed to have it on when he's about.'

'Exactly, mother. That's why I told him to go to his room.'

'But you're meant to be looking after him, not playing inappropriate games on the PlayStation! That's what you get your allowance for.'

'Yes mother, but in case you hadn't noticed, you're late and I clocked off forty minutes ago.'

'Oh for God's sake! Where's your sister? Is she home? Maybe she can keep him entertained whilst I get on with the tea.'

I drag Small Child to the attic hideaway which Delightful Daughter inhabits. I'm about to knock, when she pops her head out with a welcoming smile.

'Hi Mum. You're back late. Hard day at work?'

'Well, a long one. A telling-off about register abuse, followed by Abdul confusing adjectives and adverbs, despite it being the third lesson on the subject! Then a course this afternoon, which was interesting but meant I had to make notes afterwards. Same old, same old. How about you, sweetheart. How's your day been?'

'Oh you know, Mum. Same old, same old. Planned some youth sessions this morning, then lunchtime shift at the pub, followed by an hour's peace before the brothers returned. When the bickering got too much I escaped up here.'

'Oh dear, that bad, eh? I just wondered if you'd keep an eye on your big, little brother, whilst your little, big brother cools down and I start cooking.'

Once again, my eldest lives up to her name.

'No problem, mum. But there's no need to cook. I knew you'd be exhausted so I've already made a lasagne. It just needs heating up. In the meantime, have a break for half an hour. I'll build some Lego with baby bruv. Oh, and the district nurse called. Something about *Granddad* and *cognitive tests*. Can you ring back?'

I force a smile, go downstairs, and finally take off my coat. I close my eyes and attempt to reconnect with some inner peace and reflect on what I've learnt today. I manage a few minutes of golden silence before the incessant voices interrupt me.

'Mmm, you're obviously the resentful worst of your Enneagram type!'

'You'd better ring first thing in the morning!'

'Let Your Bev deal with it for a change!'

Then I sigh and pull myself together. It's going to take more than the Enneagram to sort out my life.

11

Love on Tour

'I can't believe you're off again. You've only just got back.'

'Well, you *did* say it was time I got a job, mum.'

'I know, I just imagined it'd be something sensible with the council, not more gadding about!'

You see, I'm now a professional tour guide, taking unsuspecting sightseers around Europe and have become a Surprising Success. The tourists feed off my every word and the feeling's amazing. I don't have to fight any *voice of an angel* for their attention or be embarrassed about my state school education. They think I'm both adorable and clever. Love's my new drug of addiction.

To be honest, it's not that difficult to keep my punters happy. Whilst they relax in their luxury coach, I provide them with fascinating, albeit not always historically accurate, commentary. When we stop, I sweep a passage through street hawkers and pickpockets, taking them safely to be fed, watered and photographed with the local attractions.

I work mainly with Americans, the occasional Canadian, the odd Ozzie and accidental Kiwi, with a few random South Africans, and Indians thrown in for good measure. To them, Europe's an exotic and unknown entity, where no one speaks English or uses the same money. They need guidance and I'm the one to offer it.

I'm assigned to what's affectionately known as the *Pyjama Tour*, a schedule so action-packed that getting dressed in the morning is a luxury. Day One starts with breakfast in Belgium, coffee in Luxembourg, lunch in France and dinner in Switzerland! It's no wonder the tourists, totally bewildered by the foreign phrases and confusing coins, cling to me like a life raft.

I, in turn, cling to my experienced, Italian drivers, despite my inability to speak their language. The first phrase I pick up is 'Porca miseria!' when they discover I'm a new guide and I can tell this isn't good by the way they hang their heads dramatically in their hands.

Each evening we join the other guides and drivers for the local excursion - *Paris by night, Swiss Yodelling with Fondue* or *Waltzing with Strauss*. This is when I get my daily Italian lesson, as my driver recounts humiliating 'Oggi, mia guida ...' - 'Today my guide...'- stories of my latest mishaps.

To be fair, there are many tales of disaster:

- losing a tourist up a mountain in Switzerland
- driving the wrong way down the one-way streets of Nuremburg
- recommending the Paris Cabaret to a Southern Bible Belt family, forgetting that underneath the feathers and sparkles, the dancers are topless…

The experienced guides look down at me and my incompetence but strangely I'm getting rave reviews from the feedback sheets, and my reputation of being 'a great tour director' is spreading.

At the next coffee stop one of the ancient, sour-faced guides sidles up to me.

'So what do you know about the history of the Abbey at Melk?'

'What? Oh my God! Is that huge building an abbey then? I've been telling them all season it's a castle!'

'Unbelievable! You're such an amateur! Why is it that the tourists seem to like you so much? Not all of them can be that stupid. You're obviously not giving them any information. So, what exactly *is* it that you do?'

Her question stops me in my tracks. I've never thought about it before. I just do what comes naturally. So I try to break it down for her.

'Well, I create a *family*. I get them talking to each other and tell them stories about the terrible things that have gone wrong on previous tours. That way they're always prepared for inevitable disaster!

Oh, and on the journey home, after a night out, I always lead them in the *Chicken* dance.'

'Dear Lord! What's our profession coming to?'

But, indeed, I believe this *is* the secret of my success. Out of a random selection of strangers I create a single unit and strive to keep them happy. And, of course, by my second and third seasons as a guide, I finally acquire some facts to dazzle them with too.

Each tour brings new challenges as people from diverse nations and backgrounds are forced together in the close confinement of a fifty-seater coach.

The Afro-American family of Mom, Pa and five teenage sons, who pose in snappy white suits on the Spanish Steps in Rome, has the Italian paparazzi convinced they're a famous boy band. Their warm humour and natural kindness endear them to the white South-African, who, for the duration of the trip, leaves his home-grown apartheid in his luggage.

The group of Sikhs from the Punjab in India chat happily with members of the Baptist congregation from Washington, USA. And the intrepid traveller from Auckland, New Zealand, in his eighties, swaps addresses with the twenty-year-old newly-weds from Quebec, Canada.

Of course, there are the inevitable, difficult clients but I spot them from the outset, determined to integrate them into a harmonious group. I deal politely with their complaints and embark on a charm offensive to win them over, ignoring their annoying habits, and focussing instead on the hidden diamond I know lies somewhere inside. And, miraculously, it works. I genuinely get to like them, and before long they're like putty in my hands.

I'm guide, interpreter, teacher, fellow party animal, and, occasionally, confidant. What's more, I'm constantly amazed at the number of couples who book these tours to celebrate a major marriage milestone only to discover that sixteen days of enforced togetherness brings them to the brink of divorce.

One such wife wails to me, in obvious distress,

'He's out of the house all day at work. This is the most I've seen of him in twenty-five years! And now I'm not sure he's the man I fell in love with.'

And no, he's not the man she first wed, just as the years have changed her too. Mostly, the gondola ride in Venice and the magic of Paris by moonlight sort out their issues but it leaves me with the impression that marriage isn't an easy train ride.

I vow I'll never settle for second best. Somewhere out there waiting for me is *The One*.

Part of my heart will always belong to the Baptist and I seek him out when I slip away from my tourists and find stillness and comfort in the quiet anonymity of an out-of-the-way church. There I linger a while, breathing in the centuries of hopeful prayers and heart-felt praises. The incense of faith and love wraps around me like a warm, protective blanket against the trials and tribulations of everyday life.

For to me, these holy places, be they churches, mosques, synagogues or temples, are built of more than bricks and mortar. My travels have shown me that they contain our innermost longings, our supplications to something greater than our individual selves. And if I sit in silent reflection, I find myself momentarily transported above historical and religious labels to a higher awareness that unites, rather than divides.

But for now I'm enjoying a nomadic, carefree, lifestyle, and, like a stereotypical sailor, I have a love interest in each port.

Italy sees me meet up with the poetic policeman who dedicates incomprehensible verse to me, whilst Austria has me comfort the unhappy hotel porter who wants to be an artist. In Germany the earnest-looking border guard slips his phone number into my passport and in Switzerland the cashier in the bank flirts outrageously with me. But France is home to the wealthy hotel owner who pursues me with ardour and declares I am his 'amour'.

My tour passes his hotel every two weeks, and he does his best to woo me with fine dining and romantic gestures. Once I have to fight my way through a forest of flowers into my room. Another time I find a string of pearls draped elegantly over my breakfast croissant. He pulls out the stops and secures us impossible-to-reserve seats at the famous Paul Bocuse restaurant north of Lyon. But his extravagance is wasted on me, his 'petite Lady Dee'.

The eye-wateringly expensive, speciality oysters aren't to my liking.

'I'm sorry, but they taste like snot! A drop of Hendo's on them might just about make them edible, though.'

However, instead of being frustrated by my lack of finesse, Monsieur Hôtel finds it charming.

'You're so amusante, cherie. I love your honesty and your famous English cooking. Turkey with jam, meat with fruit and mint! My countrymen turn up their noses at these extraordinary dishes. But not me. I love these unusual mixes and 'ow the British embrace the cuisine of other nations. Spicy Indian, exotic Asian, fiery Mexican - none of these are acceptable to your typical French palate. 'ow I would love to meld all these flavours and create something quite incredible. Mon Dieu! That'd be a restaurant worth eating at! But for now, this little part of France is not quite ready for my ambition. They're content to celebrate a rugby win against Marseille with a glass of Côte du Rhône and a plate of Cervelas de Lyon.'

Yes, indeed, Monsieur Hôtel isn't blinkered in his quest to discover new tastes and textures. Moved by his passion for all things culinary I get him to give me free rein in the hotel kitchen and rustle up our family secret recipe. As he bites into my flapjack, he lets out a deep sigh of satisfaction.

'This, mon chou, is the taste of love!'

He chews slowly, savouring the taste, then spoils the moment.

'But maybe it could become a dessert of 'eaven with the addition of some Chantilly cream and an 'int of fire.'

'Flipping heck. You'd better not say that to my mother! This recipe's sacrosanct. She wouldn't want anyone messing with it. And by the way, why don't you come over at the end of the season? You can try our famous Yorkshire puddings for real then.'

'Ah oui, mon amour. I most definitely will, when I 'ave a spare moment. In the meantime, let us make the most of these moments we 'ave together.'

And he sweeps me into a passionate embrace that ends all conversation…

But come New Year's Eve there's no sign of my fickle Frenchman. Instead a squat, scary Caveman with no neck, rugby-tackles me as I stand by the bar, dragging me over to meet his friend, the Boy Scout, dressed in comically large hat and shorts. They're part of a gang of rowdy sportsmen, hanging out in the Nursery Tavern in Broomhill before an inevitable fancy dress party. I eye Boy Scout suspiciously, as he's listing to one side and seems somewhat the worse for wear.

Unhappy with this intrusion into my night-out, I huffily smooth down my Indian, mirrored skirt and fringed scarf, and look daggers at Boy Scout, preparing to give him the brush-off. But I'm momentarily wrong-footed as I find myself staring into deep pools of vivid blue that make me catch my breath.

He slurs endearingly.

'I like your coshhtume. You make a great gypshhy, isnt't it? Are you coming to my party?'

It's not a good start to his chat-up routine, but there's something kind and soulful in his eyes that kindles a spark of recognition.

'I'm not in fancy dress! These are my normal clothes. But I guess oversized shorts, felt hat and woggle mean you should be socialising at the Scouts' Jamboree rather than rubbing shoulders with a Romany!'

Annoyed, I turn to go.

'No, stop!'

Once again I find myself floundering in the azure abyss of his eyes.

'Just give me your number. You won't regret it.'

I hesitate, then, letting caution to the wind, recite 'three-six-five-two-five-nine' into his ear, and head towards the exit.

'No, wait, isn't it? I haven't got a pen.'

'You'll remember if you want to.'

And I close the door firmly on Boy Scout.

But a few days later I receive a phone call.

'Remember me? The Boy Scout, isn't it? I wrote your number on my arm with a friend's lipstick. But when I woke up on a couch with Superman and a Gorilla, the last two digits were smudged. I've called two wrong numbers so far and this was my last try. Third time lucky! Must be fate. So, what do you reckon? I think I deserve a date, isn't it?'

Well, I'm impressed by the effort he's gone to, his voice has a pleasing lilt and, besides, my social diary's hardly full, so I agree to meet up that evening.

As I wait for him to arrive, my mother asks with interest.

'What's he like, this new beau of yours?'

'To be honest Mum, I can't really remember. He's not the usual, tall, dark, handsome type I go for. For a start he's got blue eyes.'

'Oh well', replies my mother, remembering my pet hate, 'as long as he's got his own hair, you'll be fine.'

At that moment the doorbell rings and I open it to a tall, handsome, bald guy. He smiles at me with his eyes of deepest blue and for a moment I'm caught off-guard. Then I remember what was troubling me.

Bald? Was that why he was wearing the Scout's hat - to disguise his lack of hair and rugby prop ears? Before I can conjure up a mysterious, quick-onset illness, my mother pushes me out of the door, and my destiny is decided.

Despite being follicly-challenged, Boy Scout turns out to be kind, attentive, and good company, isn't it? Oh, and very Welsh too! The conversation flows easily and he makes me feel special.

'You're amazing! All your experiences abroad - quite the free-spirit, isn't it? You're clever, talented and beautiful. I'll even forgive you your love of the royals!'

'But I'm not sure I can forgive *you* your love of rugby! My dad's brought me up on football.'

'Well, that's because no one's shown you its magic...'

And, that evening Boy Scout, weaves a powerful spell. Instead of my eyes glazing over with boredom, I find myself enthralled by the passion with which he tells the tale of the rugby in his blood. I can't explain what happens, but somehow, in the style of his beloved sport, he succeeds in crossing the touchline of my heart and scoring a try.

My mother raises her eyebrows as I prepare for yet another outing.

'You're seeing a lot of this young man...'

'Yes, I really like him. Despite being Welsh, he's definitely embracing Sheffield culture! We've been to Owlerton Stadium, done a few West Street pub crawls, had a game of bingo at the Mecca, caught a band at The Limit and a play at the Crucible. He's certainly good company and he's even a fan of Hendo's! But the season starts in a few weeks, so I don't know...'

But Boy Scout knows. He's very clear about what he wants, despite my warnings.

'You don't have to hang around for me, you know. I'll be on the road for another six months.'

'I know, but you're worth the wait, isn't it? And to prove it, here's a love spoon necklace. We Welsh don't give those out lightly, mind.'

And this time, the touring life starts to lose its appeal. The effort I put into making my groups love me no longer brings that heady euphoria. Trying to please everyone all the time's exhausting. I'm only loveable if judged so by others, so the two feedback forms that grade me as merely *good* negate the forty-eight that tell me I'm *excellent*.

My romantic dalliances no longer hold attraction for me either. I give up poetry, grow tired of the failed artist, blank the border guard and change my bank. Monsieur Hôtel, however, is more persistent.

'What is this round your neck, cherie? I gave you pearls, not ridiculous cutlery to wear! Are you trying to make me jealous?'

'Well, you didn't visit like you promised. And you've never committed to me.'

'Eh bien, so I commit now. Let's toast our love with champagne and caviar.'

'Can't we stay in? I'm always eating out!'

'You strange anglaise. Of course, we must go out. Then afterwards we will stay in.'

His intense gaze and chiselled jaw are hard to resist and his Gallic charm wins me round. I take off the love spoon to assuage my guilt.

Tellingly though, whenever I feel sad or lonely, I pick up the phone, and it's always Boy Scout's number that I dial.

He visits me on a rare weekend off in Belgium and I find him chatting at the bar with Old Sour Face, who seems unusually good-humoured.

'Hello my lovely. I've been telling this gorgeous lady how much you've learnt from her. Now is it Michelin restaurant tonight or a bag of chips on the beach?'

I know I'll always be able to rely on him and he puts everything in perspective.

'Look, stop worrying, isn't it? Forty-eight tourists think you're the bees' knees. Who cares if two think you're only the bees' ankles? I think you're great, isn't it? And that's what counts.'

True to his scouting promises, he's trustworthy, loyal and courageous. So what if the Romantic inside me yearns for a fairy tale *love at first sight*, an electrifying *coup-de-foudre*, or a tear-jerking *soul-mates for ever*.

Instead, what I get is an itch of *inevitability* a *Really? You? Well, I guess so then*. It's a strange sense of inner-knowing, a connection to some deep awareness that tells me I definitely have no choice in the matter.

At the end of the season I fall happily into the arms of Boy Scout, and, in a grand gesture, he turns to me one day and surprises me with a ring.

'See. A true boy scout - always prepared! This cost me a bloody arm and leg, which means we should definitely get married, isn't it?'

So, we arrange a date, book a venue, and send out the invitations.

The big day arrives.

I'm in my wedding dress, nervously waiting for the car.

The phone rings.

'It's not too late, mon amour! I beg you!'

But it is too late.

I bow to the inevitability of love.

12

Never Say Don't

It's been a morning of *don'ts*.

- 'Don't run. You'll drop the plate.'
  (Crash and wail from Small Child)
- 'Don't switch on the PlayStation. You've got homework.
  (Devil-Teen feigns deafness.)
- 'Don't forget to complete that form for your youth work
  course.'
  (Delightful Daughter nods passive-aggressively, meaning it's
  a lost cause.)
- 'And all of you. Don't forget to flog those raffle tickets to
  buy school sports equipment.'
  (Brilliant - they've sneaked them back into my handbag and
  Boy Scout *forgot* to take any. Bloody typical.)

The final straw comes when I call at my father's before work.

'Dad, please don't be difficult. It's just some routine tests.'

'No. Your mother says I'm fine.'

I arrive at work a broken woman with the voices rampaging in
my head.

'You're pathetic! No one listens to you.'

'You should make them pay attention.'

'Just get a one-way ticket out of here!'

As I rest my head in my hands, Amanda walks in.

'Heavens, you look as awful as I feel. Are you ok?'

Her words start me blubbing and pouring out my troubles to the staffroom.

Nadim looks away in embarrassment, but Mehmet offers me a pristine handkerchief and the pointless advice - 'You should take better care of yourself.'

Scott plonks a cup of tea in front of me whilst Nancy suggests -

'Why don't *I* take your class and *you* go on my NLP course - less stressful than teaching.'

'Yes, but...' Jenny interrupts, 'it's exams all day today, so no teaching anyway.'

'That's true,' says Claire, giving Nancy the evil eye. 'But maybe *doing* something would be better for you than just invigilating?'

Manuela's decisive - 'I agree. Now pull yourself together and get going.'

I enter the Old Queen's Head - a fifteenth-century, timber-framed, city-centre pub - the surprising, but obviously cheap, choice of venue on college's budget. As I clamber up the creaking stairs to the function room, half-expecting to encounter a ghost, I'm greeted by our trainers, Dave and Eileen - a middle-aged Sheffield couple.

She's got blonde, helmet hair, a *private trainer body* and designer outlet clothing. He's tall and skinny, dressed in a suit and polo neck combo, with a shaved head. His face is gaunt as if he's recovering from an illness, and there's something familiar about him ...

Eileen talks... a lot! Before I've made my way across the beer-soaked carpet to the coffee machine, I learn she worked in payroll and Dave was in sales before they *found* NLP. They're evangelical about their new religion.

'You wouldn't believe it, duck. Since we discovered NLP, our Dave and I 'aven't looked back.'

'Our lass is raight there. Just by focusing on t' words we use, we can change what we or others do. Straight up. I could've done wi' that when I were a lad.'

So, what *is* this NLP? I grab a coffee and a leaflet.

Neuro-Linguistic-Programming, or NLP, is an approach to communication, personal development and psychotherapy, created in the States.

Well, now it's arrived in Yorkshire, in a cut-price, watered-down version. But maybe there'll be some tips on how to deal with teaching and life more effectively. God knows, I need it! But I'm disconcerted to discover all the other group members are suited and booted sales professionals with sleek company cars.

I'm like a lamb to the slaughter.

By the time they finish their coffee I've already agreed to have my carpet cleaned and booked a life insurance review. If NLP's promising to give them even better skills of communication and persuasion, then I'll be penniless by lunch time.

We start off learning that we experience the world subjectively in terms of our five senses and the language we use. Pseudo-science or not, I'm buying into this idea straight away. I have a German student who never looks at me in lessons but doodles all over her notebook. How comforting to believe she's simply an auditory learner with no need for visual contact, rather than a stroppy Fräulein bored to death by my teaching.

Then we look at *modelling,* the process of recreating excellence by mimicking the behaviour of someone who's already good at what we want to achieve. What I currently need is to save myself a £50 loss by getting rid of the raffle tickets in my handbag.

Eileen comes to support me.

'Na then duck. Thae's already seen that lot in action, selling stuff, so it's thae turn now. Thae's got t' convince them that buying them tickets is a good idea. Go on, 'av a go.'

So, during the next break I imitate the slick sales patter of my course mates. I sidle up to Mr Car Dealer.

'You look kind-hearted. I bet you're always willing to help a friend, aren't you?'

He straightens his tie and the corners of his mouth twitch. Well at least he's not walked away yet, so I soldier on.

'I can tell you're educated too and care about your health. Do you have school-aged children by the way?'

Mr Car Dealer nods with a barely concealed grin.

'Well, then I'm guessing you'd be happy to buy a few raffle tickets to support local children keep fit, wouldn't you?'

Alas for me, Mr Car Dealer's seen through my sales pitch, as do all the others. They're the crème de la crème of wheeler-dealing, and my amateurish attempt to offload my wares misfires. Instead, by the time the next session starts, I've ended up with a brochure on food mixers and an invitation to a property time-share evening. However, all's not lost, as, out of pity, Dave buys two books of tickets.

'Ta lass. Na then, did thae use t'work in Probation Service? Thae looks raight familiar.'

After lunch, we have to think of occasions when we felt really successful, so that we can access this emotion in times when we're less confident. My sales colleagues scribble furiously but my paper remains blank and the voices have lots to say.

'You're a failure!'

'You should've done more with your life!'

'Is the bar open downstairs?'

But Eileen's reassuring - 'Relax, duck, *failures* are nowt but *feedback* 'elping us towards a desired outcome, int that raight, our Dave?'

'Spot on, love. We 'ave to *reframe* negative experiences. I 'ad a few of them in mi life but I've learnt from 'em and moved on. Na then, trick is t' avoid negative words like *don't*. See, t' brain filters out the word *don't* and just 'ears the rest of t'sentence, so it understands *Don't be late!* as *Be late!* So, it's better t' say *Come on time!*'

120

Strangely, this makes sense. So, with this positive reprogramming, instead of judging Small Child's plate throwing as a disaster, I see it as an expression of his willingness to help. Teen-Devil's obsession with the PlayStation, rather than his homework, can be attributed to a silent cry for parental guidance. And Delightful Daughter's procrastination is just a preference for working to last-minute deadlines and a feeling that asking for help is a weakness. As for my father, he feels cornered, rather than having options.

The day finishes and we head to the Tap Room for a farewell drink. The course has distracted me from my problems and I've learnt something, if only to leave my wallet and bank cards safely at home.

Dave downs his pint in one, causing his polo-neck to slide down and reveal his throat and his true identity.

'Apple!'

He splutters out his beer and stares hard at me.

'Chuffin' 'ell … Princess? It can't be … Thae's shoved on some weight. Must be them Lemon Drops.'

He points at the seat next to me, where two shiny, yellow stones are innocently imitating sherbet sweets. I quickly scoop them up and put them in my bag.

For a moment there's the satisfaction in having worked out our connection, but it's quickly replaced by the recollection of our last encounter. There's an awkward silence.

'I wouldn't have recognised thee if thae'd said nowt. But I'm glad thae did. It were a long time ago. A terrible thing. Difficult to forget. Sent me down t'wrong path. But finally I'm back on track, thanks to our Eileen and this NLP. I 'ope life worked out for thee too.'

'Yes… yes…It did… Thanks… I'm fine… Would love to catch up but … got to be going now…'

I stumble out of the door of my past onto the street of my present.

Gulping in great breaths of air, I wonder what if, instead of saying - '*Don't go!*'- that day, I'd said - '*Please stay!*' Would it have made any difference? My heart's pounding with unresolved questions. There have been too many incursions from my past lately. It's unsettling. So, there and then I decide that the simplest solution is to bundle them up and triple lock them in the deepest recesses of my memory, for the past is past and I'm choosing a new NLP future.

I'll start by eliminating the *don'ts* from my life and paying more attention to my family. Then maybe I can tackle the house? And who knows, perhaps a miracle will happen and I'll fall back in love with both my job and my husband?

As I walk through the front door, avoiding the mountain of shoes, I monitor my language, refashioning dark, negative commands into lighter, positive ones.

- 'Walk carefully with that heavy plate. You're so good at clearing up.'
- 'How about I give you a hand with your homework? Then, once it's done, you'll enjoy your PlayStation game more.'
- 'That course deadline's next week. Would you like some help with it?'
- 'I'll feel so much better once I know your blood tests are clear.'

The results are encouraging and even the voices take note -

'Not a bad effort.'

'You should keep up with this.'

'You could be an NLP trainer!'

But for every step forward there are two steps back.

13

Checking in at Church

My new NLP perspective has worked wonders on my father's mood if not his mental state.

'So, you'll agree to the tests dad?'

'Yes, it'll stop you worrying, mum says. Now, candle.'

'Thanks, dad. And yeah, I can't believe it's been ten years ... I'm going to that factory opening with Prince Harry today. A fitting tribute. She'd like that.'

'Yes, loved royalty, your mother.'

At work, Nadim nods as I enter, then averts his eyes. Amanda hugs me theatrically -

'Soo glad you're feeling better. Wish I could say the same for myself!'

Nancy pipes up from the corner - 'Wow, you're looking pretty in pink today!'

'A bit tight though?' - adds Manuela.

Mehmet has his own opinion - 'Lovely but is it appropriate for teaching? You'll get marker-pen all over it if you're not careful.'

Jenny has a solution - 'Use the interactive board in room 314 rather than the white-board.'

'Yeah, I'll swap rooms, no problem,' offers Scott.

'Only til 2.30 though. I'm leaving early to catch Prince Harry. That's still ok, isn't it, Claire?'

'Of course. Who am I to refuse a royal command?'

It's half past two and I'm trying to exit the classroom but Abdul's blocking the door. He's twenty but young for his age and exudes a nervous self-consciousness. He's the middle child of nine and craves one-to-one attention, which is why he always hijacks me at the end of each class.

'So, Mrs Teacher. You go soonly to see king?'

'*Soon*, Abdul not *soonly*. And he's a *prince* not a *king*.'

'But is adverb not adjective. You say adverb always end in *ly*. And why you have no king?'

'It's an exception to the rule and we don't have a *King* because we have a perfectly capable *Queen*.'

'Why you like king family? My host mother say they all lose taxi money.'

'Sorry? Oh! You mean they're a *waste of tax payers' money*?'

'Yes, I say that.'

'Well, good question. Actually, many people agree with your host mother but for *me*, the Royal Family are like my own family. We celebrate their births, watch them grow up, and attend their weddings. Unlike politicians, they don't give their opinions in public, so they don't upset anyone. They're all things to all people. They help us escape our own lives. And of course, the magazines love to talk about their beautiful clothes.'

'Maybe you princess then, Mrs Teacher?'

'Why do you say that, Abdul?'

'Because you look beautifully today.'

'Thank you.'

Smiling at his compliment whilst wincing at his adverb, I slip past him into the corridor and head off for my date with royalty.

By the time I get to the manufacturing research centre at Catcliffe, there's a big crowd waiting outside, but I ninja my way to the front, brandishing my phone. Buxom Royalist to my side elbows me forcefully in the ribs.

'Eee, I remember that poor mite at 'is mum's funeral. Must 'ave broken 'is 'eart, But 'e's grown into a lovely lad, innit?'

I nod in solemn agreement as I think of my own mother. But before my emotions get the better of me, Prince Harry, charming in his tailor-made suit and hand-crafted shoes, exits the factory to a sea of photo flashes. I raise my phone, but Buxom Royalist's beaten to me it. She makes a sudden turn and her impressive chest sends my phone flying over the barrier towards Prince Harry.

Years of Public School sport have honed his reflexes and he catches it to loud applause. As he looks round for its owner, Buxom Royalist jiggles and shouts.

'Over 'ere, 'arry! Woman in pink. It's 'ers.'

And the next thing I know, I'm captured forever on news reel, thanking a true-life prince for coming to the rescue of a damsel in distress.

As Harry's whisked off, no doubt to a good telling-off from his security team, I handle my mobile with new reverence. Maybe I could sell it on E-bay? Just then, it pings. I have a new message... from my father's neighbour. That's unusual ...

- Your dad's throwing everything out of the shed into the garden. Seems agitated. Thought you should know.

Oh great. That's all I need! I'll have to call in again, after I've been to light a candle.

The voices that were silenced by my brush with royalty, start clamouring for attention.

'Even in that pink dress you're nothing special!'

'You should think of your father not Prince Harry!'

'Sell your story to The Sun and jet off on the proceeds!'

On my way to my father's I stop off at the first church I see on Psalter Lane. Although God and I have never made up, this is an annual ritual I can't forego. The building's dark, stone exterior reveals a surprisingly bright interior as the late-afternoon sun streams through a central, stain-glassed arch. The dancing rays recall a distant memory of a forest of light, and my heart yearns once more with supressed longing.

I light my candle and slip into the front pew. I miss my mother. She had a certainty about her that made the world feel safe. She had her standards, which I never quite met, but she'd always fight my corner. But now there's no one to do that and I'm all alone, abandoned. Tears stream down my cheeks as I realise with a shock that I'm tired of life.

As I sit there mired in misery and loss, a shaft of light sends a kaleidoscope of colours swirling on the seat next to me as if something or someone wants me to know there's beauty and hope to be found everywhere. That dark, all-consuming void retreats and a sense of calm replaces it. Here in this place of peace, the burden of duty is lifted from my shoulders, feelings of hopelessness subside and my soul's raised above the mundane and transported towards the heavens. Unbidden, an image of an orange-robed saddhu flits through my mind, cackling - 'Mehmsaab, nothing in life is a coincidence.'

And then someone speaks in heavily-accented English.

'I don't wish to disturb you but I think this is yours.'

I open my eyes. A woman, older than me, hair streaked with grey, is smiling kindly, a small, pointed fluorite in her hand. The Russian inflections in her speech sound familiar but it's her striking, green eyes that give her away and bring me back to the here and now.

'Oh my goodness! I'm fine. Honestly… Just a bit …'

I dab my face quickly with a tissue.

'You know … menopause… whatever… Thank you.'

She nods encouragingly and I continue to burble.

'But … This is so strange… I think… I know you… Aren't you Tatyana, Vanya's wife?'

'*Vanya?* You mean, *Fred?*'

'Yes, yes, Fred's wife too of course. Do you remember me? We bumped into each other at a Christmas concert many years ago. My sister, Beverly, was in the church choir. I was about to leave for the Soviet Union and you gave me Vanya's address.'

Tatyana stares hard at me, then, at last, there's a hint of recognition.

'Oh Gospodi! Yes, you're *that* girl, with *the hat and shoes*, who was going to Moscow to study Russian. My goodness but you're so much …'

I swear she's going to finish the sentence in brutally honest Russian style, but her years of training in England kick in.

'Yes, so much… unchanged … Tell me, how was your time in Moscow and what have you been doing since?'

I give her a potted version of my life and learn that she has one grown-up son, who's now married and that, unfortunately, *her Fred* died two years ago.

'Fred always was a church-goer but I was an atheist, as we all were in Soviet times. He got me to join the choir and, when he died, I found solace in prayers and the peacefulness of the church. Now I come here often. I've changed a lot since those old days. It's been a long time since I was back in my motherland.'

There's a pause and an unasked question. I decide to answer it.

'I'm still in touch with Vanya, you know. I haven't seen him for years, since before my youngest was born. Our correspondence used to be sporadic but now we've got the Internet, we've re-connected. Would you like me to give you his email address?'

Tatyana pales and shakes her head.

'Nyet, no! The past's over. I'm settled here now. My life's calm and I've found peace through my faith. I don't wish to know about

Vanya and please don't tell him about me. It's better that way. But it'd be lovely to meet up with you again and speak my mother tongue. I get so little chance these days.'

'Yes, it'd be nice to practise my Russian - like old times. Do me good. Thanks again. I feel much better now.'

And it's true. My encounter with Tanya has re-energised me and I'm prepared for what I might find at my father's.

He comes to the door, looking distracted.

'Hi dad. How are you doing? The neighbours say you've been having a clear out?'

'Yes.'

'Well, can I help?'

'No. All done.'

I peer into the garden and see it's tidy.

'Did you find what you were looking for then?'

'No. Footy's on, love.'

I take that as a sign all's as well as it can be, so say my goodbyes and make my way home.

As I walk through the front door, Small Child runs towards me.

'Mummy, you're a celebrity! We saw you on *Look North*.'

'Yeah, mum. Your dress looked great.'

I smile at Delightful Daughter but Devil Teen's not so impressed.

'Bit embarrassing, mother.'

Boy Scout, home early for once, is disparaging.

'A rubbish catch, isn't it? Old Ginger nearly dropped it. And why weren't you at work? Thought I'd come home and at least find some tea on the table.'

I look at him pointedly.

'Crisis with my dad, so I had to stop off there and - oh, sorry - I wasted time in church, lighting a candle for my mother...'

He has the grace to look embarrassed.

'Oh, ok, my lovely. I'll get us a take-away, isn't it?'

As he goes off to fetch the delivery, the voices give their verdict.

'You're worthless. See how little he cares about you!'

'You shouldn't expect him to read your mind!'

'You're better off without him!'

14

Honeymoon Highlights

'A round-the-world honeymoon, my lovely? Haven't you got that travel bug out of your system? I was thinking a week in Majorca.'

Boy Scout, my about-to-be husband, needs more convincing.

'But we'd see the world through new eyes' - I say - 'and discover different cultures. We'd learn more about ourselves. It'd be fun doing it together.'

'Sounds great, isn't it? But be realistic. Work will only give me a fortnight. We want to buy a house and for that I need a job.'

In the end we compromise and book a return flight to Hong Kong for three weeks. This is the first-time we've been together, twenty-four-seven, in a land and climate vastly different from the UK.

For now, still under British rule, Hong Kong's a strange mix of east-west, old and new. Traditional rickshaws cycle alongside London buses. Tiny wooden sampans crisscross the harbour avoiding busy commuter ferries and huge container ships. Beneath the skyline of steel and glass skyscrapers, street stalls, shrines and red pillar boxes fill the crowded streets.

Boy Scout's overwhelmed by the experience. He's been battered by Hong Kong's non-stop commotion, its incessant noise and oppressive heat. He's nearly passed out at the night market and spent more time in the toilet than at the temples. But whilst the 'I'm not sure he's the man I fell in love with' excuse might work on your Silver Wedding, it seems a little feeble after just three days of marital bliss.

We're sitting in a bustling, gold and red dining hall where waiters push round trolleys laden with baskets of *dimsum* - little dumpling parcels of meat, fish or vegetables. My new husband palls at the sight.

'I'm sorry, my lovely. It's the humidity, see. Doesn't agree with me.'

'I know. You haven't travelled anywhere like this before. It's a bit of a shock.'

'Yes, all that rice and noodles is playing havoc with my stomach. Are you sure they don't serve chips?'

I sigh and wonder, not for the first time, if I've made a terrible mistake. Perhaps we should've tried living together before we so rashly got married? Monsieur Hôtel would've been in his element here, tasting birds nest soup and hundred-year-old eggs.

But thankfully, by day four, Boy Scout starts to acclimatise. We stroll along Golden Beach Bay, fringed with palms and fragrant plants, and wander hand in hand up Victoria Peak. We gradually leave the city behind, climbing upwards through lush greenery, past luxurious mansions where cicadas sing out a welcome. And at last, I'm Happy Honeymooner.

'Let's take a helicopter flight' - I suggest.

Boy Scout laughs - 'That's what I love about you - you're always pushing my boundaries. Go on then, you've twisted my arm.'

Forgetting my Yorkshire thrift, I book a private ride for two and we head to the helipad. For a moment I have second thoughts.

'Ooh, it's very high and the pilot looks rather young.'

'It'll be fine my lovely. Just hold my hand.'

As we relax into the journey, we marvel at the skyscrapers, giving the impression of a *vertical* city. Then the scenery changes to rolling mountains, golden beaches and an expanse of blue sea, with no sign of civilisation for miles. It's so calm up here with just the comforting whir of the rota blades and the breeze blowing softly outside.

I'm admiring the view of Lantau Island far below, when suddenly the engine splutters, coughs, then stops, to be replaced by an ominous silence. I glance anxiously at Boy Scout, who, in turn, looks for reassurance from the pilot.

But sadly, this is lacking. His neck's running with sweat and he's shouting in rapid Chinese as he fights to gain control of the lurching machine.

Peering down, I desperately try to make out flat ground to land, but there's only mountains and sea.

It's now that our British upbringing kicks in. I grab hold of Boy Scout's hand as he leans calmly forward and asks,

'Is there a problem?'

A problem? We're about to die!

Inside, I'm a screaming, hysterical mess. My first thought, bizarrely ironic, is that my mother will kill me.

But outwardly I remain stiff-upper-lipped and repress my internal scream - *'We're too young to die!'*

The sound of the silence and the heaviness of the fear beating in my heart is all-consuming. Time's stopped still and I'm alone.

Yet I'm not alone.

I'm holding the hand of the man I love and in that moment I *surrender* to my fate. And with that surrendering comes a glorious calm, and an awareness that everything will be okay. For a moment, the *Everyday-I* disappears and melts into the blue sky outside. A great peace floods through me, a silent stillness envelops my beating heart and I'm embraced in a loving, golden light.

Maybe it's all my imagination? Could I have passed out for a moment from shock? But when I open my eyes again, the engine's restarted and I can't shake off the feeling that someone or something was watching out for me.

When we finally land, I have the urge to get out and kiss the ground. But being British, I just thank the pilot for the interesting ride.

I ask Boy Scout - 'Do you think an angel was looking out for us today?'

'*Angel?* That's fanciful thinking! If your number's up, my lovely, then it's up and that's that. Thankfully, we live to see another day and get money back for our trauma, isn't it? But I tell you what, I couldn't half murder a pint right now.'

And who'd know that a pint would taste so perfect or that rugby could be such a fun and exciting sport? For somehow my beloved has timed our trip to coincide with the Hong Kong Sevens and his enthusiasm's catching as he explains the rules of this fast-paced version of his favourite game. Yes, married life suits me - we're both learning from each other. And whilst he prefers the down-town bars to my quiet shrines, we're the halves that together make a whole. I find it endearing how he tidies up after me, folding my towels and hanging up my clothes. And he's opening up to the new experiences I push his way.

And so, I recklessly persuade him to explore mainland China, at a time when independent travel's unheard of. As we cross the border, we enter a new reality. We stick out as westerners in the sea of Chairman Mao suits, but no one makes eye contact with us. It's obviously not advisable to be seen with foreigners and the best thing to do is pretend they don't exist. It reminds me of the closed atmosphere of the Soviet Union but, without speaking the language, it's impossible to penetrate into the culture.

The country, however, is amazing and we marvel at the Forbidden City in Beijing with its yellow glazed tiles, the symbol of the royal family from long ago. We walk along the Great Wall, surprised at how steep it is in parts and how we're the only western tourists there. Then we travel on to Xian to see the not-yet-famous Terracotta Warriors.

And it's here in Xian that we hit a major obstacle.

We learn from fellow travellers that train tickets to Hong Kong are booked up two weeks' in advance but our flight back home leaves in four days! Boy Scout does his best to reassure me.

'Never mind, my lovely. We'll sort it out.'

'But you don't speak a word of Mandarin!'

'You've forgotten, I'm a Valley boy and we don't give up so easily, isn't it?'

Luckily, we discover a secret booking office so, armed with our train request helpfully written in Chinese characters, we set off. But when I see the queue snaking out onto the street, I realise we're in for a long wait. We finally reach the counter four hours later but our slip of paper's pushed back at us with a shake of the head and a - 'No train, gaijin. Full.'

At this point I burst into tears of frustration. But Boy Scout comes into his own. He refuses to move away from the window and pushes the paper back to the 'job's worth' cashier. Whilst I continue bawling, my better half stands his ground and won't take no for an answer.

'I know for certain there's a bloody train!'

But the official doesn't back down.

'No train, gaijin.'

As the queue behind rumbles with impatience, a strange battle of *push and pull the paper* takes place.

'I think you'll find there *is* a train.'

'Train *full* gaijin.'

'Look see, there's my lovely wife crying on the floor.'

'No train.'

'Breaks my heart it does, seeing her upset, so, unless you want something breaking yourself, you'd better find a train, isn't it?'

Steadfastness, the refusal to give up, and an aggressive height advantage finally win the day as my hero of a husband leaves the station with two first-class tickets for that evening's train.

We slide open the door to our four-bed compartment, and, to our dismay, find three occupants already in place. If they're surprised to see our western faces, they disguise it well and make way for us to squeeze onto one of the bottom bunks.

But something illegal is going on with these characters. There's Movie Star, with a Jacky Chan appeal, Brains, a wheeler-dealer with glasses the thickness of milk bottles, and The Bouncer, the muscle of the trio. They're definitely up to no good.

Whilst The Bouncer shuts the blinds and keeps watch outside, the guard, and various other individuals keep coming into the compartment, goods are exchanged, and money passes hands. Is this some Chinese mafia racket? We sit silently, unmoving, in the hope they'll forget us.

But once the deals are done, they turn their attention to us. Movie Star points excitedly at the latest model Walkman we're listening to our music on, He makes it clear he wants to hear the songs. With trembling hands, we give up our prized possession, no questions asked. He puts the earphones on and with no further ado, disappears out of the sleeper.

We're preparing ourselves to lose all our valuables, when he reappears, bopping along to our Phil Collins soundtrack, and carrying a feast of Chinese food. He gives us a thumbs up, then puts the banquet in front of us, motioning us to eat.

Brains, who's watching with interest, points at our shiny wedding rings and for a moment, my heart sinks. But then it becomes clear that robbery isn't his intention. He just wants to know how long we've been married. By award-winning miming, we convey we're newly-weds. There's a round of applause, much winking and elbow-nudging and then, as one, they leave the compartment to reappear two hours later with more winking, nudging and raucous laughter.

Altogether we spend twenty-eight hours on the train with our new companions. We have no language in common but somehow, we communicate. We learn they come from Guangzhou in the south and, with the aid of Boy Scout's *Little Mesters* pocket knife, we inform them that our city's famed for its steel and cutlery.

Time passes quickly as Brains shows us his magic tricks, then Boy Scout impresses us with his knot-tying prowess. Movie Star throws some break dance moves, and in return I show him how to *Walk like an Egyptian*. We all beat The Bouncer at cards but, in revenge, he becomes the compartment's *Rock, Paper, Scissors* champion.

Every hour a crowd congregates outside the carriage and more individuals are ushered in to exchange their wares. But now, curiously, a second queue forms under the watchful eye of The Bouncer, whilst Movie Star relieves them of their money. Then one by one they shuffle past us newly-weds, take an unsolicited photo, bow reverentially and disappear again.

Boy Scout's non-plussed.

'What's going on? Anyone would think we're famous, isn't it?'

I laugh, remembering similar moments with the Enigma.

'Maybe they think you're Prince Charles. Your ears give you away!'

Boy Scout smiles - 'You and your royals. Just remember you married a republican, my lovely.'

And all the while, the train rumbles along on its epic journey past flat agricultural land and small villages dotted amongst paddy fields until at last the scenery changes to the rolling hills and bountiful greenery of Southern China.

We return to Hong Kong with new friends and light hearts. As we part at the station, The Bouncer gives me a bear hug that nearly crushes my ribs, Movie Star demonstrates one last time how he's learnt to *dance like an Egyptian*, and Brains presents us with two beautiful, silk dressing gowns, embroidered with red dragons.

Embarrassed at their generosity and not knowing what to give in return, we look at each other. Boy Scout reaches into his backpack and brings out the pocket knife.

'Well that's the last I'll see of that.'

I nod and he hands it over, then reaches in again. I hesitate then agree reluctantly.

'Our Bev gave us the Walkman. I'll have to tell her we were robbed.'

But our presents have the desired effect as Brains looks overjoyed and The Bouncer comes in for a second bear hug.

As we walk away Boy Scout puts his arm round me and sighs.

'What a start to our marriage it's been, isn't it? I'd never have done any of this without you! It's such a far cry from my home in the valleys.'

'Well, it's team work. We'd still be stuck in Xian if it weren't for you.'

'Well, as long as you're with me, I don't care where I am, my lovely. You're the light of my life and you're stuck with me forever now, isn't it?'

15

Whirling with the Dervishes

Today I'm trying to get Abdul to leave the classroom, so I can have my lunch.

He stays behind to ask *important questions* but stands too close for British comfort, turning these after-class interrogations into a ballroom bonanza as I dance backwards to reclaim a culturally appropriate body space.

Taking a step forward, he says - 'Mrs Teacher. You famous now. King's friend.'

I step back.

'*Prince*, Abdul and sadly not a *friend*, just a *loyal subject*. Can I pass you, please?'

Abdul blocks the door and launches into his list of questions.

'Mrs Teacher, why we say *ring-rang-rung, sing-sang-sung* but not *bring-brang- brung*?'

I free spin away.

'Interesting point. I don't know.'

Abdul tangos after me.

'And what this *wodger* everyone ask me? I no understand.'

'*Wodger? Wodger?* Oh, for goodness sake, wodger doing breathing down my neck? In Britain it's rude to stand so close.'

I shoe-shuffle backwards but Abdul grape-vines towards me.

'Really? This not *close*. This *far away*! Maybe this standing close is why my host mother were not happy with me.'

'*Was*, Abdul. She *was*n't happy with you'.

'No, she say I *weren't.*'

In his defence, he's probably right. The host families here have strong northern accents and dubious grammar to boot.

Abdul free-spins in my direction but I execute a quick heel turn and jive step away as he moonwalks a bit nearer.

'But in my country is unpolite and imfriendly to stand so far away.'

He waltzes around me as I line-dance out of his way.

'My host mother, she lovely but I worry about her. She too old to dance like Miley Cyrus.'

'What? Sorry, Abdul. I'm not sure what you mean.'

'Yes, she twerk. Every day she tell me she go twerk. It not good.'

'Oh? Oh! No, Abdul. Here in Yorkshire, people often say 't' instead of 'to'. She's not dancing like Miley. She's not *twerking*, she's just going *to work*. That's all!'

I shimmy towards the door with exaggerated jazz hands, grabbing for the handle. As I twirl Abdul out of the classroom, he reaches into his bag, in a last attempt to keep me from my lunch.

'Mrs Teacher. This book and heaven papers for you.'

He bows, handing over an English version of the Koran and some tickets. I accept with gratitude, just to escape.

That evening I sit down to read, knowing Abdul will quiz me on my progress, like I quiz him on his grammar. And as I study the Koran, I'm struck by how it's not so different from the Bible stories I grew up with.

Indeed, my first, albeit cursory, impression is that there are far fewer differences between the two religions than I imagined. The basic rules are the same. There's to be no murdering, no stealing, no coveting, and no dishonouring of parents, which I feel is a good foundation for any community.

I don't discover any rules about dancing, but later that week, I have my first encounter with whirling. Abdul's *heaven papers* are in fact two tickets for a concert of Sufi music.

At breakfast I vainly offer the tickets to my family. Boy Scout rolls his eyes, so I try Delightful Daughter.

'Sorry mum, I'm working.'

I look pointedly at Devil Teen, who snorts - 'What? You can't mean it? No, mother. Just no!'

So, thinking Bubbly Brazilian might like the chance for a whirl, I phone to invite her.

'Oh, my dahleeng, normally I'd love to but I'm feeling a little tired today. Another time maybe?'

English Rose declines as it clashes with her favourite cooking show, so in the end it's broad-minded Zen Mother who comes with me.

The concert's being held at *the Hubs* - four futuristic Sheffield-steel orbs, topped by what look like spouts. Originally built to house the centre for popular music, it was too pretentious and expensive for the sensible locals and was eventually bought by Sheffield Hallam to become their Student Union building.

Tonight's concert has attracted a diverse crowd of spectators. Many are adherents of the Sufi faith and are wearing striking, shirt-like outfits with colourful sashes, topped with impressive-looking conical headgear.

I remark to Zen Mother.

'It's a shame our Brazilian friend isn't here. She'd have loved all this spectacle.'

'I know, it's right up her street. Actually, I'm concerned about her. She's been looking rather peaky lately, don't you think? And she's lost some of her curves. Plus she's avoiding the school run.'

I immediately feel guilty as I've been so wrapped up in work and family that I haven't even noticed. I reply glibly.

'Maybe it's all that dancing she's doing that's wearing her out?'

'No, I don't think so. Something else's bothering her but she won't tell me. Maybe *you* can get her to talk?'

I'm about to ask more, when the lights dim, so I mentally put Bubbly Brazilian at the top of my to-do list and settle down to watch the performance.

Before it starts, the leader of the group, dressed in white flowing robes and a red felt hat, explains that Sufism is a form of Islamic mysticism and that the music is devotional and arouses a longing for the divine.

It's been a tiring day and my only longing is for sleep but I console myself with the thought that at least there'll be no *twerking*.

The music starts slowly and is hauntingly beautiful. Flutes combine with the chants of the singers and the rhythmic beat of the drums. It reminds me of the soulful music I heard in India and it chases away the busyness of my day. As the tempo increases, I realise that some of the group have started to move in circular motions. As they rotate, their arms lift to the sky and the skirts on their robes sail out impressively.

The music gets quicker and louder, filling my head in a restorative way, like medicine for the mind. The dancers spin round faster and faster. I'm transfixed by their twirling and their expressions of euphoria. My head, in turn, starts spinning as the music circles round and round in my brain, banishing all thoughts.

Then suddenly, for a fleeting moment, my mind stills completely and I have a sense of oneness with the dancers, the musicians, the audience and the light that lies within. I am the steps. I am the rhythm. I am the beat. I am the voice. I am the colours. I am the ears. I am the eyes. I am the light.

I am.

And then all too swiftly, I'm not.

The moment's lost. I'm back in the room, back in the noise and busyness of my *Everyday-I* self. If only I could sustain these moments for longer. For while I'm gaining the impression that devotional practices - whatever the background - can lead me to a place of unity, stillness and peace, it never seems to last! Part of me is glad that Abdul's had the confidence to share his religious and cultural traditions with me. I feel enriched by this knowledge. But another part of me thinks, *what's the point?* Am I ever going to find what I'm looking for? Do I even know *what* I'm looking for? What is it within me that's driving this search for something *other?* Why can't I just be content with living a *normal* life?

The next lesson Abdul and I continue our daily foxtrot around the class.

'Mrs Teacher, wodger think of the concert? You finded heaven?'

'Do you know, Abdul, I think for just a minute, I did.'

'And Mrs Teacher, I founded this lovely blue and white stone under your desk. Is it yours or can I keep it? It's beautiful.'

'Actually, Abdul, it's an Angelite crystal. And yes, you can keep it. Who knows, it might help you find heaven too.'

But finding heaven and staying there for any length of time are two different things entirely. My time for quiet reflection is limited to the all too infrequent breaks from my job and household duties. And right now I'm working my way through my to-do list, so at the end of the day I knock on Bubbly Brazilian's front door.

She opens it with a look of surprise.

'Oh, my dahleeng! How lovely to see you! Come in. What brings you here? How's your father?'

'Oh, no recent incidents and he's agreed to the tests. So, it's just a waiting game.'

I go through into her vividly decorated kitchen, where for once there's no music playing. This is definitely serious. I notice now that she *is* a lot thinner and has dark circles under her eyes. So, I channel my inner Russian and get straight to the point.

'We're worried about you. You look exhausted, you're losing weight and trying to avoid us. What on earth's going on? I'm your friend - so whatever it is - just spit it out!'

Even I am surprised by my directness but it seems to have the desired effect. Bubbly Brazilian, sinks down onto one of the bright blue and yellow kitchen chairs and says so softly, I can barely hear her - 'I think I may have bowel cancer...'

My stomach lurches at the *C-word*.

'What? No! What makes you think that?'

'Well, as you say, I've lost weight, I'm always tired. Plus, there's blood when I go to the toilet. And not to mention that my mum died of it too...'

My stomach lurches again and a dull pain circles my temples. It doesn't sound promising. But this is not the time to show weakness. I put on my most encouraging voice.

'Yes, but your mum was a lot older than you are now and those symptoms could be explained by something else. Have you *actually* been to see the doctor?'

Bubbly Brazilian looks shame-faced.

'Well, no, I'm terrified of what he's going to tell me!'

'He'll probably say it's haemorrhoids or you've been overdoing the dancing with that Kiki. But you won't know unless you go and see him. Look I'll come with you if it'll help. But you really must go! Promise me you will.'

Bubbly Brazilian knows I'm not taking no for an answer and to cheer her up I produce a tin of flapjack from my bag.

'See, I've even made this especially for you. So now we've agreed you're going to ring the GPs tomorrow, put on some music and show me your salsa moves. It's a shame you missed the Sufi whirling. It was strangely hypnotic and meditative. Maybe you could do with something like that? Why don't you come with me to the Buddhist centre? Our Zen friend's persuaded me to go. Now that my free trial at Spirit Mind Studio has ended she thought it would be helpful.

Bubbly Brazilian smiles.

'If I decide to follow any spiritual path then I'll probably go back to my native *Candomblé* faith. And, ok, I *will* go to the doctors, even though your flapjack's a far better medicine!'

16

Breathing with Buddha

Zen Mother's outside the Buddhist centre, checking her watch as I approach, scattering shimmering tiger eye stones as I run.

'You're very late. Lunch has just finished. How are things? Have your dad's results come back yet?'

'Sorry, yeah, just come back from his appointment. They were inconclusive. Which proves nothing, as he then told me my *mother* wants me to have more fun in my life! I'm just trying to ignore it until I get the inevitable phone call. To be honest, I'm more worried about our *dahleeng* Brazilian.'

'Well, you've persuaded her to go to the doctor's, and that's all you can do. Sounds like an hour's meditation is exactly what you need.'

She guides me into the Buddhist centre - no purpose-built temple, but a converted terraced house that used to be a B&B before its owners decided to dance with Dharma. They've combined their spiritual lives with their catering background, as the centre offers alliterative, food-based meditation options, with a meal or snack before the main event.

- Marmalade and mantras
- Coffee and contemplation
- Soup for the soul
- Dinner and deliberation

Well, I may have missed the meal but at least I've made it for the meditation. So I join the group waiting outside the cloakroom, where it becomes clear that I have to leave not only my coat but my footwear too. It's at this point I nearly escape, as the thought of entering a room full of strangers with my toes sticking out from holey socks does nothing to *still my mind*.

But before I can turn round, a chime sounds and I'm caught up in the flow of people heading towards the main room, which is laid out with chairs. The décor's all white and at the front is a small stage where a golden Buddha beams serenely at the audience. There's a smell of incense and an atmosphere of calm tranquillity.

Despite it being early afternoon, the room's full, with an interesting mix of ages and ethnicities. I'm forced to sit apart from Zen Mother on a hard-backed chair, too close for comfort to an earnest-looking youth with a man-bun and an ancient crone with no teeth.

Nobody speaks, which is disconcerting. Maybe they've talked themselves out over soup? But at least, whenever eyes meet, smiles of acknowledgement are exchanged.

Then another chime sounds, the door opens and two Buddhist monks enter, with an air of untroubled stillness. One's short and stocky, the other's tall, well-toned and imposing. But both are well past middle-age, have shaved heads and are dressed in orange robes.

For some reason I'm expecting the kung-fu, Shao-lin hero of my teenage TV show to come high-kicking in, so am disappointed to see both are Western, with not a staff or sword between them. They welcome us and explain they'll lead us in some chanting, philosophy and short meditations.

Man-bun and Ancient Crone are obviously regulars here as they get straight into the chanting, which, apparently, helps prepare the mind for meditation. My mind, however, is struggling to keep up with the Sanskrit words, which mean - *May all beings be happy and free from suffering.*

Unfortunately, the chant doesn't apply to Man Bun, as I sense, from the frown on his face, that I'm disturbing his inner peace whenever my out-of-tune *Om* echoes two seconds after everyone else's.

The experience isn't so different from my church-going episodes. The chanting reminds me of hymn-singing, but with bell-chiming rather than guitar-strumming. It's less manic than Trendy Vicar's pacing up and down and lacks the fervour of the happy-clappy services that Delightful Daughter attends, but I find the repetition of the chants strangely soothing. The busyness of my day settles and I'm hopeful that, with a bit of luck and no rumbling of my empty stomach, I might even find some inner peace. God knows I need it. I can't keep ignoring my past for ever. I'm the person I am because of it. The problem is I don't always like the person I am! Maybe Buddhism can help me accept myself.

When we move on to the *talk for the day*, with its thought-provoking questions, I'm reminded of a church sermon. In fact, the tall monk's deep baritone is strangely reminiscent of my childhood Sundays. We're asked to consider how outer peace is impossible without inner peace and that, in order to break the cycle of suffering, we must learn to control our minds. The messages are welcomingly upbeat:

- The purpose of life is to seek happiness
- If you can't do good then at least do no harm
- Respect other religious beliefs as they can all make an effective contribution for the benefit of humanity

Then, with an attempt to harness our *monkey minds*, the teachers lead us in a breath meditation. They demonstrate how to put our fingers in the correct *mudra* position and I can't help noticing a faded, crescent-shaped scar on the tall monk's left hand. I wonder idly where I've seen something similar before, but then realise my monkey mind's already taken control and stolen my focus.

I sit up straight and bring my attention back to the room where we're being taught to concentrate on the sensation of breathing, experiencing how the *in* breath is colder than the *out* breath. If thoughts pop into our heads we're advised to notice them but not follow them, just as if they were clouds which scud through the sky.

Man Bun shuts his eyes with what looks like a grimace of pain and dutifully begins breathing. Ancient Crone catches my eye, gives me a toothless smile then also starts the practice. So, I too close my eyes.

The problem is that Monkey Mind, with all its voices, starts a schizophrenic conversation with itself.

'Why can't we even Om in tune? No wonder they kicked us out of the school choir!'

'Look, we've finished with the **omming**. We're onto breathing now. Focus on that!'

'Or focus on **her** breath. Why's it so annoyingly noisy?'

'Look, we can't even manage the breathing. This is hopeless!'

'Well, shut up and stop thinking!'

'Or think about **her** and her lack of front teeth. Maybe that's causing her breath to hiss and crackle so disturbingly?'

'No, this is just a thought, let it float on by.'

Ancient Crone wheezes a deep breath in. I wait for her to exhale. A familiar wave of anxiety crashes though my stomach as I wait. And wait...

Monkey Mind chatters on.

'Oh, she's very old. Maybe we should check on her?'

'No, I'm keeping my eyes shut and focusing on not having any thoughts.'

'Yes, no thoughts. Be free from suffering. But she still hasn't taken a breath yet.'

'I wouldn't know because I haven't been thinking about her.'

'That's very good. No thinking. No thoughts. No thinking about the corpse we might be sitting next to…'

'Oh, for God's sake!'

I open my eyes, just as Ancient Crone splutters back to life in a shower of spittle. I wipe my face, trying to erase thoughts of harm, and continue my breathing.

We then go into a guided meditation which asks us to visualise ourselves in a golden light. I close my eyes again, relax, and start to melt into the warming rays of sunlight I'm envisaging.

Monkey Mind's having none of this.

'Is that our stomach gurgling? We should've made it here in time for the soup. What a loser!'

'I'm not listening. I'm becoming a golden light.'

'No, it's definitely not us. I think it must be Man Bun's stomach. It sounds pretty alarming. Listen, there it rumbles again.'

'A cloud in the sky. That's what you are. I'm not chasing you. You will pass by. I am the sunlight. You are a cloud.'

And amazingly, as I imagine these thoughts as just clouds in the sky, they float away without disturbing me. I have the sensation of sitting at the bottom of a deep lake. Silence surrounds me. I'm aware of sounds and movement coming from the surface but they're too far to be distracting.

I'm held in a warm embrace of watery darkness, until a dappled light filters through. Gradually the light intensifies and the heaviness lifts from my head. The darkness becomes a golden light and I rest there in stillness and love.

I sense a genuine desire for all beings to be happy. I sense a genuine desire for all beings to be free from suffering. I sense a feeling of peace. I sense …

I sense a terrible aroma coming from Man Bun!

Even though my eyes are closed, they start watering. I try not to wrinkle my nose and wonder how long I can hold my breath. But the moment's lost, the golden light's been replaced by a malodorous fog and hopes of happiness have been thwarted for now.

At the end of the session, I exit quickly in search of fresh air. Zen Mother intercepts me.

'Did you enjoy the meditation?'

I reply truthfully.

'Yes, I did actually. It was calming. I like the respect Buddhism has for other beliefs. I'm not keen on religions that exclude people who aren't in their club. I found the whole session inclusive and caring.'

Zen Mother agrees.

'Yes, it *is* helpful and inclusive too - one of the monks even used to be a vicar. You should definitely come on time next week for the shared lunch. You missed a delicious five-bean soup.'

17

Book Bound

'Are you one of those Hairy Christians now, my lovely? I can't keep up with your religions! Last week you were a Buddhist or was it a Sufi?'

Delightful Daughter corrects her father.

'You mean Hare Krishna, dad. And yes, mum, you really should settle on one belief system - preferably Christian. And by the way, some books have arrived for you.'

Boy Scout groans.

'Oh God, more bloody self-help books. Why can't you go back to reading trashy magazines? They cost a lot less, isn't it? They don't involve chick peas or couples therapy, and at least I get to look at bikini bodies.'

'They're fine if you want to know how to apply fake tan and lose weight' - I reply -'but what I want to know is how to *live my life.*'

You see, I'm hoping these books will serve as a means of self-improvement, an attempt to foster better relationships, and a source of wisdom to help me find my path.

The first book focuses on the importance of a healthy body and advises me to ditch refined sugar from my diet. This is a great sadness to me, as life's only made bearable by flapjack for breakfast and hidden stashes of chocolate for emergencies.

But I'm determined to make a fresh start, especially as my stomach's been playing up recently and I could do with dropping a few pounds. At least I'd have control over *one* aspect of my life. Losing weight's surely got to be easier than sorting out my marriage and my father! I wait until the end of the week when the sweet cupboard's nearly empty. I have a last banquet with Mr Kipling and his apple pies, covered in grated Mars Bars with a topping of Smarties. Then I shut the door forever and resolve to be a *clean eater.*

By the end of day one I have a banging headache, furry tongue, and evil temper. The children are hiding upstairs in the teen cave and Boy Scout's wisely retreated to the Holiday Inn.

Day two sees me desperately searching down the sides of the sofa in case Small Child's dropped a chocolate button there. But all I find is a tiny pebble of rainbow tourmaline.

On day three I'm tempted to head for the shops and hit the sweet aisle but when I wake up and look in the mirror, I realise I can never leave the house again as my face is a sea of seething spots.

Days four, five and six - I cry all day.

Day seven and I wake up feeling different. My head's clear, my face is blemish free and my eyes are sparkling. I feel full of energy and ready to implement the wisdom of my second book on keeping fit.

I'm going to ensure I do ten thousand steps every day and to help me with this, I've invested in an Activity Tracker, which I tentatively strap on then take a few paces. Immediately two little footprints appear on the screen with the number ten underneath them. I walk to the door and the number increases to twenty-five. I go upstairs, then back down again, and to my great satisfaction, I realise I've already reached a hundred steps!

It's my new, healthy addiction.

I potter about the house for the rest of the day, with my step count continuously increasing. However, by 7 p.m. I've still not reached my target. So I feign a milk shortage and heroically offer to pop down the shops for a bottle. On the way back, the Tracker starts fizzing, there's a drum-roll, and fireworks appear on the screen. I feel like a champion and go to bed sugar-free, smug and self-satisfied.

A week into the new regime, Boy Scout calls a family conference.

'You're wearing out the carpet with your constant walking, isn't it?' he complains.

'Checking labels for sugar content is soooo lame,' sighs Delightful Daughter.

'You don't do my homework any more. You're always on the move,' moans Devil-Teen.

'Chocolate!' wails Small Child.

Well maybe they have a point. But my friends have already noticed a difference.

English Rose scrutinises me in the playground.

'You're looking well.'

'Yes, it's the meditation. It's really helping. It quietens my mind. You should try it yourself.'

'Mm, not my thing. It'll be quiet tonight when my ex takes the kids and I'm binge-watching the last season of *Bake-Off*. But I'm disappointed. I thought your new glow might be down to a secret lover. Reconnecting with your French heart throb on Facebook, maybe?'

I laugh - 'Chance would be a fine thing. I could certainly do with exchanging my husband for a new model!'

But now I've made inroads into improving my physical health, I decide to work on my relationships and turn to books three, four and five for help.

In book three I learn Men are from Mars, Women are from Venus and Boy Scout's from Wales, isn't it? The *female language* I speak isn't one his *male brain* understands. It's a hopeless prognosis. But in book four I'm introduced to the *Language of Love* and how we each show our love in different ways. My personal preference is giving and receiving *Words of affirmation*, telling people how great they are and how much they mean to me. Boy Scout, however, opts for *Acts of service*. He rarely tells me he loves me because 'Honestly, my lovely, that's obvious.' Instead, he washes my car, which I never appreciate because

'I didn't notice it was dirty in the first place.' Devil-Teen requires *Quality Time* but I'm a busy working mum so 'Can't you leave me in peace and go on the PlayStation?' Delightful Daughter hankers after *Physical Touch* but 'You're an adult now. Stop hugging me.' And Small Child likes *Receiving Gifts* which makes me feel I'm bringing up a spoilt brat.

However, realising that we all communicate in different ways helps me promote family harmony, as I put this new knowledge into practice. I get the children to tidy up the house before Boy Scout returns from his Holiday Inn paradise. I reward Small Child with a Kinder Surprise for his efforts. Then I sit down with my arm round Delightful Daughter and we all watch the film version of the book that Devil Teen's supposed to have read for his English exam.

When Boy Scout arrives home, there's none of his usual huffing and puffing at the chaotic state of the house. Instead he opens the living room door cautiously and pokes his head round.

'What's going on, my lovely? Have alien body snatchers kidnapped the children? Where's the shoes on the floor and the coats on the stairs? Why's everything clean? Why isn't everyone fighting? Ah, must be you're all ill, isn't it?'

Boy Scout's suspicious nature and lack of faith in my abilities means book five turns out to be a challenge, with its advice to *give what you want to receive.*

What I want is love and kindness. What I get is being ignored or taken for granted! I bet life would have been very different if I'd married Monsieur Hôtel all those years ago. But I'm on the road to self-improvement and I'll give anything a try.

Boy Scout's been away for two days now relaxing in his Holiday Inn haven. I've had a hard day at work. Small Child's tired and hungry. No one's started making the tea.

Boy Scout arrives home.

Deep breath! I vow to keep my thoughts to myself and only offer words of love and kindness. I fake a smile and welcome my beloved home.

'Hello darling. It's great to have you back. We've missed you.' *(You miserable s***! You left me to cope on my own whilst you ate out in fancy restaurants and got a good night's sleep!)*

'Why don't you get changed and catch up on the newspapers? I'll call you when dinner's ready.' *(Yeah, you just swan home when it suits you and expect the dinner on the table like I'm a bloody Stepford wife!)*

Boy Scout looks surprised at this unusually pleasant welcome home but, not chancing his luck, disappears quickly upstairs. When he comes down, he eats his dinner without commenting on what herbs I've missed out or how the meat could've been cooked a bit longer. Then, in an almost unheard-of occurrence, he actually *thanks* me for making it and offers to wash up and put Small Child to bed, whilst I go out for a run.

My head's reeling. Is this tiny shift in thinking and communicating all that's needed for better relationships? Sorting out my life's proving to be less difficult than I imagined. And one bonus is that the voices have all but disappeared.

Occasionally they surface -

'Self-improvement? You're beyond help!'

'You should concentrate on the everyday, not the super-natural!'

'Read Celebrity magazine. It's far more fun!'

But, as I tick more books off in the Amazon *Body, Mind and Spirit* section, the voices fade away and I feel I'm making progress. I'm lighter both in weight and heart. Maybe I can rekindle that love I once experienced? Maybe I'm not such a bad mother after all? Maybe I'll be able to cope with my father and the challenges of the future? After all, there's lots of support for dementia these days and people can live a good quality life for much longer, can't they? And our life expectancy is rising all the time. Just my mum was unlucky and my lost boy unluckier still.

That familiar wave of anxiety crashes through my stomach and the voices have suddenly turned up the volume.

'You're deluding yourself.'

'You should know better!'

'Ok, but what if you just faced your fears?

And maybe, just maybe, it's time now to unlock that chest and confront my demons? I've faced Death already. He's won some battles. But he's not yet won the war. Knowledge is power. And forewarned is forearmed.

So, I study books about how modern society's fear of death is due to our lack of frequent contact with it, unlike in the past when infant mortality was much higher. I learn that other cultures, like the Tibetans, have a very different attitude to dying and even meditate on it throughout life to help them prepare better for it.

I read end-of-life stories from hospice workers, stating that many people approaching death appear free and light - almost eager to leave their bodies. I start to think there may even be a soul in me hiding somewhere but am not sure how to go about finding it.

Other books tell me that living in the moment, fully experiencing the *Now* is what I should strive for but somehow, I'm rooted in the past or focussed on the future, never managing to stay in the present. I still have no answers but the questions are coming thick and fast and there are so many books yet to read, I'm running out of space on the shelves.

18

Minimalist Mess

'For God's sake! It doesn't take much to keep the house tidy!'

An avalanche of tattered paperbacks and miscellaneous stationery land-slide onto Boy Scout's head as he vainly slams the cupboard shut, trips backwards over a mound of laundry and lands on the tower of papers teetering on the table top. Bills, bank statements, mail shots and take-away menus fly in all directions.

'You *woo-woo* on about making sense of the world and your role in it, but you can't even control your physical surroundings!'

I stop searching in Small Child's bag and snarl - 'Well, I don't exactly see *you* pulling your weight around the house. And at least *I* make an effort to improve myself and our relationship. What do *you* do?'

Just then Small Child appears, triumphantly waving a ruler under my nose.

'It's ok mum, I found it. It was in my sock drawer.'

'Typical' - says Boy Scout stomping out of the house as the phone rings.

It's my father's neighbour.

'Just thought you should know, dear, your father's talking a lot to himself lately. We hear him through the walls at night. Sounds like he's looking for something. A bit of a worry...'

'Yes, it is'- I reply - 'Thank you... He's had some tests done. It looked like everything was okay... but ... well... He's coming for his tea later, so I'll see if I can get to the bottom of it... Anyway, sorry if he's disturbing you ... and ... thanks for keeping an eye on him.'

I put down the phone and wince as a sharp cramp hits my stomach. God! What's the point of all my truth-seeking? It's a waste of time. The voices delightedly agree with me.

'*Told you, you loser!*' shouts the Critic gleefully.

'*You should get a grip on yourself!*' admonishes the Nag.

'*Get on that plane!*' coos the Temptress.

But just then the cupboard door falls open again and the last remaining book flings itself into my hands. It's by an acclaimed Japanese *organising consultant*, whose speciality is *decluttering your life*. Coincidence? I decide it's a sign to take action…

Apparently, the secret of success isn't tackling one room at a time, but targeting *key areas* in a specific order, namely - clothes, books, documents, photos, personal mementos. The idea is to focus, not on what to *get rid of*, but on what *brings you joy* in life so that you wish to keep it.

Surveying the mound of weary-looking garments I've retrieved and piled on my bedroom floor, I sense very little joy coming my way. Perhaps this is the point.

Out goes that ancient bobbled sweater, along with six, once-black, now greying T-shirts. They're closely followed into the bin bag by a gang of rowdy odd socks and ugly underwear. That adorable French mini skirt flutters its eye lashes at me, but I'm no longer taken in. I know that mutton and lamb don't mix, so it's time to say *Adieu*, and send it, together with shoulder pad shirt, too tight trousers and 80s leg warmers on a *bon voyage* to the charity shop.

Two hours and seven bin bags later I'm left, slightly stunned, with just fifteen items of clothing on their hangers, and a series of empty drawers. For a moment I have a wobble. There's hardly anything left! What on earth am I going to wear? But I realise that, in fact, I now have an on-trend *capsule wardrobe* that can be augmented with seasonal accessories. I head off to the recycling bank, feeling virtuous, and with a desire to keep decluttering.

I move on to the books. This is a hard call, but I'm ruthless and after another hour's hard graft, my bulging bookcase is more than half empty. It's a strangely cathartic process. However, there's still a long way to go and my next stop is to deal with documents. So, like a demon, I whirl through the house until the paper bin's overflowing.

Then I cull my photos. I have several albums and numerous old snaps dating back to my university and pre-marriage days and I spend the entire afternoon reminiscing about the good times over a pot of tea, before consigning the evidence, with a nostalgic farewell, to the bin. It's just that I can't quite let go of Monsieur Hôtel, with his strong jaw-line, aquiline nose and seductive eyes. Look, there's that photo of me eating lobster for the first time and him looking ridiculously proud of me. And one of him toasting me in champagne in the Roman amphitheatre.

The voices can't help interfering.

'He wouldn't recognise you now, you old fatty!'

'Just consign them to the bin.'

'A small memento wouldn't hurt.'

So, that photo of him, enticingly Mediterranean, with a cheeky wink, slips unbidden into my bed-side drawer.

I'm nearly done with my memories of India and my long-forgotten travelling companion, The Enigma, when the children come home. I regale them with some of my stories, and point out my younger self in the faded photos. Then I proceed to bin them.

Delightful Daughter is outraged.

'Mum, you can't erase your past, just like that!'

At that moment Boy Scout walks through the door and she appeals to him to stop me.

'Dad, do something. Mum's deleting history! She'll wipe us all out soon if you don't stop her. Your wedding album will be next.'

Boy Scout looks at me and raises an eyebrow. I redden uncomfortably and stutter.

'No, of course I wasn't going to throw *that* out…'

Devil Teen sticks his oar in too.

'Mother's definitely lost the plot. Nothing's safe anymore. She's thrown out half my socks and sorted out your man drawer.'

Boy Scout is not impressed.

'Listen my lovely. You do whatever that mid-life crisis is telling you to do, isn't it, but I'm warning you, my collection of rugby programmes is strictly off limits!'

Small Child says nothing, but can be seen hurriedly picking up Lego from the lounge and removing it to the safety of his bedroom.

I try to explain.

'Look, you should be happy. I'm only *tidying up*, like you asked. I won't remove anyone else's belongings but really, you should all do a little sorting out of your own.'

'Hmmph! If anything needs clearing out, my lovely, it's those piles of rocks and your royal memorabilia. I bet *they* don't go in the bin, isn't it?'

And Boy Scout's right. I'm never going to part with my collection of crystals. But those commemorative plates, which have been gathering dust and annoying Boy Scout for too long now, could be culled. With a sigh, I choose my three favourite ones and decide to donate the others to my royalist neighbour at number 93.

'See, it's easy when you put your mind to it'- I say - 'I'm going to do the same with all my personal stuff, keeping only the things that bring me joy. All the rest can be given away or go to the charity shop. I feel wonderful, no longer chained down by *stuff*. Anyway, I'm off to fetch my dad now, so while I'm gone, why don't you do some de-cluttering of your own?'

And it's true. For a brief moment I feel lighter, released, unlimited. But how long's that going to last, with my family of *hoarders* and *shoe-mountaineers*?

My father is particularly impressed as he surveys the clutter-free rooms.

'Tidy.'

'On that subject, dad, have you been looking for something yourself? The neighbours say you've been making a lot of noise at night. Talking to yourself? Maybe we should do a few more tests, eh? It wouldn't hurt.'

My father scowls.

'No tests. Thank you. Just, your mother's instructions aren't clear…'

'Dad, mum's not really talking to you. You *do* know that, don't you?'

He ignores my concern.

'Footy's starting.'

I give up. I've done enough sorting out for one day.

And, whilst I can only take responsibility for my *own* space, in the days that follow, a ripple effect takes place. Small Child sorts out his unwanted toys and tidies his room so that the floor's visible once more. Delightful Daughter bags up a boutique's worth of last season's fashion and Devil Teen finally parts with a drawer full of *Age 12* underpants.

An air of calm order descends upon the household. But the biggest victory comes when I catch Boy Scout sneaking downstairs with a swag bag over his shoulder.

'Are you by any chance decluttering?'

'Absolutely, not. I'm just taking those rugby programmes to be valued. Probably worth a mint, isn't it?'

My friends pop by to see the difference and feast on my latest batch of flapjacks. I was in a hurry to get them out of the tin, so they're a little worse for wear but English Rose still sighs in rapture as she bites into the syrupy oatiness.

'Oh my God! Why won't you give me the recipe for this? You're not a true friend, you know. And now your house looks like it should be in a designer catalogue, whereas mine looks like it's been in a war zone. It's only fair you share your secret recipe, or do you want me to go away feeling a complete failure?'

Zen Mother's also impressed.

'Wow, you can actually see the carpets. The whole house has a calmer energy. I'll suggest this technique to Luke's dad. He could certainly do with it.'

English Rose pricks up her ears.

'*Luke's dad*, eh? You're spending a lot of time with him. Is there something we should know about?'

Zen Mother colours and answers a touch too quickly.

'Don't be ridiculous. It's just that Ethan and Luke get on well and it makes sense for us to do things together and help each other out with childcare. Besides, as I keep saying, he's a really nice man. Surprisingly sensitive too.'

I raise my eyebrows.

'He didn't seem that sensitive at the Handball match, what with his flash car, sharp suit and executive career.'

'Well, that's the point. He's not r*eally* like that. He's quite unhappy in the job as it's a bit *dog eat dog*. He'd much rather go back to illustrating books. It's just he feels he has something to prove. Anyway, as I've already told you, I'm looking for a fellow yogi, and that's definitely not him!'

Bubbly Brazilian, who's been understandably quieter of late, nods thoughtfully.

'Yes, it looks great, my dahleeng. Maybe I should declutter too? It might take my mind off things…'

We gather round and give her a collective hug. I'm concerned that her health issue hasn't yet been resolved.

'But didn't the GP say he thought it was nothing to worry about - probably just haemorrhoids and overdoing it?'

'Yes, you're right, my dahleeng, he did, but because of my family history, he's referred me to a specialist. Only it's going to be a few weeks before I see them.'

My stomach tightens. A few weeks? That could make all the difference! This is not good at all. This is just like my mother all over again! But I compose myself and force out the words she needs to hear.

'Well, that's positive. If the doctor thought it was something sinister, then he'd fast-track you. But it's still tough, not knowing for sure. Can't the handsome Kiki help you take your mind off things?'

'My dahleengs, all I can say for now is that Kiki's certainly helping me keep toned with the tango. He's even asked me to dance with him at the opening night of the new restaurant!'

English Rose ignores the potential romance, being more interested in food, and jumps straight in for an update about the restaurant.

'Have they given it a name yet? Do you know what's going to be on the menu?'

'My dahleengs, I only have the inside information on the *dancing,* I know nothing about the food. But Big John at Breakfast announced the radio competition results. Apparently, it's going to be called *Fusion 3* and they'll be interviewing the owner and staff nearer the time. You never know, I might even get on the radio myself. Not as good *as Look North* of course.'

I smile sheepishly as she continues.

'But in the meantime, I'm going to try my dahleeng friend's latest weird minimalist trend.'

'Hang on a minute!' I object - 'It's not a *weird trend.*'

English Rose jumps in to wind me up.

'Yeah, maybe. But admit it, you've been dipping your toes into all sorts of waters - Buddhism, Christianity, Sufism, Philosophy, meditation, self-help books… Shall I go on? Not to mention the flipping stones that fall out of your bra whenever we go anywhere!'

She means it jokingly I know, so I parry back light-heartedly - 'Well, you've blown your chance of ever getting my flapjack recipe!'

But unexpectedly I feel my nose tingling and tears pricking my eyes. I swallow quickly as my stomach knots with that familiar tension. Why can't I just be *normal?* What *is* it that my heart truly yearns for?

Sensing the change, Zen Mother intervenes - 'We love you for all this stuff, don't we girls? You're not afraid to focus on the big questions in life, rather than just the contents of your stomach, like some others I shan't name! And who knows what you'll surprise us with next.'

19

Embracing Eccentricity

A crowd of middle-aged hippies, with rainbow hair and age-inappropriate piercings and tattoos, have congregated in next door's garden. Boy Scout is most put out by their antics.

'They should keep their eccentric behaviour inside, isn't it? All that vegetarian, teetotal rubbish and bare-foot chanting. It's not normal.'

But this being Britain, politeness is our religion, so who are we to object to the witches from the coven next door? And, in reality our neighbours run a complementary clinic specialising in nutrition and healing. They have a constant stream of pale-faced clients, who leave their clinic laden with bottles of super vitamins and bags of dried herbs but, as far as I know, there's no spells or bubbling cauldrons full of children's bones ... So, whenever we encounter our neighbours, we feign ignorance of unusual behaviour and keep our over-the-fence conversations firmly focussed on that safest of topics - the weather.

Today the High Priest, with his long Merlin-like beard and the High Priestess, with a turban wrapped round her head, are holding court in matching kaftans, shoeless in the garden, whilst I'm hanging out the washing.

I nod sociably in the direction of the High Priestess.

'Good day for entertaining.'

'Absolutely, my dear' - she replies - 'My darling angel and I have been picking nettles for a nutritious soup, haven't we?'

'Yes, sweet soulmate' - replies The High Priest turning to me - 'Perhaps you'd like to try some?'

I try not to pull a face -'Oh that's kind of you but I've got a roast in the oven.'

The High Priestess 'hmms' absent-mindedly whilst peering intently at a space above my head - 'You know, my dear, your aura's looking dim. You should slip your shoes off and connect to the earth. It'll ground you.'

'Er, maybe later, thanks.'

She smiles then points excitedly at my new plant pot.

'Oh, just look at that. So gorgeous. Such memories! Do tell me where you got it.'

'Er, yeah. Glad you like it. Got it in the Antiques Quarter yesterday. It has a kind of ancient Greek feel to it, don't you think?'

'Oh no, it's typical of the ones we had in Atlantis, don't you agree, my angel?'

The High Priest nods nostalgically.

'Oh yes, very similar. How I miss those days…'

I'm hoping I've misheard *Atlanta USA*, but have the strong impression they actually meant *Atlantis* - the fictional island in my childhood storybook.

Perhaps I shouldn't worry about my father after all!

I decide to cut the conversation short.

'Er, sorry, got to get on pegging this lot out.'

But for some reasons their conversation sticks in my brain.

Whilst Boy Scout views these neighbours as the eccentrics of the street, I'm curious about their different world view. I'm not a vegetarian and I can't pretend to see auras or believe in mythical cities but, since dipping into different faiths and reading various spiritual books, I'm now more open to the idea of the mind-body-soul connection, inexplicable phenomena and reincarnation. Who knows where it all might lead?

One morning, not long afterwards, I wake up feeling unwell, with a terrible stomach ache. My head hurts and I'm alternatively sweating, then shivering. This is no common tummy bug. Appendicitis maybe? I phone the GP. There are no appointments available today but, if I prefer, I can pre-book a session with the doctor a week on Tuesday.

With typical British stoicism I acknowledge I'll either get better on my own or end up in A&E. So, I give up and stagger down to the pharmacist to stock up on all known medicines. But just outside the house, I have a funny turn and the next thing I know I'm lying on a velvet couch inside the coven itself.

The High Priest hands me a goblet full of suspicious-smelling, blood-red liquid.

'Here, drink this. You nearly fainted so we brought you inside to recover.'

The High Priestess wafts some burning leaves around my body, while incanting strange foreign-sounding words.

'Yes, your chakras are all out of balance. I can give them a temporary fix for now. I'll just lay my healing hands on you.'

I drink the potion but the voices in my head are panicking that I've been kidnapped for a ritual sacrifice.

'You idiot! How have you ended up here?'

'You should've insisted on seeing a doctor!'

'Chill out and see what happens.'

The High Priestess rests her hands on my forehead. I feel a pleasant warmth that begins to dissolve the heaviness in my head.

'Oh, you have three guardians watching over you. That's unusual.'

The voices in my head switch on to red-alert.

'She's definitely batty-bonkers!'

'You should've left straight away!'

'But this feels very soothing.'

'Oh, I'm not making them up, if that's what you're thinking' - says the High Priestess as if she's tuned into my thoughts.

The voices are unconvinced.

'See, she's crazy!'

'You need to leave!'

'No, this is getting interesting.'

'Oh, it's only crazy if you can't see' - says the High Priestess as if I'd spoken out loud - 'It's just that not everyone has their eyes fully open to see what's right in front of them.'

The voices are getting agitated.

'What's she on about? Your father's saner than she is!'

'You should definitely close your eyes if there's a gang of celestial bodyguards following you around!'

'Intriguing, though.'

The High Priestess leans closer, to drown out the voices - 'But they need you to *wake up* and get on with your work.'

'We are awake!'

'Oh, no dear. Properly awake is what they mean.'

'She's weird!'

'She shouldn't read minds. It's rude!'

'Incomprehensible but ...'

'Never mind, my dear. You'll understand soon enough. In the meantime, your spirit guides aren't asking you to believe in anything, just to *suspend your disbelief.* I've always found that helpful myself.'

Thankfully, the High Priest interrupts.

'You're talking too much, sweet soulmate. Let her finish her drink.'

He forces more herbal tincture into my mouth, where it burns my throat like acid.

'Now then, go and lie down with this peridot under your pillow and you'll be as right as rain when you wake up.'

And with that he hands me a lime-green crystal and escorts me round to my house.

An hour later the phone goes. It's the GPs' surgery phoning back to offer me a cancellation that afternoon. But as I answer the call, I realise my head feels much lighter, my stomach's stopped aching and the fever's passed.

I can't believe this is due to the eccentric administrations of my neighbours. But then, unbidden, the Indian saddhu comes into my head once more, reminding me - '*Nothing in life is ever a coincidence!*'

As for this talk of being properly awake, is it linked to the idea of *waking sleep* and being fully *present* that I've learnt about in my philosophy classes? If I start believing that healing hands, guardian angels and quack remedies have cured me, does that mean I'm going to start believing in chakras and spirit entities? How tightly suspended *is* my disbelief?

That evening I recount my experience to Boy Scout, who guffaws loudly, then stops in concern when I don't join in the laughter.

'Oh, come on, my lovely. You know that's a load of baloney. It's all in your mind. You just needed a rest, that's all. Now don't start going even stranger on me, isn't it? I know it's that *time of life* but better HRT than ESP.'

He chuckles at his joke and I excuse myself to leave the room. Then I go out into the garden, take off my socks and reconnect with the earth …

It feels remarkably pleasant, walking on the damp grass, as if I've somehow plugged into a magnetic force that's powering up through my bare soles, filling me with a peaceful energy. I know Boy Scout thinks it's rubbish and I reflect, not for the first time, how we seem to be on such different pages. He's so matter-of-fact whist I'm striving for the

169

skies. How can I make spiritual progress if he's forever weighing me down? Or maybe he's right and it *is* just my age. Maybe I *should* go to the GPs and get myself checked out?

20

Cherishing Your Chakras

It's the third time I've been to our health clinic. Dr By-the-Book has ruled out appendicitis, kidney stones and stomach ulcers and given me a diet sheet. Dr Anything-For-An-Easy-Life has sent me away with industrial-strength indigestion tablets. Now it's Over-stretched GP's turn.

'Well, stomach problems can be tricky to diagnose. I guess it could be diverticulitis.'

But before I have chance to ask him what that is, I catch him glancing at his watch and realise my allocated NHS seven-and-a-half-minutes is up and I'll just have to google the diagnosis myself.

'Here's a prescription for some mild anti-biotics.'

He sighs, knowing that soon half the population will be resistant to their effects. He shrugs his shoulders, under the weight of a system close to collapse. Knowing he's given me the cheapest, least effective tablets available, he adds apologetically - 'Come back in a week, and if it hasn't cleared up, I'll refer you for tests. But unless it develops into an emergency, I'm afraid you'll have to wait a few months.'

A few months? I'm not sure I can cope with the problem much longer. But then I don't hold out much hope of them solving it anyway. As usual, I've already consulted Dr Google and there's clearly no remedy for what I've got.

That's because what's wrong with me is somewhat unbelievable.

Just imagine if I spat out the truth - 'Ah, you see, it's not really a stomach ache as such but more like a stream of energy whirling around madly inside me.'

Exactly! I know how unhinged that makes me sound, even to myself! But it doesn't solve the fact that I'm left walking around with this unwanted, energetic tornado and a strange sense of imbalance. I'm at my wit's end and may have to consider the possibility that, in fact, my wits have actually ended and I need *psychiatric,* rather than medical help.

But then I recall the throw-away comments not long ago from my neighbour, the High Priestess. Something about chakras and things being out of balance and suspending disbelief. Surely this is worth a try before I'm prescribed Prozac?

I tentatively knock on High Priestess' door, hoping to start a conversation on the pretence of asking which bin needs putting out this week.

'Ah yes, my dear. It's the blue paper bin. But, looking at you, I'd say it's *orange* that you need.'

'Er, sorry?'

'Well, your sacral chakra's spinning wildly. It must feel very unpleasant. You need to get it sorted.'

'What? You mean, you can actually see this weird swirling I'm getting?'

'Oh yes, of course. Look I'm sorry. I'm in a rush today. I've got to pop out to do some dousing, so I've no time to chat. But wait a minute. I have something that might help.'

And with that she disappears, returning shortly afterwards with a well-thumbed book, that she hands over before dashing off. It's all about chakras, so I make myself a cuppa and sit down for what may well be a *suspending disbelief* read.

I learn that around me is an electro-magnetic energy field which interacts with the physical body by flowing through concentrated spirals of energy, known as chakras, the Sanskrit word for *wheels of light.* There are seven main ones from the top of the head to the base of the spine, and they feed energy into our bodies and dispose of any that's unwanted.

All a bit iffy, I think to myself as I slurp back my Yorkshire Tea, trying vainly to ignore the rotating vortex in my stomach. But hold on. There may be some science behind this.

I read on to learn about a Russian scientist called Kirlian who discovered a new type of photographic image able to show electrical corona discharge around parts of the body. And it appears that, throughout the ages, many cultures have been aware of this human energy field.

Ancient Greeks talked about *vital energy* and in Hindu tradition it's called *prana,* whilst in Japan and China it is known as *ki* or *chi.* Surely, if so many cultures believe in it, there must be something in it? But in my head, I can hear the voice of Over-stretched GP with his scientific western thinking, muttering a weary - 'Yes, obviously your chakra's the problem. Go ahead and smudge it with a sage stick. Only don't come crying to me when you drop dead with a twisted intestine.'

He has a point and I for one am the greatest champion of our free health service and the first to reach for a paracetamol at the slightest sign of a headache. However, surely there's no harm reading up about alternative approaches, is there?

In my imagination, Over-stretched GP leans over and rubs his hands cheerfully.

'*Placebo effect*, of course. But by all means, try whatever you like, as long as it keeps my waiting list down.'

So, I continue reading until I come to the section about the sacral chakra, situated at the navel. Hmm, that must be my problem area. It's associated with the colour orange, is concerned with our ability to give and receive love, and is considered to be our centre of creativity. Well no wonder that chakra's knackered - orange is the one colour I loathe. I run around like a headless chicken all the time, taking care of everyone, juggling work and home and with never any thanks in return. As for being creative, chance would be a fine thing, if I only had a spare half hour in the day.

I leaf through to see if there are any remedies for bringing my energies back into balance. *Dancing your chakras awake* is one suggestion, accompanied by a photo of a beautiful Indian girl, moving gracefully in the sun-filled grounds of a temple. Other solutions include eating food or wearing clothes of an orange colour, and practising certain yoga poses. None of this inspires me but I've nothing to lose, so putting my faith in eastern traditions, I look around the house to see what makeshift medicine I can magic up.

For a start I have no orange clothes whatsoever, but then I remember that Boy Scout has some hideous tangerine-coloured overalls in his bottom drawer. I drag them out, and by rolling up the legs and sleeves, find they just about fit. I do a clandestine recce into Delightful Daughter's room and discover some orange beads that match.

Now for the food. Obviously, being the end of the week, pre-supermarket day, any once-orange fruit or veg is lying comatose on a rack in shades of green or black, so I'll just have to improvise. A foray into the forbidden *Christmas cupboard* reveals a pirates' chest of Terry's Chocolate Orange and mini-slices of carrot cake. These will do nicely.

I'm already starting to feel better.

And right at the back - the jackpot - a bottle of Grand Marnier. Well if that isn't orange, I don't know what is. I take a quick swig to wash down several segments of chocolate and put my mind to the dancing issue.

Obviously, I have no esoteric Hindi music to sway along to but I've found a better option. At the back of my *secret drawer,* underneath the photo of a certain old flame, is my guilty pleasure - the CD that still brings me joy - *Hot hits of the 80s.*

Forget the antibiotics, *this* is the cure I'm looking for.

Several hours later, Boy Scout comes home to find his chocolate-stained, orange-clad wife, bopping wildly to *Katrina and the Waves.*

'*Walking on sunshine,* Oh yeah,' I wail into my Grand Marnier microphone - 'and don't it feel good!'

Boy Scout raises an eyebrow.

'Oh, there's lovely to see you having a nice time, for a change. A bit of booze and dancing - far better than liquorice tea and chanting. And while you're, err, *busy,* I'll just go and watch a bit of rugby, isn't it.'

With face now flushed to match my fetching prison jumpsuit, I collapse in a cheerful heap on the floor, my chakra wheels of light rotating in happy harmony. The standing yoga poses look too challenging for my current state so I settle on a lying pose with my legs resting against the kitchen wall. It's surprisingly comfortable and I feel a stream of energy trickling down my legs and pooling soothingly in my stomach, as I fall into a welcome slumber.

A week later I'm back in the surgery with Over-stretched GP, who surveys me from behind a mountain of paperwork.

'How's your stomach now?'

'Actually, it's sorted itself out.'

'What? Those anti-biotics worked then?'

'Well I'm not sure *what* worked, but *something* certainly did.'

On the way out I throw my unused prescription into the bin... I've just signed up to be a *Suspender of Disbelief.*

21

Stones in My Bra

I've always been fascinated by stones.

As a child, a visit to the museum was never about history but about lingering in front of the mineral and gem displays with their flamboyant colours and fascinating geometric forms. I longed to feel the jaggedness of the large clusters or the polished smoothness of the tumbled versions.

So when a new stall - *Magic Minerals* - opened in the city's Moor Market last year, selling affordable crystals, I was in seventh heaven.

Its vibrant display of tempting goodies had all the seductiveness of the sweet counter but none of the associated calories. I filled my basket with, red jasper, orange carnelian, yellow citrine, green malachite, pale blue lace agate, deep blue lapiz lazuli and purple amethyst - a veritable rainbow of crystals. Then I handed over my gem delicacies to the stall owner, Magic Mineral Man, with his calloused hands and Australian accent.

He smiled at me knowingly.

'G'day, seems these little beauties are out to get you balanced.'

'I'm sorry?'

'Well you've chosen a crystal for each of your chakras. And for good luck I'll lob in a clear quartz and a rose quartz.'

I had little idea what he was talking about, but I nodded appreciatively, then took my stones home to my study, where I laid them out in a colourful arc on the window sill.

Over the next few weeks, Magic Mineral Man showed an uncanny insight into my personal life. Carefully bundling up the turquoise that hopped towards me, he asked -

'Off on a journey then?'

'Yes, how did you know?'

'The stones always choose you and this one protects travellers.'

He glanced at the milky, translucent pebble in my hand.

'Thinking of changing your job?'

'In my dreams!'

'Well, moonstone is a crystal for new beginnings...'

Nodding at the green and red bloodstone in my basket one Saturday, he asked in concern,

'Feeling crook? A bit iron deficient?'

'Oh, I've just had tests for anaemia. How do you know all this stuff?'

So, Magic Mineral Man told me his life story.

'I worked in Oz as a miner for many years. Then I got the travel bug. Left down under, went to South America and ended up in South Africa. I've mined them all - opals, gold, diamonds, emeralds... It was working with the locals and listening to their stories of how medicine men and shamen used the gems for healing that got my attention. So, I decided to find out more. Before I knew it, instead of *mining* minerals, I was *selling* them. And, fair dinkum, I've never looked back since.'

Because he was so down-to-earth about using crystals to heal and enhance the quality of life, or maybe because he was such a canny salesman, I walked away with a hefty tome about crystals.

I discovered they've been used for thousands of years and that they're believed to channel energy, working through resonance and vibration. Science has yet to embrace their validity but ultrasound machines use a piezoelectric crystal to produce sound waves, and quartz has been shown to increase the frequency of light passed through it.

I've hidden the book from the mocking eyes of my sceptical family, but I've continued to build up my collection of stones, picking out ones on instinct to take on outings with me.

Sometimes I keep them on a tight lead, next to my skin. At other times they roam freely through my handbag. Occasionally they break free, only to reappear some time later with unexplained fractures and no apologies.

My stones know intuitively what's needed. If I have an important decision to make, mookaite grazes contentedly nearby. If I'm lacking in energy then sunstone trots over with a delivery of vitality. And if life becomes too hectic then ametrine curls up in my lap, bringing peace and tranquillity.

The older children view my menagerie of minerals as a source of humour.

'Oh-oh mother's getting angry. Stick a bit of amethyst on her third eye.'

'No, a nice crystal elixir infused in camomile tea will calm her down.'

So, I keep my addiction to myself and Saturdays have become my guilty pleasure. On the pretext of sourcing fresh fruit and veg, I slip away to the market and let my fingers stroll through the savannah of stones, where I have an uncanny sense that the crystals are connecting with an inner energy, a hidden light within me.

Today I'm drawn to a piece of black jet, so I pocket it and head downstairs. Boy Scout, as usual is engrossed in his phone.

I mutter in irritation -'Honestly, you're setting a terrible example to the kids - always on that bloody thing.'

'Actually, my lovely, I'm doing some research for you.'

'Oh yes?'

'Looking up *dementia*.'

'Dementia? But dad's tests proved nothing.'

'Exactly. But our observations prove otherwise. Your father's obviously losing it and it says here that *delusions* and *hallucinations* are part of the symptoms. You can't stick your head in the sand for ever, isn't it? Better to forward-plan.'

'Well, what are you suggesting?'

'Just, care-proof his house for a start. Make sure he has a routine. Look into having some paid help and maybe investigate Homes.'

'No!'

'I know you don't want to hear that, my lovely, but forewarned is forearmed.'

'Yes … I suppose you're right...' - I say - 'Thanks for that. I appreciate it.'

And for a moment, I remember what I love about my husband - his *taking charge* of a situation, his *reliability*, the way he shows he cares through his *acts of service*. But then he ruins the moment.

A small, shiny hematite glints invitingly on the floor under the breakfast table. Small Child, makes a grab for it.

'Dad, look at that silver stone. Ooh and there's another pretty blue one under the chair. Where have they come from?'

'They'll be some of your mam's crazy rocks, isn't it? Probably fell out of her *bra*.'

'Uuugghh! Yuk!'

Small Child drops the stones as if they're contaminated. I retrieve the offending items and correct him.

'Out of my *jeans pocket*, actually.'

I show him the jet as proof.

'Mummy, why do you have stones in your bra?'

'Because she's a mad woman, isn't it? Your mam's half-barmy. She's having a mid-life crisis and this is part of her weird quest to *find herself*. But if there's one thing I've learnt, son, it's never to question your mother's actions.'

And with that statement, Boy Scout returns to scrolling on his phone over his cornflakes. Small Child, however, is more persistent.

'Mum, why do you carry stones about? Do you really keep them in your bra?'

I hesitate before answering. Small Child's the only family member who still offers me unconditional love and views my eccentricities with wonder rather than exasperation. I don't want to plummet in his estimation, so choose my words carefully.

'Well, you see, these crystals give you superpowers, especially if you wear them next to your skin. Now if I'd married a *rich French hotelier* who could afford to buy me diamond necklaces, sapphire earrings and emerald bracelets, then I'd be laughing and bewitching everyone with my gems on the red carpet at Cannes.'

Boy Scout snorts into his orange juice. I ignore him and continue.

'But I married your *dad* instead, so I have to keep the magic hidden away close to my heart where it works undercover making amazing things happen.'

I can see that Small Child, who's a Harry Potter fan, is eager to be convinced by the fantasy element but not necessarily by the logistics.

'But do you really keep them in your *bra,* Mum? That's a bit icky!'

I opt for a blatant lie.

'Of course not. Daddy's just being silly. That's what jeans pockets are for.'

Small Child breathes a sigh of relief and makes a grab for the hematite and blue celestite.

'Can I have them? Can I take them to school with me? Please mummy.'

I glance at Boy Scout, who's looking despairingly, as he realises his younger son is lost to him. I savour my victory and tell Small Child.

'Here's the thing, I'm no expert on crystals, but if these ones have grabbed your attention, then yes, you should definitely take them with you. But don't mess about with them in class. Just put them in your pocket.'

Small Child pounces on his treasure and disappears before I change my mind.

It's the end of the school day, the door slams open and Small Child runs in.

'Mum, we had a surprise test this morning in arithmetic. And then we had Art all afternoon.'

My heart sinks. Small Child's not known for his ability in either subject.

'So, I rubbed my stones for luck and, guess what? I got seventeen out of twenty. I'm a genius! And I got a gold star for my painting!'

The genius artist is rewarded with some flapjack whilst I read out the entries about the crystals.

'See' - I tell him -'it says here that hematite is a *useful stone for the study of mathematics*. And celestite is *an angelic stone which helps creativity*.'

'Wow, that's magic mum. What does it say about *your* stone?'

'Hmm, let's see - jet - *alleviates fears and promotes taking control of life*. Sounds useful.'

At that moment the phone goes. It's the hospital. My father's had an accident.

22

The Parking Angel

'How's your dad doing?' asks English Rose as we sit in the school yard waiting for the bell to go.

'Oh over the worst now' - I say -'but he'll be in the Hallamshire for another week. He suffered a bad concussion and his ulcerated leg got a bashing.'

'How did it happen?'

'He fell off a ladder. I'm not sure *what* he was doing. Kept saying my mother had hidden something and he was looking for it.'

'Will he be able to go home soon?'

'Mmm, that's the problem. They need to sort out his meds and won't let him go until everything's stable. Then, until his leg's healed, he'll need looking after. So, he's going to stay with *us* for a while.'

'Oh, good luck with that!'

'I know. But at least I'll have him under my wing.'

'Ooh, talking of wings. Have you managed to get out of that *angel* workshop?'

'What angel workshop is that?'

'Oh, you know - the alternative clinic lady - she's posted leaflets through everyone's door. Then she accosted me on the street. I found myself saying yes, just to get rid of her, even though it's totally not my thing.'

'But you think it's *mine?*'

'Well, you're more up for weird stuff, aren't you?'

English Rose passes me an escaped pyrite stone as evidence of my guilt.

'What about our fellow Musketeers?' I ask.

'Well our Zen friend's busy - going camping in the Peaks with *Luke's Dad* and the boys for the weekend.'

I purse my lips as she continues.

'And our *dahleeng* Brazilian's down in London. Something about *condoms…*'

'What?'

'It's *spiritual.*'

'Seriously?' - I struggle to make sense, then inspiration strikes - 'Oh…you mean *Candomblé.*'

'Yeah, that's it,' nods English Rose - 'She says it's helping her keep calm whilst waiting for her appointment. Whatever works for her I suppose, even if it's a bit *mumbo-jumbo.*'

'Well, no more than *angels!*'- I point out.

'I know, but what can I do. Sometimes I wish I wasn't so damn British. It felt rude to refuse, especially since she's a neighbour. Please come along. I'll bake your favourite lemon polenta cake.'

As English Rose's baking skills are legendary, I capitulate.

'Ok, you've twisted my arm. After all, we should be supportive.'

The room's full of angels, or so The High Priestess, would have us believe. For my part, I can't sense any celestial presence, but I'm glad to be having a Saturday off from housework and taxiing kids around.

The workshop's being held at my old haunt, Spirit Mind Studio, with its positive *angel-friendly* vibes.

'So, did you tell your other half you were coming to commune with angels?' asks English Rose.

'Are you mad? I told him our neighbour was running a course and one of us needed to attend for the sake of community spirit. So, he quickly volunteered me. Looks like we're the only suckers on the street to fall for it.'

'No, that new mum from number 87 is here too. Well *physically* here.'

I look over to the corner, where a rusk-splattered body's lying comatose on a yoga mat. Apart from us, there are three other women and two men but surprisingly not a single kaftan or Jesus sandal amongst us. Of the two men, one's in his twenties with long hair and a Led Zeppelin T-shirt, whilst the other looks suspiciously like a middle-aged accountant.

English Rose laughs.

'Perhaps he's here undercover on behalf of the Inland Revenue to see if she's declaring her angelic profits?'

But before we can interrogate him, The High Priestess launches into a detailed description of angel hierarchy. Apparently, there's a whole class system going on in heaven.

The Seraphims top the angel pop charts with their accapello hymn version of *Holy, Holy, Holy*, pushing *The Cherubims* and *The Thrones* out of the limelight, despite their fiery prayer lyrics. *The Dominions* also make it into the top five with their sceptre and orb instrumental numbers, just ahead of *The Virtues,* whose brilliant shining outfits are always a crowd pleaser. Down at number six are *The Powers*, just out-performing *The Principalities*, who are more of your Eurovision candidates. This leaves *The Archangels*, very popular here on Earth, to come in at a disappointing number eight. With seven members of this heavenly band, there's an angel for every terrestrial taste, but, although their harmonies are out of this world, they don't have the X-factor.

Finally, at the bottom of the list, despite their millions of downloads and occasional Christmas novelty success, are your bog-standard *Angels*. We have, seemingly, all got our own *Guardian Angel*, who'll never leave us. The problem is though, that some of them sing slightly out of tune, which is why we humans don't always hear them.

We're now up to speed with the Holy Hit Parade and when The High Priestess asks the group if they've ever encountered an angel, I wonder if anyone will confess to listening to their own heavenly tracks.

To my surprise, Led Zeppelin raises his hand and admits that, in times of stress, he hears an angelic choir, with melodies so beautiful that it reduces him to tears. English Rose and I exchange raised eyebrows, and she sniggers.

'Heavy metal - gives you tinnitus.'

A few others offer up tales of a shining presence that kept them feeling safe as children.

My sceptical friend rolls her eyes - 'Duh! Night light on the landing'

But then it's the Accountant's turn and he hesitantly recounts how he's never subscribed to any religion or held any particular beliefs. He tells us his wife was terminally ill and when she died, a few months ago, he saw her being carried away in the arms of a massive being of brilliant white light. He thinks the grief's sent him mad but he's here today to try and make sense of what happened.

'Definitely gone crazy,' whispers English Rose

Annoyed by her snide remarks, I snap back.

'Look, I know you didn't want to come but at least keep an open mind.'

And when The High Priestess asks me if I've had any angelic visitations, I say pointedly - 'Not that I'm aware of, but I'm willing to suspend my disbelief.'

She beams - 'Excellent, my dear. Sometimes angels don't show themselves in case we get scared, so they leave a gift, like a feather.'

I nod, whilst thinking, as presents go, I've had better.

The High Priestess now announces we're being instructed from on high to sketch our own guardian angel. I groan inwardly. I hate drawing almost as much as singing. English Rose knows this and elbows me conspiratorially.

'You'd better not draw anything rude.'

She winks, showing me her anatomically accurate angel, making me laugh despite myself.

My angel has wonky wings, psychedelically coloured robes and a turned-down mouth. The High Priestess looks at it with interest.

'Ah yes. Your angel's doing its best to get your attention but is disappointed by your lack of awareness, and wishes you'd be more giving.'

'D minus,' chuckles English Rose, showing The High Priestess her own picture with its huge clown's mouth.

'Well, your angel loves your sense of humour but wishes you'd take them seriously.'

And with a sad smile, The High Priestess signals it's time to stop drawing and begin our meditation. English Rose sighs.

'Thank goodness. I could do with a siesta.'

The High Priestess then leads us into a powerful visualisation, in which we imagine ourselves climbing a ladder, surrounded by angels and going to a place of great beauty, where we feel safe and loved, to meet with our own guardian angel.

I wake up with a start to realise I've been fast asleep on a collection of colourful gemstones and, apparently, judging by the wet patch on my shoulder, I've been dribbling heavily. I've no recollection whatsoever of my guardian angel. I say as much to English Rose, who's looking slightly shell-shocked and, for once, is unusually quiet.

'Did you have a heavenly experience then?' I ask.

She hesitates for a split second too long.

'Don't be daft. It's all a load of rubbish!'

I don't press the point but sit back and listen to the other group members as they recount their visions of meeting with their angels. For most, the visualisation's produced a positive effect and I'm pleased to see that the Accountant seems more relaxed and at peace with himself than before and Exhausted Mother's managed several hours' quality sleep.

I reluctantly admit to The High Priestess that no angel showed up for me today.

'Well, they only come at your request, my dear. You have to invite them in. Maybe you should start with the parking angel?'

'The *parking angel*?'

'Yes. Just ask the parking angel out loud to find you a space. Make sure you specify where and when exactly, and always be sure to say thank you.'

'Right, I'll give that a go then,' I agree, all the while thinking that suspending disbelief may not be the best idea after all.

As we head back home, I remember that roadworks on the surrounding streets mean that everyone's now parking their cars on our road and I'll be lucky to find a space. With an ironic grin, I call out - 'Ok parking angel, if you *are* there, I'd be grateful if you found me a prime spot in front of my door in the next three minutes.'

As I drive up, I see the road's chock-a-block with vehicles. Absolutely no chance! But then a van pulls out in front of me, leaving a space right outside my house. Hmm, just another coincidence?

English Rose's been silent all the way home. It's most unlike her and I start to feel sorry for her. After all, she's spent her day at a workshop she didn't really want to go to, where something's obviously upset her. She has no partner she can share her problems with and in a short while her four demanding children are going to be back, destroying any chance of peace and quiet.

I take a deep breath. If I'm really serious about working on myself and trying to be a better person, then maybe I do need to be more *giving*. Before I can change my mind, the words are out of my mouth.

'I've been thinking. It's selfish of me not to share, especially with good friends like you. I'll email you my flapjack recipe tonight.'

English Rose looks up in disbelief.

'Oh my God! Really? You'd do that for me? Wow, that's incredible. Email it me right now, before you change your mind! I'll make a batch as soon as I get in. It'll keep the kids quiet and we might get through the evening with no fights. Thank you. Oh, thank you so much.'

And amazingly, despite having given away the secret recipe that allows me to shine, I somehow feel shinier for having done so. It's certainly cheered up English Rose as she skips out of the car.

Meanwhile, I head indoors, careful not to mention the word *angel* to my family. But over the next few weeks, the *A-word* catches on, as everywhere I go, I call on the parking angel, who always finds me a space. I never see evidence of the angel, but I'm happy to have the help, celestial or otherwise. Of course, I mention nothing of this to Boy Scout but, as is often the way, Small Child dobs me in.

On one of our rare family outings, Boy Scout's driving us around the cinema complex, desperately trying to park in time to make the start of the latest film. The air's blue with profanities.

'Dad, why don't you just ask the parking angel like mum does?'

'A *parking angel*? We need a bloody *traffic warden*, boyo, not an angel, isn't it?'

But then, cheered up momentarily by yet another example of his wife's unbalanced mind, he chuckles.

'Oh, your mam's definitely lost it now. Perhaps that's what explains the feathers I find in the car each time she's been driving.'

I know he's laughing at me and that he thinks my soul searching's a waste of time. I know he'd rather see me buying trashy celebrity rags than reading my new favourite, *Spiritual Destination* magazine. But let him laugh! I'm on a journey of transformation and there's no stopping me now.

23

Gong Ho!

'Not *another* workshop, my lovely. It's getting to be a weekly event!'

I ignore my husband. I'm in a good mood. Despite traffic jams and diversions, I'm now forging ahead along the *motorway of enlightenment*. My father's settled in well with us. And, despite the inevitable squabbles resulting from my two boys sharing a room, harmony reigns.

My father's leg is healing well. He's not made a single reference to my mother since he's been here. And he takes himself off for a 'little walk' every day. As for me, I'm meditating regularly, working with my crystals and making good use of my self-help library. *Suspending disbelief* has proven a powerful fuel, improving my performance in this race towards self-realisation. And those annoying *voices* are all but silent these days.

By now my soulful searching on the internet has identified me as an adherent of alternative experiences, so when a half-price deal for a new therapy pops up, I immediately accept. So today I'm wrapped in a blanket on the floor of St Mary's, an inner-city church that embraces the wider community. The sun rays flooding through the arched, glass windows in the high-ceilinged room spotlight the tiny figure of our Thai instructor. Surely she's not strong enough to lift that huge hammer and hit the massive, metal disc suspended above my head?

Dotted around the room are ten other cocoons containing fellow *suspenders of disbelief*. They are here to experience the dubious delights of a *gong bath*, with its healing and meditative sound effects on the body. I'm nervous, as I have a poor track record with sounds, having failed to distinguish my *do-reh-mis* in a school audition. Since then musical notes have filled me with anxiety, rather than calm.

Tiny Thai, who could fit into one of my trouser legs, has a huge smile, encouraging eyes and a logical explanation - 'So yes, sound is energy form. It touch and shape every cell in our body with its vibration. It physically rearrange molecular structure. So yes, many ancient traditions recognise vibration and sound. It important way for returning to balance and healing. They use music, chanting, prayer. So yes, and use instrument like drum, bell, singing bowl and gong. So yes, sound wave move through water five times more efficiently than through air. So yes, is true! And human body over sixty five percent water, so it really receptive to vibrations. Now first we do exercise to prepare.'

So, I take my *mighty ocean* of a body and follow her *diminutive stream* in a series of exercises tapping up the outside and inside of my legs and arms to *warm up my energy.*

'So yes, imagine pulling down light from above. Make protective bubble round body. Now connect to Earth. When ready, please lie down on mat and wait for gong.'

But relaxing is hard, even with a pillow under my head as, with two strangers on either side of me, invading my personal space, I feel like I'm at an enforced sleepover. Still, I smile politely at Random Larger Gentleman and Intense Spiritual Lady then screw up my eyes in the pretence that, if I can't see them, they're not really here.

Tiny Thai picks up her hammer and moves towards the gong. I brace myself to be jolted off the mat but instead she barely tickles the metal and a light, pleasing sound dances gracefully into the air. It's followed by a deeper sound, more melancholic in tone, but still agreeable to the ears.

She continues striking the gong in various places and wave after wave of varying notes wash over me. My brain settles into a pleasant Alpha state as my mind empties and my eyelids gradually unscrew.

The frequency wave of the sounds now deepens and I feel the vibrations travelling through my body as if being shaken like a duster. It's like leaning against a washing machine on full spin. Whilst not unpleasant, it's a little unnerving.

What becomes more unnerving is when I sense shuddering at my side. My eyes flash open to witness Intense Spiritual Lady next to me, convulsing as if possessed. Before I can jump up and call for medical assistance, Tiny Thai appears with a small metal bowl and spoon. She smiles reassuringly and holds Intense Spiritual Lady by the shoulders.

I rue the fact that I bunked off the First Aid course at college, otherwise I might know what to do in the case of epileptic fits. I scour my mind for half-remembered episodes of *Casualty*. Meanwhile Tiny Thai rubs the spoon rhythmically round the rim of the bowl, creating an intense, high-pitched vibration very close to my soon-to-be-ex-neighbour, who goes into another seizure, clenching her fists and arching her back.

I'm definitely calling an ambulance now! But as I rise, Intense Spiritual Lady lets out a death rattle, relaxes her muscles and a look of complete joy and peace appears on her face. I stare in bewilderment but Tiny Thai just nods and motions me to return to my mat.

She now beats the gong repetitively and a low growling stalks the room. The sound's definitely having a sedative effect on Random Larger Gentleman. His stomach's wobbling, his snoring's harmonising with the gong and then he splutters explosively in my direction, turning this Gong *Bath* into a Gong *Shower*. Why is it that all my meditations end in precipitation? I wipe my face with the blanket then put the pillow over my head to forget the experience and drown out the sound.

But the sound's all pervading, bouncing off the walls and rising up from the floor. It reverberates up my spine and through my skeleton, unblocking whatever lies in its path. I feel a sense of lightness as if my bones have crumbled into powder and I'm now the gentle breeze carrying the shimmering specks of their dust.

The phrase - *In the beginning was the word* - comes unexpectedly into my head as the sound changes subtly to a softer, higher frequency.

Many spiritual traditions speak of sound as being the formative force of creation and for one ecstatic moment, as the gong resonates in all my cells, I experience a deep awareness of the unity of the universe.

I am no longer this body, this *Everyday-I*.

I am the eternal sound.

I am the harmony of the universe.

I *am*.

Then the gong stills, the sound retreats and *Everyday-I* gradually returns to the room.

Random Larger Gentleman, yawns - 'Best sleep I've ever had!'

I nod, feeling sympathy for anyone unlucky enough to share his bed.

Intense Spiritual Lady leaps up - 'It's incredible! I've shaken off years of emotional baggage.'

I smile at her. Too right. You've definitely shaken it out baby!

As for me, I've experienced sound in a profoundly physical way that's brought me into contact, once more, with that deep awareness, that eternal flame that lies within. It fills me full of love for mankind in general and my family in particular. So instead of stopping off for my usual Saturday fix at the Magic Mineral stall, I drive straight home to be with my loved ones.

As I come through the passageway that leads to the garden, the sounds of Boy Scout and the children outside laughing and talking reach my ears. It's such a rare and special event when they're all getting on that I pause to savour the moment.

Instead, I overhear what they really think of me.

'So is Mum's coming back later after her *gong thingy*?' - asks Delightful Daughter.

'Who knows what weirdness your mother's up to? She's probably joined some hippy cult! I hope she snaps out of this *woo-woo* stage soon. I'm fed up of finding *Cosmology* magazine in the loo.'

'Oh dad, don't be mean. She's trying to *find herself,* that's all. It's just a shame she didn't stick it out with the Church, instead of going down the wacky New Age path.'

'I don't think so, big sis. Having one Christian in the family is bad enough. But she's just hoodwinking herself. You both are. Richard Dawkins' *The God Delusion* tells it as it is and all mother's crazy chanting, dervish whirling and chakra balancing is a load of rubbish.'

'Well at least you kids don't have to share a bed with all her bloody stones, isn't it? I sometimes feel like I'm lying on a mountain not in a bed!'

'Granddad found some in his bed too. He likes mummy's stones and so do I.'

'Well, you're a stupid poo!'

I've heard enough. So much for all my sacrifices for my family! The voices return with a vengeance.

'You're a joke!'

'You should stop being so embarrassing!'

'Or find someone who appreciates you for who you are...'

But, *Who bloody am I?* That's the question that started all this mess. So, what if I just stop asking it? What if this road to enlightenment is all a figment of my imagination? What if I just accept that there's a pile-up on the highway, stop the car and come to a standstill on the hard shoulder of life?

24

Positively Mean

It's Monday morning and I'm still smarting from the knowledge that my family think I'm crazy. On top of that, my job sucks, and my life has no point to it.

Small Child's also woken up in a despairing mood and is clinging onto the doorframe, refusing to leave the house.

'I hate school. It's rubbish! Why do I have to go?'

I feel like joining in - '*I hate college! It's rubbish! Why can't I do something else?*'

But if I don't get Small Child to school soon, I'll be late for work.

Devil Teen helpfully shoves him onto the street.

'Well, I hate A-levels and sharing a room with you, little-poo! You don't know how good you've got it! Two playtimes a day, kind classroom assistants and a climbing wall in the yard. Just wait till you get to big school, with no breaks, evil teachers, feral gangs and pointless exams. Then you can start whining!'

He smiles with the satisfaction of having asserted his alpha-male status. As Small Child's face collapses in shock, I hiss back - 'Great! Thank you. Can we just deal with Junior School first before freaking him out about his future? Besides, you don't know how good *you've* got it, sunshine! Just wait till you're forced to work every day at a job you no longer love.'

'Well, give it up then, Mother. Stop moaning on about it all the time!'

'It's not that easy. Money doesn't grow on trees. It's impossible to find a new job at my age. In case you hadn't noticed - with your Economics and Politics A-level - there's a crisis going on. It's not that simple to earn money. Then when you do, you never get to see it because you spend it all on your ungrateful kids!'

'Shouldn't have had us then, eh Mother? And no wonder little-poo's having issues if he wears *pink* to school!'

'That's very non-PC,' I counter

'I like pink!' wails Small Child.

'There's *PC* and *real life*, Mother.'

Devil Teen jogs off coatless up the road in the rain, as I take a proper look at my youngest, who's wearing what used to be a *white* T-shirt, pre-laundry.

Taking a deep breath, I resort to that trusted old chestnut - bribery.

'Look, maybe he's right. Go and change and I'll get you a piece of flapjack and instead of walking we'll drive.'

It may not solve the problem of school but at least it gets him there.

Later that morning my phone pings with an uplifting *thought for the day* sent by Zen Mother, who subscribes to a *feel-good* website. Today's little nugget fails to raise my spirits.

- *The happiness of your life depends upon the quality of your thoughts....*

I message back.

- *Well then, I'm doomed to misery as my thoughts are dark and depressing.*

She replies with a row of hearts and a link to a website for positive affirmations. Really? I roll my eyes. But, faced with the choice of marking students' homework or clicking on the link, I find myself reading how developing a positive mind set, can transform your life.

Apparently, we all use affirmations daily without realising it. The only problem is our heads are full of *negative* ones, like:

- *I'm not clever enough.*
- *I'll never have enough money to do that.*
- *I can't …*
- *I shouldn't …*

And this is why we limit ourselves.

But, it seems, by using a *positive* statement always in the present tense, you can re-programme your thoughts to change the way you think and feel about things. Hmmm? Am I suddenly going to win the lottery, just because I keep repeating 'I'm rich?' I don't think so.

But with a mountain of essays confronting me my finger hovers over the heading, *Abundance,* and before I know it, I've arrived at a page covered in currency signs, with the following affirmations in bold.

- *I am a money bank.*
- *I attract abundance.*
- *Money flows towards me easily.*

I like the sound of that. Glancing round the staff room to check I'm alone, I stand up and intone the affirmation out loud. It sounds good, so I chant it again in an American billionaire's accent, then once more in the style of Her Majesty. My eyes fall on my students' work and I groan inwardly - Abdul's assignments always take ages to correct.

To procrastinate further I switch into my best French impression.

'Je suis un munnay bonk.

J'attracte abarndunz.

Munnay floss towaaardzz mi issily.'

It's entertaining, so I try out the affirmation in various foreign accents, until I realise ten minutes have passed and no marking's been done. With a final affirmation, in my best Japanese, I take the first book off the pile and get started.

Two hours later, with Abdul's writing covered in red ink, the last mark's been inputted and I'm dying for a coffee. But guess what? Because of Small Child's stroppiness this morning, I've left my wallet on the kitchen table. Great! So much for abundance!

Just then my phone pings again with another post from Zen Mother.

- *Every day may not be good, but there is something good in every day.*

Seriously? I'm about to send a rude reply, when I notice a piece of paper sticking out from the pocket in my phone. Only on closer investigation, it's not paper but a £10 note. Hallelujah! Maybe all those affirmations have done the trick after all? I sing my abundance song cheerily in my head all the way to the coffee bar.

When I get home that evening, I find Devil Teen, as usual, tormenting Small Child by holding a biscuit just out of his reach.

'You're smelly, old and mean!'

'Well you're an annoying stinky-poo!'

In the meantime, I sift through the mail. Oh no! An official letter for me, from the Tax Office. This is never good news. With trembling hands, I tear it open but have to re-read it twice before the truth sinks in. I've been given an unheard-of rebate of £250. Coincidence, yet again?

So, I decide this is a sign for me to continue on my *inner road* and make the abundance affirmation part of my daily routine. It connects with a deeper knowledge that all will be well and that there's always light at the end of the tunnel. Yet, when I'm in the midst of a meditation, swallowing *Bach remedies*, or attempting to *feng shui* my room, I can't ignore those nagging voices in my head.

'Crazy woman, who are you kidding?'

'You should enter the lottery - your only chance of escape.'

'Just pack it all in!'

But the affirmations, however wacky, are my only concrete plan for career change and future wealth, so I carry on regardless. I also encourage Small Child, who's the only family member I have some influence over, to make his own affirmation, which he repeats obediently every day.

'I'm clever and capable. I enjoy learning.'

Devil Teen sniggers outside the bedroom door.

'You're a stupid poo!'

I lose patience with his teenage sneering.

'Look if you're jealous because you haven't got an affirmation of your own. I'll give you one. Try saying - *I'm always kind, wear my coat to school and have a vocabulary that doesn't include the word poo.*'

'Ha ha, mother, very funny. Not.'

A few weeks later, Mrs Stickler takes me aside to say how much more confident Small Child appears in class and how pleased she is with his progress. I relate this news victoriously to Devil Teen.

'See, the affirmations *do* work.'

'Gullible mother.'

He raises his eyebrows in despair.

'It's nothing to do with affirmations. When I look after little brother it's about proper parenting. Unlike you, I never let him have a biscuit until he's done all his sums and spelling. Being mean works. Homework and hard graft have improved his grades and confidence, not positive affirmations. He'll turn into a crystal weirdo like you, if he's not careful. Forget your New Age nonsense, Mother, and get some scientific perspective, won't you? You're always so busy preparing lessons or chanting that you just neglect your kids. I don't even know why you bothered to have us!'

And, on that damning note, he stomps noisily out of the room.

Small Child emerges from behind the sofa, where he's taken refuge. Despite being too gangly now to be comfortable, he clambers onto my knee and kisses the tear that's sliding, unbidden, down my cheek.

'Don't worry, mummy. Neither of us is weird. He's just in a bad mood. He had an argument on the phone with Jess.'

'Who's *Jess*?' I ask, uncomfortably aware that the accusations of neglect hold some truth.

'The girl with hair like Parma violets. The one he really likes.'

That night in bed I toss and turn. Devil Teen's words have hit home, tapping into the reservoir of self-doubt inside me. Maybe it's because he's so certain of his logic - so unswayed by feelings unless they're backed up by facts - that it makes me falter in my own convictions?

I thought I was making progress but maybe they *are* all right and I've just been deluding myself? Is the *New Age* really just the superstitious *Dark Ages* in disguise? Have I been deceiving myself - wasting my time and money on madcap practices? It's certainly an effort - reading all those books, attending various religious services, studying philosophy and going on alternative workshops. Why am I bothering?

Maybe Devil Teen's spoken the truth. I've got no scientific proof that any of this works. All those tiny glimmers of inner peace - they're just a feeling. I've got no concrete evidence. It could all be in my head. After all, I'm at that *funny time* of life…

A depressing disillusionment settles like a dark cloud over me. He's right. And those voices, now getting louder again, agree.

'You've always been a weirdo!'

'You should act like a proper mother!'

'Let's party instead!'

Yes, it's time to give up on this quest and live a *normal* life again. I'll start by taking proper notice of my family, catching up with friends, and - why not - enjoying myself a bit more. I'll throw out all my spiritual magazines and cancel that kinesiology taster session on Saturday. Instead I'll ring Bubbly Brazilian and tell her I've changed my mind about that 'fun day out'.

25

In the Zone

'Dad, what on earth are you doing?'

I walk into the room and find my father applying a strong-smelling paste and some dried leaves to his leg.

He turns round with a guilty look.

'Chinese medicine.'

'What? Why aren't you using the cream the hospital prescribed?'

'Never worked. This does. Your m…'

He pauses, changes his mind and pointing at his watch, reminds me - 'Park run.'

'Oh great. I'm going to be late! We'll talk when I get back, okay?'

Thank goodness I'll have a chance to clear my head. I thought things were going too smoothly. My father's obviously still *talking* to my mother and now he's blatantly disregarding medical advice.

I set off for the park run - a weekly, nation-wide event, with the aim to get the general public out of their armchairs and into the fresh air. It's the only chance I get to exercise these days and, despite getting out of breath and suffering the occasional stitch, there's something about this activity that brings me joy. There's no soul-searching effort involved. It's all very simple.

Down at Endcliffe Park, I pass the early morning Tai-chi aficionados and duck under the tape, squeezing in amongst the four-hundred-plus runners. Then my heart sinks as I realise who's next to me - Luke's dad.

'Remember, this is a *run*, not a *race*!' announces the organiser.

Luke's dad, in his go-faster spikes and top-of-the range sport-tracker watch, ignores this reminder and, on the starting gun, elbows me into the railings, crashes past an elderly jogger, kicks a small child aside and hurdles over a dog as he shoots off.

Picking myself up, I start off slowly but surely, conserving my energy for later. I go past a sporty family, and give a thumbs up to their valiant six-year-old. Then I gradually pick off a few more runners by the cafe, before taking a deep breath in preparation for the hill.

Luke's dad, however, has a different tactic and has set off at break-neck speed. I can see him, in his designer sportswear, shoving his way through a group of hungover students and cutting in between the visually-impaired runners with their sighted guides, causing them to collide.

At the top, I look back at the long snake of participants making up the park run. Hundreds of people are running in formation. Each of us is an individual but, for this one moment, we're all part of something much bigger than ourselves. It's as if the park run is an entity on its own and for just a second, *Everyday-I* disappears and melds into something larger and more significant.

I shake my head and the moment passes. In the distance I see Luke's dad, struggling now, despite the energy drink he's just thrown on the path. I recover my breath and head downhill at speed, noting with pleasure that I've overtaken a twenty-something.

We're over half-way now and my tactic of a steady pace is beginning to pay off. The fast starters are running out of stamina and I now have Luke's dad in my sights. But this is a *run* not a *race*. So, when I find myself next to Zen Mother, Ethan and Luke, I slow down for a catch-up.

'What are *you* doing here?' I ask - 'I didn't think running was your thing. '

'Well, Ethan and Luke were keen to come but they're supposed to run with a *responsible adult*.'

'Err, yeah. So why isn't *Luke's dad* running with him then?'

She looks sheepish.

'Errm… Well, he's taking it more seriously than me, so I volunteered to run at their pace.'

'Right, I see. Well, I've got my second wind, so I'll crack on and see you at the finish.'

Spurred on by the injustice of Zen Mother's good nature being exploited, I go up a gear and start closing the gap between myself and the runners in front. As I pass by the monument next to the stream, time suddenly stops still. I'm *losing myself* in the pounding of my feet and heart.

I'm *in the zone.*

My mind is empty of all voices.

Each movement seems natural and effortless.

Every day I is no longer running.

Running is just happening on its own.

The body is still. It's the scenery that's moving past at speed.

Thoughts have disappeared.

Feelings have disappeared.

Then the body's disappeared.

A vast, boundless lightness replaces it.

Only the breath is present.

There is a great calm.

How ironic that once I stop my searching for inner peace, it finds me on its own!

The moment passes quickly but it touches the awareness within me, and brings an aching to rest more often in this silent stillness.

But then the finishing line comes into view and I see Luke's dad nearly knock over one of the park run volunteers in his eagerness to get a good place. I can't help myself from feeling annoyed. *Everyday-I* with its competitive ego and its persistent voices resurfaces.

'You're pathetic. You'll never beat him!'

'You should train properly!'

'Go on, show 'em all!'

I grit my teeth, pushing my body to its limits. This may be a *run* but just for now, it's a *race*. I strain every muscle, put on a final spurt, and find myself neck and neck with Luke's dad.

We're seconds away from the end.

Ha! Just as well I've given up on enlightenment and self-improvement! I can't resist a comment.

'Hi. Fancy seeing you again!'

Luke's dad is so surprised by my sudden, smug appearance, that his attention falters and I take the opportunity to sprint past him to victory. Who knew that running could be such fun?

As I hobble back into the kitchen, done-in by my Olympic feat, I ask Boy Scout - 'Where's my dad?'

'Oh, has he disappeared, my lovely? Probably gone for another of his 'little walks' - been doing that a lot lately, isn't it? Soon be time for him to go back to his place. Looks like we were worrying about him for nothing, isn't it?'

26

The Voice

Bubbly Brazilian's idea of a 'fun day out' and mine turn out to be somewhat different as I tell her in no uncertain terms.

'I hate singing, am tone-deaf and got chucked out of the school choir! Why on earth do you think I'd enjoy this *Sing the autumn blues away* workshop?'

'Because my dahleeng, I think you have an inner songbird just waiting to be uncaged. And because you have a heart of gold and want to support me at this stressful time.'

'But I thought the colonoscopy showed you just had polyps. Didn't they remove them?'

'Yes, my dahleeng, they did. But now it's yet another waiting game for the results. That's the NHS for you.'

My heart skips a beat. I've been here before. But now is not the time to be negative. I fix on an encouraging smile -

'True, but on the bright side it's cost you nothing and if they were *really* worried, they'd have fast-tracked you I'm sure.'

'I hope so my dahleeng but in the meantime - don't think me crazy - I've been praying to Iemanjá,'

'Who?'

'Iemanjá, powerful goddess of the sea in the Candomblé faith. We have a big celebration in her honour every February. I've always been drawn to her since I was a child and recently I've found myself talking to her. She's very motherly and protective - just what I need right now.'

'Well, I'm hardly one to judge! And if your goddess makes you feel better, then carry on. Maybe she'll join us in a sea shanty!'

So, here we are today at Sharrow Perfoming Arts Space. It's a modern, purpose-built facility with the advantage of underfloor-heating to keep this rag-tag group of strangers warm inside and a sound-proofed hall to keep my voice from escaping outside.

Our tutor is middle-aged, slightly rotund, with a washed-out perm and *ban the bomb* earrings. Dressed in black leggings and a multi-coloured floral tunic, she has smiley eyes and a motherly look to her, so maybe everything will be okay.

Earth Mother coughs loudly to gain our attention.

'So, why have you come here today?' she asks.

There's an awkward silence as we all look at our feet. But then my extroverted friend from sunny Salvador starts the ball rolling.

'To take my mind off my problems and fill my spirit with music!'

Her enthusiasm unlocks the floodgates of British reserve.

'I've come to learn to harmonise better,' states an operatic-looking gentleman.

'I'm here to sing my heart out,' trills an excited twenty-something.

'I want to share my hobby with others,' says an older male singleton, looking hopefully at the twenty-something.

It's like a meeting of Warblers Anonymous, where we swap tales of what brought us to this sorry end. In this group of twenty people of varying ages and backgrounds, what unites us - apart from me - is a love of singing.

Earth Mother's picked up on my pain and asks with gentle kindness.

'So, what's your reason?'

The voices in my head aren't so kind though.

'You can't sing. You're hopeless!'

'You should just go home!'

'A few cocktails and you're the karaoke queen!'

Everyone's staring at me. I'm not sure I can go through with this. But at some point, I'll have to own up to the truth. Eyes downcast, I take a deep breath.

'Well, I've never been able to sing. My sister's the musical one. So, my ambition is to take one small step by learning to make a noise that's not too awful.'

There, I've said it! And to my amazement, there's a ripple of polite applause, a few sympathetic nods and even a pat on the back. Earth Mother's encouraging.

'You just need to find your voice, that's all. So, we'll start by doing a few warm-up exercises.'

She instructs us to lie down on the floor, stretch our arms over our heads then move our bended legs from side to side. Am I in luck? Is this turning into a gym workout? I'm just thankful no music's been involved so far.

'We're opening up our ribcage and allowing our breath to flow more freely'- says Earth Mother - 'Next I want you to sing with your stomach.'

Ah, I think, in confusion - not my mouth, my stomach! And I follow her instructions to let my abdomen rise and fall, with wonderful wobbliness, whilst panting like a dog. It's fun lying on a mat, imitating animal sounds and unexpectedly I realise I'm enjoying myself.

As I 'whoo, whoo' like a steam train, I catch the eye of the bespectacled teenager, dragged along to the workshop by her over-enthusiastic mother, and we burst into a fit of giggles. After rolling round the floor for several minutes, we march around the hall, shrugging shoulders, waving arms around and intoning 'ma-ta-ba' at each other.

The sounds rumble through my body, shaking off the cobwebs of winter. I'm struck, just as with the Gong Bath, by what a difference notes can have on your mood. I'm now feeling much more light-hearted and upbeat.

We look ridiculous, but at least it's postponing the moment of proper singing, so I'm happy to keep going. And it's definitely breaking down barriers too as I notice that whenever Male Singleton 'mas', Twenty-something 'tas' back and they both 'ba' in flirtatious unison.

But now things get serious. As we sing a 'ma' together, we're asked to group ourselves in a line according to how deep or high we sound. Obviously, I place myself next to Bubbly Brazilian, who nudges me further down the line.

'I think, my dahleeng, your voice is a little deeper than mine.'

But I'm having none of this. I can't be separated from my only friend here, so I screw up my eyes, constrict my throat and reply with an unconvincing falsetto 'ma'. She gives in and makes room for me.

We're now divided into groups of four. Our quartet consists of two sniffy, would-be professional singers - members of several choirs and a claim-to-fame appearance on TV's *Sunday Singalong*. I resolve to mime any songs from now on.

Earth Mother apologetically hands out a series of badly photocopied, barely legible, coffee-stained song sheets and we get started with an old favourite, *Bobby Shafto*. Because this sea shanty was part of every music lesson I ever had, even I can manage a whispered harmony. Bubbly Brazilian, of course, has no idea who *Bobby Shafto* is, but is able to hold a tune well and together with the two Sniffies - and maybe an omnipresent Iemanjá - we produce a pleasing performance.

Just as I'm thinking this singing lark isn't so bad after all, Earth Mother throws a curve ball by introducing an unknown Old English folk song. This is a disaster! She sings out the melody for us to copy, but seconds after it's reached my ears, it disappears from my brain and reappears from my mouth in a new, discordant arrangement.

The Sniffies give me the evil eye, so I close my mouth abruptly in time to hear Bubbly Brazilian belting out the chorus at full volume -

'I love the sweet maker,

The filthy-minded heart'

I stare at her in bafflement. What the hell is she singing? She stares back with a look of confusion. In the pause between the next verse, she confides in me - 'Strange words, my dahleeng, aren't they? Is that typical old English style?'

She then blasts once more into the chorus:

'I love the *sweet maker,*

The *filthy-minded* heart'

The Sniffies look at her aghast, whilst my teacher-brain whirls into action, glancing at the lines which are only just blurrily visible on the poor-quality handout. I realise, that despite having lived in the UK for many years, and having a near-perfect command of the language, Bubbly Brazilian's never encountered the *thee* or *thou* form used to replace *you*, or seen a verb ending in *est*.

And old-fashioned words for *girl* and *my* have obviously passed her by. Quite understandably, she's interpreted the fuzzy print into something she can make vague sense of.

What she should be singing is:

*I love **thee** sweet **maiden***

*Thou **fillest mine** heart*

My shoulders heave and, as I explain the language to Bubbly Brazilian, we both burst out laughing. I'm definitely singing from my stomach now, it's aching so much. I may well not have sung the autumn blues away but I've certainly shaken them out of my system!

Eventually we gather ourselves together, and get ready for the grand finale. We start singing and for once I forget to be self-conscious. The melody streams naturally out of my head, the words and the notes mingle with the voices of those around me, drowning out any voices in my head. We're no longer individuals, but somehow have become one. Our voices are united in tone and harmony. There's a joyous feeling of being lost in the moment, in the awareness that's eternally there.

'I love thee sweet maiden

Thou fillest my heart'

On our way out, Bubbly Brazilian gives me a spontaneous hug.

'Thank you, my dahleeng. That made me forget my worries. How about you? Did you manage to switch off from all your family issues?'

I smile back.

'Yes, amazingly, I've managed not to think about my dad all day. He wants to move back home you know. They've signed him off at the hospital - said his leg's healed miraculously and his cognitive tests are fine.'

'So, what's the problem then, my dahleeng?'

'I don't know. He's definitely hiding something from me and I'm sure he's still *communing* with my mother.'

'Well maybe you should go back to *suspending your disbelief,* my dahleeng?'

'No way. I'm finished with all that stuff. I'm leaving soul searching to concentrate on family and friends instead.

27

Community Counts

'Dad, I can't move you home today. It's the street party, remember. Besides, don't you think you're better living with us for a little longer?

'No, thanks. Time to go. Tomorrow then…'- my father says determinedly.

I turn to Boy Scout for support.

'Bloody Hell, isn't it? Not another street party. A bit late in the year, my lovely? I thought we'd seen the last of the neighbours after our summer barbecue fiasco!'

'Well, yes, it was unfortunate you set fire to half the garden and the guests! But about my dad ….'

Boy Scout puts on a concerned face.

'Obviously your dad can stay as long as he wants, isn't it? But the doctors say he's fine now and if he wants to go home, who are we to stop him?'

'Well, are you at least coming to this party then?

'I'd love to, my lovely, but it's a rugby international this afternoon so I'm afraid I'll have to pass.'

It's clear from Boy Scout's objection that he prefers to focus on sport and, actually, maybe it's best if he lies low for a few more months. However, I'm not going to let him off lightly.

'Well, thank you for your wonderful display of neighbourliness and setting a great example to the children, as usual.'

'Hmm, talking of bloody kids - they're always hogging the TV, isn't it?'

He looks daggers at Devil Teen.

'That's you I mean, boyo. You'd better get off that PlayStation right now. It's nearly time for kick-off.'

'Dad, I was playing online with friends! We must be the only family on Earth with just *one* TV in the house. Why can't you go to the pub to watch the match? This is so unfair.'

Devil Teen stomps up the stairs to his Teen Cave, deliberately knocking Small Child over as he exits.

I pick my youngest up and smile fondly at him.

'I guess it's just you, me and Granddad going to the party then? Unless your sister wants to come too?'

I look in Delightful Daughter's direction. She's glued to her phone-screen, and without even glancing up, snorts - 'Little kids? Old folk? If you don't mind mum, I'll give this one a miss.'

Well perhaps it's a good job that neither older child, with their current left-wing opinions, is coming, and certainly safer that Boy Scout, with his inbred republicanism, has decided to stay at home. For today's party is being hosted by Tory Monarchist, who lives in the end house of our row of terraces in a bohemian, inner city suburb. Politics aside, she's delightful, like all our neighbours, and it's her turn to open her doors to allow in the eclectic rabble that makes up the residents of our street.

Small Child, my father and I make our belated way over to the manicured lawn of Tory Monarchist. I've forgotten to bake anything, so have raided the cupboard for shop-bought brownies.

As we arrive, we're greeted warmly by the small crowd already gathered. In one corner, the Smiley Family, of Jamaican heritage and the Friendly Wavers, who hail originally from Pakistan, are debating the merits of cooking with cloves. In the other corner, Sensible Health Visitor is discussing the difficulties of modern family life with English Rose. In the meantime, her four hooligans rampage around the garden, with Small Child now enthusiastically in tow.

I realise with horror that he's already syphoned up two bottles of coke and demolished half the brownies. He's about to trample over

Tory Monarchist's prize dahlias when he's intercepted by Human Dynamo, my American next-door-but-one neighbour.

She laughs merrily, depositing him at my feet.

'Caught you buddy!'

But before I can thank her, she dashes off again, this time to retrieve a crawling baby heading towards the ornamental fish pond. The baby belongs to the Exhausted Parents at number 87, but, as they're currently fast asleep on the swinging couch, she tucks their offspring under her arm and bounds off to help the hostess hand out plates of cucumber sandwiches.

Mrs Smiley accepts the food gracefully, then surreptitiously takes out a bottle of Tabasco sauce from her bottomless bag and adds liberal sprinklings, whilst Mrs Friendly-Waver opens her embroidered shoulder bag and proceeds to hand out spicy, home-made pakora and bhajis to all around her. She may not be extroverted but her friendly waves say it all.

The Musical Christians, our modern day Von Trapp family, who head the local church choir, are providing the entertainment in the back room. There's dad on keyboards, little brother on bass guitar, Mum and small sister as backing vocals, whilst cool big brother beats the drums and belts out the latest pop hits with true professionalism.

I note with interest that the oldest hooligan, Clementine, is captivated by this act and has stopped her usual mischief-making to look soulfully in the lead singer's direction. I hope this puppy crush doesn't end in tears.

I go over, followed by my father, to chat to our enchanting eccentrics, the High Priest and Priestess, who are deep in conversation with Tory Monarchist, and Mr High Heels, the street's cross-dressing lawyer. Today he's wearing a fetching lime trouser suit with matching kitten heels, and is discussing the mysterious Chinese Triad who've recently moved into the rental house at the far end of the road.

No one's yet met them officially but they've been spotted on the street - an earnest-looking, bespectacled, young man in his twenties, a child-model of a boy, about the same age as Small Child and a formidable mountain of a granny with greying hair and a steely glint in her eye.

Tory Monarchist announces loudly that she's detected a strange smell coming from their house and cool drummer winks knowingly in a very un-Christian manner at Clementine and mouths 'weed' to her, making her blush.

Mr High Heels smiles, casually adjusting the strap on his glittery handbag.

'I think we'd know if there was a drugs cartel on our doorstop.'

The High Priest nods in agreement.

'Oh yes. In fact, I recognise the aroma. It's nothing illegal - just ginger and ginseng tea, I believe. Delicious stuff. I used to drink it all the time when I was a soldier in the Qing dynasty.'

'Yes, refreshing,' my father announces unexpectedly.

Tory Monarchist adjusts her pearls and looks pointedly at Small Child's sticky face.

'Well, we'll soon find out if they're respectable or not. I've invited them along, of course, but they've yet to turn up, which is a shame, as *someone*'s already eaten all the scones and cream.'

Also, yet to turn up are the child-free Bigs. They reside on the opposite side of the street in a big detached house, which takes up the same space as all our terraces put together. They have a big garden with two big white dogs, the size of polar bears and with barks louder than your average house alarm. They drive several big cars, which makes Boy Scout weep in jealousy, and they obviously earn big money. Rumour has it that they're big players in the Asian electronics market but thankfully, they also have big hearts and bring big contributions to any neighbourly gathering.

As if on cue, they arrive, pulling behind them a big trailer full of cold beer and quality wine. Human Dynamo whizzes alongside them, baby now draped around her neck, tempting them with trays of sausage rolls or bowls of trifle. The Bigs wave away all offers of food and in big voices apologise for their late arrival and announce they want to introduce us to some special guests.

Mr Big turns round to reveal the Triad.

'I'd like to introduce you all to Changming, the nephew of my business partner in China. And this is his younger cousin and their grandmother who'll be staying in Sheffield for a while.'

Grandmother, a formidable-looking Asian matriarch, barks out an order in military Mandarin and both grandsons pale and bow politely.

Changming greets us in impeccable English.

'I'm so honoured to be here, Madam. My uncle's a huge fan of Sheffield.'

Tory Monarchist looks surprised.

'Really? Most foreigners have only ever heard of London or Manchester.'

'Oh no, this city's very famous to us. My grandmother loves football. She's always reminding us that Sheffield's the birthplace of that great sport. And, of course, we know how kind and funny the people of Sheffield are. Grandmother's already made a friend here, despite her lack of English. Ah, in fact here he is now.'

Changming bows to my father who looks sheepish as Grandmother waves an enthusiastic 'Ni hao' in his direction.

'Dad, can I have a word?' - I mutter in his ear.

'Later,' my father replies, making a speedy exit.

Changming continues - 'And many of my countrymen come to study at your prestigious universities. That's why I've enrolled on a course here.'

'Well that's lovely to hear!' enthuses Tory Monarchist. 'Are you in the electronics business, like our neighbours then?'

'Ah, no. That's my uncle's main interest. He loves music and, in fact, he revolutionised the way we listened to it in our country. That's how he became a wealthy man and could afford to give me a good education and now send my young cousin to study here to become a fluent English speaker. But me, I've always been more interested in the hospitality and catering industry. I like the fact that here in the UK, you eat such a range of food - Italian, Asian, Mexican and so on.'

Tory Monarchist is unimpressed - 'Well, young man, some folk enjoy international cuisine but, as for myself, I'm a traditionalist. *British* food is what I'm used to and, if it's good enough for *Her Majesty*, then it's good enough for me.'

'Ah, the Queen,' says Changming - 'my grandmother's a great fan of your royalty. She even has a photograph of my uncle with your Prince Charles and Princess Diana. He met them once on a royal visit.'

Despite herself, Tory Monarchist is impressed by this news.

'Oh, how marvellous! I've always wanted to meet nobility in person. Maybe your grandmother would be interested in seeing my collection of commemorative royal wedding plates?'

'I'm sure she'd be delighted. Her English is limited, like my cousin's, but she can get by, can't you, Grandmother?'

As if on cue, Granny Triad bows her huge bulk solemnly several times.

'Oh yes. Queen we love. Charles no good. But son and Kate very ok and children so cute.'

Tory Monarchist flushes with hard-to-conceal pleasure and leads Mrs Triad away towards her precious trove of regal memorabilia.

In the meantime the Musical Christian children have politely introduced themselves to the youngest Triad, ignoring the sobbing denials from Clementine as her siblings and Small Child dance round, singing mercilessly.

'She loves him. She loves him not.'

Human Dynamo whirls past again, throwing the now sleeping baby into the air for Sensible Health Visitor to catch and offloads a plate of beautifully crafted, golden triangles into my hand.

'Sorry, got to dash. Two more parties to get to, then off to Chicago on the red eye for my meeting tomorrow. Just hand these triangles round, won't you? They're absolutely delicious.'

I look down at the plate in my hand. Those triangles look familiar. Surely they're not… I take a bite out of one. They bloody well are - it's only my special flapjacks handcrafted to look beyond enticing!

Just then English Rose spots me and comes over anxiously.

'What do you think? Are they the real deal? Do they taste as good as yours? I've been practising every day but I need your expert opinion.'

I bite back the opinion that she's aced the recipe and massively improved the presentation and sow a seed of doubt instead.

'Yeah, I think you've almost got it right. Maybe the baking tin I use makes a slight difference…'

English Rose takes my comment seriously.

'Oh yes, you could be right. I used a non-stick tin. I'll try the next batch in a stainless steel one, like you use. Thanks so much for the feedback.'

'It has to be *Sheffield* steel though, remember.'

Feeling a little guilty, I make my excuses and go off in search of my father who's vanished into thin air. Small Child is also nowhere to be seen. Typical! He's probably being anti-social and gone off on his own again. But then I hear happy laughter from the garden and look outside where I spot the smiling faces of my younger son and Little Triad, hanging upside down from a bough. They have no language in common but they've bonded over tree-climbing.

Eventually, the get-together comes to an end. I wake up the Exhausted Parents, who declare this to be the 'best party ever' until reunited with their now fully alert and squawking infant. Then I intercept Tory Monarchist, still only midway through her tour of royal plates, and thank her for her hospitality before dragging Small Child away from his new Triad chum.

Back home, rugby's over, Devil Teen's back in front of his Play Station and Delightful Daughter's still surgically attached to her phone.

Boy Scout looks up tentatively. He's aware he must be on his best behavior to make amends for not accompanying me.

'Did you have a good time, son?'

'Yeah, dad, I made a new friend. But he doesn't speak much English. And Grandad's best friends with his granny.'

Boy Scout looks at me confused.

I tell him - 'Yes, now we know where Dad's *little walks* were taking him.'

Devil Teen looks up briefly from the screen.

'Good on you both. Mum will be dead proud. She loves inviting weird foreigners round!'

Delightful Daughter peels herself momentarily off her mobile and laughs.

'Yeah, specially at Christmas. Most *normal* people invite their relatives round then but, as Mum's definitely *not normal,* she always fills the house with strangers who can't communicate with us.'

'Oh yes,' agrees Devil Teen - 'Do you remember miming the entire Nativity story to that Iranian guy, and the Albanian student who asked you to pass the *jam* when he meant the cranberry sauce?'

'How could I forget? All those endless question games we played round the table. And the Venezuelan dentist who wouldn't let us open the tin of chocolates because she said they were *bad for your teeth.*'

I feel hurt. After all, I've made the decision to dump my spiritual introspection for quality time with loved ones and this is how they're treating me. Even the *voices* are kinder to me than my own family!

'You're a hopeless case but you try hard.'

'You should've instilled your values in your children!'

'Forget your family. Put yourself first for once!'

I defend myself.

218

'That's right, go ahead and mock me! But at least it's given you some insight into other cultures and made special occasions more about opening your hearts than opening presents. I just think it's important to look after those around you and to get involved with your neighbours. That's why you should all have come along today. You've obviously got no sense of community!'

Delightful Daughter looks up indignantly.

'Well, I was busy looking after my *chat group community*, Mum.'

Devil Teen grunts, massacring his friends on screen with a machete.

'And I was involved with my *gaming community*.'

Boy Scout suggests hopefully - '*Sporting rugby community?*'

I sigh in frustration. I've already given up on enlightenment. Now I feel like giving up on my family too!

28

Friends United

I have the shopping basket of a woman on the edge - a copy of *Celebrity Snippets* magazine, a bumper selection of chocolates and a bottle of cheap wine. The shop assistant looks at me with sympathy, nodding at the contents.

'Oh, it's one of *those days*, is it?'

Yes, indeed it is.

Since giving up my *quest,* life's taken a nose dive. I feel completely empty - a shell of my former self. I'm just going through the motions because there's no bloody point to any of it, is there? We're born. We battle through life. Every now and then we're thrown a crumb of hope - a soulmate, a true love, an innocent baby, a feeling of making a difference. But then it's all snatched away - no rhyme or reason to it. Let's purge the good folk with a tragedy, a natural disaster or a fatal illness that doesn't qualify for the latest drugs. And let's leave behind the profiteers, the bloodsuckers and the mass murderers to languish in comfortable cells at public expense. Yes, that makes sense!

There's no point to any of it! I have a husband who doesn't give a damn about me, kids who barely register my presence and friends who are too wrapped up in their own dramas to care about mine.

Perhaps I shouldn't have given away all my books to Oxfam, packed away my precious stones or cut out the meditation completely? But I couldn't carry on fooling myself any longer. There's no enlightenment at the end of the road - just a black void of desolation, a pit of darkness, an abyss of despair. The only reason I'm still on this earth is my cowardice.

Yes, the light's definitely short-circuited and there's only one way to reconnect it. Goodbye crystals. Hello Cadburys. Out with the mindful therapies and in with the Maltesers. Move over relaxation techniques and make way for Rioja and reality TV to distract me from my dark thoughts.

I put on my pyjamas and red dragon dressing gown. There's no one home to judge me. Boy Scout's off on another of his weekly jollies at the Holiday Inn. Small Child's at a *Sleep-yourself-sick-with-exhaustion-and-e-numbers-Over* with his new best friend, Little Triad, and the big kids have gone AWOL. But I'm past caring, unless Government authorities knock on the door.

You see, Teen Devil's right. All that self-help rubbish is nonsense. Every time I feel I'm getting closer to being a kinder, less judgmental person then something will happen at work or at home to turn me into a screaming harridan. Every time I feel I'm starting to live mindfully, in the moment, I'll suddenly realise I've driven half way home with no recollection of the journey. Every time I feel the awareness is right at my fingertips, it slips from my grasp, so that I'm left wondering if it's always been an illusion.

So what's the point of striving for self-improvement when I so evidently suck at it and the scientific evidence is stacked against it? Better to just give in and switch on to the latest episode of *Celebrity Sandcastles*.

The voices are delighted with my decision.

'Yeah, you sucked at all that stuff!'

'That's right. You should concentrate on family life now.'

'Or maybe have an adventure of your own?'

But then the phone rings. It's Zen-Mother, excited about her good-news website.

'Have you watched that podcast I forwarded?'

I put the corkscrew down reluctantly and with one eye still on the now muted TV, I mumble through a mouthful of chocolate.

'Errrr, which one do you mean? The one where the Franciscan monk explains how Christianity and Eastern religions aren't so different? Or the one where meditation and prayer are compared?'

I note with satisfaction that the celebrity sandcastles are pretty much alike in their lack of originality.

'No, the one about the law of attraction. It's amazing.'

'Really?'

I'm unconvinced by her enthusiasm, although the law of attraction is obviously playing out on the screen with Handsome Himbo making seductive eyes at Buxom Bimbo.

It's time to confess.

'To be honest, I'm not in the mood for any of this right now. I'm taking a break from self-improvement and soul-searching. In fact I've packed it in altogether. I've come to the conclusion it's all hocus-pocus.'

I'm hoping to cut the conversation short as the celebrities are now being shown the errors of their engineering efforts by a professional sand sculptor. But, undeterred by my lackluster response, Zen Mother continues with her spiritual sales spiel.

'Nooooo! You can't give up now. That's what I love about you - you're always open to new ideas. You're always questioning things. Look, you're just having a blip. We all do that. You can't go back to sleepwalking through life! There's got to be more to it than work, home and reality TV. Look, just watch the clip about the law of attraction. It's incredible. You put out positive thoughts and the energy they create attracts whatever you're focusing on into your life.'

'Hmm. Well, I've been putting out positive thoughts for a long time now to change my attitude, my job and my life but much good it's done me. Number One Son's right - it's all a load of rubbish. See, I'm still hopelessly flawed and unenlightened. Mindfulness makes my head ache. My work sucks. The meaning of life will forever elude me. My family take me for granted. And my friends don't care.'

I shout petulantly down the phone, then let out an uncharitable cheer as Ancient C-Lister's painstakingly created turret tumbles into the sea. My less-than-perfect-self sniggers with satisfaction as Buxom Bimbo's beautifully brushed sand bridge collapses, scoring her 'nul points' but a sympathetic, slightly flirtatious, look from Himbo.

Zen Mother's suspicious.

'Why are you cheering? You're watching Celebrity Sandcastles, aren't you?'

'Well, yes I am. I'm allowed to now I've given up mindfulness in favour of mindlessness. But it sounds rather like you are watching it too. And you've got no excuse!'

'Okay, I admit it. I'm not perfect either and to be honest this show is so bad it's good! But, look, your friends *do* care. *I* care! You're obviously having one of those days. It happens to us all. Give yourself a break and veg out by all means, but don't get sucked into inertia for too long. And remember, you *do* have friends and we all think you're great. But not as great as that fortress that footballer's wife's just built.'

And with that she rings off, leaving me to admire the awesome architectural prowess of a WAG.

I'm about to turn up the sound and pour myself a glass of red when my tablet pings and I see a message from my old comrade, Vanya, in Russia.

- You've been on my mind a lot lately. Even when distance separates us, our friendship is strong enough to survive.

Ah, that's nice. He usually only messages at New Year. I open another bar of chocolate and settle down to watch the second stage of the show, where celebrities go head to head to create the most perfect sand angel in the fastest time.

The tablet pings again with another message from Vanya.

- Great news! I've finally got a visa to come to the UK. I'll be over to visit you next summer.

Well, that's unexpected. But it'll be fine, I'm sure. Just today's not the time to sort it out. As I click off Messenger, I notice a new friend request in my Skype account. It's a name from my distant past. A name I last spoke in India. Could it be…? Is it…? Surely not…? Today seems to be the day where past meets present.

223

And for now, thank heavens, I have control of the present moment, courtesy of live pause TV. The sand angels will just have to wait, as, without thinking, I press the *accept friend* button and moments later a slightly older but still familiar face appears on the screen.

It's the Enigma!

I shriek in excited amazement.

'Oh, my life! Is it really you?'

The Enigma replies with his unchanged unflappability.

'Well obviously. But the question is - is it really you - I scarcely recognise you!'

I'm hoping he means in a good way but the expression on his face suggests otherwise.

'How on Earth did you find me?'

I gasp in astonishment, sending spittle flying everywhere.

The Enigma smiles with the patience reserved for a small child.

'Erm, the Internet?'

'Sure, sure, of course. Duh!'

I gabble on, suddenly aware of my podgy, dishevelled appearance. I wish now I'd taken time to prepare properly for this chat. Too late now though. I'll just have to disarm him by going on the offence, with a full-blown interrogation of what he's been up to for the last twenty-odd years.

As we chat, I learn that after we parted ways he continued travelling and ended up in Australia, where he opened a shop in Sydney selling exotic instruments from around the world. He married a local girl and has five children of his own.

'Wow, five kids! Just like your family growing up then?'

'Mmm, yes, only with a mother instead of the holy sisters ... '

I gulp at my mistake, remembering his Spartan upbringing and Scary Nun's soulless soup. But he continues unperturbed - 'It's fine. It all worked out alright. That's part of the reason for contacting you. Our eldest son's planning on a gap year and it made me think of you.'

Oh Lord! My mind races from Delhi to Kashmir, Varanasi and back, wondering what misdemeanors he's about to bring up from my past. He coughs in his endearingly stiff-upper-lipped way.

'Yes, well. I just needed to tell you that travelling to India with you changed my life.'

Oh my God, please don't let this be a declaration of unrequited love! Although, on the other hand, it wouldn't be totally unsurprising and would obviously be an ego boost that I could use to my advantage with Boy Scout. But this high opinion of my own attractiveness is mercilessly dashed as The Enigma continues.

'You know, I thought I was in love with you but I soon realised I'd had a lucky escape. My God, you would've driven me mad. Your incessant enthusiasm about everything totally freaked me out and your frenetic energy was exhausting. I'm so glad I didn't return with you or I'd never have met my wife.'

'Yes, well, that's lovely. Thank you for sharing.'

The Enigma carries on, unaware of my finger poised over the *end conversation* button.

'Yes, but even though you were really hard work to travel with, what you told me about my mother was a game changer. You made me understand that she left us because she was ill, not because she didn't care. So, I just wanted to say *thank you* for that. It made a huge difference to me. It meant I was able to forgive both her and myself. And in a way, you're right - I've repeated history with five children of my own. But I was lucky. I was able to support my wife and be there for her in a way my father never knew how to.'

Goodness! I can barely remember saying those words and yet they obviously had a huge impact. I spend a few minutes basking in this heady feeling of power, amazed that somewhere inside me there once was a wise woman, who obviously decided to jump ship and stay on in India.

But then I'm brought rudely back into the moment by The Enigma, who's asking a question.

'So, that's agreed then? He'll arrive at Manchester airport next summer. He's got a working visa, and hopes to get a job so you won't need to host him for too long. Anyway, thanks awfully. Delightful talking to you. Cheerio now.'

I nod in confusion, as The Enigma vanishes from the screen. It appears we'll be having another foreign visitor to look forward to.

I groan inwardly, wondering how I'm going to explain away a twenty-something Australian and a middle-aged Russian to Boy Scout. But before I can get my thoughts together, the doorbell rings. Oh my God, the older two! What have they done now? Please don't let it be the Police or the Social Services.

With trepidation I open the door to discover Bubbly Brazilian and English Rose with a bottle of wine apiece and what appears to be a child's sand-set in their hands. They barge their way into my living room, where Bubbly Brazilian lets out a delighted shriek as she sees the long-frozen image of Celebrity Sandcastles.

She shouts triumphantly at English Rose.

'You see, my dahleeng, I told you she was avoiding us because she's addicted to that rubbish.'

English Rose looks at me apologetically.

'Sorry for the invasion. But we were concerned about you. We haven't seen you for a couple of weeks. You haven't seemed yourself lately and you haven't posted any of your usual upbeat messages. Is it ok if we stop for a while? We have things to celebrate.'

'Well sure,' I say, unfreezing the screen to see Buxom Bimbo out-sand-angel Himbo and be crowned *Queen of the Castle*. Then I remember Bubbly Brazilian - I've been so wrapped up in myself I'd forgotten she was due her results back. I look at her questioningly.

'Ah yes, my dahleeng! I went back to the specialist yesterday. I've been given the all-clear. I just have to go back for annual checks because of my family history, but they're routine, so I can relax finally - thanks to Iemanjá and the NHS!'

'That's brilliant news,' I say. 'We should go out properly nearer Christmas and have a big celebration. I never get to go out in December as my scrooge of a husband says it's over-rated and over-priced.'

'We should go to *Fusion 3*,' says English Rose pointedly, looking at Bubbly Brazilian.

'I know, my dahleeng, you're desperate to come to the opening night. But I've told you already, I've only got *two* complimentary tickets but I have *three* good friends! You'll just have to draw lots or get in to the final of the Radio Hallam competition.'

'What are you on about?' I ask - 'What competition?'

'Well, my dahleeng, Big John at Breakfast did an interview with the main owner of the restaurant. He's French apparently, but has a high-profile Asian partner backing him. Anyway, it turns out one of the reasons he chose Sheffield as his new venue was its reputation for producing amazing desserts.'

I'm flabbergasted.

'Really? Amazing stainless steel I can understand, but amazing desserts?'

English Rose looks exasperated.

'Honestly, you work at the college. Don't you eat in their restaurant? It's incredible. The catering department has a world class reputation, producing 5-star chefs. This French guy obviously knows his stuff. Anyway, Radio Hallam's running yet another competition to design a signature dessert for the opening night. And I've decided to enter. So, tell me what you think of these.'

She opens a tupperware box and brings out an assortment of golden triangles.

'Is that my flapjack recipe you're using?'

'Well, yes, but I've added a different twist to each triangle. Go on, try them and tell me what you think.'

227

I'm about to tell English Rose exactly what I think but then I see the excitement on her face - she's so passionate about her baking - and to be honest I'm interested to see what she's done to the recipe.

Bubbly Brazilian delivers her verdict.

'Well, my dahleeng, the orange blossom's delightful, the cranberry sauce's very Christmasy and the coriander's *interesting*. But in my opinion, you shouldn't tamper with the original.'

'It's true,' I agree -'You can't improve it but you definitely *present* it better. So if you want to enter with my family's original recipe then give it a go. But *flapjack* as a *dessert*? Are you sure? It's more of a *snack*.'

'That's where you need *vision,'* says English Rose, thoughtfully.

'I'm thinking... Mmm... Yes! The original version with Chantilly cream and a hint of ...'

'*Fire*?' I add with a sense of déjà vu

'Oooh, now you're talking!'

'Look, my dahleeng, just get through to the final then we can *all* go to Fusion 3's opening night. But for now there's celebration, Sauvignon and sand...'

Two hours and several bottles of wine later, the lounge looks like a beach hit by a tropical storm and the winner of the sand competition is declared to be Bubbly Brazilian for her impressive sculpture of the Christ the Redeemer.

As she does a victory circuit of the sofa, the door opens and in fall my older offspring, somewhat the worse for wear. Devil Teen's carrying a bucket of wilting flowers that look suspiciously as if they've been pinched from outside a garage. Delightful Daughter sees my quizzical expression.

'Don't ask! You don't need to know! But we just wanted to cheer you up and tell you that, even if we take the mickey out of you, we *do* appreciate you, Mum. *Don't* we?'

She elbows Devil Teen in the ribs and, surveying the Mediterranean mess in front of him, he grunts - 'Yeah, of course we do, Mother.'

'Well, the gesture's definitely appreciated. Thank you both. Have you had a nice evening out?'

Delightful Daughter smiles mischievously.

'Oh yes, mum. We bumped into my old friend, Jess, down at the Leadmill, so *some* of us had a *really nice* time, didn't we, little, big bruv?'

Devil Teen flushes.

'Yeah, it was a good night out, Mother. Anyway, I think I'll leave you, er *adults,* and head up to bed now.'

English Rose sighs wistfully, 'Ah, wish mine were so appreciative.'

In bed that night I reflect on the evening's events.

How quickly we can fall into despair, feeling we've lost our way. It's so easy to give up when life gets hard. But maybe there's something to be said about the law of attraction after all? Just when we're at our lowest ebb, positivity bounces back in many ways. Small, kind words can produce unexpected changes. And castles in the air can sometimes turn into castles in the sand.

But that doesn't mean I'm going on a spiritual treasure hunt again, whatever Zen Mother might think. No, instead, I'm changing my quest for enlightenment into a quest for more *fun* in life. If Boy Scout can't be bothered to take me out and romance me anymore, then I'm just going to have more nights out with the girls on my own.

29

Family Fortunes

Just when I'm used to Boy Scout ignoring me, he starts paying me attention. For some reason he's worrying about me.

'Are you alright my lovely? Just you've been a bit grumpy lately. Probably *that time of life*, isn't it? Would you like a lift down to the church or Buddhist centre?'

'For Heaven's sake,' I reply - 'I'm not menopausal. And I've told you before, I've given all that stuff up. Just get out of the way of the telly. You're blocking my view of *Clean for your Life.*'

'Alright. No need to snap, isn't it? Just thought some of that medication might do you good.'

'It's medi*tation* and it sucks! You can bring me another glass of wine though. That's all the *medication* I need!'

He sighs but he's not giving up.

'I think you've probably had enough wine, my lovely. Here's a nice cup of liquorice and mint tea instead. And I've bought you a copy of that *Power of the Light* magazine.'

I can't deny he's trying hard. But it's too little too late. I don't know why I feel so cross all the time. It probably *is* my hormones, although deep down, the now-banished, wise woman's shaking her head in disagreement.

I decide to test how serious his commitment is to me.

'Our Bev's coming over tomorrow for a pre-Christmas visit to exchange presents. You'll be here, won't you?'

He pales and burbles excuses about having to take a client out. Bloody typical. All talk and no action. He never makes the effort with my sister.

I have a flashback to my student days, studying Russian literature, where the great writer, Tolstoy, proclaimed - *All happy families are alike. Each unhappy family is unhappy in its own way.* In essence, in order to be happy, he implied a family must be successful in a range of criteria, such as money matters, parenting, religion and extended family.

Is it any wonder then that I feel miserable? I'm forced to earn money for my ungrateful kids. My parenting skills are, at best, inadequate. Religion is, by necessity, a banned topic, and relatives are a test of patience!

The next day Our Bev arrives with photos of her feline friends and fascinating information about the difference between a whip and a crop. As usual, I zone out.

'Typical, you're not listening, Squirt! And by the way, when will you learn to make a decent cup of tea? Never mind. *I'll do it my way.*'

And even though I'm now a middle-aged matron, I revert to my subservient role of younger sister and meekly agree, that unlike my superior sibling, I can't cook, clean or sing.

And this is one of the issues with family relationships - we're conditioned from an early age to stick with the attributes we've been assigned in our personal genetic soap opera. We can be either *pretty* or *intelligent, fat* or *sporty, funny* or *serious* but not both. These aren't minor roles either - they'll define us for life. If the character of *charming, successful, future banker* has already been taken, then we must audition for another part.

Our Bev, being the elder, got first pick and went with *practical, musical, animal lover.* So, as there were no handed-down cookery tips, singing lessons or family pets left for me, I opted for *clever, athletic, people pleaser.*

In senior school there was that brief moment of rebellion when I auditioned disastrously for the school choir and, in revenge, she took up cross-country for a week. But it was doomed to failure, as everyone knew she was the singer and I was the runner. So, we gave up and accepted the way things were.

In my own parenting I've tried to avoid this stereotyping, offering Devil Teen guitar lessons to go with Delightful Daughter's clarinet tuition, whilst buying *her* racing games so she can compete with him on the PlayStation.

Devil Teen despairs of me.

'Oh mother, you should know by now that she only likes *making* music and I only like *listening* to it.'

And sadly, Delightful Daughter agrees with him for once.

'Yes, Mum. Whilst I applaud your PC thinking, I can't see the point of driving round and round a track.'

As for Small Child, he's his own person, uninfluenced by his parents' views and family stereotyping. This is, of course, due primarily to benign neglect. His elder siblings only pay attention to him when they're feeling kind, and ignore him when they're not, whilst we, his elderly parents, are too exhausted to keep up with him. Thank goodness then that, finally, he's found a real friend.He and Little Triad are now inseparable. They build huge Lego cities together, climb trees and dangle precariously off the bannisters.

Today though, I've told Small Child he's got to stay in to see his auntie and, judging by the shriek and the sound of a breaking mug, Our Bev's just found him. I rush into the kitchen to see what's happened.

'The little horror was hiding under the table. He caught me unawares. Honestly, give me a houseful of cats any day!'

'What were you doing under there, giving Aunty Bev a fright?' I ask Small Child.

'I'm a pirate and I've made a den to hide my bounty! I've already got some Chinese treasure but I don't know what it is. I thought it was an old-fashioned phone but there are no numbers to press. It's got a head set too. Is it one of those *walkie-talkies*? It's got a *stop* and *play* button and a funny door that opens and closes and a weird, oblong, plastic disc thing inside. It looks really old. What is it, mum? Do *you* know?'

Before I have chance to reply, Our Bev's swept it away from him.

'Oh, would you look at this. What a blast from the past! It's a Walkman.'

'A *walking man*?' Small Child repeats in confusion.

'No, little Squirt - a *Walkman*. Although it's not a genuine one. It looks like a knock-off Chinese version. It plays music on the cassette - that oblong disc. See, if you press here and put the headphones on, you can listen to music.'

She presses the button and Small Child's amazed as a tinny-sounding version of *Walk like an Egyptian* belts out.

'That was my wedding present to your mum and day. They took it on honeymoon… and got robbed! Ah, that was when they were *in love*. Perhaps, I'll get a replacement for their Silver Wedding next year?'

'That's if we're still together by then!' I mutter, turning back to Small Child. 'Where did you find it, anyway?'

'At my friend's house. His uncle invented it. That's how he got rich. It looks a bit lame though and the music is pants.'

'Well, in our day it was cutting-edge technology. But, you're the generation of digital natives, so it probably does look like an ancient artefact to you. Anyway, you've seen Aunty Bev now, so maybe it's safer if you take this Walkman back and hang out with your friend for a bit.'

'Great, can I take a football too? His Granny's teaching us how to do *keepy-uppies* so I can impress Grandad.'

Small Child whips on his shoes and leaves the house, just as Delightful Daughter walks back in from her lunchtime shift and Devil Teen walks back in from goodness-knows-where.

'Hi Aunty Bev. How are you?'

Our Bev transforms into James Brown and belts out her reply.

'I feel good. I knew that I would now!'

Both children smile - they're used to Our Bev and her stage-musical way of carrying out a conversation, so when she launches into

Tom Jones' '*What's new, pussy cats?*' they give her a quick update of their lives.

Then, in turn, Our Bev informs them in detail about all her cats and every horse at the stables. So, it's to their great relief when the doorbell goes and the Mothers' Musketeers barge into the kitchen, all trying to tell me their news at the same time.

'My dahleeng, she's through!'

'Yes, I'm through! Thank you, thank you, flapjack recipe!'

'Yes, thank goodness, she's through! We can all go now. I was going to pretend I wasn't bothered and let you others go, but I'm secretly glad we've *all* got tickets.'

Our Bev has no idea what they're talking about, so channels her inner Spice Girl.

'*Woah! Stop right now, thank you very much!* What's all this about?'

The girls stop mid-sentence and I jump in to explain.

'I'm guessing our culinary genius has made it through to the final of the Radio Hallam's *Design a dessert* competition and has bagged herself a place at the opening night of the new, super-duper Fusion 3 restaurant next Saturday? Which means that because our Brazilian bestie is dancing in the show, she also gets to take two friends with her to watch her strut her stuff. Which means we all get to hang out with the big wigs, have a free, 5-star meal and a family-free, fun night out. Yay!'

Devil Teen rolls his eyes at me.

'That's not very kind of you, mother, saying you'd rather spend time with your friends than your family.'

'Hmm and here was me wondering where *you* were earlier. I don't think you were out walking with *your family*, were you, sweetheart?'

Devil Teen blushes and goes unexpectedly quiet. Luckily, his aunt sings away the silence.

'Oooh, *food, glorious food, nothing quite like it!* Actually, I've been reading about this *Fusion 3* restaurant and the *Design a dessert* competition. There was an article about it in today's Yorkshire Post. I was going to mention it to you, Squirt, and ask if the restaurant owner had already given you VIP seats.'

'What? What are you on about?' I ask, mystified. Sometimes Our Bev is hard to follow.

Unperturbed, she reaches into her bag, brings out a crumpled edition of the paper and stabs triumphantly at a photo on the third page.

'Look, if I'm not mistaken, that's definitely the dodgy French guy who kept phoning our house wanting to marry you! And the article even says he was hoping to catch up with an *old friend* in Sheffield. That could be you, Squirt. I'd watch out if I were you - our dad was not impressed by him at all!'

Delightful Daughter's rushed over and grabbed the paper off her aunt.

'Mum, you've got a hidden past! Let's have a look. Oh my life, mum. She's right. It's an older version of the man in the photos you showed us. You know, when you were in your minimalist phase, throwing everything away?'

She hesitates suspiciously - 'Only I don't remember you binning his photos…'

'Oh, don't be ridiculous,' I say - 'of course, I did. I threw them all away when you were at work. That's why you don't remember. Anyway, can I have a look now please? I'm sure you're both deluded, anyway.'

But when the evidence is in front of me, there's no mistaking the chiselled jaw, the unforgettable profile and the still seductive eyes. It is indeed an older and possibly even more handsome version of my very own Monsieur Hôtel!

I slump down in my chair outwardly lost for words whilst inwardly the voices thunder in my head.

'Oh, he's aged a lot better than you!'

'You should tear up his photo right now!'

*'What if he **has** come looking for you?'*

My three musketeers gather round to pass judgement on the man from my past.

Bubbly Brazilian is complimentary.

'Oh, my dahleeng, he's quite a looker! Almost as handsome as the marvellous Kiki. If I were your hubby, I'd definitely watch out.'

Zen Mother advises caution.

'Well he certainly looks a charmer, but you've got a solid marriage so don't go thinking the grass is greener...'

Aware that my children are listening, I put her straight.

'Look, I don't think for one minute he's come to Sheffield to find *me*. It's just coincidence. And anyway, he'll take one look at this plump, middle-aged version of me and either not recognise me or run a mile. So, my marriage is in no danger whatsoever.'

English Rose is more pragmatic.

'So, are you going to talk to him at the opening evening? Surely it'd be strange if you didn't?'

'Well, surely it would be strange if I *did?* He might think I'm after something - when obviously I'm not. Well, obviously, I'd like to know what he's been doing for the last twenty-five years but only out of politeness, not genuine interest, obviously. Because I've hardly thought about him at all over the years, obviously...'

'Oh, but you definitely should talk to him,' says English Rose - 'As your Bev says, we might get VIP treatment. Maybe he could give us a tour of the kitchens. If he cooks as good as he looks, then I'd definitely *design a dessert* with him any day!'

Devil Teen interrupts.

'Mother, you're not going to talk to this French guy, are you? What would dad say?'

I reassure him.

'For goodness sake, this is all turning into a soap-opera. Dad won't say anything because he doesn't need to know anything, as there's, obviously, nothing to know! I'm going for a lovely night out at a new restaurant to watch one lovely friend showcase the tango in a dance spectacular and watch another lovely friend, hopefully, win a cooking competition, whilst enjoying a delicious meal with a further lovely friend. Okay? That's it! And if this former French *acquaintance* of mine happens to recognise me, then I will, obviously, exchange polite, small talk. I'll tell him how I'm happily married with a charming family and I'm sure he'll tell me about his happy marriage and charming family too. And that's that!'

Our Bev grins mischievously - 'Except, according to this article, he's never been married. Unrequited love apparently...'

'Isn't it about time you were going home, Our Bev' I remark - 'and some of you have Christmas presents to buy and *dessert designing* to perfect, whilst others have homework to finish and work to get to?'

And thankfully everyone takes the hint so for now the subject of *Monsieur Hôtel* is mercifully closed.

Later, after dinner, with Small Child safely tucked up in bed, I settle down to watch a re-run of *Cosmetic Surgery Catastrophes* when Devil Teen unexpectedly appears in the living room.

'Is it okay if I watch this with you, mother?'

'Sure, of course' I say, amazed that my older son's considering spending time with me.

We sit there in awkward silence for several minutes until I ask the forbidden *mum* question.

'Have you finished your homework then?'

There's a long pause and I can see him struggling with the answer. Then it all comes out in a stream of words.

'Actually, I think the homework's finished me off, mum... Actually, I can't bloody do any of it! In fact, I'm doing really badly at all my subjects ... I never told you but I got crap marks in all my mocks. I

237

knew you'd be so disappointed in me. Anyway, it looks like I won't be going to uni after all… In fact, maybe I don't even really want to go to university…'

He sits back in the chair looking surprised by what he's just blurted out.

I pause the programme, mid-botox-botch-job, and turn to look at my older son. Truth be told, I haven't paid proper attention to him for some time now and I can suddenly see that he's lost weight and has dark circles under his eyes. He also looks rather wretched and vulnerable and my heart goes out to him.

I take a deep breath.

'Well, that's quite some story and one that's obviously making you very miserable. What can I do to help?'

'What? You're not going to shout at me for wasting all my time on the PlayStation? Aren't you mad I'm such a failure?'

'Well, for a start, you're not a failure. You're a boy with a great brain and a sharp intelligence. Maybe you just need a little support to help you in the right direction? Exams are tough and there's a lot of pressure on students these days. So, it's no wonder you're feeling stressed. There's still time to sort things out. I can have a word with your teachers and even get you a private tutor if you think it'll help.'

'Really mum? Would you do that? It'd be expensive.'

'Of course I would. It'd be worth the money, if that's what you want. But if you decide university isn't for you, there's also plenty of other options. After all, you're very reliable and dependable. You've never let me down looking after your little brother, even though he drives you mad. With those qualities, any employer would snap you up.'

'But I thought, you thought I was just a waste of space.'

'Oh sweetheart! Whatever gave you that idea?'

'I dunno. I guess you and I haven't been getting on lately. You've been busy with college and those weird workshops you go on… And when you *are* here, you're either hanging out with big sis or doing stuff with little-poo …'

I suddenly remember that Devil Teen's *love language* is *quality time* and that he's right, I can't remember the last time we did something together.

'Oh darling, I'm sorry! I miss our cinema nights out. We should start going again - just the two of us. It's just I thought, maybe… possibly… you might have someone else now you'd prefer to hang out with rather than your old mum? You know… someone called Jess, maybe?'

He blushes and looks away for a moment as if deciding whether I'm worthy of being let in on the secret. Then he turns to me with a real passion in his voice.

'Mum, Jess is great! I really, really like her! She's down-to-earth and honest. I've always liked her since she first started hanging out here years ago. And she likes me too! It's just she thought, in the beginning that I was too young for her, although I'm nearly eighteen. And then she thought I'd be going away to uni, so there wasn't much point in us getting together. So, I thought if I failed my exams I wouldn't have to go away, would I? But then if I'm a failure she might not want to stay with me. Aaargggh! I don't know what I should do now!'

I smile, remembering my tour guiding days and the way choices eventually sorted themselves out.

'Listen sweetheart, why don't you and Jess just enjoy seeing each other for now. You don't have to sneak around anymore - she's welcome to come here, you know. And for the moment, just concentrate on doing as well as you can in your exams. You could defer university for a year or even go to one of the universities here in Sheffield, if you want. There are plenty of options, whatever results you get and whatever happens with you and Miss Green Fringe.'

Devil Teen smiles for the first time.

'It's an orange buzz-cut at the moment, actually.'

'Well, there you go. And now I think you should come and give me a hug and stop worrying. At least you haven't had a botox disaster like that girl on the telly!'

We both laugh and Devil Teen comes and sits next to me for the first time in ages.

'Muuum?' he says hesitantly.

'Yes?'

'You're not really going to hook up with that froggie bloke are you? I mean, he looks well fit from that photo and the French *do* have a reputation for romance. And our dad *has* let himself go a bit and doesn't really appreciate you like he should, does he? But you wouldn't cheat on dad, would you?'

I'm just about to answer, when the man himself, staggers through the door after his business dinner.

'*Cheating*? What's all this about cheating? Are you and your mam watching one of those ridiculous reality shows again? Who's cheating on who, my lovely?'

30

Dramatic Decisions

'You look beautiful, Squirt! Doesn't she, mum?'

'Yes, you absolutely do, young lady.'

My mother sniffs and reaches for her hanky.

'Well, there's our car coming, Beverly. Time to go. We'll see you both shortly.'

As the door closes behind them, I'm left alone in the house with my father. He looks frail but still handsome in his smart, new suit. He smiles proudly at me and quickly blows his nose to hide any unwanted emotions.

'Time flies. Only yesterday you were stealing apples from the greengrocer's…'

I'm about to remind him of other less delinquent memories of me, when the phone starts ringing harshly. My father looks at me pleadingly.

'Don't answer. Not today!'

But the ringing's incessant and demands a reply. My father shrugs and leaves the room as I lift the receiver off the hook.

'It's not too late, mon amour! Don't do this to me! I'll give you anything you want! You can 'ave the life of your dreams 'ere with me in Lyon.'

It's Monsieur Hôtel again. He's phoned every day since I got back to England and the story's always the same - come back to France, marry him, set up a chain of international restaurants and travel the world together in luxury. It's a tempting offer and one that part of me feels is foolish to refuse. But another man has a hold on my heart and he's been waiting patiently for me for a long time.

So, today I have a decision to make. But what if I choose wrongly? As I'm bombarded with declarations of undying love and promises of a perfect future, my resolve starts to waver. My father pokes his head round the door and points dramatically at his watch. I shake my head uncertainly and he sighs and disappears again.

What should I do? What should I do?

And then, the door opens again and, completely out of character, my father strides towards me, wrenches the phone from my hand and shouts down the line.

'That's enough now, my lad. Give up! You had your chance. You blew it. It's too late!'

And then he slams the phone back down, cutting off the call.

I look at my father in disbelief.

'Dad, why on earth did you do that?'

'Well, love, it's true. He's had his chance. He's all words and no action! If he meant what he said, he'd have been here in person long ago.'

'But he's very busy running a hotel. It's not that easy.'

'Listen, love, it *is* that easy. This Frenchie's full of drama and romance. It's exciting but it's not real. Not solid. Won't last. What you need is what's waiting for you. It might not be perfume and poetry but it's reliable and loyal and lasting. You know that deep down, which is why you're all dressed up now. Both me and your mother think you've made the right choice but if you're in any doubt, then we can just stay here. No need to get in that car. It's your decision.'

I don't think I've ever heard my father make such a long speech in his life and I sink down into a chair in shock. Just then the doorbell goes and my father returns with a beautifully wrapped package addressed to me.

I open it with trembling hands. Inside there's a single, exquisite red rose and a message written in Boy Scout's neat handwriting - 'I can't wait to spend the rest of my life with you. You are the light of my life.'

And I realise, of course, that my father is right. It's too late for Monsieur Hôtel. It was always too late. My heart's always known the truth. I look at the rose and smile.

'Come on, dad. Get me to the church on time!'

31

Well Tackled

It's Saturday evening and preparations for Fusion 3's grand opening are well under way.

On Bubbly Brazilian's insistence, I've spent the day being humiliated at a beauty salon, but the results are astonishing. My legs are now smoother, my skin looks fresher and my nails have been given a professional polish. And with the help of an industrial strength corset and two pairs of Spanx, I've succeeded in redistributing the fat from my stomach to create - even if I say so myself - quite an eye-catching, hour-glass figure. Coupled with a newly purchased, flattering 50s style, scarlet dress, I reckon that at least I won't let the side down.

As I teeter down the stairs on high heels I haven't worn for years, Small Child does a double-take.

'Mummy! You look like a film star! Hey everyone, come and look at mum! She's sooo beautiful!'

Delightful Daughter raises her eyes from her phone.

'Wow mum! You're rocking your inner Marilyn Monroe. Are you sure dad doesn't have anything to worry about?'

'Don't be silly, sweetheart. But I've got to make an effort, haven't I? I don't want to ruin the photos for the others.'

Devil Teen looks up from his PlayStation.

'Mother, you *do* look amazing! But, honestly, I don't think it's a good idea for you to go out. Won't dad be upset if he knows that French guy is going to be there?'

'Your dad's not even back from watching the rugby yet. And he's recorded the international to watch this evening, so he won't even notice I'm not here!'

At that moment, Boy Scout comes through the door earlier than expected, walks obliviously past me and proceeds to give Devil Teen a detailed post-mortem of the match. I sigh in frustration that I'm so invisible to him and go back upstairs to fetch my bag.

As I'm coming down the stairs for a second time, Boy Scout appears in the hallway and catches sight of me. In an almost comical, cartoon fashion, his jaw drops open.

'Bloody hell! Is that you, my lovely?'

'Yes, it bloody well is! Now if you don't mind moving, I've got to go out in a few minutes.'

'Go out? Looking like that? Where are you going? Who are you going with? Why aren't I going with you?'

'You're watching the international and I'm going out to support my friends at the opening of this new restaurant.'

'What? You're going out looking like that? Without me?'

Devil Teen adds fuel to the fire.

'Yeah dad, she's going to that fancy, new restaurant run by her ex-French boyfriend, who's still got a thing for her, and come to Sheffield to find her.'

'You snitch!' gasps Delightful Daughter, watching her father's face turn pale.

Boy Scout's mouth is opening and closing like a gold fish struggling for breath.

'What, that bloody French hotelier is still chasing you after all these years? How did he even know where to find you? Why have you kept all this a secret from me? Or is that why you've been acting so strangely recently?'

I attempt to calm down the situation.

'Look, stop making a big deal about this. It's not a secret. I just haven't got round to telling you. I only found out last week that it *is* that French guy but he doesn't even know I'm going tonight. It's a coincidence. We probably won't even speak to each other. He's simply opening a restaurant here and as my lovely Brazilian friend's doing a tango as part of the show we've got free tickets to the opening night.'

'Well, I don't want you to go, isn't it?'

'Don't be ridiculous! Of course I'm going. I can't let my friends down.'

'Oh, is that right? Or is it Monsieur 'steal people's wives away' that you don't want to let down?'

'Seriously! I'm not having this conversation with you right now. Look you're sopping wet from the game. Go and get changed and we'll talk later, when I get back.'

Luckily the doorbell goes and I escape to the waiting taxi outside.

Zen Mother's here already, serene in a simple, white shift dress. English Rose turns up shortly after, looking slim and svelte in an emerald green, Grecian style outfit that perfectly complements her chestnut hair. I sigh enviously. I used to have a figure like hers when I was younger but still, tonight, I'm quite enjoying my new-found curves.

As for Bubbly Brazilian, she's kitted out in a spangled, fuchsia, tassels-and-sequins combo, and waving enthusiastically at us from inside the taxi.

'My dahleengs, you all look divine. And as for you...' she points dramatically at me - 'you're simply bootylicious!'

I am just settling my bootylicious body into the back seat, anticipating an evening of fun, when there's a rapping at the window and I look out to see the thunderous face of Boy Scout mouthing something I can't hear, and waving a crumpled piece of paper at me.

Oh my God, what can he want? I open the window slightly and catch his ranting.

'Oh yes, my lovely. No secrets, is it? That dress tells another story. You scarlet woman! What's this photo in your bedside drawer? Does that French chancer think he'll have better luck trying to steal my wife off me a second time? I'll give him luck! Just you wait!'

Bubbly Brazilian raises an eyebrow.

'Errm, my darling is everything alright?'

'Everything's fine,' I mutter darkly, 'drive on.'

The cab pulls up outside Fusion 3, where a red carpet's been rolled out and a queue of VIPs are waiting to make their way inside. I spot a well-known boxer, several famous musicians and a minor soap star amongst their numbers. Despite the inauspicious start to the evening, I'm looking forward to rubbing shoulders with Sheffield's elite, although rubbing shoulders with a certain French man might be a different matter…

I glance at Bubbly Brazilian, who's magically regained her voluptuous sparkle. I wonder if this is just a result of her getting the all-clear or whether romance has a part to play.

I ask her - 'Do we finally get to meet the mysterious Kiki then?'

'Oh yes, my dahleeng. He's dying to meet you all too. Especially *you* as I've told him all about your royal family scrap book. You know, the one your husband knows nothing about.'

'Well, he probably knows all about it now as he's been ransacking my bedroom drawers!'

'Oh, my dahleeng, is that why he was shouting at you in the taxi?'

'It's a long story. Basically, he's got the wrong end of the stick about this French bloke and he's a bit upset. I'll sort it all out later. But for now I'm not going to let it spoil this evening. I'm looking forward to a virtuoso dance performance from you and your Argentinian. And as for *you*, I expect fantastic results from my secret recipe and your great culinary and presentation skills!'

English Rose flushes guiltily and confesses - 'Yes, I know I probably wouldn't have got through to the final if it hadn't been for the recipe and I'm really grateful. I'm hoping it might give me a bit of publicity and be the start of a new career in catering. That'd be so amazing!'

Zen Mother is encouraging.

'In our eyes, you're already a winner anyway for getting to the final. Just enjoy your moment of fame. By the way, do you know how they're actually going to choose first prize?'

English Rose nods - 'Yes, there's going to be a tasting by the owners who will make the final decision about which dessert gets to be on the menu. Maybe *you* can put a word in for me?'

She looks pointedly at me, but I shake my head - 'I'm telling you all, there's no way I'm going to approach *that man* unless he notices me first. I'm just going to keep a low profile and enjoy the evening. My husband's already worked up enough about me going out as it is. I'm not going to make matters worse!'

As if on cue, my phone pings three times in rapid succession with messages from the kids.

- Sorry, mother. You were right. Dad didn't need to know.
- Come home mummy. Daddy's acting weird.
- Mum, ignore the boys' messages. Have a great evening!

I groan inwardly but decide to place my faith in Delightful Daughter's response, cross my fingers and hope for the best.

We finally make our way to the front of the queue, past the burly bouncers and into the restaurant itself, which is certainly different from the Pizza Express that Boy Scout usually takes me to.

All around the room, there are various potted plants and ferns, giving a slightly, tropical feel to the venue. The walls are painted in sunny, ochre-yellow and welcoming azure-blue and the floor's decked in warm, rich timber. At the front, there's a separate, slightly raised area for the dance spectacular.

Comfortable, curved chairs in a deeper shade of wood are placed around tables, crafted from Sheffield's own stainless steel, whilst tubular metallic lights, reminiscent of Chinese lanterns, hang from the ceiling. This rather bizarre combination shouldn't work on paper but somehow in reality it does, creating a fusion of Mediterranean evenings, Amazonian jungle, Asian adventures and English *cool*.

'Wow!'- English Rose exclaims - 'If this is the décor, then I can't wait to try the food!'

We're directed to a table for four.

'But where's your Kiki going to sit then?' asks English Rose.

'Here, actually, my dahleeng, I think you'll find *you* are on the *finalists'* table at the front.'

English Rose pulls a nervous face.

'Can't I stay here with you lot instead?'

'No, my dahleeng. You're with the VIPs. Seize the day and bask in the glory! We'll be supporting you from the sidelines, don't you worry.'

As English Rose reluctantly makes her way to the front, Zen Mother s sighs appreciatively - 'Oh this is a lovely secluded corner, away from the main hustle and bustle of the restaurant.'

'Well, yes, Kiki and I have to get up to dance,' says Bubbly Brazilian - 'so sitting here will cause less of a distraction and besides, it's a good location to avoid being seen, if you know what I mean?'

She smiles conspiratorially at me and I nod gratefully as I've just noticed who's sitting at the finalists' table and my heart's skipped a beat. It's no other than Monsieur Hôtel himself! And English Rose is now being seated next to him.

From my concealed spot behind a fringed palm, I take a good look at him. My God but he's aged well! Is it possible this is all down to nature, or has he had a bit of help? A slight nip and tuck maybe? And look at his hair - not a hint of grey. Definitely some Grecian 2000 going on there. I smile to myself, imagining what my Neanderthal husband would say about such an *unmanly* beauty regime.

But there's no denying Monsieur Hôtel looks great - at least ten years' younger than I do. And apparently, he still has the charm. I can see him getting out of his seat to kiss English Rose's hand as she joins the table. He's obviously complimenting her on her dress as she's blushing prettily. Still, she doesn't have a lot of competition - the other two finalists are a rather portly grandma in an unattractive, nylon sack and a tweenage girl in short socks, who's laughing hysterically at the jokes flying her way from the compere for the evening - Radio Hallam's larger than life Big John. Next to him sits a middle-aged, rather dapper, Chinese man, looking slightly bewildered by the whole proceedings.

I scan the packed restaurant, recognising a few more faces - the Lord Mayor sitting with some prominent entrepreneurs, a pitchful of overpaid footballers with their tangerine-faced WAGs, some C-list celebrities from TV and radio and … the Bigs, sitting not far away from us, with the Triads.

Changming spots me, comes over and bows politely.

'How lovely to see you here, Madam. I didn't know you were with the dancers.'

'Well we're *with* them, but not *dancing*. That's how we got tickets - because of my friend. How about you?'

'Oh, I'm here because of my uncle,' he points at the top table, 'He's in partnership with your neighbours, you know, in the electronics field. But because I'm studying Business Hospitality, he decided to go into this joint venture and open a restaurant. Eventually he wants me to help manage and expand it.'

'Wow, that's a great plan,' I say - 'I hope you'll be very successful. I'm certainly looking forward to trying the food.'

And at that very moment, the starters arrive at our table - dim sum stuffed with olive tapenade, bhajis made of onions and refried beans and a selection of garlic and chili dipping sauces. It's a definite amalgamation of tastes but the overall effect's really appetizing. As we tuck in, Big John announces the first dance routine - a Bollywood bonanza that morphs effortlessly into a Chinese dragon performance.

Zen Mother's impressed and says as much to Bubbly Brazilian.

'Very clever. The choreography was superb. Your Kiki's definitely a professional. I don't think we've seen anything like that in Sheffield before! Will it be your turn to dance soon?'

'Oh yes, my dahleeng. That's why I've just been picking at the starters. I'm feeling rather nervous. I'm the only amateur dancer here tonight but Kiki reckons I've got natural rhythm and we've certainly been rehearsing enough, so hopefully, I won't let him down.'

'Yes, you certainly *have* been rehearsing a lot with him, haven't you?' remarks Zen Mother.

'All strictly platonic, my dahleeng. Just like you and Luke's dad.'

Bubbly Brazilian winks at me and Zen Mother's cheeks redden as she makes hasty denials of any romance.

Talking of romance, I sneak another look at Monsieur Hôtel, who's deep in conversation with English Rose. He's doing that glass-swilling thing with his wine - rolling it around to let it breathe, then sniffing it like a professional. I'd forgotten how he used to do that at every meal. It was really irritating. At least Boy Scout doesn't pretend to know anything about wine and just slugs it back merrily.

Thinking of my husband, I decide to check how things are going at home, then wish I hadn't bothered, as I see the messages waiting for me.

- Dad's drunk two bottles of wine!
- Daddy's shouting. I don't like it.
- Everything's fine. Will you be long?

For goodness sake, can't I even have a night out on my own, without some drama? I decide the only solution is to hit the wine bottle myself and make inroads into the main course that's just arriving.

To the sound of drum rolls, the waiting staff bring large hunks of barbecued meat on huge rotisserie skewers to each table and then, using the sharpest of Sheffield knives, cut slices for each guest. The meat's accompanied with plates of steamed jasmine rice, stir-fried vegetables and a rich, red wine sauce. Again, it's another synthesis of South American, Asian and European cuisine, and it's both striking and delicious. I have to hand it to my French hotelier - he's succeeded in melding all these contrasting flavours to create something quite incredible.

I gobble my food down then sneak another look at him. He's definitely still a dish himself! But he's only half way through his main course. That's right - I remember now - he used to take so long to eat anything, telling me how it was important to chew each mouthful thoroughly to savour all the tastes.

He's waving his fork around and obviously explaining the finer details of the recipe to English Rose, who has, apparently, got the hang of *savouring* the tastes far better than I ever could. They're ignoring Changming's uncle and the rest of their table, leaving Big John, the consummate professional, to keep the conversation going with Portly Grandma and Tweenage Girl until it's time to announce the next dance act - the Argentinian tango.

A silence falls over the room as the first melancholic notes of a violin and accordion fill the air and onto the stage step an exotic, dark-haired couple in a close embrace. They move stealthily, in an almost cat-like manner, improvising a story of a tragic relationship, encompassed in dance. It's intimate, personal and deeply emotional as they dip and sway together in a passionate and sensual courtship. I can understand now why Bubbly Brazilian is so obsessed with the tango - it's as if she's a different character and the audience has been swept up in her masquerade. Finally the music finishes and, to thunderous applause, she and Kiki take a bow, then make their way over to join us in our hiding place.

It's only when I really focus on this Kiki and his beautiful, chocolatey-brown eyes and luscious, long lashes that I realise, despite time having aged him, I've definitely met him before.

I wave an accusing finger at my friend.

'You've been lying to me all along! His name's not Kiki. That's Enrique, my fellow royalist from Moscow.'

Bubbly Brazilian looks in confusion at her dance partner.

'My dahleeng, is this true. Is your name Enrique?'

Kiki's staring at me with a puzzled air, as if trying to place my face.

'Yes, of course it's true. There's no dark secret here. My given name's Enrique, but its shortened form's Kiki. And *you* are...?'

He looks at me again more closely and then gradually recognition dawns.

'Could it be? But you have... you have... you have... changed so much... Ay Caramba! It *is* you! My Lady Dee. My devushka from Moskva.'

So, whilst Zen Mother congratulates Bubbly Brazilian on her amazing performance, Enrique gives me a hug and a potted history of his life over the last twenty-five years. He tells me how he'd tried to track me down when he knew he was coming to Sheffield but, not knowing my married name, drew a blank. He seems genuinely pleased to see me.

'Now I can finally discuss the royal family with someone who understands my passion. What a happy coincidence we've found each other again.'

All too soon though, Kiki disappears to organise the next dance number and Bubbly Brazilian's rewarded for her efforts by the arrival of the desserts, complete with extravagant sparklers. I'm just about to get stuck into the mouthwatering lychee soufflé on a soft croissant base, when my phone pings annoyingly three times.

What now? Haven't things calmed down at home yet? Apparently not.

- Dad's on his third bottle!
- Daddy's gone quiet now. It's scary.
- Mum, hope you're having fun. Are you home soon?

I sigh - all being well, wine will take effect shortly and Boy Scout will fall asleep. I can't imagine Monsieur Hôtel ever being the worse for drink. Probably just as well then that we didn't end up together - his habit of *sipping* and *savouring* might've clashed with my lifestyle of *guzzling* and *gorging*!

As I peer out from behind the palm fronds and spy on my nearly-ex-fiancé, I have a sudden moment of clarity that he is not and has never been the one for me! Yes, it's true there was an initial frisson of excitement when I first saw him tonight, but now I've got as far as the international cheese platter, the spark has definitely gone and I can view him with complete detachment. Which is just as well, as he and English Rose seem to be getting on famously. I watch with interest as their hands brush *accidentally* over the selection of crackers.

Bubbly Brazilian interrupts my thoughts.

'So, my dahleeng? How are you feeling? Has seeing your former French love stirred up old memories? Are you ready to quit married life for an old flame?'

I shrug - 'No, it's funny. The grass always seems greener on the other side but I think I'm wise enough to stay in my own garden these days. But how about you and the amazing Enrique? He's still as gorgeous as he was in my day and no girl's yet caught him. Maybe you'll be the lucky one to reel him in?'

Bubbly Brazilian laughs loudly.

'Oh, you English girls! You can be so naïve sometimes! Your *gaydar* is obviously not as well-developed as ours.'

'What? You mean?'

'Of course. It's obvious. Such a beautiful man with a love of dance? Never married? And surely his fixation with the royal family gives it away?'

'Awh, that's such a shame. I had high hopes for the two of you!'

'No, it's for the best. It means I'll always have a wonderful man in my life but with no messy complications. Now sit back and enjoy his final choreography.'

And at that moment, the first bars of the famous French can-can boom out and a bevy of dancers come whooping and high-stepping onto the stage. It's wild, exciting, fun and a fitting end to the dance spectacular.

Now all that remains before the tables are cleared and the restaurant turns itself into a night club, is to announce the winner of the *design a dessert* competition. In readiness, Big John takes centre stage with his microphone.

'Now ladies and gentlemen, I'm sure you'll agree this evening's been a resounding success. We at Radio Hallam are proud to have been responsible for the competition to name *Fusion 3* and just as proud to be here to discover the dessert that will become its signature sweet. As you can tell from my waistline, I've tasted everything our viewers have sent in! But now we're going to leave the final decision to our judges, who will be asked to give marks out of ten for each dessert. So please give a warm welcome to the owners of Fusion 3 and our three talented finalists.'

The restaurant erupts into noisy clapping as Monsieur Hôtel and Changming's uncle are led onto the stage, where a small table's been laid out with the three winning desserts. Tweenage Girl stands coyly at the front and lifts up a sign, naming her dessert as *Jam Roly Poly*. Both judges take a spoonful and make appreciative noises. She's awarded eight out of ten from each and looks rightly pleased with herself. Next Portly Grandma parades past with her sign for *Spotted Dick*.

Zen Mother whispers - 'I think that one's an acquired taste if you're not British.'

Monsieur Hôtel, being an Anglophile and therefore used to dried fruit in desserts, finishes his mouthful, smiles and declares it to be another eight out of ten but Changming's uncle is having trouble finishing his portion, so delivers a meager six out of ten. Portly Grandma's about to kick off but Big John sweeps her away as English Rose appears with her *Fiery Flapjack*.

The tension at our table is palpable.

'Come on my dahleeng! You can do it!'

'I know it's the taking part that counts. But I do so want her to win!'

'Come on, do it for my mum and her secret recipe!'

The judges take a bite each out of the perfect golden triangles in front of them. As they chew slowly, you can almost feel the flavours being released - syrupy crunchy oats, sweet Chantilly with a chilli-flake kick. I see the delight form on their faces. Changming's uncle shouts - 'Ten. Yes, ten!' whilst Monsieur Hôtel nods in silent agreement - 'Oui, dix. I mean ten!'

The crowd erupts and English Rose flushes modestly as Big John declares her the winner. Changming's uncle bows solemnly to English Rose as the Sheffield Star and Telegraph journalists move in for photos.

Monsieur Hôtel, however, is still seated. He's in a state of shock. Suddenly he jumps up and runs towards Big John, who's making a congratulatory speech on behalf of Radio Hallam. His breathless voice can be heard around the room.

'Oui, yes. But who made this? There is only one person in the world who can make this dessert! Where is she? Where is mon amour?'

Bubbly Brazilian and Zen Mother look at me anxiously as I slip lower in my seat. For whilst *I've* spent all evening spying Monsieur Hôtel out of my system, *he's* yet to meet me! Oh Lord, perhaps now is a good time to go home?

I'm about to phone a taxi but realise I've had three missed calls. I check my messages - there's an *amber alert* from Delightful Daughter.

- Dad's lost it. We couldn't stop him. He's on the way to the restaurant RIGHT NOW!

Oh God! Now what do I do? Big John's obviously thinking the same thing as Monsieur Hôtel rounds angrily on poor, confused English Rose.

'But no. I 'ave only tasted perfection like this once before in my life! And you are not… This can't be …This is a mistake… This is not your recipe is it? Admit it, you are a thief!'

English Rose is taken aback but saved by Big John's timely announcement - 'Ladies and gentlemen. We've enjoyed our amazing fusion meal and dance spectacular and just crowned our *design a dessert* winner, so now the floor's open. Get down and shake your moves. It's that all-time classic - Boogey Nights!'

The music blares out, drowning the heated discussion that's going on between Monsieur Hôtel and English Rose. I'd forgotten how dramatic he could be! Still English Rose, with her experience of dealing with unruly children, is holding her own. But oh dear Lord, she's pointing our way. I sink further under the table but there's to be no escape. Moments later I hear his unmistakable accent.

'Is it really you? Mon petit chou? After all these years! 'ave I finally found you again?'

I rise slowly from under the table, pretending to have picked up a dropped spoon.

Monsieur Hôtel steps back in surprise and exclaims to English Rose -

'Mais, non. This is a mistake! This is not ma cherie. She was like Lady Dee - so slender. Like you Mademoiselle.'

Bloody charming! All these years and I thought it was my inner beauty he was in love with, when it turns out it was my looks and my flapjack he was after! And just like that, any last flicker of longing for my French amour dies out.

I decide, however, to call on my years of philosophy training and silence my inner critic. I can be the better person here. I smile sweetly at my ex-love.

'Actually, I *was* your *cherie*. But, sadly, it wasn't meant to be. Time's changed us both and I really hope life's treated you well. It's wonderful you've fulfilled your dream of setting up an exciting, new dining-out concept. You must be very proud. *I* am very proud of you. And I'm delighted you've chosen Sheffield as your starting point, and one of my good friends to create the dessert.'

That's certainly wrong-footed the man. I can see now that, underneath my extra padding, he's finally recognised the young girl he knew in Lyon, and is silently congratulating himself on his lucky escape!

But there are many years to catch up on and he *is* still very charming, so he joins us at the table and recounts his culinary exploits over the last two decades. English Rose is mesmerised, hanging onto his every word.

'What? You actually got to cook with the legendary Paul Bocuse and eat in his Michelin star restaurant? I'd die for that!'

I recall the snot-like oysters I once had the misfortune to eat and wonder if I'm now witnessing the start of a match made in heaven. Monsieur Hôtel looks at English Rose with admiration and a touch of embarrassment.

'Mademoiselle!'

What a smoothie! He knows full well she's a mother of four, but is just buttering her up.

'Mademoiselle, I do so apologise for calling you a thief! I was just overcome at tasting that dessert once more. Of course, a recipe is only as good as the cook who makes it, you know…'

English Rose suddenly becomes animated and reaches into her bag for yet another of her Tupperware boxes.

'Yes, I know that and I was desperate to get through to the finals, which is why I stuck with the original recipe. But I'd be honoured if all of you, would just taste one of these and give me your honest opinion.'

English Rose hands us all a bite sized triangular flapjack. Oh God, it's not the coriander one again, I hope! Tentatively, we take a bite. It tastes so deliciously familiar and yet at the same time, so deliciously different.

Whilst Monsieur Hôtel looks on in awe at English Rose, Bubbly Brazilian nervously breaks the stunned silence.

'Oh, my dahleeng, I hate to say it, but I really think this is *better* than the original!'

And thankfully, all those meditation practices and positive affirmations come to the fore once more. Instead of being consumed with petty jealousy, I find myself strangely at peace and happy for my friend's success.

'Do you know, I actually agree! What on earth have you added to it?'

English Rose smiles cheekily at me.

'For now, that's *my* secret recipe. My lips are sealed!'

Unfortunately, someone else's lips are definitely not sealed, as a familiar, Welsh voice can be heard booming above the noisy disco beat.

'Let me in, dammit! My wife's in there! I don't care if I haven't got a ticket! I'm warning you, stand back, isn't it, or you'll regret it!'

There's a sudden kerfuffle at the door and both bouncers disappear from sight as Boy Scout, looking much the worse for wear, rugby tackles them to the ground. He picks himself up, dusts himself down and ploughs through the crowd on the dance floor.

'Where is she? What have you done with her?'

Like a mad man, he surveys the room, and homes in on me like an Exocet missile. Spotting Monsieur Hôtel sitting nonchalantly unawares next to me, he grabs him by the collar, lifts him off his feet and thunders into his face.

'Now then, boyo! That's my wife there. *My* wife, get it! You tried to take her away from me once before. I'm not letting you try a second time, isn't it? If you do, I'll *have* you, I will!'

To his credit, Monsieur Hôtel keeps his cool, quickly sums up the situation and digs deep into his nation's reputation for diplomacy.

'Ah, yes you are right, Monsieur. I admit defeat. The better side won! Just like Wales versus France in the 2005 World Cup. It was a close call but Wales played a stronger game on the day. And by the way, that was a tremendous tackle back there. Do you still play?'

Boy Scout shakes his head in confusion. He isn't expecting this reply and like a Welsh Pavlovian dog, he's fine-tuned to answer any question to do with rugby.

'Well, not any more since I got injured, isn't it? But I used to play for the first team. Do you play?'

'Unfortunately, mon ami, no. But I'm a big supporter of Lyon, of course.'

'Lyon? Where are they in the league?'

Boy Scout's about to continue on the rugby theme then suddenly remembers why he's here.

'Ermm, my wife…'

'Ah oui, your beautiful wife. You're a lucky man indeed. We knew each other many years ago. And now, by complete coincidence, we 'ave met again! She's been telling me 'ow 'appy she is with 'er life and family 'ere…'

Boy Scout looks even more confused.

'Has she, really?'

'Ah, oui, yes of course. Sometimes we don't appreciate things until we are in danger of losing them, n'est-ce-pas? Now please forgive me, but I 'ave other guests I must see to. Please make yourself at 'ome here. 'ave a dance, a drink - a coffee maybe? Perhaps our paths will cross again. But for now, Bon Soir!'

And just like that, the crisis is diffused.

Whilst English Rose plies Boy Scout with flapjack to soak up the wine he's consumed, I text Delightful Daughter.

- The Eagle has landed. Code red downgraded. Don't worry. All is well.

The evening's drawing to a close. We drag Bubbly Brazilian and Kiki away from the dance floor, wake Zen Mother up from the couch in the corner and round up English Rose who's spent the rest of the evening in the company of Monsieur Hôtel. The three musketeers commandeer our pre-booked cab, leaving Boy Scout and me to face a long wait in the taxi queue.

But tonight luck's with us.

'Perhaps you would like to share our taxi back with us? Our other neighbours had to leave early, so we have space' - a voice offers and I look up to see the welcome face of Changming.

We hop gratefully into the back of the cab and smile at his uncle, who stares at us both for a long while, then starts pointing and shouting, 'Charles! Diana!' before going off into a long stream of Chinese.

Changming looks bemused. 'My uncle's saying he's sure he's met you before - on a long train trip many years ago. He says you taught him a special dance and gave him a present.'

Meanwhile Uncle's searching wildly in his inside coat pocket and brings out a very battered old pocket knife. Boy Scout looks at it in amazement.

'Bloody hell, my lovely! That looks like my *Little Mesters* knife from our honeymoon!'

We take a closer look at Changming's uncle. Could it be ...? Surely not?

I ask Changming - 'Did your uncle use to wear glasses with extremely thick lenses?'

Changming nods - 'Yes, one of the first things he did when he became rich was to get himself contact lenses. Granny said it completely changed his appearance. No one even recognised him when he came home!'

'Well, let's see if he recognises this' - I say, going into my old *Walk like an Egyptian* dance routine. Uncle, aka, Brains from the Chinese Mafia of our honeymoon trip, laughs out loud and *walks like an Egyptian* right back at me.

That night, as I finally settle down to sleep, I reflect that it's been an evening full of drama and chance meetings. So, it's no surprise then when my dreams are populated with the image of an orange-robed holy man reminding me - 'Mehmsaab, remember this. Nothing in life is a coincidence!'

32

Hypno-what?

The next morning Boy Scout looks at me sheepishly.

'I just thought… Well, I put two and two together…'

'And made five?'

'Well, alright, isn't it? I'm sorry but you have to admit you've being acting strange lately. Then finding his photo and all … Well, I couldn't bear the thought of you... you know… Anyway, my lovely, I know I'm not a man of many words and I don't say what's in my heart often enough, but I was saving this to give to you at Christmas. But perhaps it's best if you have it now.'

He hands me an envelope.

As I open it, I feel a surge of love towards this man of mine. My father was right all those years ago. It might not be *perfume and poetry* but it's always, *reliable, loyal and lasting* and, just occasionally, there's *drama and romance*. For Boy Scout has come up trumps and booked tickets to Rome to celebrate our Silver Wedding. He's even reserved seats in business class on the plane.

However, as the festive season ends and our anniversary draws closer, an increasing sense of anxiety and unease pervades my daily life. I'm secure in my marriage once more, so that can't be it. Work gets me down but I've come to terms with sitting it out until retirement. So what's changed? Why do I feel like a vital part of me is missing? It must be my age because, for some reason, my monkey mind's gone hyper-active and the voices have taken control again, turning me into Tiresome Worrier.

'Flying? Remember Hong Kong!'

'You should keep your feet firmly on the ground!'

But I can't cancel the trip as Boy Scout's even arranged the childcare, with Delightful Daughter stepping into my shoes for the weekend.

'Don't worry mum,' she says - 'I'll make sure those boys behave. You deserve a break. You've been quite stressed these last few months. And that fandango with dad can't have helped! But, honestly, you seemed a lot happier when you were going to your philosophy classes. And I know we made fun about the stones in your bra - but maybe they *did* actually work - for you at least. Anyway, go and have a good time with Dad.'

And I wish I could but each night I wake up in a cold sweat from a nightmare where twisted metal falls from the sky and Small Child's left an orphan. Maybe if I got our affairs sorted out before I went then I'd feel better?

So, I march Boy Scout off to the lawyer's to make a will, despite his protesting - 'This weekend away has suddenly got very expensive, isn't it?'

But I feel calmer now I know that Delightful Daughter, being over eighteen, will get custody of her siblings. She laughs at the news, sticking her tongue out at Devil Teen.

'Ha! I'll be your legal guardian, so watch out!'

Devil Teen responds by throwing a cushion at her.

'Oh great!' I say - 'I knew I should've made Our Bev the guardian instead. Perhaps I'd better not go?'

'Mum, don't be silly. We're messing about. Why don't you want to go?'

'I don't know. It's stupid really. It's just I keep getting that dream where the helicopter's falling from the sky and dropping into a deathly darkness...'

'Mum, you're going to have to do something about this! Dad's really looking forward to this break with you. Besides we've flown as a family countless times and it's never bothered you before. Look I have to admit, I… we… have all been concerned about you lately. You seem kind of down in the dumps. I know you were a bit wacky before but at least you were happy-wacky! Anyway, I came across this bumf on hypnotherapy at the library. I thought you might be interested.'

'Oh no, I'm done with all that stuff! Unless there's scientific proof that it works, I'm not going.'

'Oh Mum. Come on! You used to be so open-minded. What happened to all that *suspending your disbelief* you preached? I know you won't go to the doctor's, so at least give it a try?'

She pushes a leaflet into my hand. She's right. I don't want to take anti-depressants and what do I have to lose? So, a few days later, here I am wandering along a row of identical terraces off Abbeydale Road, trying to find the home of *Hypno-Healing*. I ring the bell and the door's opened by a young girl, with long pink hair and an interesting eyebrow piercing.

'You!' we say simultaneously.

'What a coincidence,' I continue, 'Is your mother at home?'

Eyebrow Ring looks nonplussed then breaks into a grin.

'Ha ha, I love your sense of humour! We've missed you at philosophy classes. Welcome to *Hypno-healing*. Please come in.'

I groan inwardly at the thought of putting myself into the hands of a child, but then decide to revert to *suspending disbelief* and go with the flow.

Eyebrow Ring leads me up three flights of stairs into a cosy attic room. Hanging on the wall is an array of credible certificates and there's no sign of any pocket watches, which is a relief at least.

We talk about my flying phobia and how a possible root cause might date back to my honeymoon experience. Eyebrow Ring explains she's going to use music and visualisation that'll put me in a relaxed state where she'll be able to bypass my conscious mind and access the sub-conscious, where the root of my problem's stored. Then she can re-programme it with a more positive attitude to flying.

Thinking of stage-show hypnotists, who play their volunteers for laughs, I ask - 'You're not going to make me howl like a dog, are you?'

'Certainly not! In fact, I can only put you into a trance if your subconscious allows me to. So, are you happy to give it a go?'

Happy is perhaps not the right word, but there's a comfortable couch waiting and I've nothing to lose.

Eyebrow Ring puts on some therapeutic whale music and I close my eyes. As I relax I'm asked to visualize a set of steps that I'm walking down one at a time to a place of peace and tranquility.

In my mind's eye I see myself high up at Higger Tor - my favourite rocky outcrop in the Peaks, overlooking the purple-heathered moorland that stretches out as far as the eye can see. Strange formations of grey gritstone dominate the landscape and down below, a mysterious Iron Age fortification rises up from the valley, where a brackish stream cuts a path down to a wooded gorge. This is a special place to me - a place I've known since childhood and where I still go today to be close to nature and leave the stresses of city living behind.

'You can return to this place anytime you want and you'll always be safe here,' Eyebrow Ring assures me in a mesmerizing voice.

'But now,' she continues in the same transfixing tone, 'I want you to return to the past, to that helicopter where the engine's just cut out.'

And as if by magic I'm transported back twenty five years in time to see the sweat trickling down the pilot's neck as he radios frantically over the airwaves.

'What emotions are you feeling at this point?

It's odd that, despite Eyebrow Ring's soporific speech, I can still hear and understand her. Somehow I thought being hypnotised would be like being under an anaesthetic.

I'm expecting to feel *terrified* but when I view the scene dispassionately, there's a strange sense of being watched over and unexpected words come into my head.

265

'I feel *calm, accepting, trusting.*'

'Good. Well, hold on to this peaceful feeling and remember that whenever you're flying, you're safe and looked after. Nothing can harm you. So maybe your anxiety isn't about flying after all… Let's go further back in time. Have you had any other shocking experiences?'

Apart from Boy-Scout nearly suffocating me with a pillow every night, I can't think of anything off-hand. I let my thoughts drift and … all at once I'm back in an onion-domed church in Russia. My body jolts suddenly on the couch.

'It's ok. You're safe. What do you see?'

'It's a little *babushka* - a Russian granny - she's lying exposed in an open coffin … I don't like it!'

'Ah, *death*. It's fine. Now, look at the body and tell me what you notice. Remember you're safe.'

The voices beg to differ.

*'Safe? This is **death** she's talking about!'*

'Yes, you've sorted out your flying phobia. Now head back to that rocky outcrop.'

'But a little peek won't harm…'

And somehow, I'm no longer afraid. I'm disassociated from the scene in front of me. I'm not in it, but watching it, as if it were on a cinema screen.

I approach the deceased babushka and see she has a garland of fresh flowers on her head. Her white hair's been lovingly brushed and, despite her obvious age, she looks like a sleeping child.

'She's peaceful, and at rest, like her body's there but she's gone home.' - I tell Eyebrow Ring.

'Good, that's right. Remember death's a natural part of life - a return to home.'

The voices are unimpressed.

'You'll regret this.'

'Don't open another can of worms!'

'Hang on, who's that?'

Everything's gone misty and a figure in a hat, carrying some kind of box, appears out of the haze.

'Can you see anybody else?' asks Eyebrow Ring with alarming intuition.

I consider lying - after all I've fixed the flying problem - let's not delve deeper. But the subconscious part of me is intrigued to see who's there…I gasp - 'It's my mum!'

'What do you want to say to her?'

I'm about to tell her I miss her, but instead I find myself shouting.

'I'm so angry with you! Why did you have to go first? I wasn't ready for you to go. I haven't made you *proud* of me yet!'

Oh, this is getting weird. Why can't my mother stick to appearing in my *father's* hallucinations? But annoyingly she's going nowhere. Instead she smiles knowingly and points behind her to another shadowy figure.

'Is there someone else there?' asks Eyebrow Ring.

My heart starts to pound. I don't want this to be … and yet I do … My hands feel clammy as I recognise the long, flowing hair. My breathing is labored as I look once more into the soulful doe-eyes of the boy who stole my heart forever.

'Oh my God!'

'Remember you're safe.'

It's … It's my first love … He died tragically…'

'What do you want to tell him?'

I feel myself tremble as I whisper the words - 'I'm sorry. I'm *so, so* sorry.'

The Baptist comes towards me with open arms that encircle me and I feel an overwhelming sense of love and loss.

'I should've been there for you. I should never have left you alone. I was meant to protect you. Please forgive me!'

But his embrace doesn't last. His arms aren't solid. It's just an illusion. He fades away from me once more.

Then I can hear the strangest sound.

I've turned myself into that hypnotist's stage-show dog after all.

I'm howling and shaking and sobbing…

And, just as suddenly, the storm passes and I'm left in an ocean of calm under a golden sky. For one exquisite moment I have the sense of being unconditionally loved, the feeling that *the truth* is just within my reach.

But it's a fleeting sensation.

'I think there's somewhere else you still need to go to…' says Eyebrow Ring.

And yes, there is.

I'm alone in that monkey mind with the questions that haunt me - *What is death? What happens to me when I die? Who am I?* I shudder as an impenetrable darkness sweeps over the horizon, casting warning shadows into my oasis of peace.

I go inwards - '*Who am I?*' - I ask.

And suddenly something really bizarre happens. My notion of *self* is disappearing. The *Everyday-I* - daughter, wife, mother, teacher - retreats into the background. My physical body fades into the surrounding shadows and I have the sense of losing *me* as I hurtle towards a void of impenetrable blackness. I am teetering on the edge of a bottomless pit and I know that if I let go, *Everyday-I* will cease to exist.

It's completely and utterly terrifying!

'I've had enough! I don't like it here! I want to go back *now*!'

So, Eyebrow Ring takes me gently home to my moorland haven before returning me up the steps and back into the attic room.

'Great work, you've done a lot of clearing out and releasing of emotions' she says.

I nod, glad to be back to normal again and vowing to stay well away from any further *self-discovery*.

'Hopefully, you'll feel fine about flying now but maybe you have some other issues, you'd like to work on in future - about death and dying? You know, some psychologists and spiritual thinkers say we need to *face death before we die*. By that they mean the *death of our ego* - our *everyday self*.'

Oh no! This is all sounding like a return to my soul-searching. No, thank you! I came here to tackle my *fear of flying* and now I'm bloody leaving with a *fear of dying*! Typical! It would've been simpler to go to Dr. Anything-For-An-Easy-Life for a prescription of Diazepam!

'Hmm. Maybe another time...' I say in a politely British manner, knowing I'll never come back again.

I've had enough of death. I'm not ready to face my deepest fears. Let's lock those memories away, erase all questions and concentrate on *real life*.

For, phobia cured, it's time now for Rome and a revival of romance - a celebration of twenty- five years without killing each other!

33

Muddling through Marriage

I awake with a start, in a sea of sweat, to find loving spouse poised murderously above me with the pillow inches from my face.

He sleep-slurs at me.

'You must never leave me! I scored a try for you!'

Then he thuds wordlessly back onto the bed, with a self-satisfied smile on his face.

We resume our synchronised sleeping. A nudge of the elbow and he turns at my command. A tap on the back and we settle into sleepy spoons.

Next morning though, he's not speaking to me.

'What have I done now?'

'Well I dreamt you were having an affair, isn't it?'

'Exactly! You dreamt it! And we've been through all that before. You're lucky those bouncers didn't press charges!'

'Yes, I suppose so. But I still can't help feeling cross.'

'Well, if anyone's cheating, it's *you* with all your nights away at the Holiday Inn! And besides, I'm too wrinkled, knackered and menopausal to even consider an affair.'

Boy Scout looks at me appraisingly, about to nod but, just in time, thinks better of it.

'Come over yer and give us a *cwtch*. We haven't done so badly. Twenty-five years, eh? Who'd believe it? A life-sentence! Still, Rome will be pretty special, isn't it?'

And indeed, Rome *is* special. A silver wedding present to show how much he loves me, even after twenty -ive years.

He loved me so much back then that, much to the annoyance of the Welsh guest list, we got married on a snowy Rugby International day in February at Hassop Hall - my mother's upmarket choice. The result was that the wedding speeches were interrupted by constant updates on the score and the bar was drunk dry in the ensuing victory celebrations. And he still loves me so much that he's taking me to a city of culture that he knows I'll enjoy. He's sorted out the kids and he's even booked the weekend away in April so the sun will be shining on us.

Well, that's the romantic scenario of my dreams. The reality is somewhat different.

'What do you mean, we're going to Rome to watch Italy play Wales? What happened to Michelangelo and the Vatican City? When did romance turn into rugby?'

But this is marriage - the land of concessions, where the Colosseum clashes with conversions, the Trevi Fountain is tackled into touch and the prop pinches your pizza.

Many of those fellow travellers who started their matrimonial journey at the same time as us have already jumped off the train of togetherness. They've staggered into the swamp of separation, dragged themselves through the desert of divorce until they finally arrive at the oasis of opportunity.

Somehow Boy Scout and I have muddled our way through the mangroves of marriage and ended up in the caves of compromise.

The older children are less than impressed.

'Honestly, it's not as if you two are happy! Everyone else's parents are divorced. But we have to put up with your bad moods whilst missing out on two exotic *guilt* holidays a year.'

'Yes, Big Sis is right for once - no expensive, one-upmanship Christmas presents for us. Why can't you just split up and make everyone happy?'

Committed singletons or newly unshackled friends are no better. They purr smugly, avoiding eye contact with me.

'It's bliss! I only have to think of *myself*. I can do exactly what I want, when I want. I don't need a partner to make me happy. After all, so many married couples are downright miserable.'

Well, yes, they may well be right. But to my mind they've misunderstood the whole point of the marriage game, which is to *stay on the train*.

When you get married, you board that compartment of coupledom full of joyful anticipation of the journey ahead. But then an extra carriage or two gets added on, and, if you're complete masochists, a baggage car too. So now, the train's getting busy and requires attention to keep it running.

This involves steering the engine, clipping the tickets, serving second rate snacks and cleaning the corridors. It's a full-time job, done in shifts, often thankless. The train rarely stops, and you never reach your destination, but every now and then you get to sit down in first class, enjoy the panoramic views and realise that it's actually not such a bad way to travel.

It helps too if you have a map of the eight stops on the marital rail loop.

Love is the most sought-after destination, with its neighbouring, popular suburb of *Familiarity*. A few stops down the line brings you to the outskirts of *Disillusionment,* followed by downtown *Irritation* and finally the inner city of *Outright Dislike*. It's best not to linger too long there but head for the residential area of *Resignation,* before enjoying the avenues of *Acceptance* leading to the forests of *Fondness* and round, full circle, to the lake of *Love*.

I've travelled this route many times over and believe the secret of staying on track is to make sure that if one of you hops off to stretch their legs at a slightly dodgy station, then the other has to stay on board, set their sights uptown and drag the escapee onwards with them.

If both parties disembark in the inner city then a crash is inevitable!

272

For now, despite our recent near-derailment, Boy Scout and I are still bumbling along on the locomotive of life. And, for once, Rome lets us uncouple our cumbersome carriages and peer out at the passing scenery.

We hop on an open-top bus and in the balmy, spring sunshine we take in the sights of this ancient city, passing over the chance to visit the Forum and the Colosseum as we decide that cappuccino, not history, is calling to us. We get off and then opt for wine not coffee, just because we can - with no incumbent children to tie us down.

We amble along the cobbled streets to the Trevi Fountain, where like excited teenagers we throw our three coins into the water thus securing our return to Rome in some distant future. Boy Scout realises that culture, if accompanied by Chianti, is relatively bearable. He tells me - 'I can't believe you remember all these interesting back alleys from your guiding days. Very impressive, my lovely, even if I'd rather not know Charles and Di were here in 1985!'

Then we join the throngs of rugby fans making their way to the Stadio Olimpico. There's an atmosphere of heady excitement as, kitted out in ridiculous daffodil hats, the Welsh fans mix with their Italian counterparts, whose faces are discreetly painted with their national flag. And, after a few beers, I discover that, twenty-five years later, I almost understand the rules. Seeing Boy Scout's passion for the game, I recall with fondness the night that he and his rugby anecdotes *scrummed* their way forever into my heart.

On our final evening together Boy Scout declares - 'It's nice to see you relaxed for a change. I've been worried about you. You haven't seemed happy for a while now. You know, my lovely, if work's getting you down, then pack it in. Money would be tighter, but we'd manage somehow.'

'But what would I *do*? Who would I *be* without a job?'

'Well you'd be your lovely self, wouldn't you? I don't know.Maybe you'd get fitter, do more running, isn't it? Or take up your meditation again. That seemed to calm you down. And actually, here on our own, we're doing okay, aren't we, my lovely? You know there was a time, after your mam died and all that followed, that I thought things would never be the same again. You kind of withdrew from me and focused on the kids, like you didn't need me…'

'The opposite! I *did* need you, but you were never there!'

'Well, yes, I understand that now, my lovely. And I'll make sure I'm around more. Hopefully things should get easier for us. The kids are growing up, mostly alright, and your dad seems back to *normal* now. Must've been an infection after all, isn't it?'

'Yes, he's not mentioned mum in ages and he's done a massive clean-out. He's *finally* taken all her clothes to the charity shop. It must be the influence of his new *friend*. I even caught them doing *tai chi* together in the garden.'

'Does that make you feel odd, your dad seeing someone again after all these years, my lovely?'

'Well, I'm not sure it's progressed to *romance* but, despite the language barrier, they get on really well and that's good to see.'

'It certainly is, my lovely, and this weekend away has made *me* realise I still love being with you, even after all these years. You'll always be the light of my life, isn't it?'

These rare words of tenderness touch me and I look at my husband for the first time in ages. I mean, *really* look at him. As I stare into those deep pools of vivid blue and lose myself in their intensity, I remember the inevitability of our love.

For a rare instant, the light in me meets the light in him.

It's beautiful and overpowering.

The awareness connects us and the universe stands still.

We're two jigsaw pieces, that, let's face it, sometimes take a bit of forcing into place, but when one part fits into the other, then the whole picture comes into clear focus.

Yes, Boy Scout has his feet firmly planted on the earth, whilst I yearn to fly upwards towards the heavens. But I realise, for the first time, that he's not holding me back on my path, he's simply anchoring me to the ground, making sure I don't blow away when the wind gets too strong. For my part, maybe my aspirations to reach the skies lift him higher on his own journey?

It's not something we articulate in the busyness of our routine world but every now and then something jars us out of our regime and we're forced to open our eyes to the light within. And when it connects, then the principles of Adveita come into play, and two become one. The *Everyday-I* in each of us drops its ego self and relaxes into its natural *Eternal-I* state, where all is peace and light and love.

But that powerful love within us is terrifying in its energy. What heights of greatness we could achieve if we only let it loose in our daily lives! Far safer then to look away and settle for easy contentment.

Boy Scout is the first to break the spell.

'There's no need to cry, my lovely.'

'Well, you've got tears in your eyes too.'

'That's cos I've just seen the latest international results, isn't it?'

And just like that, we leave the Lake of Love, get back on the train and let the familiar loop restart.

Little do I know though that, thanks to my beloved, another journey is about to restart.

34

Let Your Feet Do the Talking

It's all Boy Scout's fault!

For a Silver Wedding present I get him tickets to Cardiff Arms Park and he gets me a three-month gym membership and a voucher for a *foot treatment.*

I've made subtle hints about a deluxe pedicure. I dream of transforming my toes and harmonising my heels. I want a beauty therapist to take me under her wing, nourish my nails and soothe my soles. I want feet worthy of movie star shoes, with no effort entailed on my part.

Instead, Boy Scout's filtered out the original message, focusing on *transform* and *therapy.* Mistaking *sole* for *soul,* and *relax* for *reflex,* he's booked me in for a session of *reflexology.*

On the plus side it shows he's been paying attention recently and noted my interest in alternative therapies. It's just he obviously switched off when I told him I was *giving up the inner seeking* and *going normal.* And really, I just wanted a session of pampering, not an encounter with an *ology.*

Anyway, here I am, in the therapist's functional but cosy room, with the smell of incense lulling me into drowsiness. I'm resting in a comfortable chair, covered in a comforting blanket. There's a map of reflexology acupressure points on the table in front of me and several artistic photos of beautiful feet, dotted around the wall. This, however, turns out to be the problem. Faced with these air-brushed images, I can only shudder at my pasty, varicose-veined horrors that are poking out in humiliation from the blanket.

Reflexology's meant to be a pleasant, therapeutic experience, but I'm too ashamed of my bunioned, gnarly trotters with their deformed, discoloured nails, to be able to relax. This treatment is meant to promote well-being and restore the body's balance but I'm too busy apologising to notice.

I burble in embarrassment - 'I meant to have a pedicure before I came. I just never had the time.'

The therapist, a beautiful thirty-something with long black hair and enlightened eyes smiles serenely at me and lies graciously.

'Oh, your feet look perfectly fine to me. But they *are* an expression of your inner self. So maybe you need to allow yourself more *me* time?'

'Hmmppphh, *me* time. Chance'd be a fine thing! I'm always giving, giving, giving and never getting any gratitude for it, I tell you!'

The therapist nods empathetically whilst pressing various points on my soles, heels and tops of my feet. And before I know it those inner voices have *outed* themselves and are bad-mouthing my family, friends and work colleagues. Serene Therapist nods and presses in sympathetic silence.

'And he promised he'd change after our little *misunderstanding* but he still rarely tells me he loves me and he never listens to what I say!'

More silent nodding and pressing, which I take as permission to vent all of my problems.

'Oh and even though I've got nice friends, somehow I can't be bothered to make the effort any more. I'd rather watch a royal wedding replay on the telly. If I don't occupy my mind, I just start worrying about everything. Owwwww! That hurts! Why does that hurt?'

'Well, yes, that's no surprise really,' says Serene Therapist - 'That spot coincides with your shoulders, where you hold all your tension. You see reflexology's based on the theory that different points on the feet, correspond with different areas of the body. Sometimes the energy field in your body gets blocked and causes problems, so by manipulating the feet, the blockage can be removed and the Chi can flow more easily.'

'Ah okay, I've heard about this Chi before. It's something to do with chakras isn't it?'

'That's right. Chi is seen as being a universal life force that flows through everything and connects everything. Here in the west, people are starting to accept it more. For example, when I first started out in reflexology, it was seen as pretty weird but now it's more or less mainstream.'

I nod vigorously - 'That's true, otherwise my husband would never have booked me in for it! I'm sure he thought it was a beauty treatment but with an *ology* in it to impress me. To be honest, I actually wanted a relaxing pedicure.'

Serene Therapist smiles - 'Well pedicures are all well and good but I think you'll benefit a lot more from this session. You seem to have a lot of blocked areas, but the Chi's flowing much better now. You know, in the east, Chi's just accepted as part of life. All kinds of martial arts are based on it and so is yoga, which by the way, I think you'd find very helpful. Particularly if you're feeling anxious about life in general.'

'Mmm. I'm not sure yoga's my thing,' I say, not wanting to get back on the Eastern bandwagon - 'But there again, who knows…'

'Well, maybe not yoga then,' says Serene Therapist - 'Actually, to be honest, what I think you'd really benefit from is reiki.'

'*Reiki?* What on earth is that?'

'Oh it's a fantastic way of balancing your energy. It's really helpful and relaxing. I have a Scottish friend who does it, if you're interested.'

'Oh no, thanks. I've been trying to wean myself off any *airy fairy* stuff - present therapy excepted!'

Serene Therapist smiles to herself and presses even more firmly, until the pain magically disappears and I feel myself relaxing. I'm not sure whether it's due to auto-suggestion, as this therapy's yet to be scientifically proven, but having someone massage your feet, even if it's slightly painful at times, is actually quite soothing.

'As for work,' I continue - 'Well, I spend every evening preparing my lessons in front of a computer. It's giving me migraines and sending me blind! And do the students appreciate all my hard work? Do they hell! It's relentless. Owwww! What's that bit you're pressing?'

'Ah, that. Well, it corresponds to your eyes and your head. Once I've worked on it, you should feel more comfortable'.

Serene Therapist hoovers up my negativity with calm composure and keeps on prodding, nodding and poking. Eventually I run out of things to complain about and tune in to the whale music that's been playing all the time in the background. Before I know it, I've drifted off into a refreshing sleep where beautifully varnished nails and baby soft skin slip seductively into impossibly high heels…

I wake with a start to wipe the dribble from my mouth and realise with sadness that the horny hooves attached to my legs haven't been magically remodelled. Somehow, though, they look less hideous. And whilst I've not experienced the stillness, light and unity I encountered when I was on my soulful searching journey, I do feel as if my whole body, not just my feet, has had a full M.O.T. I can almost sense the energy flowing unhindered through me and my fingers and toes have a pleasantly alive, tingling sensation about them.

The session ends and Serene Therapist glides with me to the door, slipping a couple of business cards into my hand.

I skip home with a spring in my feet and a lightness in my heart. I feel ten feet taller, my head no longer aches and, is it my imagination, or do my eyes look brighter? I'm not sure whether it was the pressing of the acupressure points or the fact that someone was listening, unjudging, to me for an hour, but I certainly feel better.

I vow to take better care of myself so I pumice my feet into submission, slather them in cream and steal a nail varnish from Delightful Daughter's collection. Small Child's intrigued by my sudden interest in self-grooming.

'Mummy, that looks fun. Can I join in too?'

'Sure darling, as long as you wipe it all off before daddy comes home. He might not appreciate your handiwork…'

So, we while away a happy hour in a mother-son, toe-and-finger-painting extravaganza. When Boy Scout comes home, early for a change, he actually notices my new look.

'Oh, very nice, isn't it? That *reflexologist* did a very good job my lovely.'

35

The Yogi Warrior

Something about the reflexology session calms me down and makes me start questioning again. Perhaps I should *suspend my disbelief once* more? What's the harm in trying out new practices?

If Devil Teen can buy me a rose quartz bracelet for my birthday, maybe he's trying to tell me something? At least when I was on my quest, I didn't feel anxious, like I have done recently. And I've slammed on even more weight since I've taken to telly watching. So, I decide to take up Serene Therapist's suggestion and try out the yoga classes at my new gym as a way of balancing my Chi. And if I feared this was going to shunt me back onto a spiritual pathway then I needn't have worried - all the other participants here are more interested in flirting than enlightenment.

But Boy Scout can put aside his jealousy. Hook-up highway is closed to me, for I'm the only one wearing baggy tracksuit bottoms in a sea of tight-fitting Lycra. And I'm at least twenty years older than my fellow yogis in this zoo of a class. It's full of alpha-males competing to hold intricate postures for as long as possible, in a bizarre mating ritual aimed at the bendy, beach babes striking impossible poses.

Even the positions are all animal-themed. Cobras morph into lizards and eagles chase pigeons, whilst dogs roam freely and uncontained in upward and downward packs. After fewer than four lessons, I give up trying to fit in with the *in* crowd and switch to a women-only class, more suited to my age and shape, in Sharrowvale community centre.

The session's calming, apart from the disco beats and manic shouting from the Boxercise class next door. Once we've listed our litany of physical complaints to the instructor, she finally starts the class in time for three poses and a cool-down. Still, I learn to breathe correctly for the first time in my life and get light-headed as my bloodstream becomes saturated with oxygen. But sadly, it comes to a chilly end when the council can no longer afford the heating bills and closes the centre down.

To warm my bones, I travel across the city to Walkley to sign up for some *Hot Yoga* classes. I envisage some easy stretching in a Mediterranean climate but instead I'm treated to a forced SAS route march in forty degrees of Equatorial heat.

The idea is to move from pose to pose fluidly, as muscles stretch better in the warmth. However, the only fluid part of the activity is the amount of liquid flooding from every pore. I'm lying in a rain forest of my own making. As I lower my exhausted body onto the floor and lay my weary head down in *Child* pose, I'm in danger of drowning in the lake of sweat that's pooled on the mat.

My body's definitely had a full work-out and my monkey mind's successfully quietened as, in this oven-like studio, it takes full concentration just to breathe. I soon realise this jungle version is past my capabilities, so I leave the forest floor and head up into its canopy, with a foray into *aerial yoga*.

This involves ropes and hammocks in a bizarre cross between an S&M dungeon and the big top, with the contortionist-instructor obviously on loan from a circus.

'Now just hop into the hammock,' she instructs, leaping nimbly into the flimsy material hanging precariously from a rope attached to the ceiling.

I try and haul my bum over the side but succeed only in pulling a muscle in my arm whilst lifting myself two inches off the ground.

'Try a bigger jump and pull harder on the ropes,' the Contortionist suggests from her upside-down position.

I gather my strength and my best, Olympic, high-jumping technique. With a mighty roar I back-flip into the air, over the hammock and crash onto the mat below. Contortionist unravels her legs from behind her ears and cartwheels over to me.

'Could I have some help here?' she asks, as a team of aerial-yogis shimmy one-handed down the ropes. They form a pyramid, swinging me in synchronised rhythm upwards and into my hammock, which rocks dangerously due to its unexpected load.

Contortionist handsprings back across the mat and forward-rolls neatly into her hammock. She leads the class in a series of impossible moves, where their bodies intertwine with the ropes, and I watch, spinning helplessly in all directions, hoping she'll forget about me.

No such luck.

'Here I'll help you do a head stand, supported by the hammock,' she says, trussing me up like a kidnap victim before I can object.

Dangling downwards for the first time in many years, the blood rushes to my head, bringing a strange sensation of euphoria and a wonderful feeling of lightness. Then as I come out of the inverted pose, my mind is totally focused working out which limb to move.

'Bravo,' claps Contortionist as I collapse into the folds of my hammock, laughing uncontrollably. I've obviously awakened my inner child as I feel a joyous sense of fun.

'Quiet time now,' she says so I cocoon myself in the hammock's multi-folds. Swaying gently in the womb-like darkness, I experience a feeling of inner peace and stillness.

But, whilst I'm attracted to this acrobatic take on the traditional eastern discipline, I'm less attracted by the price of it. My northern love of thrift thwarts my burgeoning meditative awareness and my yoga journey comes to an abrupt end.

But the universe doesn't give up so easily. Zen Mother calls round one day. She's never spoken much about yoga, but I know it's played a significant role in her life. She's a busy social worker by day but hasn't suffered the burn-out that many in her profession do. She attributes this to yoga, saying - 'It clears my head after a hectic day. I can feel the energy in me settling down and I get a real sense of peace and stillness. That's before Ethan comes home from school of course! And now I've decided to take it one step further and complete my instructor's training. But I need some guinea pigs to practise on for my course and thought you'd help me out…'

She's my friend. So, what can I do? I find myself conscripted into her *Iyengar* army.

I turn up for the first class at a converted knife-works in John Street and see, to my annoyance, that Luke's dad has also signed up.

'What have you invited *him* for?' I hiss at our first class when I see him in his designer yoga gear, already limbering up so he can prove he's suppler than the rest of us.

Zen Mother replies with her usual calm.

'We're all on a journey in life. We need to let go of expectations and *cultivate kindness*.'

Then she welcomes us all and reminds us -'Yoga's not about competition. It's about discovering yourself.'

I glance knowingly at Luke's dad, who has the grace to look embarrassed. And besides, I reason to myself, *cultivating kindness*, he has at least come here to support my friend, so he can't be all that bad.

Zen Mother starts each session with a group chanting of *Om*. The sound reverberates through my body, shaking off the dusty drudgery of the day and replacing it with a higher energetic note. I can feel, as with the Gong Bath, how sound has an immediate, transformative effect. This type of yoga though is very precise and focused on having complete alignment in the performance of the postures. Zen Mother transforms into a slightly scary, *she-who-must-be-obeyed*, precision major.

Each stretch and bend must be meticulously executed and limbs are carefully manipulated to create the perfect pose. The precision major commands us with yogic authority as we try vainly to follow her often incomprehensible instructions.

'Lean forward with your hip a fraction more and breathe in through your left nostril!'

'Pull your buttock flesh to the side and down.'

'Lift up your middle ribs and bend with your heart.'

'Let the roots from your feet grow into the ground and pull up from your knees.'

I follow as best I can, twisting legs and arms into corkscrew combinations whilst, at the same time, remembering to release the tension from my eyebrows and let my cheeks soften. I even exchange a comradely look with Luke's dad as we both try to keep our balance and avoid toppling over.

It's a struggle to keep track of all Zen Mother's minute instructions but in order to do so the mind relinquishes its incessant chatter and homes in on the task in hand. The classes empty my brain of the trivialities of daily life and fill it with a welcome calmness.

After a while I find myself looking forward to the sessions, and Luke's dad and I now often stand companionably together on one leg in the playground, practising our *Tree* poses. He's dropped his competitive spirit and become quite chilled. Could it be that yoga and Zen Mother have influenced his decision to pack in his high-flying career?

I wish that I too could make the leap of faith to resign from my job, especially when I see how much happier he looks. He's gone back to illustrating books, his beard's growing back and his clogs have made a return. He's no longer putting on a macho act, and he's a much nicer person for it. As for me, I may not be a nicer person but I'm certainly a calmer one. Yoga's definitely helping battle those feelings of anxiety that once threatened to overwhelm me.

Today I'm poised in *Warrior* stance and Zen Mother's adjusting my wrist fractionally.

'There, now you're in as powerful a stance as you can get!'

At that moment, I feel a surge of energy coursing through my body and down along my outstretched arms. I have a feeling of invincibility, a oneness with all warriors, past, present and future. For a second, I have a sense of being pulled just slightly out of my body, as if I were a card being gradually slipped out of its envelope. I'm still attached but like a jigsaw piece that's not been properly pushed in.

Zen Mother puts out a hand to stop me over-balancing.

'I feel a bit weird, a bit light-headed. A bit, sort of, out of my body!'

'Ah yes. It's probably an energetic surge though your chakras.'

I don't know what that means exactly, but I'm returning *to suspending my disbelief.*

'Do you see yoga then as something more than just good exercise and physical stretching?' I ask.

'Well, yes, of course. But it's not something I talk about much. Not everyone's open to its more spiritual aspects.'

Here we go, *spirituality* again. I can't seem to escape it!

Yet it's comforting to know that, just as with the philosophy classes, there are others trying to make sense of their time here on earth. Some do it through traditional faith, some through seeking knowledge in books and some through finding a physical connection.

Something in the practice of yoga has touched a deeper awareness within me, and I realise that my journey has re-started whether I like it or not...

36

Holiday of Surprises

It's the olden times - the days before cheap air flights. Long-distance coach is the only way to reach summer sunshine and Our Bev's not impressed.

'This has been the journey from hell! It's the last time I let you talk me into coming on holiday with you, Squirt. Next year I'm going to Skeggy.'

She's right. Thirty hours of her singing *Y Viva Espana* on a packed coach full of screaming kids and irate parents has definitely been an endurance test. But we've finally arrived at the Costa Dorada.

We're immediately bowled over by a wave of heat, the like of which we've never encountered. In fact, it's all a new experience to us. Our Bev and I have never been abroad before. This is the end of my second year at university and in September I'll be heading to France then Russia to improve my language skills. I'm terrified that the shock of the unfamiliar will get the better of me and I'll be sent home, unable to cope, so this trip to Spain is meant to wean me off British culture gradually.

I've been invited, of course, by my Bristol classmates, Arabella - for the winter season in Montreux, and Piers - to his condominium in Bermuda - but the wages from my pub job never quite stretch to the ski hire or flight ticket. So, Spain is my first affordable foreign trip.

Strangely though, British culture has transposed itself to the Costa Dorada and the high street is full of pubs selling full English breakfasts and restaurants that offer fish'n'chips with curry sauce. Our Bev, once over the trauma of the journey, is in her element.

'It's just like home from home' she says, happily scoffing a 99 ice-cream with chocolate flake and strawberry sauce - 'only the beaches are genuinely golden and the water is actually warm.'

Whilst I too appreciate the endless beaches fringed by fragrant pines and palms, and the unaccustomed sunshine, I hanker for a taste of the *real* Spain. So, under duress, I make Our Bev take a trip to the walled, medieval city of Tarragona, to see its Roman heritage and to nearby Sitges, where we visit a gallery of Catalan art. There we find a local restaurant and dine out on gazpacho and whitebait. Our Bev has a few things to say about the meal.

'No, Squirt, I don't care if you say it's good for my education. How can they call that tomato soup? It's ice cold and reeks of garlic! And from now on I'm sticking to fish fingers. Anything with eyes on it, is going nowhere near my mouth.'

She also has a few things to say about the locals.

'It's surprising how they hold hands all of the time, even the men. I suppose they're just being friendly. Rather un-British though and I'm not sure Our Mum would approve.'

But I keep her happy by organising a half-day horse-riding trek in a nearby nature park, where she enjoys communing with the horses and I enjoy the cool greenery of the forest trail. In return she agrees to take the train with me to Barcelona, capital of Catalonia, so that I can wander through its medieval centre and soak up the atmosphere of its famous street, *Las Ramblas*, full of colourful stalls and street artists.

It's the end of the day and we don't have much time left. I really want to see *La Pedrera*, a landmark building, hailed as one of the brilliant architect, Gaudi's, most inspired creations, but Our Bev's insistent she wants to visit *La Sagrada Familia*, the iconic cathedral.

'Honestly, Our Bev, why have you got to bring religion into everything? Over the centuries the Church has spent millions on building massive cathedrals, whilst on the streets the poor freeze and starve. I don't want to have anything to do with supporting that corrupt institution!'

'Well, I'm sorry. You're always banging on about discovering the *culture* of a country and my guide book has the cathedral as the *number one* sight to see. And the architect's still that *Gaudi* guy, so you can tick him off your list too. Plus it's only a ten-minute walk away. Plus you *made* me come when I could've been sunbathing on the beach. So I definitely win!'

And when Our Bev is in her bossy mood, there is, indeed, no arguing with her, so we head off to *La Sagrada Familia.*

It certainly is an impressive building even though it's still not finished. Our Bev is in raptures as she circles the outside, 'oohing' and 'aahing' at the different scenes depicted from the Bible, very few of which mean anything to me.

'Can we go now?' I ask like a petulant toddler.

'Certainly not. The inside has an even greater write-up in this book, so we definitely can't miss it.'

I groan, 'Ok. Let's just get on with it. Afterwards we can stop for churros and hot chocolate at the station café.'

Then, expecting to enter the sombre, dark house of a God I've long since stopped believing in, I step through the doorway… and gasp… This is not at all what I imagined. This is unlike any church I've ever been to! Instead I've stumbled across a radiant jungle of colour, where tall trunks lead your gaze upwards to a glowing canopy.

The first thing that hits me is the light. It filters through the stained-glass windows in dancing shafts of greens and golds, dappling the lofty columns that reach up and up, into the heavens. The twisting pillars, like mighty trees, move towards the ethereal glow, seemingly fusing with the sky above. I'm in a forest of light! As the sunrays seep through the coloured glass I get the distinct feeling of being lifted up towards a divine unknown. My heart aches with a supressed longing and the beauty of this moment resonates through my whole body, bringing an unexpected tear to my eye.

Our Bev catches me wiping it away.

'It's incredible, isn't it? No wonder they called him *God's architect.* He certainly brings the building to life. And don't tell me you didn't feel the power of it too.'

She's right. For a moment there I felt transported to a higher realm. But her untimely interruption has brought me swiftly back down to earth and I'm certainly not going to give my big sister the satisfaction of seeing me waver in my atheist beliefs.

'Yeah, Our Bev, it's very beautiful. I'll give you that. But then it bloody well should be - the amount of time and money that's been spent on it!'

And just like that, the divine becomes the mundane. The celestial forest reverts back to a cleverly designed building where light is simply used for pleasing effect. I'm no longer taken in by this architectural trickery. And, whatever my heart might say, my head tells me there's no place for *spirituality* in my life.

But later at the station café, as I sip an industrial-strength, black coffee and Our Bev pushes her inferior cuppa to one side, I can see that the visit to *La Sagrada Familia* has affected her. She looks pensive.

'What's up, Our Bev? Can't you wait to get home and have a proper brew? Is that it?'

She smiles ruefully.

'You and I, Squirt, we're so different. You love all this travelling, different cultures and food. Me, I'm happier at home, where soup is soup and tea is tea. And don't get me wrong, I've enjoyed the experience and even hanging out with you! But *home* is where I want to be. Only I'm not sure home is Sheffield any more...'

'What? What do you mean by that? You love Sheffield! You've always said you'd never move away. Where are you thinking of going?'

'Scarborough, maybe?'

'*Scarborough?* Why there?'

'See, you know I've always wanted to run my own stables...'

'Yeah, despite Our Mum trying to convince you to become a vet.'

'Tell me about it! Well, Sheffield's too expensive but I could afford it if I moved to Scarbs.'

'Wow, Our Bev. You certainly are a dark horse. Mum's not going to be happy though...'

'No, it's bad enough I didn't go to uni or find Mr Right, now I'm abandoning her to a life of Our Dad!'

'Relax, she'll come round. And Scarborough's hardly the Soviet Union, is it? If I can go and live *there*, without mum freaking out, then I'm sure you can move to the east coast. You should do what makes you happy, Our Bev.'

'Thanks, Squirt. And, besides, mum's given up on me - her hopes are riding on *you* now. Back there in the cathedral, that light really touched me. It made me think of *you know who*... Yes, life's too short not to seize the moment. And I reckon if I can travel thirty hours to Spain with you, then what's three hours to Scarborough?'

'You're absolutely right Our Bev. Only just let me get back in one piece from Moscow before you tell mum, won't you?'

37

Light and Love

After my experience with Serene Therapist, the AA of spirituality has found me broken down on the roadside, injected some reflexology into the engine, pumped up the tyres with yoga and towed me back onto the highway of inner discovery.

The business card she presses into my hand has somehow led to me being here today. I can't explain why I phone and book a session in the first place. Perhaps it's my positive experience of yoga, and a curiosity about what exactly reiki is? Maybe it's linked to a new determination to *suspend my disbelief?* At any rate, I'm here now, slightly regretting it and feeling rather sceptical.

Reiki (pronounced Ray-Key) is a combination of two Japanese words - *rei* and *ki* - meaning universal life energy. It's an ancient healing technique used to balance the subtle energies within our bodies and it's believed to address physical, emotional, mental and spiritual imbalances.

Serene Therapist's friend couldn't be more different from her. She's a forthright Scottish practitioner, stocky with wild, red hair and an unconvincing sales pitch - 'I kan nae really explain what it is. Just trae it!'

I can get my head round acupuncture and reflexology and the way they target certain pressure points to release blockages. Although not fully accepted in the scientific world, these complementary therapies have some logic that appeals to my common sense. But waving your hands around someone's body and accessing an *intelligent energy*, seems a bit far-fetched to me! If the therapist had been a flower power, incense wafting stereotype, I'd probably have run a mile. But she's so down-to-earth and normal - and a Scot to boot. There's no way she'd be wasting time or money if she didn't think there was something in it!

'Wael, if youse think there's hundreds of mobile phone signals zooming through the air. We kan nae see them kan we? So why kan there nae be an invisible energy there too? Just coz we kan nae see it or science has nae found it yet, it does nae mean to say it's nae there, does it?'

Well, she does have a point I suppose. Dogs can hear sounds that humans can't perceive. Primitive tribes view a solar eclipse as something magical because they don't understand the science behind it. Perhaps reiki is something similar. I won't know unless I try it.

So here I am, lying fully clothed on a couch, as Forthright Scot places her hands lightly on, or above, different parts of my body, whilst in the background, the ubiquitous whale music pulses on.

I'm finding it hard to relax. I've come with a nagging toothache and there's a huge pile of student essays waiting to be marked on my desk back home.

Forthright Scot places her hands over my eyes and I try to clear my thoughts but my monkey mind is having none of it and rushes around opening drawers full of past actions to review negatively, and future jobs waiting, futilely, to be done. What on earth am I doing on this couch when I could be using my time far more productively? It's not like I'm getting a relaxing massage or a physio work-out.

Forthright Scot moves her hands to my head. The movement jars my jaw and my tooth starts throbbing again. I add *phoning the dentist* to my mental to-do list and fret about the fact the therapist is touching my hair, which I didn't have time to wash this morning.

I should've listened to Boy Scout when he questioned where I was going.

'*Rocky*? Sounds a bit ridiculous to me, isn't it? Still, I don't mind you going back to all those mumbo-jumbo books or trying weirdo stuff, if it makes you happy again.'

Oh well, it's just a one-off, I reason. Absolutely nothing is happening so I won't be coming back again. And in the worst scenario, I'm just going to have another forty-five-minute lie-down in peace and quiet.

Forthright Scot now moves position to the sides of my head. It takes a while to register that her hands are getting very hot. Not just hot but positively volcanic. The whole side of my face is on fire! I open my eyes in shock. Forthright Scot is grinning at me.

'Youse seem to be taking in a lot of energy raeght here. Kan youse feel anything?'

'Uhh, yeah, it's uncomfortably hot.'

'Dun nae worry. It'll balance out in a moment. Just trae and relax.'

She's right. After a few minutes, the heat subsides and she moves her hands to above my chest. I then feel her move her hands to my waist, then my hips. But hang on… How many pairs of hands has she got? If her hands are now at my hips, how can they still be at my chest! I open my eyes again and see her hands are actually at my feet.

'Uhh. That's weird. I can feel your hands at my chest, but they're obviously not!'

She grins again.

'Ach, yeah. Dunnae panic lassie. They call it *phantom hands*. I've no idea how tae explain it. They say it's the energy still working on a particular spot even though yer hands have just left it. I suppose it's a bit like people who lose a limb but can still feel it… Never youse mind. Just trae and go with it.'

I decide to take her advice and go with the flow. Before long the whale music has pulsed me into a dreamy drowsiness.

After what seems hours, I'm woken up by the Gaelic grinner. I feel a little spaced out but very chilled, as if I've had a refreshing night's sleep. And amazingly, my toothache's entirely disappeared!

After that, I keep getting drawn back to have a reiki session.

Each one is very different. Sometimes I feel heat, sometimes cold. On occasions I find my body involuntarily twitching, or energy pulsating through it in waves. Once I sob uncontrollably. But mostly I bathe in a sea of beautiful light. It reminds me of the forest of light I experienced so many years ago inside the cathedral of *La Sagrada*

Familia. I feel my body is floating in a golden haze. Every now and then, brilliant bursts of purple, green and yellow fireworks cascade down towards me. I feel safe and protected, cocooned in a warm blanket of love

After several sessions, Forthright Scot takes me aside.

'Yer know. I should nae be saying this to you. I'm doing ma saelf outta business but really yer should do the reiki course. Yer paying me a fortune when yer could save money and learn te do it yersaelf...'

So, I enrol on a weekend course with Forthright Scot and discover more about reiki and its founder, Mikao Usui. I learn that although reiki is spiritual in nature, it's not a religion, has no dogma and can be accessed by anyone, regardless of their beliefs. It's a loving, intelligent energy and can never do harm. All you need to do is be *attuned* by a reiki master, just like tuning in a radio to your favourite station.

After my first attunement I practise giving reiki to another of the course participants. Neither of us feel anything. I am disappointed. Maybe it hasn't worked. I go home dejectedly.

But that night in bed the palms of my hands start pulsing. I feel an energy surging in circular motions, gradually making its way up my arms, down my torso, into my legs and out through the soles of my feet. There's a sensation of light pervading every cell in my body.

It's exciting but somewhat unnerving. It's reminiscent of having your first child - the feeling that you've done something that can never be undone. Will life ever be the same again? But then I reason that, like a radio, I can just tune in or out of the different stations or choose simply not to switch it on. I have a flash vision of myself as a superhero, shooting reiki energy from my hands into the universe. I stifle a laugh.

Boy Scout grumbles.

'Will you just quit fidgeting now a minute? Have you got cramp?'

'Mmm, yes,' I mumble in reply, knowing he's not ready to hear the truth yet.

I practise reiki daily on myself and it makes me feel much calmer and more centred. The brief encounters with light, stillness, harmony and oneness that I've had on my journey so far seem to last longer with reiki and affect me more powerfully. I realise now that *the path* has found *me*, not the other way round.

Naturally I'm keen to share this blissful experience with friends and family, hoping that my new-found *healing powers* will transform others' lives for the better. Sadly, this is not to be the case.

Bubbly Brazilian finds it relaxing but prefers to spend her free time dancing with Kiki, whilst English Rose jumps up half-way through a treatment, declaring it's definitely not for her and that, anyway, she has to go and practise a new recipe with Monsieur Hôtel.

My reluctant guinea pigs thank me politely for my efforts, telling me how nice it was to 'have a little lie down' but they never come back a second time and I never cure anyone of any ailment, however minor. What am I doing wrong?

It takes Forthright Scot to put me right.

'Ach lassie. It's yer *Ego-Self* that's getting in the way of the reiki. Just cos youse are open to the energy, does nae mean everyone is! Some folks actively shut it down as they are nae ready fer it. Yer kan nae force it on people. It's nae about youse being a great healer. Youse is just a channel fer the energy. When yer get out of the way of yer self, that's when healing happens best and when folks are ready, they'll come and find yer themselves. Just stay open-minded and trae te trust.'

So I stop pushing reiki on others and wait to see what happens.

Zen Mother shows an interest and declares her session to be 'relaxing and energetically restorative' whilst The High Priestess claims that a whole host of angels were present at hers.

But it's Boy Scout who surprises me. Usually he feigns disinterest in any of my *weird goings-on* and has been resistant to what he refers to as my *ridiculous rocky* but one day he actively asks me for a session. He winks at me in a rather perturbing manner.

'I've been reading up on this *rocky* malarkey. If it's good enough for Sting and Trudy, then it's good enough for a boy from the Valleys, isn't it?'

Oh no, I fear he's got the wrong end of the stick! Is he thinking of those trashy magazines of my past with their tales of celebrity tantric sex? After twenty minutes of whale music, he opens his eyes impatiently.

'Bit boring this, my lovely. Not doing much for me. Now if you move your hands here… There's better, isn't it!'

I realise then that the reiki path is not for everyone.

'Oh, for goodness sake, you've just got a one-track mind!

'Well, be glad I still fancy you, my lovely … as well as appreciating your inner beauty, of course, isn't it?'

I feel my frustration rising.

'Don't you feel the energy? Don't you have any sense of there being something greater than your physical body?' I ask.

'I don't know what you want me to say, my lovely!'

'Just say you feel *something* - *anything*. Different colours? A sense of light maybe?'

'Well I *was* feeling something, but now you've killed the moment, isn't it?'

Typical! He always brings things back to basics. I feel myself snap - 'Oh, I give up trying! Sometimes it feels like we're on a completely different wavelength!'

'Well, I give up too. I'm going downstairs to watch the rugby, isn't it?'

I sigh, for, whilst I know now that Boy Scout loves me, I still worry that we're walking separate paths in life, and it makes me sad that I can't share these often profound experiences with him.

But those friends, and friends of friends who find their way to me for reiki, reaffirm that it's not my imagination. Something energetically inexplicable happens in those sessions. It's always positive and seems to help in both physical and emotional ways.

I sense that the energy is connected to the light that, though often neglected, has always been with me. I'm starting to understand that the love and peace I've been looking for have been with me all along.

38

The Other Side of the Void

My return to the road of self-discovery has seen a return to my self-help reading. I've been through all the *How to...* series and worked my way through diet, exercise, relationships and careers.

Despite the pages of excellent advice, I'm still an unfit sugar addict, with family and friends who get on my nerves, and a job I no longer enjoy. Still, I live in hope that some nuggets of wisdom will eventually make their way into my life.

I'm currently hooked on *inspirational stories* of how individuals have overcome childhood abuse, horrific injuries, and life-threatening situations, and have just started leafing through an auto-biography of an American woman who cured herself of cancer.

It's not dissimilar from other stories I've read but suddenly my attention is grabbed by the mention of *confronting the void*. The author's words paint a picture of that very same terrifying, bottomless pit which I encountered in my hypnotherapy session.

My body is poised on full alert, my nerves jangling, as if I myself were facing that immense, fathomless black hole once more.

I read on.

In a leap of faith, the author of the book jumps into the void... And passes through to the light beyond!

My heart is pounding, but no longer with terror. I know now that I'm not the only person to have faced this darkness. I know now that it *is* possible to come through to the other side. I know now that this is what I must do.

Two weeks later, after a cup of refreshing, Himalayan, yak tea, made with activated healing water, I'm sitting in a comfortable chair, eyes tightly shut, as a therapist, skilled in this particular journey, guides me through a series of relaxation exercises and visualisations. When I encounter negative emotions, instead of running away from them, I'm asked to notice where in my body they occur, then accept them, experience them and actively *surrender* to them.

At first this sounds counter-intuitive. Why should I want to re-live the anger I felt towards my father or the grief of my mother's death? But bizarrely, the very act of surrendering opens up a space around the feelings, allowing them to dissipate. As each strong emotion fades, another takes its place, until finally I am faced with the fear of dying, the fear that my *Self*, the *Everyday-I*, which I so strongly identify with, will disappear into nothingness.

As I contemplate the extermination of *Everyday-I*, I'm gripped by an overwhelming sensation of dread and realise that, once again, just as in the hypnotherapy session, my physical body has melted away and ahead of me is an impenetrable pit of darkness.

The therapist gently encourages me to let go and surrender to the darkness, but *Everyday-I* is having none of it.

'Just step into the void.'

'No! No way!'

'Why don't you want to step into it?'

'Because it's terrifying!'

'What exactly about it is terrifying?'

'I don't know. It's just so black and awful!'

'But what would happen if you did step into it?'

That blackness - it's insufferable. I, I, I ...would disappear. I'd cease to exist! I'd be dead! It would be awful!'

'But you don't know that,' says the therapist - 'You can't know that for certain. The only way you'll find out is if you surrender and step willingly into the void. So why don't you just have faith and go for it?'

This word *surrender* has a powerful meaning. In religion, having faith and submitting to the will of a higher power is often seen as the path to peace. I want to find that peace and I'm here because I've read an account of someone who faced the void and passed through it unscathed.

I have a choice now. I can stay in this room with the therapist, playing our interminable questions game, or I can choose to take a leap of faith and submit to the void.

I take a deep breath.

I silently intone to myself - '*I surrender. I surrender. I surrender*'.

Then I step forward into the darkness …

For a moment, the terror grips hold of me as the inky blackness swallows me up. I feel like I'm being buffeted in waves of dark shadows, careering towards a waterfall of impending doom. As I'm hurled over the edge, I hold on to the mantra '*I surrender*', as if it were a life jacket. I am falling, falling, falling …

Then suddenly the fear recedes.

The darkness remains.

There is complete silence.

I have the sensation of being a seed planted deep in the earth.

The darkness and the silence are my friends. I rest in this place of nurture and solace, with an overwhelming sense of peace and stillness.

Everyday-I has indeed ceased to exist. It has been replaced by an *Eternal-I* that connects with everything. I am the darkness, the silence and the calm.

As I contemplate this surprising, new, yet always known, fact, the darkness subtly changes. Small lightning flashes break through. A sky of glittering stars appears, as if the universe itself was being created.

Then, as one, the stars join up and the most brilliant beam of golden light floods my entire being. It's similar to the light I've experienced before with reiki but is far more overpowering and intense.

I am overwhelmed by a sense of joy and calm. I am beautifully weightless, floating in a sea of pure love.

'The darkness and the light are the same!'

I gasp in amazement, with the deep-seated knowledge that I am one with all things.

I am the darkness, I am the light and I am the love.

I want to stay and bask in this blissful awareness for ever.

But hang on … Something even stranger is now happening. It feels like I'm actually dissolving and melting into the golden rays.

The beam is beaming, beaming, beaming …

Boom!

I have become a beacon of light and love!

Just like that. One minute I am me and the next minute, I'm not.

My body has vanished and been replaced by a crackling electrical force field.

Energy is powering its way around my body, sparking off from me in all directions. My physical form has completely and mysteriously disappeared. Yet I have the sense of being all-encompassing, filling the entire room with brilliant white rays and the ferocious force of love.

It's most disconcerting. And even more so, as judging by the lack of reaction from the therapist, I'm apparently the only one to have noticed this uncalled for metamorphosis!

I am completely sober, drug-free, and have no history of psychotic episodes, so where the hell has my body gone? This is the most extraordinary, unexpected experience of my life but the part of *me* that still believes itself to be *me*, is screaming hysterically.

'*What the F*** is going on here?*'

Maybe I'm having some kind of stroke or an unprecedented epileptic episode? If I had visible hands, I would pinch myself, but *I* do not exist anymore!

I have shrunk to a miniscule spectator in the lighthouse of my new reality.

This is a reality far removed from my every day experience. Could this, in fact, be the spiritual awakening I've always longed for?

I've often dreamt of *finding myself* on some silent mountain retreat and spending the rest of my days spreading wisdom, peace and love to the world. But it's just my luck that when my big moment comes, I'm sitting in my scruffy trackie bottoms in a nondescript therapy room.

The *Everyday-I*, the *I* that is a mum, leads a *normal life,* does a job, the dishes and the school-run, can just be heard shrieking hysterically in the background,

*'Pull yourself together! Find your body! I knew that f****** yak tea was a bad idea!'*

But this new *Eternal-I*, this *Bodyless-I*, this *I* of blinding light and immeasurable joy whispers into my earless ears.

'This is who you truly are. You are the light! Shine down on the world!'

And who am I to argue with this ethereal command?

I am a flaming lantern in a river of joy, my power of speech sunk in a stupor of serenity.

This *Eternal-I* is intent on seducing me with its blissful nectar of love. But that trouble-causing *Everyday-I*, who has to function in the ordinary human world, is not giving up control of me without a fight. She starts up again, trying to override this craziness.

'Look, you're being ridiculous! You can't just turn into a fireball! Besides, it's obvious you're deluded as no one's noticed this explosion and gone running for the fire extinguisher! It's most likely a form of quick onset glaucoma. You definitely should have gone to Specsavers!'

Everyday-I is used to a mundane, humdrum lifestyle, where she passes mostly unnoticed, unless socks need sorting or the fridge needs filling. *Everyday-I* cannot comprehend this out-of-the-body experience. She thought she wanted enlightenment but really maybe all she wanted was a bit of peace and quiet and *me time.* This is a step too far out of her spiritual comfort zone!

She wails from a long way away.

'Please let me come back! I promise this time I'll definitely give up all the self-help nonsense for good and stick to my normal, unhealthy, work-family-TV imbalance. Just stop the shining! I want to be human again!'

The new *Eternal-I*, however, is having none of this and woos me with a tempting promise.

'Why be ordinary when you can be extraordinary?'

And indeed, I have a sense that this new existence of euphoric ecstasy and pure perfection is who I truly am. But if I surrender to the light, there may be no turning back. *Everyday-I*, after all, has a foot firmly on the Earth. I can almost feel her reaching for her mobile to google *strokes, epilepsy, glaucoma* and *hallucinations*. You see, if that foot is lifted, then living in this human world may well become impossible.

But this experience is so beautiful that it cries out to be enjoyed, at least until my body returns …

Then from somewhere in the burning blaze of bliss that is currently *me*, I hear the voice of the therapist telling me my time is up.

'Well?' she asks, no doubt eager to continue her game of questions. 'Did you get to the other side of the void?'

But I have no answers, I have no voice, I have no *me*.

For whilst I may look human to the therapist, in my own, now non-existent eyes, I have no shape or form and am simply a vision of pure light. I have no legs but somehow manage to float out of the door. I am high on love, drunk on life, fizzling with electricity. I am as tall as the sky, deep as the ocean, and endless to all sides.

As I flow out of the building and down the Moor - the busy high street - tossing light and elated laughter in all directions, I cannot believe that nobody has noticed the dazzling steps I dance.

But they have.

'Make way for the nutter!'

A shout goes up from the crowd. The pedestrians around me nervously drop eye contact and let me, the chortling hysteric, pass by.

I drift on the breeze to the no 81 bus stop and hover in front of the driver. He looks at me intently. For a moment I recognise a small, familiar spark in his eyes, but then it dies out and somehow, despite my apparent lack of arms, money is exchanged for tickets. As I sparkle and glitter onto the bus, a toddler points delightedly at me.

'Shiny lady! Shiny lady!' he calls out in excitement before being shushed into reluctant silence.

The *Everyday-I* in the glow of other-worldliness registers that it is nearly 3 p.m. and time to pick up Small Child from Juniors. I need to get off the bus and regain my physical form right now!

The Shining Brightness, however, shows no desire to dissipate, so I glide along the pavement and into the school yard, allow Small Child to melt into my loving warmth and sail back towards home.

'Are you alright, Mummy? It's just, you seem a bit spaced out.'

I stare at him blankly through the mists of my magnificence. *Everyday-I* starts to fight back. I need to snap out of this now!

'You are not a beacon! You are a mother! Stop this at once! Get a grip and grow some limbs! When was the last time you checked your make-up?'

And finally, with this heart-felt wish, the fire within me dies down into a flickering candle. The beacon of light switches off and with a last sad call, *Eternal-I* sighs in disappointment.

'I am always here. Just look inwards.'

The outline of my body becomes perceptible to me once more. The silhouette of my skeleton shivers back into existence.

Small Child prattles on obliviously about classroom dramas and playground skirmishes. A heaviness returns to my bones with each step I take. *Everyday-I* is back. She checks in the mirror. Great! My mascara's run and I've got huge panda eyes. No wonder everyone was staring at me!

'Mum, can I have some flapjack? I'm starving!'

Duty and daily routine snuff out the light.

Back in my human frame, I look down at my hands as they fetch his snack. I can still feel my palms pulsating. It's a reminder that something quite monumental has taken place. Or did I actually have a mini stroke? For now I'll just blame it on that yak tea. For who can I share this incredible incident with? Who would believe me? *Everyday-I* is all for keeping schtum. We don't want people thinking I'm *losing it* after all!

In bed that night when Boy Scout dutifully enquires what kind of day I've had, I find it safer to lie.

'Oh, you know, just the usual.'

But as I sit there, sewing last-minute name tags into Small Child's PE shorts, the embers of the light are still glowing. There is a profound awareness in the depth of my soul and a feeling that my whole life has been leading to this moment.

Boy Scout glances across at me and carefully puts down his toast.

'What's up my lovely? You look different somehow. Good different, mind, in a strangely glowing kind of way, but a bit *not quite here* too! What's occurring?'

The point is I have no idea *what's occurring*, but before I can even engage my brain, the words come tumbling totally unexpectedly out of my mouth.

'You know, I really think it's time to make some big changes in my life. I'm going to hand in my resignation tomorrow.'

Boy Scout looks momentarily taken aback, then announces, with uncustomary sweetness,

'Yes, my lovely, you're right. You don't have to do this anymore. You've been trying to make yourself happy with all that self-help mumbo-jumbo and touchy-feely therapy when maybe it's the job that's been the problem all along...'

The next day I wake up to find I am, reassuringly, myself once again. There is no light seeping through my tatty nightwear, no golden glow bouncing off the shabby bed sheets. I poke my stomach to check I possess a physical body and am disappointed to note there's still more flesh than bone wobbling in waves over my frayed pyjama bottoms.

The palms of my hands show no signs of pulsating and all four slightly arthritic limbs are intact and electricity free. There's no more elegant drifting, gliding or flowing, just an abrupt lurching out of bed, a sorrowful shuffling to the bathroom and a reluctant return to the dutiful trudging through day to day life.

It's all a bit of an anti-climax. One minute I'm an extraordinary beacon of light, an *Eternal-I* with endless possibilities. And the next minute, I'm ordinary *Everyday-I* with a things-to-do list.

I somehow expected my life to magically transform overnight. I mean, once you've been a flaming lantern, it's hard to be happy with a spluttering candle! If only I'd given myself fully to the experience, abandoned the school-run, let go of the last ties to earthly life and sailed off into the celestial horizon. Maybe now I'd be sitting in eternal ecstasy instead of daily drudgery.

But the problem is that once you've been a beacon of light, it's a bit hard to *un-beacon* yourself.

I'd like to say the experience has made me a better, more enlightened human being, but that's clearly not the case. I'm still an ordinary, middle-aged mum, with half a century of hang-ups and a life-time of mistakes. I'm still that flawed *Everyday-I* I've always been, only now the light has finally *outed* itself.

If I was religious, I could run round proclaiming I'd found God, join a nice church, mosque or temple and live happily ever after with my fellow believers. Unfortunately, there is no *House of Light* I can visit to tell all in the confessional, no *Path of Light* to guide me on my way. Or could it be that, in fact, there are many houses and many paths all leading to the same destination? For this light refuses to compartmentalise itself. It doesn't believe in labels, in the 'if you are this, then you can't be that' mentality. It's a unifier not a divider.

My task now is to acknowledge this light within me, not be afraid of it. I can't un-live my experience and I can't yet tell anyone about it. But one thing is certain, it is time to make a change.

39

End of an Era

This is not quite the change I had in mind!

I wake up with the uncomfortable awareness that I'm not in my own body and that overnight I've down-graded to an inferior model.

This vessel I'm occupying feels lumpen, heavy and unmoveable. Indeed, trying to raise my eyelids takes an inordinate amount of effort, and my eyes have narrowed to slits, caved in to their sockets and been bathed liberally in road grit.

My head's grown to gargantuan proportions, so my neck is folding under its weight, whilst, conversely, my brain's shrunk to the size and mental capacity of a walnut, and is struggling to make sense of the situation. My hair has clumped into spikes so brittle I fear any movement may shatter it and my teeth have transformed into tombstones, coated in thick, rotting vegetation.

I'm not sure if I still have limbs, but a trial attempt at lifting my arms confirms these have now turned into octopus tentacles, flailing wildly around the bed, knocking random objects off the chest of drawers.

I become aware of a loud persistent buzzing in my ears. I feel it may be a language of sorts, but one that's entirely foreign to me. I concentrate really hard, trying to block out the thunderous sound of the veins pulsating in my temples. I think it could be some kind of robotic SOS message, set on a loop recording.

'Get up! Get up! Get up!'

Then a light, so blinding it is of biblical proportions, singes my retinas, forcing waterless tears out of my crusted ducts. Slowly, and tortuously, an image forms. It's the face of Boy Scout, but in this new, parallel universe, his smile shows little warmth and his decree is tinged with malevolence.

'You need to get up *now*! I have to go to work and that bloody Australian boy you've invited over will be turning up today, isn't it? What on earth is he going to think? Honestly, I can't believe you came home in such a state! Thank God it's only once every twenty-five years.'

I try to formulate a reply but my tongue has collapsed somewhere over my right cheek and my throat's been obstructed by a Saharan sandstorm. A strangled 'Mmmmeurrrgggghh' is the best I can manage, and I hope my beloved interprets this as 'Have a great day at the office, darling. Love you too!'

As I lie still, tentatively checking out body parts for signs of co-operation, memories swirl in and out of the fog in my brain:

A leaving do in All Bar One. Wine. Colleagues. Manuela making a speech. Wine. Reminiscences of long years of service. Wine. A presentation. Wine. Feelings of love for aforementioned colleagues. Wine. Inviting all colleagues to a summer barbecue. Wine.

Effusive hugging of all colleagues. Wine. Amanda crying in the toilets and Scott comforting her. Wine. Nadim taking incriminating photos. Oh God! Wine. Feelings of love for all of humanity. Wine.

Nancy ordering champagne. Jenny saying it's not a good idea. Champagne. Attempt at effusive hugging of all humanity in the pub. Mehmet, sober, and taking charge of me. Forcible removal of champagne.

Dancing with Claire on the table. Forcible removal of my body from pub to taxi. Feelings of love for taxi driver. Forcible eviction from taxi and rapid home delivery. Then, blessed darkness…

And now, the morning after, here I wallow, facing cursed punishment, as just-desserts, for an evening of overindulgence.

Thank Heavens farewell debacles are such a rare and historic event for me, for my body couldn't survive more frequent mistreatment. Still, the current pain is worth it, for it was a great night out, full of fun and laughter and the fitting end to an era.

It's an era that lasted a quarter of a century at college and for the most part I loved every minute until, in the last few years, a jadedness took over, an apathy of the soul. Something was out of synch. My heart was no longer in teaching.

But the moment I handed in my resignation a huge weight lifted from my shoulders. And although the first day of the rest of my life has not been particularly auspicious so far, surely the only way is up now?

I gingerly get out of bed, mix a cocktail of drugs to get me through the day and stand under the shower until my eyelids unglue themselves. A few hours and several episodes of daytime TV later, the doorbell explodes. I fix my best welcoming smile onto my face and shuffle towards the door.

'G'day. You must be my dad's long-lost travelling partner. Wow, you haven't changed a bit from the photos I've seen of you! It's fantastic to meet you at last. I'm so grateful you agreed to put me up for a while. You're one kind lady.'

I've never met this tall, bronzed, blonde, surfer dude, with an air of Prince William about him, but he's already making a favourable impression on me with his blatant lies. I search my addled memory in vain for his name.

'And you must be…?'

'Bruce.'

'Really?'

'Yeah, I know! Everyone thinks it's my dad's idea of a joke, what with me born in Australia and all. But in fact, my old man's family tree goes all the way back in history and we're supposedly related to *the* Robert the Bruce. I don't quite believe it myself but it's always best not to argue with dad.'

I nod in sympathy, remembering our university days when the Enigma made mince-meat out of anyone who disputed his facts and figures.

'Well you'd better come in then. I hope you don't mind, but with three children, we've got no spare rooms so I'm afraid you're sharing with my youngest in his bunk bed.'

'No worries, I'm the eldest of five, so I'm used to little brothers! Now, once I've put away my stuff, are there any tasks I can do to help you out? I don't want to be a sponger. I want to pay my way in kind.'

And, amazingly, Bruce turns out to be my ideal house guest. He does all the odd jobs around the house that Boy Scout's ignored for the last decade. He compliments me on my cooking, even when it's clearly inedible. He joins me on the weekly park run and has even shown a genuine interest in my rediscovered crystal collection.

He's also got the rest of the family on board.

Small Child adores him for his *New South Wales' Lego Champion* status and his knack for building state-of-the-art tree houses. Boy Scout's impressed by his knowledge of rugby and enthusiasm for sport of any kind. Devil Teen finds an ally to play with on the PlayStation and Delightful Daughter seems rather taken with his Aussie charm, recommending him for a job at her pub, before he has chance to look elsewhere.

And Bruce's arrival coincides with the start of a new chapter in my life - one that Bubbly Brazilian and English Rose are eager to discuss.

'My dahleeng, that's fantastic news. It's about time you created some space for yourself.'

'Yes, now you're around more, you can be my new recipe taster, if you like. I'm so enjoying being creative with Fusion 3's summer dessert menu. You could help me improve my French too - I thought I might have a holiday over in Lyon at the end of the summer.'

Zen Mother is more discerning.

'I don't think that's a good idea actually. Can't you see how different she looks? So much lighter. She doesn't want to be weighed down with a list of things-to-do for other people. She needs time to reflect about what *she* really wants in life.'

And Zen Mother's right. For so long I've played the part of wife, mother and teacher that it's almost as if I've forgotten what brings me joy. My forays into religion, philosophy and alternative therapies have gradually revealed new insights. I've learnt to *suspend my disbelief* and be open to new ways of thinking. I no longer fear death and I have a real sense of the light inside me. I am *of this world* so I need to live in it as my *Everyday-I* persona, but it's a huge comfort to know that *Eternal-I* is always there if I just look inwards.

In the same way that I uncluttered my house of unnecessary *stuff* I now repeat the process on myself. I start peeling away all the labels I've stuck on myself over the last half century, gradually revealing the *I am* that is the nature of my true essence.

Having stripped back the layers and got rid of the job that weighed me down, I now choose to live more *authentically*. I decide to return to my childhood for inspiration. What was I passionate about? What brought me joy and made my heart sing?

With more free time, I rediscover my love of reading. I turn away from the self-help books and devour the classics. I reactivate my Russian and, in the poetry of Pasternak, find myself once more transported to a snowy winter's day in an Orthodox churchyard.

To my delight, I've also discovered the *Geronimo* running club, who meet in Millhouses Park for a gentle jog in the woods, some training in technique and quite a lot of nattering. Whilst many are far from spring chickens, they don't believe age is a barrier, are up for any challenge and regularly beat much younger runners. I find this inspirational and it encourages me to run most days out to my favourite rocky outcrop. And I'm ridiculously pleased that my now much slimmer body still does as I ask of it.

I start to write again - a weekly blog, discovering humour in the mundane. I find the creative process exhilarating and an entire day can pass without me noticing it. And, whilst Bubbly Brazilian isn't a great supporter of my singing, she's a firm fan of my writing - posting smiley faces and thumbs up emojis to encourage me. My readership gradually increases from five to a record-breaking forty! So what if I never go viral? That isn't the point. If I only touch one person's life and make them smile then I'm happy. And so how great that Bruce, who has a tricky relationship with his father, uses my blog as a basis for neutral conversation with the Enigma in their weekly skype talks.

Meanwhile, I continue to *embrace eccentricity*, tie myself in yoga knots under the beady eye of Zen Mother, and practise reiki, weighted down with a selection of stones in my bra.

I dip in and out of church services and Buddhist meditations and search in vain for that wise woman with my posse of philosophers. I keep an open mind and watch inspirational internet videos from all faiths, whilst still allowing myself one trashy TV programme a week.

There is a freedom and lightness now to my life.

I suspend disbelief and affirm positively every day - 'I trust in the universe. All my needs are taken care of. I enjoy earning money. I am safe.'

And magically, job offers appear. All temporary, but reasonably paid and fun.

I discover the healing power of joy and laughter. I am following my passions, living more soulfully and allowing that diamond of awareness within me to finally shine through.

With no permanent job, I become a minimalist extraordinaire, keeping on top of the clutter my family of hoarders try to bring in, even if I never keep on top of the housework. Now I cook more nutritious, although not necessarily more delicious, chakra-enhancing dishes, and the Parking Angel always accompanies me on my trips to the health food shop. I even have time for a home pedicure, so the reflexologist is no longer conveniently busy when I try to book an appointment.

I find that these days it is so much easier to use positive rather than negative wording in my speech with others and I try to remember that no one is better or worse than myself. We are just different. And the *voices* are all but silent…

The only thing missing in my life now is the courage to share my transformational experience with others.

40

Nothing in Life is a Coincidence

It's August and the day of the promised barbecue.

There's a lot to celebrate -

- My new, *authentic* life.
- Boy Scout's promotion at work, which means he won't be away on business so often.
- Delightful Daughter's acceptance on the youth work course and her decision to defer it for a year to go travelling around Europe with Bruce, her now, very close *friend*.
- Small Child's award for the *most improved student* in his year group, but, more importantly, him finding a best friend and finally being happy at school.
- Devil Teen passing his A-levels with the grades he needs and his choice to study in Sheffield because of a certain hair stylist, who's virtually taken up residence with us.

In fact, our house is rather crowded at the moment as my old friend Vanya arrived from Moscow a few days ago and is currently sleeping on the sofa. Luckily, he doesn't seem to mind too much.

'Devushka, it reminds me of the Soviet days in my communalka. Since then the government's done a lot of building work and I have my own studio-flat in the suburbs. But I'm used to sharing facilities and at least, so far, no one has stolen my possessions!'

Indeed, Vanya is an enthusiastic guest. He's impressed by everything, from the city centre with its thriving, multi-cultural, artistic scene, to the dramatic landscapes of the Peaks and my favourite rocky outcrop.

315

'This is a city I feel strangely at home in, devushka. It's not as grand as my Moskva, but the people are very welcoming and the city is so green, with all its tree-lined streets.'

He's particularly taken with our garden and eager to help out with the barbecue. But this year, I'm playing safe. No unwanted calls to the Fire Brigade and visits to A&E! I've outsourced the catering to Fusion 3, so Monsieur Hôtel and his very able assistant, English Rose, are in charge of all the food and drink. This leaves me to play the welcoming hostess to my selection of friends, neighbours and ex-colleagues.

It's all going well. The Musical Christians, now with the addition of young Clementine in their band, are providing the entertainment. Kiki and Bubbly Brazilian have set up an impromptu dance class at which Claire, my ex-boss is apparently excelling, and Magical Mineral Man is, surprisingly, holding his own.

Bruce and my eldest have organised some games for the children, even taking charge of the Exhausted Parents' toddler, much to their delight. For some reason though, Granny Triad - giving a tai chi demonstration with my father - keeps waving in their direction and shouting, 'Will and Kate!'

The High Priest and Priestess are walking bare foot on the grass and attempting in vain to make Amanda do the same.

'Oh my goodness, no. I couldn't possibly do that. The last time I took my shoes and socks off I got badly stung by a bee - nearly died! I had to be helicoptered to hospital. It was an absolute nightmare. Soa I think I'll give it a miss, if you don't mind.'

In one corner, Zen Mother's trying to initiate Human Dynamo into the joys of yoga, but she's too impatient to stand in the *Tree* pose for more than five seconds and rushes off to help the Bigs unload their crate of champagne. Still, Ancient Crone and Man Bun from the Buddhist Centre are up for a yoga challenge and copy Luke's dad as he demonstrates proficiently what to do. Maybe Zen Mother, with her positive affirmations and the law of attraction, has finally found her yogi, after all?

In the other corner, Mehmet, Mr High Heels and Sensible Health Visitor are putting the world to rights, whilst Nadim silently nods and Boy Scout can barely suppress his glee, as Manuela and Our Bev discuss my shortcomings.

'Oh, yes, I stopped asking her to make me a cup of tea at work! Absolutely hopeless - she could never get it right!'

The food, as expected, is going down well, particularly with Nancy, who's already on her second helping. And Monsieur Hôtel and English Rose are engaged in animated conversation with the Friendly Wavers and The Smiley Family about Asian and West Indian cuisine.

Just then, Vanya comes over to me, looking shell-shocked.

'Who's that woman who has just come through the gate? Those unforgettable green eyes! Am I seeing a ghost? Tell me I'm dreaming!'

Ah yes, I'd completely forgotten I'd invited her, and now I think of it, this might not have been one of my better ideas. For the woman who's just walked into my garden is no other than Tatyana Higinbottom - Vanya's ex-wife!

As if aware that a pair of eyes are boring into the back of her head, Tanya turns round, spots Vanya and her legs buckle under her in a faint. Vanya rushes to catch her before she falls.

'Gospodi! Tanya! Is it really you?'

'Vanya! This can't be happening! What are you doing here in Sheffield?'

I decide it's probably best if I don't get involved, so scuttle off in the opposite direction and lie low behind some convenient bushes. It turns out, this is an ideal place to eavesdrop on some rather interesting discussions.

Delightful Daughter and Bruce are deep in conversation with Devil Teen and Jess, whose red hair today is waist length, due to some cunning hair extensions. They're explaining their travel plans.

'After that we're stopping in Barcelona, aren't we Bruce?'

'Yeah, that's right, possum. *The Sagrada Familia* cathedral's on our bucket list of places to see, isn't it?'

'Oh for God's sake Big Sis! Why have you got to bring religion in to everything? Far more interesting to see Camp Nou football stadium, if you ask me.'

I hold my breath, expecting an argument to break out but Jess has got it all under control.

'Actually, the *Sagrada Familia* is raight good. I went to Barcelona last year for an 'airdressing competition and did some sightseeing. The light inside the cathedral is proper amazing. I'm not religious meself but I were completely blown away when I walked inside. The colours from the stained-glass windows were like summat from a different world. I actually started blubbing.'

She turns to look at Devil Teen with a teasing smile.

'You know, when you're a bit *older,* love, you might not see the world in such black and white terms. Maybe traditional religion isn't for you but you there's nowt wrong with keeping an open-mind, innit?

Devil Teen looks as if he's about to argue, thinks better of it, then smiles and says -

'Well, as it's *you,* okay. But for now, I think we should make the most of that crate of champagne. We're not likely to be able to afford our own until your chain of hair salons is up and running!'

They wander away to be replaced shortly after by Our Bev, English Rose, and Jenny - who's chatting to The High Priestess.

'So, you must be *the angel lady* then. I have to say, it all sounded a bit ridiculous to me at first but now I never go out in the car anywhere without invoking the Parking Angel.'

'That's good to hear my dear. Not everyone's as open-minded as you, are they?' says The High Priestess, looking pointedly at English Rose, who blushes uncomfortably.

Jenny continues - 'Oh, I did a bit of research on it actually and found out that angelic beings are common in many faiths. Then of course, I've had my own strange out-of-the body experience when I nearly died giving birth to my second child. I was surrounded by an amazing light - maybe it was an angel? Who knows? But I think people nowadays are much less likely to judge you as crazy if you have an unusual experience, don't you?'

English Rose looks as if she's about to say something, then thinks better of it as Our Bev joins in.

'Well I know my little sister was very judgmental as a teenager. She was a fanatical atheist growing up.'

'Was she?' interrupts English Rose in amazement.

'Oh yes, really in-your-face about it at times. But she's been on a bit of a journey since then and, well, she may not have embraced my Christian beliefs, but I think she's discovered what she was looking for. She certainly seems happier in herself since she gave up work. But I think it's more than giving up work - she seems *lighter* somehow.'

If only Our Bev knew the truth! But now that I've overheard this conversation, maybe telling her of my *beacon* experience wouldn't be so much of a big deal after all? As everyone heads off to sample the desserts, I take a quick look around the garden.

Oh yes, I can see Vanya and Tanya sitting on the bench, chatting intensely to each other. They haven't killed each other yet, so it's safe to come out and make a beeline for the sweet trolley.

Monsieur Hôtel hands me a portion of beautifully-presented toffee roulade and smiles ruefully at me.

'It'll never be as delicious as your flapjack, ma cherie!'

'Well, I think you've found someone who can make an even better version of it than me, haven't you?' I ask, hoping he'll reveal his true feelings towards my friend.

'Oui, it's strange, mon chou. I spent twenty five years regretting the fact that I put my passion for my job above my passion for a woman. But as your dear papa so rightly told me - I 'ad my chance and I blew it! When the opportunity came for me to open my dream fusion restaurant, I couldn't believe it was in your 'ome town. And, I 'ave to admit, a part of me 'oped I'd bump into you and find you were single and available. But fate 'ad other, better ideas. And now I 'ave found a new love - someone who shares my passion for cooking in a way that you never did. It's a recipe made in 'eaven!'

'Even though it comes with four side dishes you didn't order?'

'Ah, the children! Well, it's not straight-forward, I agree, but I think we could be a *fusion family*, n'est-ce-pas?'

I'm glad to hear his intentions are honourable and wonder if English Rose thinks the same. I go off in search of her and find her sitting, strangely silent, under one of the trees.

'Are you ok?' - I ask - 'I've just been talking to our French friend and he seems to think you're more than ok!'

'Yes, he's the best thing that's happened to me in years! I think we might have a real future together... But that's not the problem. What I want to tell you is... Look I'm just going to come straight out with it.'

'Ok...' - I'm intrigued to know what's bothering her.

'Look, you remember that angel workshop? Well, I only bloody well imagined I saw an angel, didn't I? Hovering there, right in front of me. Clear as day. Completely freaked me out! I thought it was all in my imagination but when you did your reiki stuff on me, it bloody appeared again! Do you think I'm cracking up?'

'What? You mean turning into *me*?'

English Rose smiles, despite herself.

'I don't know. It's just very weird, isn't it?'

Well, not as weird as becoming a beacon of light, I think to myself! I weigh up my words carefully before I reply.

'You know, I'm coming to believe we all have to walk our own path in life and if yours involves seeing angels, then who am I to dispute that? If I were you, I'd try talking to them. They might have some interesting insights to give you. At the very least, I can assure you that they'll help you find a parking spot!'

We both laugh, the tension gone.

'Yeah, I wanted to tell you before. I should've known you'd understand. And by the way, you've just dropped this.'

English Rose hands me a purple charoite stone that makes me instantly think of Magical Mineral Man. I wonder where he's got to… Then I spot him laughing and joking with Bubbly Brazilian as he tries to perfect his salsa moves. When I come over to them, she grabs me.

'Would you believe it, my dahleeng, this guy knows all about my Iemanjá!'

'Yeah, fair dinkum,.' he says - 'Remember me telling you I'd travelled in South America? Well, I rocked up in Salvador - this gorgeous lady's city - one February, just in time for the festival. It was mind-blowing to see so many people come and leave their offerings by the sea. I found it very moving. See, I was brought up a Catholic myself, so Iemanjá reminds me of Our Mother Mary - very nurturing and protective.'

'Yes, my dahleeng. I honestly believe she's protected me and it's nice to talk to a non-Brazilian who knows a little bit about her and doesn't dismiss it as rubbish!'

'Well that's great' - I reply - 'and nice to see you chatting for once with a man who isn't Kiki! What have you done with him by the way?'

'Ah my dahleeng. He's over there with your Scott from college.'

I look over, and to my surprise, see Scott with his arm very comfortably round Kiki's waist. My eyes widen and Bubbly Brazilian bursts out laughing.

'Honestly, what did I tell you? You English girls have no *gaydar* at all!'

It's getting late now and people are starting to say their goodbyes. Vanya comes up to me looking victorious, his arm around Tanya. There's no beating around the bush - he gets straight to the point.

'You know, we've been talking all afternoon and it makes no sense for me to stay in your crowded house, when Tanya has an empty flat. I'll get my bags and move out now.'

Tanya smiles sheepishly and, with her years of training from having lived in the UK, offers a half-hearted apology.

'So sorry if this upsets any of your plans but we thought it might actually make your life easier. Is it ok with you?'

And of course, it's ok with me. I'm happy for them both.

As I stand there contemplating how strangely things have turned out, my father with Our Bev in tow, grabs me.

'Girls. Something to give you. Front room.'

I exchange a surprised look with Our Bev, then follow him inside. On the settee are two boxes. My father points at them awkwardly.

'Sorry, ten years late. I didn't want to let go. But then...' - he looks at me - 'you started that *decluttering*. Thought it time for me to do the same. Anyway, took a while to find.'

'Is that what you were looking for when you fell off the ladder, dad?' I ask.

'Yes. They were with her hats all along.'

Our Bev smiles. 'Our Mum did like a good hat! So, what's in them Dad?'

'Memories mostly. Your mother wanted you to *know*. Maybe that's why she came back? Anyway, she's gone now. I'll leave you to it.'

He disappears off back to Granny Triad and his tai chi.

Our Bev raises an eyebrow - 'Well, he was never really normal, let's face it. And he seems to be coping fine with his new *friend*, so I think we can stop worrying about him for a bit, eh, Squirt? So, let's take a look in these mystery boxes. This one's got your name on it, in Mum's beautiful calligraphy.'

Like kids opening Christmas stockings, we rip off the lids and gasp simultaneously.

'All my singing certificates!' - says Our Bev.

'And my running awards!' - I say.

'Aaah, there's a photo of me with my first pony.'

'Oh, and one of me with each newborn.'

'God, look at the collection of my old paintings and craft work!'

'And she's kept every one of my school stories.'

We stand there for a moment, looking through the mementoes of our lives - a lock of my once-curly hair, Our Bev's tiny first shoes, a newspaper clipping of me at a teaching conference and one of Our Bev opening her stables.

'I always felt I never lived up to her standards' - says Our Bev.

'Me too... But now... We... *know*...'

And two sisters hug to mark a sense of loss, love and closure. Life has a funny way of working itself out.

Just then Delightful Daughter comes in, waving a phone in front of my nose.

'Hey mum, glad I found you. I thought you'd like to see this picture that Bruce's dad's just scanned in - especially since you chucked out all your photos in your great minimalist purge! It's of when you both went travelling in India.'

And there on the screen, an orange-robed holy-man with ash-daubed forehead stares prophetically out at me. I still remember his ancient bony fingers waving excitedly in front of me and his voice proclaiming, 'Mehmsaab, remember this. Nothing in life is ever a coincidence!'

Getting ready for bed that night I reflect on the events of the day. It seems that more people than I imagined have been given a glimpse into an alternative way of seeing the world. Some open the door to conventional religions, some slam it completely shut, and some, like me, let a little chink of light escape, unaware that one day a beacon will blast its way out and change their life forever.

For, underneath all those labels I've given myself over the years, right there in the core of my being, resides *Eternal-I*, the essence of my soul, with its message of profound simplicity - *'I am a beacon of light and love.'*

So, as I warily pick up one of Devil Teen's pungent socks, wrench Small Child out of his week-old underpants and add them to the mountain of dirty washing found under his sister's bed, I resolve to love those around me as best I can. And loving also means sharing, so perhaps now, after all, it's time to share my experience with Boy Scout?

I decide to bite the bullet, so before he settles down in bed with his rugby magazine, I jump in with my story - 'You know, love, that night I decided to pack in work... that night you said I looked kind of different ... *glowing* different? Well ...'

As I recount my experience, Boy Scout, to his credit, does not burst out laughing. In fact, he nods along, almost seriously. When I finish my account, he's strangely silent, then replies with one word - 'Namaste.'

'What do you mean *Namaste*? I've just told you I turned into a beacon and all you can say is *Namaste*!'

'No, see my lovely. Since you've been doing all your *soul-searching* stuff, I've been doing a bit of research too. After all, I don't want you beating me in a pub quiz, isn't it? Anyway, *Namaste* - it's a Sanskrit word, used as a greeting by Hindus, and in yoga too. It means *the divine light in me meets the divine light in you*. It just came to my mind when you were talking, that's all.'

'What, so you believe me when I say I turned into a beacon of light?'

'Well, I can't say I really understand it, my lovely! I'm just a simple bloke from the Valleys, isn't it? But you ... You are a wonderful and complex woman! Sometimes, it seems to me that you overthink things and make life far too complicated, isn't it? But I can tell you one thing though. For me and the kids, you have been, and always will be, *a beacon of light*. You are the centre of our universe and we love you for it.'

He looks at me with those deep blue eyes and, once again, I really *see* him. The divine in me meets the divine in him. The *Eternal-I* in each of us unites. It is a beautiful moment of pure love.

And then the moment is lost as *Everyday-I* resurfaces and normal life resumes. Boy Scout shuffles uncomfortably in the bed, reaches under the sheets and removes a selection of crystals. He sighs dramatically - 'Just, I get a bit tired of sleeping on a pebble beach at night, my lovely! Could you perhaps cut down on the number of stones you keep in your bra?'

Author's Note

I really hope you enjoyed reading my book as much as I enjoyed writing it! I'd love it if you joined my Readers' Club at **judithwatkins.co.uk** where I'll let you know when I've got a new book coming out and give you free access to exclusive downloads. Get my **free story download** at **judithwatkins.co.uk** to discover all about 'The Pyjama Tour'.

And if you liked *Stones in my Bra*, then please do leave a review as that helps attract more readers who can enjoy the book too.

Finally, if you like the idea of reiki, then I've programmed a 45-minute session to be sent to everyone who reads this book. Just suspend your disbelief, find a quiet space, relax, and be open to receiving the healing energy. But if you feel it's all just *rocky malarkey*, then have a cup of tea and a flapjack instead.

Printed in Great Britain
by Amazon

49747645R00194